THE INTERLOPER

Manoranjan Byapari was born in the mid-fifties in Barishal, former East Pakistan. His family migrated to West Bengal in India when he was three. They were resettled in Bankura at the Shiromanipur Refugee Camp. Later, they were forced to shift to the Gholadoltala Refugee Camp, 24-Parganas, and lived there till 1969. Byapari had to leave home at the age of fourteen to do odd jobs. In his early twenties, he came into contact with the Naxals and with the famous labour activist Shankar Guha Niyogi. Byapari was sent to jail during this time, where he taught himself to read and write. Later, while working as a rickshaw-puller in Kolkata, Byapari had a chance meeting with the renowned Bengali writer Mahasweta Devi, who urged him to write for her journal *Bartika*. He has written twenty-seven books since. Some of his important works include *Chhera Chhera Jibon, Ittibrite Chandal Jibon* (memoir), the Chandal Jibon trilogy (novels) and *Motua Ek Mukti Senar Naam*. Until 2018, he was working as a cook at the Hellen Keller Institute for the Deaf and Blind in West Bengal. In 2018, the English translation of Byapari's memoir, *Ittibrite Chandal Jibon* (*Interrogating My Chandal Life*), received the Hindu Prize for non-fiction. In 2019, he was awarded the Gateway Lit Fest Writer of the Year Prize. Also, the English translation of his novel *Batashe Baruder Gandha* (*There's Gunpowder in the Air*) was shortlisted for the JCB Prize for Literature 2019, the DSC Prize for South Asian Literature 2019, the Crossword Book Award for Best Translation 2019 and the Mathrubhumi Book of the Year Prize 2020.

Byapari was elected a member of the Bengal Legislative Assembly in 2021. The English translation of his novel *Chhera Chhera Jibon* (*Imaan*) was shortlisted for the JCB Prize for Literature 2022. The English translation of his novel *Theek Thikanar Sandhane* (*The Nemesis*) was shortlisted for the JCB Prize for Literature in 2023. He also received the Shakti Bhatt Prize in the same year for his body of work.

V. Ramaswamy is a literary translator of voices from the margins. Besides the Chandal Jibon trilogy, his previous translations include *The Golden Gandhi Statue from America: Early Stories, Wild Animals Prohibited: Stories, Anti-stories* and *This Could Have Become Ramayan Chamar's Tale: Two Anti-Novels* (shortlisted for the Crossword Book Award, 2019), all by the anti-establishment Bengali writer, Subimal Misra. He was awarded the inaugural Literature Across Frontiers-Charles Wallace India Trust Fellowship at Aberystwyth University to translate the Chandal Jibon novels.

Praise for Chandal Jibon Trilogy

'In evocative and imagery-rich writing, Manoranjan Byapari introduces us to the devastating realities of mid-twentieth-century India: hunger, caste violence, and communal hatred. Jibon's experience in his tortured world remind us of the distance we have come, and how far we have yet to go.'
—**Dr Shashi Tharoor for** *The Runaway Boy*

'Manoranjan Byapari is an outspoken, fearless and unapologetic writer. His writings seethe with anger and indignation, and *The Runaway Boy* is no different. It is a gut-wrenching account of caste atrocities, dirty politics and crippling poverty that no discerning reader should miss.'
—**Hansda Sowvendra Shekhar for** *The Runaway Boy*

'*The Runaway Boy* is a piercing tale of human determination, shorn of hackneyed sentimentalism, and set in an unforgiving territory of death and desperation. Cuttingly frank, deeply political, and singular in feeling, this is an incandescent universe of long sufferings and of small, fleeting joys. Manoranjan Byapari does not confirm abstract theories the better-fed cultivate about the poor; he holds up a mirror that reveals, instead, through the pangs of a boy seeking hot rice, a world that feasts on the soul, and where hell is not a faraway place as much as everyday reality.'
—**Manu S. Pillai for** *The Runaway Boy*

'Manoranjan Byapari's epic narratives tell you more about our society than any number of studies by social theorists or political psychologists. Immersed in a world of caste violence and congenital poverty, here is fiction with the unmistakable sound of Indian history in the making.'
—**Jeet Thayil for** *The Nemesis*

'In the shape of a novel, Manoranjan Byapari serves us a great outpouring of pain and a hundred fierce cries for justice. This book ought to be on syllabi across the country so we may better understand how structural violence works at the intersection of caste, class and law enforcement.'
—**Annie Zaidi for** *The Nemesis*

MANORANJAN BYAPARI

THE INTERLOPER

TRANSLATED FROM THE BENGALI BY
V. RAMASWAMY

eka

First published in Bengali in 2013 in the magazine *Haatey Bajare*

Published in English as *The Interloper* in 2024 by Eka, an imprint of Westland Books, a division of Nasadiya Technologies Private Limited

No. 269/2B, First Floor, 'Irai Arul', Vimalraj Street, Nethaji Nagar, Allappakkam Main Road, Maduravoyal, Chennai 600095

Westland, the Westland logo, Eka and the Eka logo are the trademarks of Nasadiya Technologies Private Limited, or its affiliates.

ISBN: 9789360455996

10 9 8 7 6 5 4 3 2 1

Typeset by Jojy Philip, New Delhi

Printed at Manipal Technologies Limited, Manipal

Contents

1

The Man with the Stone

For quite a few days now, a twenty- or twenty-two-year-old youth had been observed roaming around in various parts of the city. He was slow-footed, with a morose, wrecked look on his face. A sense of hurt seemed to be smeared all over him. It wasn't at all clear what or who he was searching for as he went around the city. It was as if some fragments of memory scattered in the dust on the city streets, or some beloved tale, drove him to trudge in this way, like a crazed soul.

Observing him, one would think he didn't have a spot of his own in the entire universe where he could lie down to rest. Nor any address to speak of. The streets were his habitat, his shelter and his address. It was the street that was his country, his continent and world. He was born amidst the dust of the street, and it was in that dust that he would breathe his last.

This vagabond was proud of belonging to this country, but he had no formal proof of being its citizen. No record in the census archives or in the electoral rolls, no ration card either. If one conducted a search through such records, one wouldn't find his name or identity anywhere. In other words, he was devoid of an identity in this country, in this time, in human society—an unwanted, redundant man.

It was almost midnight now. Darkness all around. You could hardly see what lay five feet ahead. This was a railway station. It wasn't supposed to be so dark here at this time. But it was a new moon night, and on top of that there was a power cut. As a result, the darkness seemed dense and fearsome. This darkness had been simmering with rage since evening for being afar, but once the power went off, it pounced in blind fury and took over the whole locality, as if it had swallowed up the entire flow of life.

The youth had arrived here a little while back after wandering through various places. He had been sitting quietly since then in a corner of the platform, concealing his presence. It seemed he was trying to hide not just from the eyes of the people moving all around, but also from himself. The deep darkness that had descended seemed to have provided him that opportunity now. It provided him relief from any ugly embarrassment.

He was terribly hungry right now. It wasn't that the hunger had arisen just now. One could say that he had been starving from the moment he was born. There had been no rice in his house that could be cooked for a meal. And so, there was no affection in his Ma's womb. With all the fasting and starving, she didn't have the requisite colostrum in her breasts. The boy made for his Ma's withered breast after he was born, but didn't get even a drop of the beloved beverage. And so, from the very moment he arrived on earth, terrible hunger had become a part of his life. Which hadn't stopped stalking him to date.

Seasoned folk can look at a seed and fathom what tree it was and what it would be like. They look at the morning sun and intuit what the rest of the day would be like. The way this boy had commenced his life journey, it wasn't really difficult to guess what its conclusion would be like. And so, one could say without any hesitation that—not just today or tomorrow or the day after—his whole life would be like a penance that disavowed food.

Just as a river has high and low tides, hunger too has its ebb and flow. As morning advanced, so did the agony of hunger grow. Once it was noon, the vicious bite of hunger waned on its own. Like Devi Chhinnamasta drank her own blood and quenched her bloodthirst, hunger too consumed and mitigated itself. All the bodily agony found spontaneous relief.

The second attack of hunger commenced once daylight disappeared, and continued till midnight.

The stranger's river of hunger was now in spate. The banks on both sides were inundated by salty water. Waves lapped the shore. And with the waves came the terrible poison in foamy, churning eddies. He knew that this condition would continue for quite a few hours now. His intestines would wriggle and writhe like a python on fire. After a while, it would feel as if someone was trying to wrench out and tear his intestines. A top would spin with a terrific hum in his head, sparks of fire would dance in front of his murky eyes. If he tried to speak, the voice that was supposed to emanate from the throat would seem to have exited soundlessly through his ears. There was nothing to be done now but to bear the unbearable.

He was sitting at the far end of the eastern side of Platform No. 2. He staggered from there now, held the railing, and walked towards the overbridge at the western end. He knew there was a spot beneath the stairs of the overbridge that lay in complete darkness. That dark corner was the most safe and hassle-free spot in the railway station. No one looked in that direction. Those who wanted to hide in the station selected that corner for this very reason. The mystery behind the birth of many infants who ran around in the station on their tiny feet also lay hidden in this dark corner under the stairs.

The youth didn't want to be spotted by anyone, he didn't want to get entangled in any unnecessary trouble. He felt weak with hunger. Fear had nested in his weak body. That was why, like a snail retreating into its shell, the boy dragged his inert, powerless body towards that dark spot.

This was a difficult time. A time when a calamitous fear stalked the entire city. People were killed almost every day in some or other part of the city. No one could be certain whether a bullet aimed at one's chest wouldn't strike the next moment! That's why station precincts were completely deserted on a night like this. The kerosene lamps that burnt in the illicit liquor vend behind the mound of stone chips along the rail siding had gone off. The babble of drunks was absent. There was no sign of life anywhere at this time. It was as if all life lay dying, trembling in fear, behind the bolted doors of houses. Only the ugly cries and howls of a few mangy mongrels shattered the unbearable silence of midnight. Some people, who had no place to go to, the homeless, marginal folk, lay scattered here and there over the platform. Their dishevelled sleeping bodies reminded one of unclaimed bodies piled on the floor of the autopsy room in a mortuary. Walking slowly, the stranger skirted the sleeping folk, reached the overbridge and then slithered into the darkness under the stairs like a mouse. After that he lay down on all the dust, dirt, paan-spittle and banana- and orange-peels there, with his hands pressed to his tummy and his knees tucked to his chest, like a curled-up dog. As the youth lay there, he thought that if he could somehow get through this miserable night, then tomorrow, once the light of day emerged, some prop to survive might be found. After which the curse of the past wouldn't be able to hound him. After all, what recourse did he have right now, other than to hold on to such a bizarre hope? 'Hope' was the name of the witch who did nothing else but deceive people. But people were unable to forsake her illusory allure.

Although the youth had lain down, he couldn't sleep. All that the hungry boy could do was to pretend to sleep, as if lying in ambush. As he lay like that, he felt the tug of drowsiness. But that didn't last long. It suddenly vanished when there was an incredible sound. Scanning his eyes, he saw that right near his head, in the dense darkness, an enraged man—someone who seemed to be a murder addict—was standing with a large stone in his hand. He was drunk, which was why his legs were unsteady and he was wobbling. The niche of darkness under the stairs was filled with the acrid stench of illicit liquor. The man was trying to bang the heavy stone in his wobbling hands on the sleeping youth's head. But because the stairs of the bridge over his head sloped downwards, there was only a narrow niche underneath. And the man with the stone wasn't able to stand up straight either. Unable to take advantage of the vertical distance from which to strike the man so that he would be killed, he was stationary in perplexity. His situation was like that of a hungry tiger standing in front of a goat inside a grilled cage. He couldn't hunt, and he couldn't leave either.

The weak, helpless youth's heart trembled in terror and his throat turned dry. But his body lacked the strength to sit up, or flee, or resist the attacker. So he could only let out a feeble wail—'*Ah! Ah! Ah!*' That sound infuriated the man with the stone—'Hey you bastard, shut up, just shut up! Don't you try to scream! People will come running. There'll be a commotion. Shut up!'

The youth lying there said, *'Tumi tomar pathorda lamao. Naile ami aro jor chechamu!* Put your stone down. Or else I'll scream even louder!' The stationary man looked at the stone in his hands and then at the terrified youth. And then in an annoyed tone, he said, 'Have I thrown the stone on your head? You can go ahead and scream if you're still alive after I've thrown it on your head. If you screamed then and got a crowd of people, that would have meaning. What's the point of shouting now? Even if someone comes, what the fuck can he do? A stone is not an unlicensed gun, it's no offence to be carrying it!'

After a pause, and a bout of laughter, the man said, 'But yes, what you said is also correct. After all, you'll get no chance to shout after the stone falls on your head. You'll get, what's it called ... "final release" from starvation, from sleeping on pavements, and rail platforms. All right then, fulfil your final wish. Scream out for your life with all the power in your lungs. Once you're done screaming, I'll throw the stone. So start screaming, "Whoever's here, help me." Bastard, get it into your head that no one comes to save anybody in this country. If a pickpocket is caught, a hundred people arrive to beat him. But if a man falls from a train or a bus, no one will take him to hospital.' The man's face wasn't visible in the dense darkness. So the youth lying under the stairs could not make out anything about him to get some sense of whether he might have had some dispute or hostility with the man in this or some former life. Otherwise, no one in their senses could be so cruel as to kill anyone like this, for no reason, for no enticement or incitement. Killing a man was not like killing a hen or a goat. If he was caught, he would be hanged or sentenced for life. In order to solve the mystery, the prone youth asked softly, '*Tumi keda?* Who are you?'

'Who am I?' The man with the stone burst into a hideous guffaw. '*Arey* Bangaal, my job is to set out on the streets with a big stone once night descends on the city, and then smash the heads of the people sleeping on the pavements, under trees and in railway stations—you know, the beggars and vagabonds, all the useless people—and dispatch them to Ma Kali. I don't exactly remember how many I've killed before this, I think it must be ten or fifteen. The first time I smashed and killed a man with a stone was in 1963. I was only thirteen years old then. I've been addicted to stone-killing ever since. And I'm going to kill you now.'

The boy said raspingly, 'But I didn't do you any harm. I'm just lying in this corner like a dead man. Why do you want to kill me for no reason?'

The youth wouldn't have believed that a boy who was merely thirteen or fourteen could kill someone if he had led a life free of stumbles on its pathways. But he knew. Life had taught him that many people end up doing lots of things that, looking at them, one wouldn't ever imagine they could do. And the person who committed the act too never imagined that he could do that one day. That's why the youth was silent.

The man continued, 'I used to work in a tea-shop in Park Circus then. The hair of the Prophet, or some hair of someone, was stolen from some mosque somewhere at that time. So Hindu–Muslim riots broke out all over the country. Houses and shops were burnt down and people were killed. Although Park Circus was a largely Muslim locality, there had not yet been any riots there. The locality was peaceful even after lots of people died in other Muslim localities like Rajabazar and Khidirpur. But there was always fear, that's why there were hardly any people out on the streets once it was evening, people returned home and bolted their doors before it became dark.'

The man laughed, a mocking laugh. But it was directed at himself. 'No Ma or Baba would send their children out at such a time. They couldn't be at peace if they were outside. They'd keep looking streetwards as they waited in trepidation. But I had no one in the city to call my own. No Ma, no Baba, no home, no address. No one would look for me if I got lost, no one would shed tears if I died. I worked in the tea-shop for two meals a day. I had to do whatever the shop owner instructed me to. So that day, at around nine- or nine-thirty at night, the owner ordered me, "Go and get me a bundle of beedis."

The man with the stone was engrossed in his tale. He continued, 'The Park Circus railway station is there now, but there was no station then. There used to be some tiny shanty-like shops there. An old Bengali Muslim man sold his handmade beedis in one of those. The tea-shop owner was addicted to this man's flat-nosed beedis tied with red string. I used to go and buy beedis from him every day. So on that day, too, I went there as usual. How would I know, tell me, that someone was lying in wait, to kill me? I went to the shop all right, but on the way back I saw four boys my age, or maybe a year or two older than me, standing in the middle of the dark approach. As soon as I came in front of them, one of them took out a knife and stepped up to me. He asked me, "Which community do you belong to?"

'The way I had come lay in darkness. There wasn't a soul anywhere. There were clumps of milkweed and other plants on the two sides. Tell me, what was I to do then? There were four of them, and I was all alone. They wouldn't spare me even if I fell at their feet and wept. Those who incited riots never spared anyone. Right in this station, the goonda, Ratan, had stabbed a man in his stomach seeing the beard on his face. He was a poor man who sold eggs for a living. The basket on his head fell and the place overflowed with the yolks of the broken eggs. All the poor folk in the station began scooping them up into their palms. But no one thought to take the man to a hospital.

'I got scared. What would I do if, like it had happened to that man, they cut my belly open with the knife and my intestines fell out? So out of fear, you know, I jumped and picked up half a brick lying on the side. And I brought the brick down with all my strength on the crown of the head of the boy with the knife. With that single blow, he slumped to the ground like a felled tree. Oh, how the others ran when they saw that! The boy with the knife twitched his limbs a few times and then went still. I picked up the knife and ran away. Smashing heads has become a habit ever since then.'

Once again, the man with the stone broke the silence of the night with his hideous laugh. 'What's that you said? That you didn't do me any harm? Why just me, you've harmed no one in this world. You don't even have the power to harm anyone. The one who can't cause anyone harm can't do any good to anyone either. Harm and good are two sides of a coin. You should know that when someone comes to harm, it benefits someone or the other. It's not possible to benefit someone without harming anyone.'

'May I say something?'

'Speak.'

'Let's say someone's a thief. Whom does he benefit then?'

'It's because he's a thief that so many people work as watchmen, guards, policemen and so on. Police stations, jails, courts and so much more are established. So many masons and workers find employment. A lot of building materials like bricks, sand and cement get sold. Factories making locks, grilled doors and windows, safe-vaults, cupboards—all their sales go up. Can't one say that? Would anyone buy all these if there were no thieves? So in one sense, stealing is also a way of benefiting society.'

The supine youth was struck dumb. He had never imagined that a misdeed like stealing could have such an interpretation. And it was obvious that someone who interpreted it like that would prove any kind of wrongdoing in the world to be right with his own counter-explanation and reverse logic.

The man with the stone continued. 'It's not really necessary for me to know why you're lying here like this. But you need to know why you're going to die. That's why I'm asking you at the outset, tell me why you're lying here like this?'

The youth under the stairs felt extremely weak. Besides, all his mental faculties seemed to have been devoured by terror. The fear of unnatural death. So although his lips moved, they emitted no sound. He gazed, helpless and distressed, in the direction of the man with the stone who was shrouded in darkness. He said, 'You can't reply, can you? Let it be, you don't have to say any more. I know what you'll say. That you're not alone ... The same old story of everyone who spends the night like this in station platforms and pavements ... How different would yours be? What can it be? "Oh, I'm very poor. I don't have any place called home. That's why I'm lying here." I've heard such wailing lots of times. That doesn't soften my heart. Nor does it make my hand unsteady when I bring down the stone. What can you do if you're poor, so you ought to die. Die.'

After all this while, the youth finally mumbled timidly, 'Is it such a crime to be poor that one ought to die?'

The man at once retorted, 'Of course it's a crime that deserves death! Did anyone make you take an oath that you'll be poor?'

The youth heaved a sigh and said, 'Are people poor out of choice? It's their fate.'

'Do you believe in fate?'

'Everyone does.'

'I don't. I believe that fate does not drop from the sky. You have to create your fate through your own efforts.'

The youth twisted his chest and let out a deep exhalation that vanished into the dark night's air. He muttered, 'We lived in East Bengal. Although we had nothing much there, at least we had a roof to lay down our heads under. We had an address to our name. We had nothing, but we were content. Our contentment was intolerable to someone. They partitioned the country and snatched away our peace and tranquillity. We lost our country for no fault of ours. We finally had to leave and come to India. We were called "refugees". That country was no longer ours because we were Hindu. And because we are refugees, we don't belong to this country. Although we're Bengali, the Bengal government told us there's no place for us in Bengal. They wanted to drive us far away from Bengal—to the Andaman islands and to the Dandakaranya forests. My Baba said we wouldn't accept that resettlement. He said it wasn't resettlement but banishment. So the government said that there was nothing more they could do. That was the end of their responsibility. Whether you live or die is your lookout. That's why we're country-less and homeless.'

But the violent man interrupted him before he could say any more. 'Enough. There's no need for the same old song to keep playing on the stuck record. I know all about riots, Partition, refugee camps and all that. That's only a pretext to hide your own incapability and an attempt to gain the sympathy of others. Let me tell you about Partition. I left everything behind in East Bengal and came away. Let those who sympathise with you when they hear your tale do that, I don't get upset about it. You weren't the only one who came away from East Bengal because of the partition. Hundreds of thousands of people arrived in the same way. All the people from one-hundred-and-forty-nine *jabar dakhal,* or forcibly occupied colonies, like Bijoygarh, Azad Nagar,

Netaji Nagar and so on, were once in East Pakistan, but a bastard like you doesn't even have a patch of land to lie down and die on. Go and see how big their houses are, the roofs touching the sky. They occupy one room and there are tenants in the ten other rooms. I've heard that those who didn't have a scrap of cloth to cover their backside in East Bengal are millionaires today. Tell me how they achieved so much.'

The youth replied falteringly, 'The people in the one-hundred-and-fifty forcibly occupied colonies that you mentioned are all very fortunate. After arriving in this country, they managed to find a plot of land to lay their feet down and stand up. They were able to do that only because they belonged to the brahmin, kayastha and baidya castes. Whether you talk of the government or the political parties, after all it's the high-caste who are at the top of everything. It's because they supported the people of their own caste that the *jabar dakhal* colonies could come up on such valuable land. The first forcibly occupied colony that came up in West Bengal was called Bijoygarh. Prime Minister Jawaharhal, Chief Minister Bidhan Roy, the governor, Mr Katju—all of them went and stood around them and encouraged them. Seeing Bijoygarh, other colonies came up later. Go and find out—there's not a single household of low-caste folk like us. No one got any place there. If the people in the colonies weren't high-caste, you'd have seen how the government, political parties, leaders and ministers would have driven the people out of the places they occupied.'

After a pause, the youth continued, 'After all, the high-caste people are very clever. People occupied two or three plots in two or three colonies. There were fights between them too because of that. Say, the man whose name you hear spoken of now, as a "mastaan". He's a product of those times. So after that they retained a plot that they liked, they sold one of the other ones and deposited the money in a bank, and educated their sons and daughters so that they could get good jobs. Some built big houses and gave rooms out to tenants, so that they could live comfortably for the rest of their lives. Don't they say, *"machher tele machh bhaja,* frying fish in its own oil"—they did just that and became wealthy.'

The youth's voice swelled with helpless lament. 'I was small then, just five or seven years old. Right in front of my eyes, so many people have gone from living in bamboo-mat houses to becoming the owners of large mansions. My Baba didn't want to be crafty, deceitful or fraudulent, which you need to be if you want to become wealthy. He was a simple, straightforward villager of the Namasudra caste. He thought that he would get through his life somehow by sticking to the honest path, working hard and living frugally. That however difficult life was, he'd go to Vaikunth when he died. And live content there.'

'Stop, stop that!' The man with the stone rebuked the youth mildly. 'Stop your sermon. If you think that you can get away by laying all the blame on your Baba, forget about it. Tell me about yourself. Your Baba didn't come to sleep here. It's you who's lying here. You're the one who's going to be judged for that crime. Say what you have to in support of yourself.'

After pausing a few moments, the man said, 'Okay, let's say I accept that your Baba was possessed by the righteous soul, man of truth, Yudhishthira, because of which he couldn't do anything in his life. But do you think saying all this will absolve you of sin?'

'Sin! What's my sin?'

'Aren't you starving on the street and dying? Eating when hungry is nature. Eating when not hungry is perversion. Not eating oneself but feeding others is culture. Snatching and eating food off someone else's mouth is mischief. And not eating even when you're hungry is sinful. The soul resides in the body. And God resides in the soul. If you go without food, your body suffers, so the soul suffers. And if the soul suffers then the one who dwells there, God, suffers. The one who makes God, the Almighty, suffer, is a great sinner. He goes to hell after he dies. I want to dispatch you to hell so that you can realise the punishment you deserve. Tell me, what more do you have to say?'

The youth replied, 'I'm only twenty or twenty-two years old, I mean, my life has hardly begun. I arrived in this city from very far away after going through many paths. So many people live in comfort and contentment here. I don't want that, I'm looking for a means to survive with dignity and to be able to eat twice a day. I'm hopeful that I'll get that sooner or later.'

'You won't get that any more. If you die today there'll be no tomorrow.'

'Are you really going to kill me?'

'Yes, I'll really kill you, my dear! After all, you survived for twenty years—tell me, did you have a single meal to your fill? Did you get medicines when you were sick? Did you get warm clothes in winter? So what's the point of living? Tell me, is there any meaning to living like this?'

'But there may be a big change in my life tomorrow! Neither you nor I know what's going to happen.'

'The one who has something in him can do it by twenty, and the one who hasn't can't do it even in a hundred-and-twenty! Your grandfather lived for a hundred-and-ten years, he couldn't. Your Baba couldn't in fifty years. The same Baba's blood flows in your veins. Your life and your blood are accursed, so how can you be a successful man! You can't, it's impossible for you to be able to do anything in this life.'

There was deep darkness all around. It was as if the world was submerged in a directionless vortex. All over the world nocturnal beasts of prey were roaming around fearlessly. The murderous voice of a sick mentality resounded in the darkness. 'Do you know what a "gene" is? There are twenty-eight genes in the human body. Of which fourteen are given to you by your father and fourteen by your mother. It's these genes that determine whatever you do in life. Whether you are kind and compassionate, prone to anger, intelligent or brave—in sum, all the good and bad qualities in a man are provided by genes. Did you get that? So, what your ancestors didn't have your grandfather didn't inherit. And so, he couldn't pass it to your Baba. Your Baba couldn't give you what he lacked. The same thing happened from your Ma's side as well. That's why the minimal intelligence, audacity and skill without which it's not possible for a man to exist are absent from your head. If you had that, you wouldn't have been on the street like a dog or cat. That itself proves that as far as this country, the present time and our society are concerned, you are a useless, discarded, redundant man. Whether you exist or not makes no difference of any kind to anyone.

'Just think about it a bit, if you continue to live, you'll face a lot of starvation, humiliation and oppression. Tell me, why should you be greedy to live like that, and what does the world gain from that? It's better that you die. If you die, then at least your dead body might be of use to students of anatomy.'

The voice of the man with the stone now sounded like a snake's hiss in the night air. The youth was trembling and perspiring in fear.

'The country is full of useless people like you. I believe the population of India has now crossed five-hundred million. Who knows what it will be if you people are added to the number! Haats and markets, streets and riversides, trains and buses are all simply overflowing with people. Where's the need for so many useless folks? The fuckers don't do anything else but produce yet more, year after year. Anyway, I have nothing more to say. Move your head this way, let me smash it with the stone and leave! I don't have much time. You aren't the only one, there are countless people on the streets. I don't know, how many can I kill in a single life! Still, let me remove the garbage of the world as much as I can.'

The youth didn't want to die. Even a blind, or lame or leprosy-stricken man wouldn't want that! Even someone who was a despised shit-worm proclaimed—I don't want to leave this beautiful universe. And here was an ordinary man. Our great religious scriptures tell us—only after eight-hundred-and-forty million lives does a living being attain the rare human life. And then he expresses his gratitude for the opportunity by singing captivating songs like, 'I haven't eaten for two days, O Ma, give me a bit of rice-foam to lick'.

The youth was hoping for that which had happened many times in his life. He had escaped certain death in incredible ways. Something like that would surely happen now. Perhaps someone would unexpectedly arrive there, who would rescue him from the mad murderer. What was needed now was to snare him in a trap of words so as to buy time. He said, 'Everything you say is fine. But don't call people "garbage". Man is the greatest creature on earth. Our scriptures call him the recipient of divine elixir.'

'Recipient of divine elixir!' the man with the stone retorted mockingly. 'Let's hear who issued this certificate to man? Who wrote the scriptures? There are many other creatures besides humans. Did you go and ask them? Go and ask the donkey, the horse, the dog and the cat, all of them will thump their chests and say that they are the greatest and most important creatures in the world.' The stone-man cleared his throat and spat out the phlegm, and then he continued. 'But even if for the sake of argument one accepts that man is the greatest creature on earth, you people aren't that. You are like the dry husks in a crop of grain. And rice grains attacked by insects in a bag of rice—that's what you people are! All garbage. I'll say "garbage" a hundred, a thousand times. Bastard, if you can't secure the means to feed your belly, if you can't build four walls around you with a shade over your head, you don't have the balls to occupy a place where you can squat and shit and lie down and die—then what are you but garbage! As long as I'm alive, I'll remove the garbage of this earth with all my heart and soul. I'll make the word habitable for children, that's my commitment to the newborn.'

The man with the stone was tottering in intoxication. His speech slurred. And like a drunk, he was repeating the same thing over and over again. The youth didn't interrupt him. He let him jabber away. He blurted out four lines of a poem by Sukanta, and repeated them a few times. And then he asked the supine youth, 'Can you tell me who wrote this poem?'

The youth said in an anguished tone, 'How can I tell you that? I don't know how to read or write.'

The intoxicated man said, 'Must say, poets have great foresight. The one who wrote this poem knew for certain that sometime in the future someone would be inspired by his poem and set out alone with a heavy stone to areas of darkness to remove garbage. Perhaps this line of the poem was written specifically for me—"If no one heeds your call, then venture alone." I've ventured out all alone to clean up our society.'

The man staggered, as if about to fall with the stone. Balancing himself somehow, he said, 'You bastard, people in this country have houses that touch the sky. They have more money than they can ever count. So much land that a horse would tire running through it. Where did they get all that from? Everyone was born naked like you. It was all a result of their effort. They made the effort and so they got everything. Every kind of comfort in the world is within their reach. People like you who never made any effort are useless, lacking in energy. All lying on the streets. Whenever I see the likes of you, my hands itch to kill. I feel at peace after smashing heads with my stone, my dear. I had become very despondent once. I used to think that my life was worthless. But now I think that I too can do something worthwhile. Behind every birth on this planet lies some deep reason or the other. I think I was born to clear weeds. My God brought me into the world to do this task.'

The youth said in a distressed tone, 'Shall I say something?'

'Go on, tell me. Say it quickly and be done. The night will soon be over.'

'You won't be angry, will you?'

'Oh, don't worry. Why should I be angry! How can I be angry with someone who's going to die in a little while! So, tell me.'

'I once got the opportunity to meet and go around with some wise and educated people. They used to say that one couldn't become a multimillionaire merely through one's efforts. For that you have to alienate a lot of people from what's due to them. But that's unjust. Are you saying that people should be unjust?'

'What did I say? I spoke about making an effort. So that's what their effort is.'

'But that's unjust and wrong!'

'Who said so? You lot? All the unsuccessful people with empty hands and bare buttocks, isn't it? Just as a river has two sides, words also have two sides. Men too are on two sides. People on one bank talk in a certain way and those on the other bank in another way. You belong to the people on this bank, those who are called the "have-nots". Go to the other bank and tell the people who belong to the "haves" that all their wealth and glory was acquired wrongfully. They'll scour law books and open the pages of religious texts and prove that they didn't do anything that was wrong or immoral or illegal. If you annoy them too much, they'll kick you on your backside and drive you out.'

After a bit of a pause, the man said, 'Do you know what their philosophy is? It is that wealth is supreme. Following the supreme path means that there's nothing wrong with accumulating lots and lots of money, however it may have been acquired. They say that it's not possible to do anything good without money. So how can acquiring the means to do good be wrong? Have you seen the temple built by the Birlas? Can you tell me how many hundreds of millions of rupees were spent on that? They ask, could the seventh wonder of the world, the Taj Mahal, have been built if there was no money? Could Robi Thakur of Jorasanko have become a world poet if he didn't have immense landed property? Could Gautam Buddha have undertaken his great teaching unless he was a king's son?'

'Actually, that's simply bad reasoning.'

'Then what's the correct reasoning? You can't read or write, you're lying on the railway platform with your hands pressed to your belly and you have the audacity to argue? Who's going to listen to what useless people like you say? Their people have taken over art and literature, they run the country, the temples and monasteries, educational institutions, everything. Everyone will accept whatever they say as absolute truth.'

The man with the stone laughed now. But his laugh too was as hard as the stone. He said, 'Let me rid you of a delusion before you die. Tell me which direction the sun rises from? Think about it and tell me.'

'There's nothing to think about, everyone knows it's the east.'

'There you see, they say the sun rises from the east and so you say the same. That's what everyone says. But not for once does anyone think about whether the sun is anyone's slave that it must rise from the east every day. Let me tell you, the sun doesn't rise from the east or west or north or south, it's fixed at its own spot. When the night passes, the direction from where we first see the sun is called east. That's what we have been taught. In simple terms, where the sun rises becomes the east.'

The man was silent for a while, and then he continued. 'There have always been two groups of people in our country. You could say they belong to two sides, or two points of view. One group has everything, and the other group has nothing. Those who have everything are few in number. Those who have nothing are great in number. But those few people have the latter under their feet. It's no big deal for the many people to get together and finish off those few people. But you know what the problem is, the many aren't aware, they aren't organised, and they're not that concerned about rooting out the system that's come down from time immemorial. And even among the many, a few people emerge as their leaders, either through religious association, or by coming under the sway of political ideology, or out of attraction for wealth. That's why even after trying many times, the few haves can't be wiped out. And so, one has to start from the other end now. Like chanting "mara, mara" and arriving at "Rama, Rama".'

'How's that?'

'If I have to explain that to you, I'll have to tell you a story first.'

'Tell me. Put the stone down and sit down beside me and tell me.'

'Of what use is the story to you before you die?'

The youth replied, 'Our maxims say, "Learn as long as you live". They say, "the wealth of life is never lost."'

The man with the stone coughed and cleared his throat. 'Long ago, there was an emperor in our country called Ashoka. He embraced the Buddhist faith. He gave up all his luxuries and comforts, and led an extremely simple life. And he wanted the people of the kingdom too to forsake pleasure and luxury, and lead simple, ordinary lives. So the emperor declared that no woman in his kingdom could wear jewellery and ornaments on her body. That no man could wear expensive, attractive garments. The law to that effect was created, but it was found that no one complied with the law. Affluent folk adorned and decorated themselves in the same way as before and went about. So what was to be done? How could people be made to forsake all that? The senior-most minister of the land then advised the emperor to use the law differently. So the emperor made a new declaration. What was that? Now because of the earlier declaration, women who were engaged in prostitution could no longer adorn themselves with ornaments, and so they began to lose their customers. They were in financial distress, and so the stricture on wearing expensive garments and ornaments was no longer applicable to women who were engaged in prostitution. Similarly, those who were the customers of prostitutes were also exempted. It was found that from the next day no more men or women wore expensive clothes or ornaments. Because they would then be dressed like prostitutes and their customers. No one wanted to wear expensive garments and be disgraced!' The man pushed the supine youth's leg with his feet and said, 'What did you understand? This is what's called bending your finger to get the ghee out of the jar when you can't do it with a straight finger. If you don't heed what I say in this way then do it the other way.'

Who knows what the time was now. It was silent everywhere. The voice of the drunken, assassin resounded hideously in that silent darkness. People would soon start arriving to catch the first train of the day. It wouldn't be possible for him to carry out his murder. And so, the youth continued to hear the man with the stone rave.

'Our country is a vast one. There are people of so many languages, customs and cultures here. Do you know there's a place that's surrounded by forests and mountains? Its name is Abujhmad. A primitive Adivasi tribe by the name of Muria lives there. If someone hits someone with a shoe there, the one who is beaten is punished, not the one who hit him.'

'Punishment for the victim! That's an upside-down custom!'

'What's upside-down to you and me is as clear as water to them.'

'How's that?'

'Who wears shoes? First it was the British and now it's this country's babu class. The Adivasis never wore shoes earlier, nor do they wear them now. They hate the "civilised, babu, gentlemen" class. For the Adivasis of Abujhmad it's a simple calculus—why did an Adivasi go so close to all those despised folk that someone could hit him with a shoe? After all, a shoe is not like a bow and arrows! It's because he went near that the shoe hit him. He had to be punished for that. And not some small punishment. He was straightaway cast out from the community. That's why, if someone's shoe touches an Adivasi, you can be sure that he's got misfortune in his fate. An enraged Adivasi will cut your neck with his axe. The one who doesn't do that will be declared an offender and punished by the Adivasi community. Tell me, will a babu who knows about this custom of theirs have the audacity to strike someone with a shoe?'

The youth asked, 'In the place you spoke about, if there's a robbery, do people leave the thief behind and catch the policeman and haul him to jail? Thrash him up?'

The man replied, 'That custom's the best one. If that could be done, you'd see that there wouldn't be any more robberies and thefts in the country. Millions of rupees are spent on the police department, but is crime decreasing even by a bit? Why not? They're getting their salaries and getting bribes from the criminals too. If there was a rule that the police station responsible for a locality where there was a robbery or burglary would compensate that through deductions from the constables' salaries—then none of that would happen any more. But if you speak of Abujhmad, there's no police or suchlike there, and so there are no thieves and robbers too. No thieves, no beggars, no prostitutes. There aren't any rich folk, and so there aren't any poor either. No landlords, and so no one's landless. All of them live together. They go hunting together, they share and eat whatever they get.'

The man with the stone didn't say anything for a long while. The night advanced. Not even the sound of the mongrels howling could be heard now. Countless unknown, nameless stars twinkled in the sky. A shooting star suddenly raced towards the northeast, like a fireworks rocket. The man then said, 'Is there anything more that you want to know or say? If not, let me smash you with the stone now!'

In the course of the conversation, the youth had briefly forgotten that he was lying in an unfriendly darkness and standing near his feet with the stone raised was an emissary of death.

Perspiring profusely now, he said in a trembling voice, 'Are you joking with me? Are you really going to kill me?'

'Yes, my dear, I swear on Ma Kali, I'm really going to kill you. You tell me, what's the point of keeping you people alive? This spot under the stairs that you're hiding in, after a few days another one will join you there. A girl, my dear. Like you, there are so many pavement girls wandering around. And then the two pavement types will fuck and give birth to another pavement dweller. Nowadays this station is swarming with all those tiny pieces of garbage. Some are naked, some wearing pants torn at the backside, their hair matted and noses running. Tell me what's to become of them? They'll become beggars, petty thieves, whores, porters, maidservants and so on, won't they? But they'll never become humans. It's to avert the arrival of that nuisance that putting an end to your breathing is vitally important.'

The man moved a bit closer to the recumbent youth and said, 'This great work should have been initiated long ago by someone or the other. If a sense of panic and terror had been put into people's minds that if they slept on pavements, station platforms or under trees someone would arrive and kill them while they were asleep, then no one would want to sleep like that. In whichever way they could, through whatever means, they would try to build a secure shelter. And that would be for their own good. I want to plant that fear deep in people's minds. What people end up doing when they're afraid is not something they can do in ordinary circumstances, even if they are brave. What people do when they're in desperate straits, with the fear of death hanging over their heads, will be good for future generations.'

The man with the stone was speaking excitedly. He stopped to catch his breath. And then he continued. 'I know that whatever I'm doing now is not right in the eyes of the general public and according to the law. They can't judge my work correctly right now. That's what's been happening eternally. Not just me alone, many great sages failed to get due recognition in their times. But that recognition came from people of a future generation. I have no doubt whatsoever that one day people will realise the value of my work. And on that day, there won't be a single homeless person in this country. Words like homeless, shelterless, harbourless, derelict and destitute would need to be removed from the dictionary.'

The boy realised that there was no possibility of his survival. Usually people lost their sense of right and wrong in a fit of greed or rage or vengeance and committed a heinous act like murder. There might still be a chance, by dint of some circumstance, of rescue from the clutches of such a killer. But it was very difficult to be rescued from a man who performed his act not out of greed, or rage or for vengeance but entirely selflessly, motivated by blind adherence to an ideal. The kapaliks, who vowed human sacrifice in order to satisfy Ma Kali, were unmoved however much the little boy brought for sacrifice wept.

The youth was too weak to move or rise. Even the strength to shout and scream and get a crowd of people seemed to have vanished. He was half-dead anyway from hunger, thirst and weariness. So what could he do now! He shut his eyes and helplessly counted the moments as he waited for the stone to come down on his head.

The boy had arrived in this world some twenty years ago. He couldn't remember a single day in his life that had been spent joyfully, when he'd been able to laugh heartily for a while. It was as if he was trapped in a monstrous hell of constant deprivation, starvation, humiliation and oppression, where no light of hope or any shore of support could be glimpsed. It had then occurred to him many times that death was a thousand times better than such a life. That it wouldn't be a bad idea to commit suicide and be free of such an unbearable situation. That longed-for death was standing next to him today. A stone would descend—*smash!* Only a few seconds of agony. After that, all agony, difficulty, humiliation and hunger would come to a complete end. The reclining youth got ready—Come, O stone! Come, O death! After all, one had to die some day. So why not let it be today! When there's no way I can avoid you—let me accept you at ease. Descend, O stone!

The man said, 'I've never talked so much and for so long with anyone before you. I usually just go somewhere and bring the stone down. All of them died in their sleep with one blow. The poor wretches didn't even know why they died like that in their sleep. You're the only one who's going to die knowing everything. To tell you the truth, I'm feeling really happy now. I feel absolutely light-headed ...'

'Shall I say something?'

'More talk! You're going on and on ... How much more do you have to say? All right, tell me.'

'Aren't you afraid?'

'Afraid? What's there to be afraid of while killing sleeping folk? Is there any easier prey than humans in this world?'

'That's not what I meant.'

'Then what are you saying?'

'I'm saying that after all you're killing people. What will happen if you get caught by someone one day?'

The man with the stone laughed. 'I'll surely get caught some day or the other, either by the police or the public. What'll happen then? Nothing will happen! I'll die, that's all. Either the police will hang me, or the public will beat me to death like a mad dog—isn't it? *Aarey*, I've taken ten lives—but I'll lose only one. One in exchange for ten. So I'll still make a profit, isn't it?'

'Even if you exchange a hundred for one, it's you who's the loser.'

'I don't think so. Each person's calculation of profit and loss is different.'

The youth had realised that the man was unwavering in his blind resolve. It was impossible to make him budge. Kindness, compassion, affection and love were all great qualities of the human race. But not everyone had these qualities. If they did, bloodshed, murder, destruction and woe would have disappeared from the earth.

He reflected that the man with the stone wasn't some ghoul, or an ogre in human guise, he was a man. But there was no kindness or compassion in his heart. Why was that? If a piece of iron was kept in contact with a magnet, the iron too became magnetic. So did this man never come in contact with any kind and loving person in his life? When a handful of grain was scattered on the earth and it received light, air and rain then it came back a thousand-fold. If a seed of love had been planted in the bosom of this man by a kind person, it would have been a tree today. It would have given flowers, fruit and cool shade. Perhaps no one had given him this human quality. That's why he had none of that in him. How could he distribute something that he did not possess?

The terrible fear of death that had overwhelmed the youth when he first saw the man with the stone was no longer there. He said, 'The fear of death is more troublesome than actual death. I've been living with that trouble all my life. I can't bear it any more. Hit me with the stone. If I die I'll be freed from all the burning agony.'

'So you're ready to die?'

'What else can I do but be ready? I don't have an ounce of strength in my body. So how will I resist you? After all, you're standing at my feet. If I could have suddenly kicked you in your balls, where would you be, and where would your stone go! But what can I do, let whatever's in my fate happen.'

The man said, 'Like you're angry with me, you're also angry with yourself. Tell me, isn't that true? But just think for once, did I say anything incorrect? Can one or can't one kill by that reasoning? Almost half the people in the city live on pavements, railway stations, under trees, beside rail tracks, on the banks of foetid canals, in slums and shanties, where people die every day like dogs, cats, jackals, vultures, mosquitoes and flies, of disease, starvation and from eating foul food. Bastards—when you're dying, at least die like humans. Turn around just once and say—"there must be a fundamental transformation in this system".' The man spat out a glob of phlegm in contempt and continued. 'They're all a bunch of cowardly, half-dead eunuchs. The bastards will die of starvation but they won't snatch food. During the Bengal famine in 1943, almost three million people died of starvation, yet there were no food riots. I despise such people, I swear on Ma Kali, I really despise them. Thousands of boys, each one of them a gem, gave up their lives prematurely trying to make these sons of swine aware, and trying to put an end to their sorrows and misery. So many of them rotted in jail, so many were crippled for life. What was the need for them to do that? But the people they were fighting for did not take a single step for themselves, they didn't resist. The millstone of exploitation that sits heavy on society couldn't be moved.'

The man continued, 'Didn't you say that humans are the greatest beings on earth? I don't have the means to do it, or else I'd finish everyone off like how the municipal corporation pours oil in drains to kill mosquitoes. Down with your greatest being—who scours garbage bins and snatches food away from the jaws of street dogs!'

The youth thought that the man wasn't exactly cruel or unkind. Hidden under the cover of apparent intractability there was within him a secret distress for those who were bereft. And that distress must have driven him to his present madness.

The supine youth knew that there were several varieties of madness. This was a vast country and the state apparatus was infinitely powerful. Hundreds of thousands of policemen and soldiers, submarines, tanks, bomber aircraft—what did they not possess? Those who held the Red Book in one hand and in the other clutched a few country bombs, or a katta or a clumsy pipe gun made in a small forge, declared war on this state power—one had adequate reason to doubt their mental health. And yet all of them were meritorious university students. They wrote poetry, sang songs, painted pictures, acted in plays, some were doctors, engineers and lawyers. Except in this one sphere, they were completely normal, healthy people. Because of that madness they did things which could not be explained using ordinary intelligence. The man with the stone appeared to be violent and ghastly now, but perhaps once the light of day emerged, he would appear to be another man.

After remaining silent for a while, the mad drunkard said, 'Do you know why I said so much all this while? I too belong to the "have-nots". I too feel anguished and angry about the inhuman condition of these lives, I hate myself for that. Tell me, if all of us "have-nots" stand up as one, can't we change the situation? There are plenty of examples in the world to prove that it's possible. But they won't stand and rise. They won't fight and demand what's theirs by right. There's nothing but death in the fate of all these weak, cowardly, powerless people. No more talk, close your eyes and die now. Be born again after you die!'

The stone descended just after that. The boy who had borne starvation and humiliation for so many years and survived died. And then he rose once again, just like a tender sapling that survived and grew amidst the ruins of a destroyed city or civilisation, heralding the future.

2

The Vagabond

The weary and hungry vagabond who had been lying like a corpse since last night under the stairs of the overbridge on Platform No. 2 of the Jadavpur railway station, amidst all the dust, dirt, paan spittle, banana and orange peels, bread wrappers and other garbage there, woke up with a start to a crashing sound, and fully awake now, he looked wide-eyed in astonishment in all directions. He had no doubt now that he was the most fortunate person in the world. He pressed his hand on the left side of his chest and realised that his heart was thumping rapidly. That clearly meant he was still alive.

This world was most beautiful. There was nothing more pleasurable and blissful than being alive here. There couldn't be. Which was why people kept their blind or lame or bedsore-ridden and even paralysed, bedridden and comatose loved ones alive through a million means.

During the night that had just passed, so many hundreds of people had had to leave this earth and go away, whether out of natural or unnatural causes, and for known or unknown reasons. But he had been saved from being devoured by a macabre death. Like a dearly beloved one, the breezy, pure, clean air of dawn smeared a pleasant sensation all over him. The universe's message of life resounded in his ears, it lit hope in his breast, and in a little while, the lordly sun turned the eastern sky red and rose like a golden orb. That sunrise could be glimpsed to one's heart's content. This was most joyous, most blissful.

His eyes now fell on the hard floor of the platform and he realised that the object that fell with a monstrous metallic sound was not a heavy stone thrown by that murder addict. It was an innocent and innocuous fish-trough. A fish seller had thrown it. He would get on the first Down-train of the day and go to some fish market in the riverine country of south Bengal to bring fish.

With the arrival of the train, there could be no more delay. That seemed to be the message that emanated from the flow of life in the railway station as he woke up suddenly. By now some passengers of various ages had arrived at the railway station. The solitary tea-stall that was exactly in the middle of the platform was open now to quench their thirst. Cups of hot tea from the shop reached eager hands. Slurp, slurp, they sipped noisily.

If there had been food in his belly, his eyes would have been submerged in the deep slumber of dawn. And it wasn't inconceivable that any other person would have reason to be angry with the fish seller for his offence of throwing the trough and ruining his sleep. But the young man sleeping in the dark niche below the stairs, on being woken up so rudely, couldn't express his anger against him. To the contrary, he felt rather pleased inwardly. Being liberated from the terrifying nightmare that had seized him, like an octopus with its eight tentacles, and paralysed him with fear, he actually felt gratitude towards the unknown fish seller. It was as if, amidst this darkness, he was revealed as a person dispatched by God to grant a new life to someone imperilled and facing death.

The recumbent had had a nightmare. A long and terrifying one. A murderer was standing near his head, holding a huge stone raised in his hands, with the intention of killing him. He had been about to smash his head with the stone. His life seemed to be hanging by a thread. Being delivered now from that agonising moment preceding death, the supine vagabond laughed inwardly. He thanked the God of life for being given a new lease.

Just like one can't measure contentment, or say how much of it one ought to receive in order to call it contentment, unless that is weighed against misery, it's impossible to know what life is, and how valuable the breath of life is, unless one stands face-to-face with death.

The lights had come on in the railway station. Until a little while back, the entire locality had been swallowed up by a terrifying darkness owing to a power cut, but that vanished the moment the lights returned.

A religious preacher had said that however fearsome and piercing the darkness might be, and even if all the darkness on earth was gathered together, it couldn't extinguish the light of a small earthen lamp. But if the flame of the lamp was extinguished for some reason, the darkness could assume an intense form. Of course, he had said this out of anguish over the decay of belief in God and the spread and development of atheism in the world.

It was very difficult to say whether this beautiful earth would be suitable for humans to live in if a day dawned when there was no more light. But there was no need for any such worry now. Because however fierce the darkness of that world might be, and however it might conspire, it did not have the power to extinguish a small earthen lamp. But if the lamp went out for some reason, the darkness would only grow fiercer.

This was true, and it is equally true in politics, sociology, art, literature, culture and all other spheres. These were bad times. In a sense, there was no ray of light anywhere in this country. There was only darkness, a piercing, all-pervading darkness. An insidious, crippling, black, new moon's darkness seemed to have descended upon society and life all over the country. It seemed there was perpetual night, suffocating and ghastly. A band of creatures of darkness romped around in that darkness like maddened elephants.

They had no pity or mercy, no sense of good and bad, right and wrong, or fair and foul, no remorse or compunction. They roamed around with their ferocious fangs and claws bared, intent on devouring people. But they looked exactly like humans.

No one could say whose chest they would stab in the anarchic darkness, or when. No one could say which breast's warm blood would wet the city streets, which mother's bosom would be laid bare, and which woman would be widowed.

Time was a terrible assassin now. Everything was joyless, with only the great glee of murderers all around. The unfettered movement of exultant killers in the valley of death known as a country. Whether in street processions, or in public rallies or political meetings, it was killers who had hegemony. Right now, the creatures known as people had only one option, namely, death.

Although all the electric lights in the railway station were on at this time, the light could not reach the spot beneath the steps of the overbridge. It couldn't, no light could reach everywhere equally. While one set of people flew around in jet planes, downtrodden Adivasi folk were oblivious of what even a train was. It seemed that all the darkness of the land had come fleeing and hidden under the stairs like a criminal who had escaped from prison. As in prehistoric times, when man crawled out of a mountain cave into the light of this world, or even before that, when he emerged from the dark recesses of his mother's womb into the dusty earth—in the same way, the vagabond crawled out of the dark corner under the stairs, as if he had just been born. The sky above was packed with stars, as he stood on the hard cemented floor and stretched himself, and dusted the grime off himself. It seemed that it wasn't just the grime, but all the failures through life, the defeats, and every old notion that he wanted to dust off. He turned his head and gazed at the terrifying dark corner under the stairs.

The vagabond suddenly seemed to be thoughtful. He thought he was discarding his deprived, futile and humiliating past there, like a tree that shed its old leaves every spring and took on a new appearance, or like a snake that forfeited its worn-out skin every full moon. It wasn't a dream, it had really happened, a stone had been dropped on my head this night. The stone had smashed my head to smithereens. I am dead. But it was no man with a stone who smashed my head, it was I who did that to myself. The I that was alive until yesterday is no longer there. This me is a different me. I have just been born. This dark night is the mother from whose womb I was born. The moment such a thought struck him, a bolt of energy shot through his long-starved, weary body. Until just yesterday, his knees trembled violently as they bore his body. But that had vanished in a trice. He stood up straight. He clenched his hand into fists, unclenched them, and then clenched them again. He glanced at the signal post. The red glowed in the pitch darkness, like a one-eyed monster. When that turned green, it meant that a train was arriving. The tea-stall in the middle of the platform was full of customers now. They were the passengers waiting at the station, mostly labourers, and rickshaw-drivers. They blew on the steaming tea and sipped it. All of them were worried lest the train arrived on time today. They couldn't be sipping tea in that event. They would have paid for the tea in vain. That's why they were hurrying.

The vagabond longed for a cup of tea now. Who didn't want that after waking up at the crack of dawn! This small desire could by no means be seen as criminal. But his pockets were completely empty. It had been so for many days.

The man knew that there were two ways of obtaining food in this country. The first was to put the money down before the shopkeeper with a bang, order whatever one liked, and then eat to one's fill. The second was to order whatever one liked, eat to one's fill, and then flee the place. But since he did not possess even a penny, there was no question of buying food. And if he had to adopt the second method, right now he possessed neither the strength in his legs, nor the courage of mind that were required for that. He had been unable to stand up yesterday; but he was standing up today. He would be able to walk tomorrow. And sprint the day after tomorrow. He had to wait until then. For just a few days!

He pinched his throat to quell his desire for tea, and climbed slowly to the top of the overbridge. If it had been yesterday, he would have had to take the help of the railing on the side to climb up. But his mind didn't consent to that today.

The overbridge was at the western end of the station. Standing atop the bridge, the man looked both eastwards and westwards. Beneath him, the railway track stretched out like a taut bowstring. The two parallel rails seemed like the straight lines of life and death. One complemented the other. If one of them was excluded, the other was rendered worthless and unreal.

After a while, the vagabond sat down on the bridge, resting his head on the railing. The pleasant breeze of dawn lapped at his face. It was like the touch of a compassionate hand, patting the head of a dying person. The youth dozed off again. No nightmares attacked him while he slept now. There was a squalid mass of innumerable tiny shanties on both the northern and southern sides of the railway station. Hogla reed, bamboo matting, discarded tin sheets, leaves, wood, gunny and various other items were used in their construction. All the labouring folk who dwelt in these shanty settlements were also asleep now, motionless. As were the happy citizens of the cultured and polished civil world beyond the railway area. Denying the environment of cold terror that pervaded the body of society, people were now submerged in the deep, inaccessible pit of unconsciousness.

The vagabond himself was unaware of how long he slept like that. Up- and Down-trains arrived and halted one after another. There was a lot of commotion in the station precincts for a little while. The man lazily opened his eyes a slit. Once the train departed, unbroken silence once again descended upon the entire station. He shut his eyes again.

When he next opened his eyes, this time, as expected, there in the eastern sky, like a golden dish, like the big red dot of sindoor on one's Ma's forehead, was the round red effulgent sun. The city that seemed to be dead and ruined in the darkness of night seemed to have returned to life upon receiving the rejuvenating touch of the rays of the new sun.

The glow and shine of the light of the new morning had now spread to the ramshackle huts on both sides of the railway lines, and the artistry of the flickering light was also manifest in the glum face of the poor ragpicker boy with blistered hands and feet, setting off with a torn sack slung on his shoulder to collect waste paper, the scraggly hair of the girl who washed utensils in babu homes, and the eyes of the blind beggar who sang to the accompaniment of a tambourine.

The vagabond came down the stairs to Platform No. 1. All around him were large milk drums, huge bundles of newspapers and massive baskets of vegetables. Averting all these, he advanced on wobbly legs, like a child that had just learnt to walk, taking tiny steps, and with his face turned towards the newly risen sun. He didn't really know where he was going, or why. He thought he could, and so he did.

He walked till the end of Platform No. 1, stepped down and crossed the rail tracks on the left side, and hopped up to Platform No. 2. He walked westwards, and then crossed the tracks, and returned to Platform No. 1. After doing this over and over again a few times, it occurred to him, this isn't my first time here, I have come here before, some time or the other. I lived here for a while. That's why these streets, shops, markets and people all look very familiar. That mad old woman in tatters sitting with a dirty pot on a torn kantha in a corner of the station, I had seen her one afternoon sitting near the railway yard and cooking rice on a brick stove, with leaves and twigs for fuel. That teenage girl looking at herself in a broken mirror and tying her hair was attending to her hairdo before leaving with her Ma for Hari Singh's cattle shed to collect the cow-dung there. She had once jumped naked into the nearby pond. She had played around in the water. He remembered everything now. But he could not remember when exactly, or how long ago, that was. A complex black curtain swayed between memory and forgetting.

The vagabond wondered, am I remembering things from a past life? Were all those incidents from some earlier life? When I came to this station, fevered, with ugly welts on my back, my whole body in pain, and passed out as I rested against the wall behind that paan depot, and lay there all night. I don't exactly remember who it was that thrashed me badly with a bamboo stick. Who thrashed me? Why?

And thus, while travelling without a ticket on a train, on an aimless journey yesterday, when the train halted here, the footloose vagabond had got off on account of some irresistible attraction. Standing now in front of the wall in the station where he had once lain unconscious, he tried to remember where exactly he had been impelled, with all his life, to try to reach, since yesterday, or even earlier, one could say, since the time his eyes first saw light! Everything seemed clouded in mist. He couldn't remember anything any more. Once upon a time, there was a huge explosion on the sun. Many scientists have been able to provide an elaborate explanation, on the basis of their expert knowledge, of how this world was created, and how life gradually emerged on earth. But all knowledge finally failed before the behind-the-scenes mystery of human creation. No one has been able to say what kind of evolution took place, as a result of which ape was transformed into man. Scientists have identified this epoch of the triumphal journey of ape becoming man as the missing link. Also undiscovered till now, when exactly man forgot all his human responsibilities, feelings, virtues, and duties, and turned into a non-human creature. When the mother who could no longer bear the anguished cry of the offspring born of her own womb, 'I'm hungry, Ma, give me food', herself went to strangle it to death. Much of this vagabond's life involved a similar missing link. But he clearly remembered that he had been born in a thatched, twin-roof hut, from the womb of a woman who went around begging for a bit of rice foam. He wasn't alone, he had a bunch of small brothers and sisters with protruding ribs. Among whom, one sister had shrivelled up and shrunk, out of starvation, at the age of seven or eight.

His father had never been lazy, or shirked work. He could toil from sunrise to sunset like a wild buffalo. But the number of job aspirants was always far greater than the number of jobs available in this *'Saare Jahan Se Achchha'* country. Which was why the daily labourer father didn't find work every day. And if he did find work, the wages for that were too low for the hard work it involved. And so, he didn'.t get to eat every day. As a result of which he fell ill. He came down with the ailment that starvation leads to. It was known as a gastric ulcer, in English. Everyone knew that ailments were cured with medicines. But when the man was a complete pauper, how could an ailment with such a fancy English name be treated by chewing the leaves of Bengal's thankuni, or pennywort? An English medicine was required for that, which was terribly expensive. It was difficult for a man who lived from hand to mouth to afford that. Consequently, the father's ailment was never treated. The pain resulting from the ailment grew worse by the day. After a while, he lay writhing in bed like a slaughtered goat, and implored to God, 'I can't bear it any more, grant me death now!' How would a family survive when its only earning member was confined to bed? The kitchen stove was no longer lit. The business of eating came to an end. After some days, the youth's sister shrivelled up and died of starvation.

One day, the young man had been tortured by hunger. He was simply not able to bear it. As if there was a wrenching inside his stomach, like a python twisting. He left home and ran away. And he had started walking like a crazed person, along a strange and unknown path. He was very young then. Just fifteen, or sixteen. He had not really seen the cruel ugliness of the world. Illusory souls spanned the nooks and crannies of his mind. He had thought, it's such a vast world. Maybe not here, but surely in some corner or the other he would find food. Hot, steaming, red-coloured, plump-grained rice. And if there was some salt, a couple of green chillies, and a lump of boiled potato with that, what more could one ask for!

And when that rice was available, he would first eat as much as he could and fill his stomach, and then pack some in a bundle using his gamchcha, and bring that for his starving parents and siblings at home. Owing to the lack of food, his siblings neither laughed nor played, they just cried all day. His Ma too seemed to have become like a mad old woman as she went without food, and his father seemed to be dying. He didn't know then that the world was most miserly. It hadn't left even a fistful of rice for him. All that it had in store for these destitute folk was contempt, ridicule, hatred, deprivation and oppression.

After leaving home, he had arrived at the railway station and boarded a train there. He got off that later, and boarded another train. And then another. Day after day, and month after month, he moved from one place to another, solely on the quest for food. Where was the hot, steaming rice! Almost like a caged lunatic, or like a raging storm, he wandered, ticketless, and with an empty stomach, from one end of the country to another, in the hope of finding the desired food, but he didn't get that. He had observed that except for a small number of people, all the innumerable people across the country were hungry. All of them spent their nights in the endless penance for food. Even in the various cities and metropolises where all the resources of the country were concentrated, hundreds and thousands of starving folk clamoured for a couple of stale rutis as they stood with a battered bowl or plate in their hands. The hill stations that nestled visitors in comfort and joy too had poor people without warm clothes, who wailed and wept because of the bitter cold. And in our beloved, most beautiful city, Calcutta, this paradise of enjoyment and luxury, here too people lay on the streets for want of the tiniest bit of kindness and compassion. They died on the streets.

From long personal experience, the young man had realised that he was an outcaste and an unnecessary creature in this world. No one would give him anything here. And yet the quest continued. Going round and round, again and again, like a wheel, which he had begun almost a decade ago—that still continued. He still walked the streets with the lamp of faint hope lit, and thought that he would surely find a bit of soft, tender soil where a small plant could gently take root and thus extract a bit of food for survival. He relied on his own strength and ability.

A madcap had set out in search of a touchstone. After much searching, and failure, he forgot the way back and lost all hope of finding the touchstone. All that he had left was the habit of searching, and the addiction of wandering the streets. In the same way, as this vagabond too wandered, and went from one place to another, somewhere along the way he somehow forgot the very objective behind leaving home and treading the road. The entire past, and the sad faces of his loved ones had begun to fade from his memory. The indomitable will to move forward was all that remained in his blood.

Someone had once opined that the earth was round. No matter where one began one's journey, it was possible to return to the place where the journey had begun if one walked on incessantly.

This vagabond remembered the starting point of the journey, as he did the moment he had set out, but a vast emptiness surrounded almost everything else. An immense darkness overshadowed every fragment of memory. A big missing link in his life.

But since yesterday, or one could say, since last night, his mind and intelligence had started becoming active once again. He gradually remembered everything. That was why he felt terribly scared now. If this path of the world ever led me to my loved ones, what answer would I give them? After all, these two hands of mine are still as empty and bereft as before, I have been unsuccessful, a failure.

Someone had once said that life was a journey. The one whose journey came to a halt was actually dead.

Life may be a journey. But not all journeys were like life. The piece of grass carried by the strong current of the river was journeying alright, but was it alive? This vagabond's life was a lot like that. It was as if he had wheels on his feet, because of which he had not been able to stand still on any spot of land, or in any role. He kept sliding away. And he slid and slid until he reached this railway station. He still did not know exactly what role his fate had brought him here to enact.

It was eight or eight-thirty in the morning now. Like always, a busy day had begun in this part of the city of Calcutta. Up- and Down-trains arrived and then departed one after another. In the interregnum between the arrival and departure, the train halted for a while to disgorge teeming masses. Countless people—young and old, fair-skinned and dark-complexioned, short and tall, men and women, gentlemen and lowly folk. A major part of the life of this newcomer here had been spent on the platform of some railway station. The crowd of people in every station seemed the same to him. The same commotion, running around, shouting and screaming, shoving and jostling, quarrels and fisticuffs.

Observing another train arriving now, the man moved away. He wasn't supposed to like being shoved and elbowed in his present bodily state. That's why he was a bit wary. The Up-Lakshmikantapur suburban train arrived in a few moments and halted at the platform. Although it was morning, all the Up-trains were frightfully crowded. The passengers were bathed in perspiration, and flattened like chira. There was no longer any food, money, or work in rural Bengal. The modern city had wrung the villages dry of their lifeblood, turning them into a heap of refuse, like sugarcane bagasse. That's why village folk were headed to the city now. The city didn't deprive them entirely. It was like the cunning milkman who fed the emaciated cow some of its own milk after he had milked it dry.

The vagabond was looking in front. Once the crowd thinned a bit, he spotted a woman who was in her thirties, dark-complexioned, of medium height, and in reasonably good health; she was staring at him unblinkingly, with a look of great astonishment and bewilderment on her face. The woman had a heavy bag in one hand, and her son's hand held firmly in the other.

After staring at him like that for quite a while, she shook her son's hand, and said to him, 'See who's standing there!'

'Who is it, Ma?' the boy shot back.

'Can't you recognise him? It's your Jibon Mama!'

'Where's he?'

'There, behind the paan-depot.'

The boy would have been about twelve years old. He was curly-haired, like Lord Kartik. He had a round face, and a simple, innocent smile that could only be seen on the faces of children. But in this case, it was different. Not all children could smile like this. Everyone wasn't so fortunate. Yet this boy could smile.

The boy left his mother's hand and ran towards the newly-arrived vagabond. And then he held his arm firmly. The smile on the boy's face vanished, and a fierce complaint arose. 'Where were you all these days, Mama?'

The vagabond was twenty-four or twenty-five- years old. So he could well be called a youth. He was shocked at this sudden attack. He fell into utter confusion. He could simply not remember when and where exactly he had seen this boy and his mother before now. Although both the faces looked extremely familiar! He wasn't able to view them as strangers. But there was a problem as regards this vagabond youth, his memory simply refused to cooperate with him. A chapter of his life had been washed away, swept and plastered over, wiped clean, leaving no mark behind. So he looked at the boy with much embarrassment. The woman picked up her bag and slowly came and stood before the youth. She echoed the same query, 'Where were you all these days, dear?'

'How many days?' The stranger suddenly retorted.

The woman flared up at that. 'Don't you know how long? It must be at least two months!'

The boy shook the stanger's arm again. 'I came long back to Ma for the summer vacation. Why didn't you come even once to our house, Mama?'

The woman said, 'So many people said such a lot of things about you. Some said that you had been murdered. Some said you are sitting in prison. One person said that you had got married to the only daughter of some fishery owner somewhere, and are living as a *ghar jamai* in Sindeshwar or somewhere. Whom shall I believe or disbelieve? Every person says something different. So you tell me now where you were after you disappeared!'

The stranger felt quite unsettled at being suddenly accosted by kin in this way. Of course, the very next moment he controlled himself too. His footprints were to be found in various places, including those in which he was out of place, and which were bad places. He had had to confront many unimaginable incidents in his life. Where he was required to speak the truth, he had told the truth, and where lies were called for, he had lied. He had learnt from his own life experience that a lie was more powerful than a piece of truth. It was sometimes truer than truth. But seeing that there wasn't really any need to be untruthful, he told the truth. 'I was wandering around.'

'Where were you wandering around?'

'Did I ever know that! I went wherever my eyes and my feet took me.'

'Why did you do that?'

'I don't really know why I went.'

'Have you got married?'

'Oh no. How can I get married when my own food and shelter are uncertain!'

The woman's voice now turned tearful. She softly said, 'Forget about me. After all, I'm no one to you. But there are definitely some people here who really love you. They worry about you. What kind of person are you? Didn't you think of them even once? No word of where you were, or how you were.'

The stranger was stunned by the flurry of complaints. As far as he could remember, this was probably his first time in this station. And if he had indeed been here before, that was not six months or a year ago. By no means. It could well have been in his previous life. He felt at a complete loss now, that there could be someone here who considered him kin, or loved him!

The woman continued, 'Raju has been with me for almost three weeks. Every day he asks me, "O Ma, why doesn't Jibon Mama visit anymore? Did you ask him not to come?"'

The stranger gathered that the boy's name was Raju. A very nice name. But he couldn't fathom why the boy had been so upset. Because of him? How could that be! Also surprising was the fact that the woman was referring to him as Jibon.

After the youth thought about the matter for a while, it became clear to him. There used to be a person here whose name was Jibon. Who looked exactly like me. He is missing now. And seeing me here now, these people have come to the conclusion that the missing person has returned.

False! This was a falsehood of Himalayan dimensions. People were very foolish, they did not know that those who leave never return again. Even if the man who had got lost returned, he would no longer be the person who had left. His body and feet would be covered in the dust and grime, and whorls of filth, of many pathways, which was called memory, or experience, or maturity, which would constantly impede his return to the former position. But right now, in this moment of crisis, the stranger did not have the heart to point out the perfectly plausible error on the part of a simple woman and her naive son. The truth that was not in anyone's interest, which only brought sorrow, was inferior to a huge lie. Let there be a gross mistake. If that made someone happy for a while, so be it. Since no one was being harmed or made worse off. In a little while, these people will return to their respective destinations, and I will go my way, and then it won't matter a whit whether it was true or false.

In order to ease the ruinous and distressing atmosphere, the stranger said, 'Where I went, why I went, why I was away so long, why I couldn't send word—oh, that's a long story. How can I finish telling you all that right now, standing here on the platform! You are busy, and so am I. Let all that be for now. I'll tell you some other time. Tell me about yourself now. Where are you off to in the morning?'

The boy by the name of Raju began giggling when he heard him speak. He said, 'O Ma, who's this Jibon Mama! He talks just like an educated gentleman. No one will guess that he's Bangaal. And he's addressing you respectfully as *"tumi"* all the time!'

The woman laughed too. He thumped him gently on his back, and said, 'Just watch, he'll start addressing me as "Didi" very soon.' And then looking at the stranger, she raised an eyebrow and continued, 'No, that won't be wrong, after all I'm quite a few years older than you. Elders should be spoken to respectfully. That's what you've finally learnt in all this time. So what were you telling me?'

Raju asked, 'O Mama, don't you say *ailam, khailam, halar po* any more? Have you forgotten it?'

In reply to the boy's query, the woman replied, 'It happens. Such things do happen. Isn't it said that when a pussycat goes into the forest, it becomes a wild cat! And when a wild cat goes to a pilgrimage site, it becomes a renunciant! That's what's happened to your Jibon Mama now, dear. He has dropped the Bangaal language, and speaks proper Bengali now. You couldn't pinch a single strand on his head earlier because he used to crop it so short, but now his hair is so long that if you put earrings on him, he'll look like a girl. It's good, great, everything's changing, why shouldn't you change too!'

The woman paused for a while, laughed at her joke, and continued telling her son, 'Just think about how you were earlier, Raju! You used to play with the basti boys, and be covered in dust and mud, like some monster boy. And see how you are now, after joining the missionary school! Will anyone be able to say that you are the son of Anjali, the liquor seller? Tell me, will they? People are like clay, they turn out the way they are moulded. Just you see, you'll hesitate to call me your Ma one day.'

Raju burst out in protest, 'No, I won't hesitate. I'll never be like that. You're my Ma, and I'm your son. That's what we'll always be.'

'You're the son of my womb. You'll always be mine, that's no lie. But not everyone is from my womb. Why on earth should they remember me? When someone needs you, they're full of praise, but when they're done with you, you're called rotten. That's what I am to some people.'

The stranger realised that the final barb was directed towards him. The look in her eyes hinted at that. But there was nothing he could say now. He had not yet been able to figure out how the missing person by the name of Jibon happened to be Raju's Mama, and how the woman was his sister! So he thought it was best to remain silent. Let the attack grow more fierce. Let the poison-arrows of her words rain on him fiercely. Some clue or the other would emerge from that. All the complex knots would then unravel. All the darkness would be gone. Everything would become clear.

After being silent for a while, the woman named Anjali began speaking again. But now the poisonous jibes were no longer there. All her suppressed anguish welled up. 'You know how tiny Raju was when his dad died? He was still suckling then. I didn't believe that I could raise the boy all by myself. I was clever enough to begin the liquor business then, and that's how we survived. Or else, who knows where this mother and son would have been washed away. So many people say such a lot of things. A single woman. The liquor business. How can drunkards be trusted?

What if someone who's drunk molests you at night? How could I handle it all by myself?'

There were tears in Anjali's eyes now. She wiped her eyes with the anchal of her sari, and continued, 'As long as you were here, I felt as strong as an elephant. All the thieves and ruffians of the locality, all the drunks and addicts knew that I had a special relationship with you. That's why no rascal ever had the guts to look me in the eye. Everyone remembered how you thrashed that fish thief, Bhoja. I felt very vulnerable after you left. I don't feel like telling you how a few people from nearby, and most of all, the pickpocket, Hara, are annoying me. I keep thinking I should abandon my customers, and go away somewhere and get work that gives me food and lodging. Or else, who's to say when someone decides to break into my room and strangle me?'

The stranger now thought he could say something. Some information had been obtained, some clues had come up. So he said what was appropriate at this moment. Actually, it was as if he wasn't the one speaking, it was as if the person who was missing was sitting inside his head and making him say, 'But I am back now. So there! I don't need to go anywhere else. Everything will be fine, like before.'

The woman by the name of Anjali squeezed the stranger's hand in gratitude. 'I knew that you would say this.'

After a while, Anjali said, 'That Asima of mine—you know her, hey, the one who drank toddy and bit your ear—she's got married again. This husband is nice, he's not a thief, or a cheat. They bought two kattahs of land near Subhasgram and moved there. I wanted to visit them, but somehow I kept putting that off. Raju's vacation is coming to an end. So I decided to go yesterday. I wanted to stay there for a few days. But I felt like returning after a day. It's in the middle of nowhere, and after dusk it's just the darkness. I was trembling all over. Meanwhile, I had to worry about the thieves here. What will I do if someone walks away with my pots and pans, kantha and saris! That's why I rushed back the first thing this morning. Asima's husband reminded me about that. But everything was intact, so I could be at peace. Why don't you come along to my place? You can have a cup of tea with me.'

He had been dying for some tea for a long time. But now the newly-arrived stranger got the chance, unsolicited, to mitigate that. If he accompanied Anjali, he would get tea, and there would surely be something else to go with that! Two country-biscuits, and a bowl of muri? He nodded his head, and said, 'Let's go.'

They crossed over from Platform No. 1 to Platform No. 2. There was a long goods train halted there. Next to that were several heaps of stone chips, one next to another. And beside that was a vast vacant tract. A temporary market came up there in the evening. It was called Sandhya Bazaar. On the southern side of that were serried rows of shanties, an entire phalanx of shacks made of various materials like bamboo-matting, hogla reed, broken bits of discarded tin sheets, gunny, leaves and wood. Next to the shanties was a long, narrow strip of foul water, full of slithering worms. A long, high wall belonging to the Railways fringed the pond. On the other side of the wall was the life of the civilised, educated folk. It wasn't as if the people on this side did not go across when required. There was an unwalled section to permit movement. People from the shanties side too went across sometimes. But the people on both sides knew well which side they belonged to. They had nothing to do with the people on the other side.

The shanties—the moment one sighted them, one could conclude that they were beyond counting—where, in the opinion of the civilised and refined folk, as well as the police, illiterate, anti-social masses lived. That is to say, thieves, pickpockets, drunkards, whores, and so on. But although they were not entirely correct, it wasn't entirely untrue either.

Anjali lived in one such shanty. The door of her hut was cheaper and weaker than the small, brass lock on it. Anjali unlocked the door, kept the heavy bag on one side of the room, spread out a torn mat made of hogla on the floor, and said to the stranger, 'Sit.' She told her son, 'Go out and play for a while. Don't get your clothes dirty.'

Anjali took off the expensive sari she had on, folded it carefully, and hung it on the string strung across the room. And then she remembered that there was a man in the room. She promptly pulled down a torn gamchcha, and wrapped it around her fulsome breasts. And then she smiled embarrassedly, and warned him impishly, 'Don't you dare look this side, or I'll gouge your eyes out! I'm changing my blouse.'

She put on a torn and dirty blouse, and wound a similar cheap and coarse sari around herself. She sat on a wooden floor-seat that she pulled out, put water to boil on the stove, and said, 'There's no milk. So it's black tea. Just sit here, let me go and see whether Ahalya Mashi has made some petai porota.'

Ahalya's shop was nearby. She had ghugni and porota ready by seven in the morning. All the coolies and labourers had this cheap breakfast before setting out for their arduous labours. She bought two-hundred grams of porota and some ghugni from there, packed in sal leaves, placed it before the stranger, and said, 'Eat. Have all of it. I can see from your face that you are starving. Didn't you have anything to eat yesterday?'

The stranger hadn't eaten anything yesterday, or the day before yesterday, or the day before that as well, but he didn't even remember that now. It was as if after going for days on end without food, he had forgotten about food altogether. He stuttered, 'I mean … I don't … I mean, the money … I mean, if one wants to eat, then …'

Cutting him short, Anjali said, 'Hey! You've gone without food because you have no money! And here I am, holding on to your hundred-rupees since God knows when. Just wait, I had put that into a bundle and kept it somewhere. Let me try to remember.'

'What hundred-rupees?'

'The man who supplies me the booze, Imran, from Hossainpur, he gave it to me.'

'Why?'

'Didn't you ask me to tell him that he has to pay you, like he pays the police and the party boys every month? Or else you wouldn't let him carry on his business? I told him that. He gave me the money the next day. And then you disappeared somewhere. So I couldn't give it to you.'

As Anjali spoke, she took out a blue-coloured hundred-rupee note from the fund tucked in a sari fold at her waist, and proffered it to the stranger. 'Keep this. You need it. I'll look for where I kept the other note later. Here, take it.'

Someone was outside the door. He called out, 'O Boudi, dear, give me a pint of booze.'

Anjali looked at the stranger, and said in a whisper, 'It's that swine, the pickpocket Hara. Once the booze goes inside him, he starts saying all kinds of rubbish. Don't say anything, just sit here and listen.'

This time, too, the stranger said what was necessary right now. 'I'm here, don't worry. Let's see how far he goes. I'll kick him on his balls and make him sober!'

Anjali poured out the liquor from a large bottle and filled a small bottle, and held it out through the slit in the door. 'Here.' As Hara took the bottle, he said, 'Where were you yesterday, Boudi? I came so many times in vain.'

Who knows how Anjali would have responded if it had been some other day. But she felt very brave today. And reckless. She replied, 'Why were you looking for me? What business do you have with me? Aren't there ten or twenty other liquor vends around here?'

'Shall I tell you? I'm scared to do that!'

'Why don't you come out with it? If you can't bring yourself to say it, take two gulps and then tell me. I won't mind.'

'Unless I have the booze from your hands, I swear, I swear on Ma Kali, I don't get high. God's given you a lovely face. If it had been someone else, she would have earned a hundred-thousand rupees ...'

Anjali laughed. Her laughter was full of indulgence. So the pickpocket, Hara, was intoxicated even without taking a drink. In order to heighten the intoxication, Anjali said, 'I've been observing you for a long time. Booze doesn't make you drunk. It's not for the booze that you come to me either. Boozing is only an excuse, you have something else in mind. Isn't that correct? You swore on Ma Kali, so tell me the truth!'

Hara nodded his head meaningfully. 'So you got that!'

'What are you? Won't I get it? Am I a kid, or what? I know exactly what's on your mind.'

'Then tell me why I come to your vend! Can you tell me that?'

'You come because you want me. Isn't that true?'

After a pause, Anjali continued, 'You got married twice, and how many women you've slept with you yourself don't remember. You've had so many women, but you haven't stopped hoping for more. I believe you told Bishu, "I won't be at peace unless I've had her." That if I don't agree to your proposal, you'll throw acid on my face. Tell me, didn't you say that?'

'So the fucker Bishu told you!'

'You could have told me directly, instead of going about here and there, telling all and sundry.'

'I don't like it at all when you taunt me.'

'What do you mean?'

'I mean, I may have made a joke sometime, but you should not take that to heart. I'll never say such things again.'

'What was that you said about a hundred-thousand rupees?'

'I wasn't talking about you. I meant what women like Rupali, Sandhya and Bisakha would have done if they had a body as young as yours. They could have earned a hundred-thousand rupees.'

There was another room in front of Anjali's room. There was a bit of space between the rooms. Hara sat down on the bricks lying on the ground there. He took out a paper packet with some boiled gram, salt and green chillies from his pocket, and placed it beside him. He lifted the bottle to his mouth, took a gulp, and then put some gram into his mouth. He was high on the booze as well as Anjali.

Anjali now said, 'I need some money.'

'How much?' Hara asked. His eyes were gleaming now. The prey seemed at hand.

'What you said, a hundred-thousand. A thousand or two less will be fine. Asima has built a house in Subhasgram. Two katthas of land for fifty-thousand, and another fifty-thousand to build the house. I'll sell myself. Either buy me, or find me a buyer.'

Hara laughed, 'Ha ha.' And then he said, 'I said a hundred-thousand just like that. But I am like a small change buyer. Twenty, or fifty, or maybe a hundred, or two hundred sometimes. I can't afford any more.'

Anjali narrowed her eyes, and smiled wickedly. She said, 'Little drops of water too fill up the pot. So bring whatever you can, and come after a little while. Someone is already waiting in my room. Let me be done with him.'

'Who's that?'

'Look.' And as Anjali said that, she opened the door wide. Seeing the stranger sitting inside, Hara was shocked, as if he had seen a ghost. Forgetting all about the gram, he gulped down the liquor. He put down the bottle after that, flung the price of the liquor at her and fled the spot.

Anjali laughed, and said to the stranger, 'Hara has seen you, he's not going to come here again! You don't know how many times a day he used to bother me. As if he can't find booze in any other place.'

The stranger said, 'But if he comes ten times, isn't that good for your business?'

'He bought a pint now. Or else he just asks for half a glass. I spit on the face of such a customer! If you want to drink alcohol, do that. But why do your eyes wander! It drives me mad.'

Anjali filled a tall glass with black tea, placed it in front of the stranger, and said, 'Here you go. Hurry up and finish the porotas. If the tea gets cold, I can't warm it again. The kerosene is finished.'

'I can't eat so much.'

'Where's it so much? It's only two-hundred grams.'

'That's quite a lot.'

'But you used to have two-hundred-and-fifty, or three-hundred grams before. What happened today?'

'Do you think I'm still the same me?'

'All right, just eat as much as you can. Leave the rest, I'll eat it.'

'You'll have my leftovers?'

Pretending to be shocked, Anjali retorted, 'As if it's the first time you're feeding me leftovers!' She paused a bit, and then continued, 'I didn't know earlier that sharing someone's food made one fonder. I guess that's why I am crazy about you, like I was about Raju's father.'

The stranger ate the porota in right earnest, and continued to listen to Anjali. She carried on, as if in soliloquy, 'I wasn't so bad-looking, you know. After Raju's father died, so many people told me to get married again. They said, how will you go through a long life all by yourself. But I couldn't forget the fucker! It didn't seem right to serve food to someone on a plate that someone else had eaten from. And then I was afraid of something else as well. What if the new father wasn't nice to my Raju, if he didn't care about him? That's why I decided that I am fine as I am.'

The stranger asked, 'How long did you say it's been since Raju's father died?'

'Oh, it must be ten years at least. The day Raju's father was run over by a train was the first time you visited our place. I didn't know you before that. I had seen you around in the station, but we had never spoken. I think you used to work in Satish's liquor vend then. No, sorry, I think you were a waste picker then. Right, I remember. You used to sell that to the buyer who sat at the railway siding. Some nasty boys from babu homes had set a dog on you, it bit some flesh off your leg. You went mad after that!'

Mad! The stranger seemed to choke. Anjali offered him a glass of water, and said, 'What else can I say, other than mad! Do you remember how many dogs you killed at that time? There wasn't a single dog left anywhere around the station. You began by killing dogs, and ended up killing people. Of course, those you killed were worse than dogs. You know, the likes of Hara, Bhoja, and so on.'

The stranger had as much of the porota as he could, kept aside the rest of it and sipped the tea. It had gone a bit cold. He made a slurping sound. Anjali giggled. 'Do you drink tea differently now? Why are you slurping?'

'Time changes everything about a person.'

'Are you still as quarrelsome as before? Or less?'

'More actually.'

'Why is that?'

The stranger put down the glass of tea, and asked Anjali, 'Did I take fourteen injections in my stomach after the dog bit me?'

Anjali retorted, 'How would you? Did you have the money?'

'The poison from the dog is lying in wait in my body. I'll come down with hydrophobia any day and die. Won't I, tell me?'

'You might.'

'So how can I forgive all the dogs that are responsible for my death.'

'Dogs? It was only one dog that bit you. And that's dead.'

'All those who set dogs on people like me are dogs too. They are still around. I'll carry on with my task as long as I am alive.'

As the stranger said that, it seemed it wasn't him speaking but someone else making him say it. Had he ever been daring enough to say something like that! He could not recall that. He felt as if he was uttering the dialogue of some character that he liked in a jatra performance. It was as if the character was compelling him to speak.

After a long time went by in silence, Anjali spoke. 'Dear bhai, I'm in terrible danger. I've been wondering ever since you came whether to tell you or not.'

'But one danger just left! More danger! What's that?' the youth asked.

'The big babu in the excise department who was there earlier has been transferred.'

'How is that a danger to you? Someone else will take his place.'

'That's what the danger is. The new babu who's come in his place is a big bastard. The payment that we made without fail every month—the new big babu has doubled it all at once! He says, it can't be any less. Either run your place, or shut shop. The prices of everything have shot up, your monthly payment has got to increase too.'

'So what's the problem? You just need to add some water to the alcohol you serve.'

'Oh, I'll manage all right, whether by adding water, or raising the price. But the problem lies elsewhere. He has sent word that the liquor shop will be raided on the fifth of next month. Apparently, they have a quota of the number of cases they have to file every month, or else their records would suffer. He said that they will pick up one person from every vendor. So he's asked for people to be ready to go to prison. Those running the other vends don't lack for people. Like Satish has four sons, there's no problem for him to go and spend a few days in prison. Gurupada has a brother, Jamuna Mashi has a son-in-law. Kalpana can send her husband. If they can give someone up, their vends won't close. But who do I have? I'll lose the business as well as my home and family. Raju's school reopens on the twelfth. Who will look after him? Who will drop him to his school? I'm terribly worried!'

Anjali sat silently for a while, and then she said, 'If only I could get someone who could go to prison for a few days in my stead. I'll pay him wages for those many days. Buno was there, do you know him? I think he lives somewhere near the ink factory. He served time a couple of times, posing as my husband. But I don't see him around anymore. If I could have found him, he would have merrily marched into prison.'

The stranger thought over the matter for quite some time, and then he said, 'What if I go?'

'Go where?'

'To serve time in prison. I'll be there for as long as it takes.'

Anjali shook her head animatedly, 'No, no, you won't do.'

'Why not? Why won't I do?'

Anjali said, 'Let's say, they charge you with an excise violation. A lot of people will see that. Tell me, won't they see you? That will include both your friends as well as your enemies. Let's say one of those enemies takes the trouble to inform the local police station. Can't they do that? So then all the old cases against you will be pulled out again. Don't you remember what happened to Harihar? He had gone to the red-light area in Kalighat to have fun. After he was picked up during a police raid, he landed up with the armed robbery charge from ages ago, in which he was an absconder. Seven years' punishment. If you get caught like that, then instead of coming out in ten days, you won't come out even in ten years! *Baap re*, the kind of cases you have against you! I sell two or five bottles of booze everyday. Will I be able to afford to pay for your bail, or to fight your case, with the few rupees of profit I make? And you'll just rot in prison. I can't send you to that doom knowingly. Get someone else if you can. There's Ganesh, the two Gopals are there, no one you ask can say no. I heard that Ghoti Naran's rickshaw got stolen. He's out of work. If you tell him, he'll go happily.'

'He'll go happily to prison!'

'Won't he? Everyone will go. Haven't you done a lot for them? To tell the truth, you jumped into the lion's den for them. That time when there was trouble with the people from Laskarpara, and you were charged, that was because of Jalil and Amal. What personal interest did you have? I can say for sure that if you have ten cases against you, eight will be on account of others. Will they be scared to spend a bit of time in prison for someone like that? Speak to them and see. They won't be scared.'

'Okay, let me see what can be done.'

'Whatever you do, it has to be before the fifth. Don't delay. The raid will take place that night.'

There was food now in the stranger's belly. He felt a bit languid. He wanted to rest a bit. He lay down on the torn mat. This shack, the woman, the twelve-year-old boy Raju, the sunlight and the foul, pungent stench of illicit liquor coming in through the gaps and cracks in the bamboo-matting wall, the buzzing flies, the loud voices of passers-by, and from time to time, the rumble of a train arriving, and then departing—nothing seemed unfamiliar to him anymore. And together with all these things, like an undercurrent in his heart of hearts, the bond of a deep, intimate relationship. It seemed he had been inside this run-down room many times before. He had played with Raju. He had held him by the hand and taken him to the Rath Mela. Bought him balloons, a papad, and a bamboo flute.

'What happened? You're lying down? Are you feeling unwell?' Losing his thread of thought at Anjali's loud enquiry, the stranger said, 'I didn't sleep well last night.'

Anjali retorted, 'Then I'm sure you slept well the night before!' She laughed, and said, 'Do you ever sleep at night? Can you sleep at all?'

Anjali stood up. 'All right, sleep then. Let me finish the work in the house. The fish sellers and rickshaw-drivers will all be here soon for booze. I won't get any time then.'

'Okay,' said the stretched-out youth. As Anjali stepped out of the hut, the stranger sat up and said, 'Shall I tell you something, Anjali-di?'

'What?' And with a mischievous smile on her face, and a saucy voice, Anjali asked, 'Shall I lie next to you, stroke your head and put you to sleep?'

'No, no! *Chhee!*'

'Why do you say "*Chhee*"? As if I've never run my hand on your head. I haven't seen you in six months, have you turned into a blushing shy bride in this while! All right, tell me what you wanted to say! But before that speak properly. All this "Didi this, and Didi that" doesn't suit you at all! It sounds terrible! Call me by my name like you did before, address me fondly as "tui". Be different with those you want to be. But not with me. So tell me.'

The stranger said in a soft voice, 'Take these hundred rupees.'

Astonished, Anjali said, 'The money's yours, why should I take it?'

'Take it. I'll explain later.'

Anjali had one foot inside and one outside. She said, 'Okay, I'll take it. And?'

'Buy things with the money. Get de-husked, fat-grained, red rice. And get large, Chandramukhi potatoes. Some green chillies, and a lemon if you can.'

'Anything else?'

'No. That'll be all.'

'And after that?'

'Cook. Rice, and mashed potatoes. It's been ages since I've eaten rice.'

Anjali gazed fixedly at the youth for quite a while, and then said, 'The red, fat-grained, de-husked rice used to be sold a long time ago, it's not available in the market now, I'll get whatever is available. Keep the money. I can afford to feed you one meal, of a fistful of rice. I invited you for a meal many times earlier, you said you would come, but never did. Today you asked me to feed you, do you think I'll take the price for that!'

'No, no, not the price,' said the stranger embarrassedly. 'It was just like that.'

'If you feel like paying money and eating "just like that", then go to some restaurant. There's no food for you here!' Without waiting for any response, Anjali left. The stranger lay down again and fell asleep.

3

The Return of Jibon

Perhaps the news spread through the railway station and its vicinity, in the neighbourhood and the railside squatter settlement more speedily than a flame in a forest turns into raging forest fire. Jibon is back! Our Jibon-da has returned!

Pa-khara Kedar, or Lame Kedar, who ran the small tea-shop at the western end of Platform No. 2 of the railway station, was the first to spot Jibon, and he passed on the news to everyone. 'When I first saw him, I couldn't believe my eyes. Was I seeing right? So I kept looking, and realised it was none other than Jibon.'

Kalipada Shikari lived on the canalside in Rajdanga. He was a rickshaw-driver in the rickshaw stand on the western side of the railway station. There were four rickshaw stands here. There was one on the left side, and one on the right side of the railway line at the end of the eastern platform. Another one was beside Kedar's shop, at the end of the western platform, and the fourth one was beside the Platform No. 1 exit, near the ticket counter, in front of an ancient banyan tree. There was a temple under the banyan. There were idols of various gods and goddesses in the temple. There was a straight road going from there to the heart of the suburb, the 8B bus-stand crossing. News of Jibon's return or reappearance spread in all directions.

Kalipada was standing at Kedar's shop now. He had just taken a sip from a cup of tea, when Kedar informed him. 'Hey Kali, do you know, Jibon isn't dead. He's alive. He's returned here too.'

'What rubbish!'

'I swear, I swear on Ma Kali! I saw him with my own eyes! At first, I could hardly believe—'

'Where was he all these days? Did he say anything?'

'I couldn't speak to him. I was busy making tea with my head down. The moment I raised my head, I spotted Jibon. But the way he looks now, I think he was in prison, or something like that. Long hair that covers his ears. He's become thinner.'

'So where's he now?'

When Anjali, the liquor seller, arrived at Platform No. 1 to tell everyone, she discovered that someone had already done that before her arrival, and taken all the credit. He had said, 'He's back, Jibon's back!' The news seemed to bring back a bunch of sorrowful, almost-dead people to life. Perhaps a dark cloud of dread descended upon the minds of some. Perhaps the veins on the clenched fists of some enraged people were swollen.

But the people who were the happiest at the news of Jibon's return, the ones whose survival and growth revolved around the station—Haat Kata Ganesh, Boro Gopal, Kalo Gopal, Shiva, Boro Bimal, Chhoto Bimal, Bachcha Amal, as well as several others—set off in a group for Anjali's place. It was like party workers going to the airport to welcome a mass leader returning to the country at the end of a foreign tour.

It was only Kaliya who stopped short. He was unable to walk in step with Ganesh, Gopal and the others. He was seized by an unknown fear, which made him tremble. It made his throat turn dry. He said, 'You people carry on, Ganesh. I need to go to the toilet. My stomach's acting up.' And he walked away in the opposite direction. It would be more accurate to say that he ran, rather than walked. An unintended crime weighed heavily on his chest. From which he was simply unable to free himself.

To the south of the station was the high wall of the TB Hospital. When the wall was being erected, hospital employees themselves had removed the bricks from a section on the station side. Or else, they would have had to go all the way around, and walk almost half a kilometre, to get to the station.

Kaliya entered the TB Hospital compound through the break in the wall, and ran breathlessly towards the east. And thus, he reached the very end of the hospital compound, with the sweepers' quarters, the waste incinerator, the morgue, the large drain carrying the city's sewage, and pigs grazing in the dense dholkamali thicket. This was where Nanu's illicit liquor den was.

Nanu was the son of a ward-boy in the hospital, he used to be a member of the action squad of a political party at one time. Because of that, he had to leave the locality for a long time, running from one place to another. A hoodlum away from his locality was something like a fish out of water. The only difference was that the fish died at once, while the hoodlum lived in fear of his life. Nanu decided to return to his locality. He had resolved that he would not leave his neighbourhood, even if that meant getting killed.

The Congress party, for fear of which Nanu had fled the locality, was, of course, not as aggressive as before. Earlier, if they got the slightest trace of a member of the Marxist party, they thrashed him, and broke his bones. They were somewhat peaceful now, and weary with inner conflicts. A leader of a small faction of the party, and a former mastaan of the station area—Sadhan-da to everyone in the locality—had assured Nanu: 'Stay in the neighbourhood, no one will tell you anything. I'll keep a lookout for you. Reopen your booze den. Once you start making some money, give me a share of that.'

Owing to lack of maintenance, what was earlier the morgue was completely dilapidated now. Someone, or some people, had taken away the collapsible gate and the grilled windows. And so, it wasn't possible to keep dead bodies there. There was a pile of torn mattresses and blankets at one end. People now used the place for their own purposes. Nanu used to run a liquor vend here all day. After he fled, the evidence of what some people sometimes did here was found the following day in the haphazardly scattered practical item by the name of 'Nirodh'.

It was this spot that Kaliya came running to, and when he found Nanu there, he breathlessly informed him, 'Nanu-da, Jibon-da is not dead. He has returned.'

'What are you saying!' said the stunned Nanu. 'Are you sure?'

'What the hell, would I lie to you?'

'No, I don't mean that. But how on earth did he survive? I saw Jibon stumble and fall with the bag, with my own eyes. You know the bag had country bombs. Two of them, powerful ones. Remember the sound of the explosion? Could anyone survive that?'

Bathed in perspiration and gasping for breath, Kaliya retorted, 'All talk of what happened or didn't happen is useless now. The main thing is that Jibon-da didn't die. I think he was critically wounded in the explosion. And then whatever had to happen, happened. The police must have arrived and picked him up, and admitted him to some hospital. He recovered and returned from there.'

Kaliya was still gasping for breath, and his wild buffalo-like dark-skinned, strong body was perspiring, but so was Nanu. The difference was that Kaliya had exerted himself, running a long distance, while Nanu was in great terror, anguish and a sense of guilt.

He clutched his hair and said in a deeply injured tone, 'I did something terribly wrong, Kaliya. But what can I do, tell me! I saw it with my own eyes, and I also read it in the newspapers the next day, that a miscreant was killed in a bomb explosion. What would I think after that?'

Nanu hit his head in despair. That was why he never sought to find out about Jibon. Since he was dead! It would have been a different matter had he survived. 'You know how we all felt at that time. All of us could have been in trouble because of him. The one who was killed is no more. But if we dug too deeply to find out about him, and the police got wind of us, we would all be finished. You remember how scared we were! That's why I told you and everybody else to simply keep mum. There's no need to tell anybody. Let it stay between the five of us alone.'

Nanu was a veteran when it came to fisticuffs, murder and bloodshed. When a stone was thrown into a pond, there were ripples for a while, and then everything returned to normal, leaving no trace behind. Nanu's character was something like that. When some incident took place, it stayed on his mind at best for a week, or ten days, and then he forgot all about it. He had witnessed many deaths in his life. He was never really upset. But that a dead person would have survived, and then returned, was beyond his imagination.

Kaliya was much younger than Nanu. He was a poor fellow, who toiled for a living. The arduous labour for his livelihood had made him somewhat harsh-natured, somewhat intolerant. He used to get into fights at the slightest pretext. Fisticuffs almost every day. The last time was when, on Jibon's request, he had got roped into a major operation to help out Nanu. That was where Jibon was killed in a bomb explosion. Kaliya was left speechless after something like that. He couldn't tell even those closest to him. That was his crime.

After a while, Nanu spoke. 'All of you know that Jibon and I were close friends. We weren't enemies. It was on my behalf that he joined the operation. But we didn't kill him. Even Jibon can't accuse us of that. Can he? No, he can't. Whatever happened, was an accident. We were about to return after completing our mission well. If he hadn't got out of the car, and then run towards the lane, nothing would have happened. Why did he have to do that unnecessarily? It's not us, but he himself who is responsible. If he blames us now, that would be wrong of him. Our only fault is that we did not try to find out about him later. And I didn't tell Ganesh or Gopal about the incident. Why me, anyone in my place would have done the same. Run for his own life.'

When Nanu finished, Kaliya said, 'But now that we've got the news, we need to meet Jibon-da. Everyone went. It'll look terrible if we don't go. I don't feel brave enough to meet him by myself. How can I look him in the eye? That's why I came running to you. Please come along. When he hears the truth—if you explain it to him—Jibon-da will surely understand. Or else, even if he doesn't say anything to you, he'll eat me alive. I'm very scared. Please come along just now, Nanu-da.'

'Where to?'

'To meet Jibon-da?'

'I mean, where is he now?'

'At Anjali-di's place.'

'What's he doing there?'

'I don't know.'

As if in soliloquy, Nanu said, 'Whatever happened was a mistake. A terrible mistake. The lane was full of smoke after the bombs went off, I couldn't see properly. And the next day, when I read in the newspaper that a person had been killed, I assumed it was Jibon. I'll explain it to him. If he doesn't accept that, there's nothing I can do. Whatever has to happen will happen.'

Nanu was extremely dark-skinned. But his face seemed even darker with the cloud of anxiety and apprehension over it. After a while, he said, 'Jibon and I were fierce enemies at one time. We were after one another's blood. And then we became friends. We stood beside each other in times of danger. I wonder whether he'll remain a friend, or turn into an enemy now. A mistake is not the same as wrongdoing. I made a mistake, but I did no wrong. Come, I'll explain it to him.'

Kaliya's fear did not abate. Who knows what might happen today! Ganesh was short-tempered, Boro Gopal was thick-headed, while Bachcha Amal loved Jibon like his own father. When they found out that Kaliya had kept something so important about

Jibon secret, for so many days and months, they could well kill him, and throw his body on the rail track. If that happened, it would all end very soon, but what if they subjected him to a social boycott?

Feeling ravaged and full of apprehension, Kaliya walked behind Nanu with his head lowered. When the two of them reached Anjali's place, there was a huge crowd of people there. It was as if the entire station had come down to welcome Jibon back. All these people were grateful to Jibon for one reason or another. They were humble folk, with whom a man by the name of Jibon had a close relationship. His activities were completely enmeshed in public life here. So everyone considered him to be their own. They had come to meet their beloved Jibon.

The entire band—of those who ate at the cheap eatery, slept on the station platform, had been abandoned by their fathers and lost their mothers—had arrived. Their leader, none other than Haat Kata Ganesh. He was an unfortunate lad, with a scorched fate. When he was very small, both his father and mother died within a span of fifteen or twenty days. His father had been run over by a train. While sleepily crossing the rail track outside his shanty, he had not noticed the speeding train under the cover of mist. And his Ma had died of grief, winding a sari around her neck and hanging from the beam. Of course, people did condemn her adequately after she died, saying, '*Chhee! Chhee!* You had to go and die like this! Didn't you think about your son as you were dying! Who will he live with now, who will feed him, how will he survive!'

Ganesh was seven or eight years old then. He ate whatever people provided him, and when they didn't, he scoured the dustbins. And thus he grew up a bit. After that he washed used glasses in a country liquor bar for some time. He finally got into the squad that was engaged in smuggling.

That was towards the end of the 1960s. Many parts of the country were reeling under food shortage. The police beat and killed people who were rallying in demand for food, as if they were snakes. Cordoning of rice was in operation in Calcutta at the time.

Bringing rice to the cities from villages was strictly prohibited. The police carried out massive arrests. To tell the truth, it was as if the police had no other work besides apprehending rice smugglers. A special squad was set up solely for this purpose. But it was true that if someone could somehow get past the prying eyes of the police, and bring a sack, or half a sack, of rice into the city, he made a huge profit.

Ganesh was inducted into this trade. His job was to get under the train, and conceal large and small pillow-like bags of rice in various spots there. And to remove those when the train stopped at a particular station. The police too were salaried employees like others. They patrolled the train compartments and searched suspicious-looking bags and baskets, but no one risked their lives and went under the train. So the smuggling of rice could not be stopped.

The rotten rice, full of insects, dust and stones, that was distributed through the city's fair-price shops was not palatable as far as the city's babu class was concerned. They looked for good rice. In those dire times, it was these smugglers, who were outcasts of decent society, who assumed the responsibility of feeding and keeping alive the babu folk. They brought sacks and sacks of rice, in the same way that some others risked their lives, evading the watchful eyes of the state apparatus, crossed the border, and brought gold, cocaine, heroin, counterfeit currency notes, weapons and explosives into the country.

Ganesh had arranged twenty small bags, containing ten kilos of rice in all, under a train departing from Canning station. He had come safely all the way too with the rice. No one stole the rice, the police didn't detect it, nor was any packet lost in transit. The mishap occurred while retrieving the packets after ten or twelve stations. Didn't Ganesh know what exactly happened that day! Had the guard signalled the driver too soon, despite having been paid? Or was he a bit slow in emerging from under the train? The train suddenly began to move forward that day, and there was no way of escaping. As the merciless iron wheel inched forward to crush him to death, he had only a few seconds to run from there. And in that situation, he cleverly lay down, lengthwise, in the narrow strip of space between the rail track and the platform. Although he could protect his body, he couldn't save his right arm. The solid wheel of the train tore away some of the flesh from his elbow.

After that, he had to spend a long time in a public hospital. When he recovered, he realised that his arm was a bit bent. It wasn't as strong as it used to be either. That's why his name was Haat Kata Ganesh.

There used to be a man called Jibon here. He was no longer here. His newly arrived replica was sitting in Anjali's house now, whom the people of the locality knew as 'Chandal Jibon'. Because that was the name of the person who was missing, or had been killed. Another meaning of the word 'Chandal' was someone enraged. People called him Chandal out of affection, or love, or respect, or anger. There were several Jibons here, several kinds of Jibon as well, but 'Chandal Jibon' referred to the person who was terrible when confronted with anything nasty.

Ram Pal, a resident of Chhapra district in Bihar, was now sitting in a humble posture, with almost folded hands, in front of the replica. He was pleading with Jibon—the one who jumped into the fray when anyone was in danger and rescued them—to solve a great personal problem of his. He believed that a single threat issued by Jibon Bhai would set everything right, like before. Ram Pal was weeping and tears flowed down his cheeks. His nose was running too, and he was wiping his eyes and nose time and again with a gamchcha. But his tears did not make any impact on the people present there. Someone smirked, some people were getting annoyed. Some were getting angry. Ganesh was itching to punch him a few times, and chase him out of here, until he was across the railway line. But he couldn't do it. Because Ram Pal had arrived before them! And 'Jibon-da' was listening to his tale of woe with full attention. 'What's wrong with Dada? There's no point in wasting time, listening to all this useless talk!'

Nanu and Kaliya arrived, and stood at the back of the crowd. They wouldn't be able to speak to Jibon unless the crowd thinned a bit. After all, what they had to tell him was not anything ordinary. After a while, Jibon raised his head and looked around. But Nanu wasn't sure whether Jibon had spotted him. He turned towards Ram Pal again and said to him, 'I heard everything you said. So what do I have to do now?'

Ram Pal said, 'Come with us to our hut. I'll gladly accept whatever you decide.'

Ganesh now roared out impatiently, 'Hey, get out from here now! Or else I'll thrash you. Dada has just returned to the locality, won't you let him get some rest? You want him to go with you now?'

Ram Pal replied, 'I'm not asking him to come right now. It's okay if he comes in the evening.'

'We'll talk about that in the evening. Be off now! I'm getting really angry. If you try to act too smart, I'll thrash all three of you and kick you out of the locality.'

Ram Pal from Bihar and Dharani Dhar from Baripada in Orissa were friends. Or at least they were, until a few days ago. Seeing them together, people used to say, 'One can't imagine a friendship like theirs nowadays.' If it had been anyone else, they would have been killing each other by now.

The two of them had come from their respective states in search of work. For the first few days, Ram Pal had sat on the pavement, selling sattu. He wasn't very successful. And Dharani Dhar went around people's homes delivering drinking water. Two metal containers hung from a curved strip of bamboo that he carried on his shoulder. He too didn't earn much from that.

After this, both of them began working in a biscuit factory in Narendrapur. They earned a bit more here, and so they were somewhat better off. They no longer feared being unemployed.

It was at the factory that the two of them met one another, and later became close friends. It was as if they were one another's soul. They decided to live together. House rent was very high in this city. Living in a rented house meant that a major part of one's income went towards the rent. They wisely bought bamboo poles and bamboo-matting and built a shanty beside the railway line. Next to their hut, was the hut of another fortune seeker, Draupadi Mal. Back in the countryside, that is to say, in a village in south Bengal, she had a husband, two sons, and a little bit of cultivable land. It was said that she lived happily there, with her husband and children. It was also said that someone brought her from the village in Gosaba to the city with the promise of making her even happier. He was the one who built her shanty.

Draupadi was five feet and two inches tall, she was fair-skinned, and she was in good health. After living with her for some time, the man left one morning, saying he was going to work, but he never returned. After some time, both Ram Pal and Dharani Dhar, from next door, desired her sexually. Meanwhile, Draupadi too thought that if she was deprived of male company for too long, she would come down with terrible ailments like insomnia and hyperacidity. But most of all, the northerly wind that blew in through the tattered bamboo matting of her room turned her bedsheet icy.

Draupadi found work as a cook in a wealthy household in Central Park, in the Jadavpur locality. She pilfered mustard oil and ghee, using a bottle tied to her petticoat string; packets of spices like cumin, coriander, turmeric and red chilli, in the cleavage of her breasts; and rice and dal, in the packet used to dispose vegetable peels. And thus, she was getting along quite well. But she was not at peace. She constantly regretted her single status. She had a husband back in the village, but she could no longer return there. She viewed her husband as an alien. The son born of her womb had turned into her enemy. Aashar was one of her sons, he had a freshly sprouted moustache. He was given the name because he was born in the month of Aashar. He was going around declaring, 'Do you think

I will let the mother who shamed us by running off with someone live? Just let her set foot here. If I don't cut her to bits and bury her in the sandbar of the Vidyadhari, I'm not my Baba's son! I'll be his piss!' After hearing about such a threat from some people who had come to the city from her village, Draupadi lacked the courage to return there. Because Draupadi's and Ram Pal's shanties were next to one another, they encountered each other every day, and expressed neighbourly sympathies for each other's sorrows. And both of them deeply felt that just across the flimsy bamboo-matting was someone suffering exactly like me.

Ram Pal and Dharani Dhar were both security guards in the factory. Their duty hours were from eight at night to eight in the morning. Or from eight in the morning to eight at night.

But now, after speaking to the factory manager, one of them was able to be at home while the other worked. There were some petty thieves in the railside squatter settlement, who stole whatever they could lay their hands on, so that they could sell it off and drink.

One night, it was raining very heavily. At such times, people's sense of loneliness assumed great proportions. Ram Pal was lying all alone in his room that night, restless. And in the next room lay Draupadi, full of regret. Both of them were yearning to remove the meagre gap of bamboo-matting so that their two bodies could merge into one. After that, one doesn't exactly know who invited whom, and who first entered whose room through the gap in the bamboo matting. But what was certain was that they had sprung into each other's arms with the same frenzied hunger with which people in a famine-stricken land pounced upon a plate of rice. And such nocturnal pouncing carried on, from time to time. Sometimes it was Ram Pal who slipped through the matting and went next door, and sometimes it was Draupadi who came over. No one had the slightest clue.

As things carried on in this fashion, Draupadi made a mistake one night. She had forgotten what day of the week it was. As usual, she slipped in through the gap in the bamboo-matting, and got inside the mosquito net hung in the room. And groping in the darkness, like a snake swallowing a frog, she devoured the sleeping man. As she wrapped herself around the man passionately and pressed her lips on his to kiss him, she realised that there was something lacking in the kiss, it was insipid like vegetable curry without salt. She then felt Ram Pal's face, and discovered that his thick moustache was missing. This face was completely shaven, like Dharani Dhar's!

But there was nothing to be done now. A snake had a curved fang like a fish-hook. Once any prey was caught in it, the snake could not let it go, however much it tried. It had to swallow the prey. If one's kite's string got entangled with that of another kite, and one tried to pull the string and bring down the kite, there was bound to be a problem. The easy option was to give more string. So she did that. And when the play of bodies in the darkness was over, as she was returning to the other side through the matting, she softly said, 'Don't tell Ram. Only you and I know what happened.'

And thus did the days go by. Draupadi had assumed that Dharani Dhar was unaware of her liaison with Ram Pal, and that Ram Pal was unaware of the liaison with Dharani Dhar. But the truth was that both of them knew everything about each other.

A few days later, food for the two residences started being cooked together, on the same stove. After all, charcoal and kerosene were expensive! Lighting only a single stove saved the cost of fuel for the other. Provisions for the two establishments were purchased from the market and brought back in a single bag. It was Draupadi who went to the market. However, the expenses were borne by Ram Pal sometimes, and sometimes by Dharani Dhar. Draupadi no longer went to work as a cook in someone's house. She had opened a tea-shop in front of her hut, beside the railway line. She sold muri, chhola sheddho, alur chop, fuluri, beguni and so on. The shop did quite well. When the two friends received their salaries at the end of each month, both of them gave some money to Draupadi. She bought saris, and got ornaments made, with the money. And the most amusing aspect was that this triangular relationship did not give rise to any problems. Ram Pal knew, as did Dharani Dhar, that a woman was like a deep tubewell. The more you worked the force rod, the more water flowed. If someone filled a pot from it, it did not run short of water for the next person.

Although no one had suspected anything earlier, now everyone in the squatter colony knew everything. They gossiped, saying, 'The slut Draupadi's really aptly named! I swear on Ma Kali, you've got to give it to her! Doesn't care whether it's Bangaal or Ghoti, Mero or Khotta, she doesn't exclude anyone! She's amazing!'

However, such nasty things were discussed in secret. No one had the audacity to say all this to Draupadi's face. Oh, what a fierce woman she was! Once, who knows what had happened, she had chased the mastaan Haat Kata Sonaiya with a fish-cutting bonti. After that Sonaiya never went anywhere near the No. 2 railway gate. Sonaiya lived in front of the Palpara Bazaar, near the rail gate on the western side of this railway station. He was earlier a porter in this station. At that time, Sadhan was a notorious mastaan of the area. Sonaiya gained repute as a mastaan by stabbing him in the back.

Be that as it may, Draupadi's household was a happy and peaceful one. Because she had got a small operation done, as a result of which the size of the family did not increase. No evidence had been presented to anyone either by which it could be said that Draupadi was polyandrous. But now Ram Pal's fate got scorched. His happy life caught fire. The beautiful garden he had nurtured with care was destroyed. Who knows why, but Draupadi conspired with Dharani Dhar and cast him out like a fly fallen into milk. So, not only did Draupadi exit his life, but he was also dispossessed of the pots and pands, bedding, floor mat, mosquito net, and bedsheet—half of whose cost had been borne by him.

Almost everyone in the locality knew about Ram Pal's tale of woe. He had called out to people, and wept as he made them hear the story. But he never got any sympathy from anyone. Some people covered their faces with a gamchhha and smirked, as they were doing now. The tears of a helpless man like Ram Pal, who belonged to another land, could not evoke any response from anyone. In the face of such inhumane behaviour from the cruel society, he did not feel like living any longer in this world. He wanted to die.

That was what he said now. 'Jibon Bhaiya, I'll throw myself under a train if I can't get Draupadi.'

Ganesh could not tolerate Ram Pal any longer. He dragged him out of the room, and pushed him towards the railway line: 'Fuck off! Kill yourself! People like you ought to die!'

The crowd in front of Anjali's shack had thinned a bit now. People who could eat only if they earned a day's wage could not afford to spend too much time on grief or joy. They had to go to work.

Ganesh had been dying to tell Jibon something for a long time. Getting the chance now, he assumed a grave tone, and asked the stranger, 'What happened to you, Dada? Where did you disappear all of a sudden without saying anything to anyone? You hadn't fought with anyone, nor was the police after you, so what was it? We ate together that night, at Chhechan's eatery, both of us slept on the platform, and then you were gone. Simply gone, without any trace. Tell us where you were.'

Nanu looked in Jibon's direction now. His eyes pleaded, 'Don't tell him, Jibon. Don't tell Ganesh anything. Ganesh and Gopal addressed Nanu as 'Dada', and respected him like an elder brother. But that was only because of Jibon. He was their Dada, and Nanu was Jibon's friend. So he too was 'Dada' because he was their Dada's friend. Or else he had no other kind of connection with such youths. Nanu didn't come much to these parts either. They loved Jibon more than their own lives because he was always with, beside and close to them. He shielded them, like an umbrella under hot sun or rain, like a blanket in a winter's night.

If Jibon now revealed to Ganesh that Nanu had called him away for a personal matter of his, and that after an accident took place there, he had left the wounded Jibon behind and fled, and then kept that secret for so long, no one would spare Nanu.

Nanu was completely alone now. All the boys from middle-class households with whom he did party work had fled the neighbourhood fearing for their lives. They did not dare to return in the current situation. Which was why the vacuum in all such localities had been filled by a bunch of lumpen proletariat. They were given to drinking and beating people up. No one had any control over them. As if they were the police, judge, jailor and executioner all rolled into one. A mastaan who could single-handedly make an entire locality tremble had once arrived at the railway station. He was drinking and making a nuisance of himself. But Ganesh and company had thrashed him. They didn't spare him on account of being a mastaan. To tell the truth, Nanu was a bit scared. If they humiliated him, he would have no face left whatsoever.

Although Nanu was preoccupied with such apprehensions, and was getting scared, some of that fear waned when Jibon spoke. Nanu realised that Jibon too didn't want the incident of that day to be revealed to everyone. He said, 'Oh, it's a long story. Let that be for now. I'll tell you later. You people tell me how you all are.' When Nanu heard Jibon say that, he felt like bowing his head low in gratitude. This was what a friend ought to be like.

The few people who were still there slowly began to leave. All the rickshaw-drivers, hawkers, porters, labourers had to attend to their livelihood. If they spent the whole day with Jibon, how would they be able to set a pot of rice on the fire? So everyone was gone after a while. There was only Ganesh, sitting beside him like a shadow. And there were Nanu and Kaliya.

Nanu then called Ganesh aside, and said to him, 'Will you do me a favour, Ganesh? Just run to my den. Bachcha Dilip is there. Tell him that there won't be any payments today. I'll pay them tomorrow. Ask him to give you all the money from the sales. I want to buy some things for Jibon. Tell Dilip I'll be late. He shouldn't let there be any trouble, tell him to handle everything properly. Take Kaliya too along with you.'

Ganesh did not feel like going anywhere right now. But it was a question of buying things for Dada. So he went. Once Ganesh and Kaliya left, the room was completely vacant. Anjali had gone to the marketplace for purchases. Plump-grained rice and potatoes. Some fish as well. Raju's father loved to eat chochchori prepared with lote fish. She would serve lote to Jibon if it was available today.

Nanu was face-to-face with the stranger now. The stranger realised that this dark-skinned, tall chap with bloodshot eyes was bursting to tell him something. And that he wanted to tell it to someone called Jibon. Not having a clue as to what he would say, or what his relationship to the person called Jibon was, and not wanting to make a fool of himself by speaking first, the stranger looked at Nanu in silence.

Nanu then spoke, slowly, and in a voice full of anguish. 'Forgive me, Jibon.'

The stranger got the cue to say something. He said, 'No, no, don't say all that. You didn't do anything wrong!'

'I got terribly scared, you know. Which was why I could not tell anyone about what happened to you.'

'Forget about all that,' the stranger said. 'Whatever had to happen has happened.'

Nanu was silent for a while, and then he said remorsefully, 'If I had the slightest idea that you were alive, I would have made sure that I brought you back somehow or the other. And if I couldn't do that, I would at least have informed everyone after I returned. I looked for you in hospitals and prisons. I had witnessed it myself, although there was smoke in the lane, but I also read about it in the newspaper the next day. I realise now that I was wrong. The news referred to the same incident, but it was someone else who died. You can understand what my state of mind was like then. Babui had died just a few days earlier, and then you. That's why I kept quiet about the whole thing. I was already in such a lot of trouble, what would I do if something else now descended upon me! Thankfully, my Dada had not given his actual name and address to that whore, or else things could have spiralled.'

Nanu paused for a while, and then continued. '*Achchha*, Jibon, the whole thing had been taken care of properly. We picked Dada up, and were on our way back as well. But why did you suddenly stop the car and run towards the lane as if you were out of your head? If you hadn't done that, you wouldn't have stumbled and fallen like that. The bombs in the bag wouldn't have exploded either. What on earth happened? Why did you go?'

The stranger smiled weakly, and said, 'How can I tell you why I went? I don't remember all that any more.'

'I got it. You won't tell me.'

'Forget about all that for now. There's no point in digging up a dead man's grave, there'll only be a stink. It's better that it remains concealed like it is.'

'I hope you aren't angry with me! Tell me the truth! Just understand that whatever happened was because of a mistake, and because we were scared.'

'I'm not angry at all!' The stranger, 'Jibon', said, 'I told you, I've forgotten about it. Just remind me if you ever hear me mentioning anything. Even if someone ever asks me something, I don't think I'll be able to answer. I no longer remember anything of the past, nothing at all. Everything between us starts today!'

Nanu said, 'Just don't tell Kaliya anything. That was the first job the poor chap did. He was trembling in fear for at least seven or eight days after we returned. I was the one who told him not to say a thing to anyone. Who knows what a novice might end up saying!'

The stranger 'Jibon' replied, 'Don't worry. I won't tell anyone anything.'

Ganesh and Kaliya had returned in the meanwhile. One had to say they had been very quick. It was almost two miles, both ways, and it had taken them only half-an-hour. Nanu took the money from them, counted it, and looking at the stranger, said, 'Come out for a while, Jibon.'

Anjali too returned after her purchases. She asked, 'Hey, where are you taking him! He's supposed to have lunch here in the afternoon!'

'Lunch? Oh, there's a lot of time before that. You finish cooking, I'll bring him back.'

'Make sure you bring him back!'

The stranger had silently surrendered to fate. Life had played plenty of games with him. And it was still doing that. But the game it was playing now was thoroughly enjoyable. So he continued to enjoy it.

Nanu brought him to a shirt and trouser cut-pieces shop on Station Road. 'I have not yet repaid you for what you did for me. Let me do something at least now. Let me at least get a shirt and a pair of trousers made for you. What you are wearing is all torn. Here, select something you like.'

After that, Nanu himself revealed to Ganesh, 'My Dada ran away with all of Boudi's ornaments, and camped in the red-light district, in Seth Bagan Lane. If Jibon hadn't come along, we wouldn't have got either the ornaments or Dada back.'

'When was that? I didn't know about it!'

'Oh, it was a long time ago.'

They then dropped off the shirt and trouser pieces at a tailor's shop, and dragged him to a haircutting salon. It was the same old Thakur, from Bihar, who sat on the pavement with his razor and scissors. He knew Jibon. He had cut his hair many times. He knew how Jibon liked to keep his hair. So why did he have such long hair on his head! But even without anyone telling him, as a barber, he knew this was the result of being in prison. So he chopped off and did away with the burden of overgrown weeds on Jibon's head. The cut he gave was called *kadamchhat*. One didn't have to use much oil, and during fights, no one could grab him by the hair.

After all these tasks were successfully accomplished, Nanu said, 'Jibon, my friend, so I'll leave now! Take your bath, have lunch, and take a nap. Come to my place at night. You'll come, won't you? It's a joyful day today. The heavy stone I was carrying on my head for the past year was gone after I saw you. Let's eat together tonight. I'll send Dilip to bring pork curry and tondoori ruti from Tollygunge. And no cholai tonight, I'll treat you to country liquor.'

The stranger had realised a long while back that the man who looked exactly like him was as indelibly bound together with life here as a fish in water, or a revolutionary living among the people. He used to stand beside people, no matter what. This was why he came to be established as a means of succour for endangered folk, and was loved by the people.

However, it was a very prosaic rule that when a weight was placed on the pan of a pair of scales, goods of the same weight were then placed on the other pan. So it stood to reason that the man who had so many friends, ought to have an equal number of enemies as well. When the love of his friends was so intense, his enemies' hatred and rage would also be fierce. If anyone was grieved by his death, perhaps some were overjoyed. Now that he was back, some people were happy, but some others should have thrown a brick on his head. The stranger was compelled to realise that just as he could stay on in this station area and enjoy the fruits of that unseen person's good deeds, he could just as well abandon responsibility for the ire the man had earned and flee the place. Nothing was to stop him. But if he left, where on earth would he go to! He couldn't think of any place worth going to, where someone would be waiting with a plate of hot rice, who would look at his sad face and guess his state of hunger. He had found such friends and kin here. He didn't have anyone anywhere else, neither friend nor enemy. I'll stay here. I'll see what happens. I'll continue acting on behalf of that Jibon until he returns.

Jibon's friend by the name of Nanu had an illicit liquor den somewhere nearby. But the newly arrived stranger was not supposed to know where exactly it was. So how would he go there at night?

The stranger asked, 'Why me alone! What about Ganesh?'

'Sure. Ganesh too. And Gopal, Kaliya and any others who want to come along. I won't say "no" to anyone today. If we run short of Bangla, there's always cholai. It's my own vend.'

Ganesh now brought Jibon to his real stronghold, the spot in front of the ancient banyan tree, in front of the Platform No. 1 exit. There was a temple under the banyan. There were idols of many gods and goddesses in the temple, including Shani, Shiva, Kali and Manasa. This was the place of worship that Jibon had established. But that was not out of any religious sentiment, but out of the public-minded urge to put an end to the railway passengers' incessant urination next to the banyan tree. The temple now had a concrete plinth. At this moment, a man was sitting on that, engrossed in smoking ganja. Another man was sitting with his head bent, immersed in writing on a satta pad. Noticing the stranger, they forgot about whatever they were doing, and gaped at him astonishedly. No words emitted their mouths. A long queue of rickshaws began from the front of the temple, where many rickshaw riders were sitting, waiting for passengers. Seeing Jibon there, they too couldn't believe their eyes.

Behind the line of rickshaws, along the wall of the TB Hospital, was Jalil Mollah's cycle-repair garage. He used to carry basketloads of vegetables in front of Kolay Market. After that he sold vegetables for a time. He rode a rickshaw too afterwards. He had a grin as wide as an ocean on his face. 'My dear Dada, you're back! I can't believe my eyes! What am I seeing! I never imagined I would see you again, Dada! Are you well, Dada?'

The man who had been writing on a satta pad was the priest of this temple. People no longer had faith in and respect for gods or priests nowadays. They didn't make monetary offerings like before. So he could no longer survive merely by conducting his priestly duties. He needed to do something else as well. He did two other things. One was writing on the satta pad, and the other was selling *puriyas*, or tiny packets of ganja. He kept a chillum, and coir-string to light it. There were arrangements for collective ganja consumption.

He almost screamed out, 'Any fucker who drinks the water from our station won't find joy even if he reaches heaven. He has to come back here. You left the station and went away a few times earlier too, were you ever able to stay away? I had told everyone, just watch, if he's alive, he'll surely return one day. Tell me, hasn't he come back? Hasn't he?'

Jalil said, 'Come, Dada, come to my garage. Let's chat for a while. Hey Bhuban, send three cups of tea and three nimkis to my garage. Extra sugar in Dada's tea.'

The stranger said, 'No, no, very little sugar in my tea.'

'Do you have diabetes, or what? You used to have two spoonfuls of sugar earlier.'

Ganesh said to Jalil, 'Take Dada along to your place, Jalil. I'll finish some work and join you there. It won't take long, I'll be back very soon.'

'Have your tea first, I've ordered it.'

'I'll have it at Bhuban's shop, on my way.'

Jalil took the stranger along most affectionately, sat him down on a locked rickshaw, and pulled up the hood. After that, he sat down to repair a cycle wheel. He spoke as he worked. 'Dada, you weren't here. Everything was in a mess with you gone. You formed a rickshaw union with such difficulty and effort, but that's gone. No one pays subscriptions any more. It's every man for himself. It was so fine earlier. If anyone fell ill, or had to perform his parents' sraddha, or get his daughter married, he could take a loan from the union fund. They found help in difficult times. But what can one do if people can't see what's good for them! Do you know what all these people are like? Isn't there a saying about a dog's tail—that's absolutely true. It'll be straight as long as you pull it. The moment you loosen your grip, it goes back to being crooked. There's no one who is public-minded like you.'

The tea arrived. Jalil sipped his tea, and continued. 'I feel angry with the people, but it makes me sad too. What can I say, Dada! Now that you are back, see what you can do. Will you let them graze, like cows and buffaloes, or thrash them and make men out of them!'

The brahmin priest stopped writing on his satta pad, and came and stood in front of 'Jibon'. 'Jibon, my son, now that you are back, do think about this temple. You are very powerful. No one can say "no", if you ask for donations and suchlike. But this year's annual function is certainly going to be a grand affair. Oh, what a voice Prahlad Baul has! See if you can get him here for the programme this time! You'll see how people will sing your praises.'

Amar Ghosh, the rickshaw owner, arrived there. He had about twenty rickshaws operating. A man from a village called Sundhira in South 24-Parganas had taken a rickshaw on hire, saying he would run it from the bus-stand. Many people like him arrived from the village, and survived here riding a rickshaw. So Amar Ghosh had given a rickshaw to Manohar, from Sundhira. He rode the rickshaw at the 8B bus-stand for a few days. He paid the daily rent too on time. After that he disappeared one day, taking the rickshaw with him. He neither returned the rickshaw, nor paid any rent. It was said that he had apparently given the rickshaw away as dowry to the groom for his daughter's marriage. And that apparently, the son-in-law was making trips on that very rickshaw in a village called Belegachhi.

In a voice full of distress, Amar Ghosh pleaded, 'I don't have any other income. All I have are those few rickshaws. My household survives on that. Help me, Jibon! Please bring back that rickshaw of mine!'

A rickshaw rider arrived next. He complained that his son picked on him, and beat him, and his mother never said a word either. Rather, she provoked him. 'Set this injustice right, Jibon!'

Hearing that his father had come to Jibon with a complaint, the son too came running, with a counter-complaint. He said, 'My

Baba drinks every day, and then comes home and abuses Ma, beats her. Ma is the one who gave birth to me. How can a son remain silent when his Ma is tortured like that?'

Another man arrived. He reported that someone snatched his wrist watch the previous night. A young woman arrived and said that someone had enticed her with the promise of marriage, and taken her out and spent nights together several times, but no longer wanted to marry her.

Life was a battle. It was a journey of uncertainty. It was also the name for an unimaginable experience. Life meant constantly breaking oneself up into smithereens, and being transformed into another new person. This game of demolition and construction had been going on from time immemorial, across the world. At every moment, something or the other was being created, and something or the other was being destroyed. Destruction for construction, and construction for destruction, were the ebb and flow of a changing word, its rule. Changing the rules of the world was beyond anyone.

The stranger Jibon thought deeply about himself: this life of mine has subjected me to many tests, of different kinds. Perhaps by subjecting me repeatedly to such tests, some unseen teacher wished to see whether this competitor could be successful. Every human life is like a piece of stone, or a dead log of wood. It is unaware of the fire it carries inside. It becomes aware only when one dry stone is struck hard against another. Or when someone throws the stone from very high up on another chunk of stone.

He continued thinking. He hadn't arrived voluntarily. Someone had surely pulled him into this life. Who was that? I don't know! However, there was another test now—perhaps he would have to face the most difficult test of his life. This was a test of 'becoming'. A test of whether I can break down my past self, and rebuild that into a new self.

Thoughts argued with each other inside the stranger's mind: I was running around from one place to another like a ball of cotton floating and whirling skywards in the wind. And then the ball of cotton suddenly fell on the rugged surface of the earth. It occurred to the stranger that he too had a seed inside him. A seed that would take refuge in soil, be nourished by the sap of life of Mother Earth, and grow into a tree, raising its head to the sky with infinite audacity.

I have to begin somewhere, in some way or another. I have to give up my vagabond life. I have to firmly grasp some roots. And then, looking to the future with the eye of a bird, throw everything away if need be. Who knows what lies ahead? The answers lay in the dark womb of tomorrow. How would one know where the path ended unless one began walking? Whether it was straight or crooked, difficult or easy! So what if it was dark, one could grope one's way, and crawl, and still move ahead. There had been no opportunity all these days. But now that life had opened the door of possibility, and a faint ray of light was visible, coming to a halt, and sitting idle, would be unfair to oneself.

It was almost ten in the morning now. Around the middle of June. The rains would have begun by now in earlier years. But who knows why, the rains were delayed this year. So the sun had begun hurling fire already. This was the most busy time in this locality. The entire station area was abuzz. Up- and Down-trains arrived every few minutes and then departed. People poured out of the stationary train. The horns of rickshaws, the cries of the porters and various other sounds made the whole place noisy. The horrible dream of last night still weighed on his mind, and he thought it would continue to do so for a long time; but apart from that, this morning had gone well. But the dream, it was as if it was no dream. It now seemed to him to be a message. A direction. It was like a prologue to a novel, which had an undeniable relation with the development of the tale.

The vagabond man, who had freshly returned to life, pondered; it was as if some unseen playwright had completed writing a script centred on him, and just as the intermediary part of a melody flowed towards a conclusion, it was the dream of curtains that moved this play along.

After a while, the sun was directly overhead. Meanwhile, Jalil had treated them to another round of tea. But there was no sign of Ganesh. Jalil said, 'Let's wait a little longer. If he's not back, we'll go and have a bath. I'm burning in this sun.' Ganesh returned soon after. He had a gamchcha, a bar of soap, and a bottle of oil with him. Oil meant mustard oil, and the soap was 501. That was a cheap brand of soap. And one could use it to bathe as well as wash one's clothes. Needless to say, it was used by all these poor folk.

Ganesh said, 'Let's go and bathe, Dada. I think Anjali-di must have finished cooking by now. Are you coming, Jalil?'

'Of course, I'm coming! If we hadn't waited for you, we would have finished bathing a long time ago! Let's go.'

Bachcha Amal too came running. 'I'm coming too!' They went to the lake in Palpara everyday to bathe. There was no waterbody as large as this lake anywhere nearby. The water was very clear. It had a paved ghat as well, on which one could wash one's clothes at ease. There was a straight road from Station Road to the No. 9 bus-stand. If one turned right there, and went across the railway line, one reached Palpara Bazaar. Past that, and a bit to the left, was the lake. There was a timber yard on the northern side of the lake. And beyond that was the railway line.

Ganesh said, 'Dada, wear the gamchcha, wash your lungi and shirt, and put them to dry. Your clothes reek of sweat, can't stand next to you! They'll be dry by the time we finish bathing.'

The stranger could not remember when he had last bathed. He had no recollection of when bathing, eating, sleeping and other such daily activities had dropped off his life. He dived lustily into the cool depths of the lake. He rubbed his head and body with the 501 bar to rid it of the dirt and grime accumulated over a long time. Perhaps with that he also washed away everything of the past. He felt as if all the sadness–failure–fearfulness, all the painful memories of his past life, had really been washed away in the waters of the lake, and that he had entered a new life, in the way a boy began his journey towards divine knowledge after his upanayan, or thread ceremony. Or in the way a householder entered the life of renunciation, following his initiation.

It was terribly hot. By the time they finished bathing, the stranger's thin lungi and shirt were dry. Wearing a clean set of clothes made him feel light.

Emerging from the lake, Ganesh laughed, and asked, 'Can you swim across the lake now, Dada, with a person on your back?'

Jalil exclaimed, 'Was it Dada who had done that earlier!'

Ganesh said, 'Circumstances drove Dada to do that. If such a situation arises again, he'll do that once more. That was the day I first met Dada. Ever since then, he has been unforgettable.'

Amal was five or six years younger than Ganesh. The time they were referring to was much before he had arrived at the stand at the station to drive a rickshaw. Ganesh told him, 'While being chased by the police once, Dada swam across this lake with a man on his back. He was in the Naxalite party then. The police were at the railway line, while Dada and his group were in front of the timber yard. There was a fierce battle between them. While the police fired their bullets, these people hurled country bombs. What a battle it was, for almost an hour! Neither side was in any mood to relent. We had come here to bathe, and we sat on this bank and watched. We were scared, but we were enjoying it too. Suddenly a police bullet hit a person on his leg. A terrible wound. But the police were unable to come directly and get him! There's a long, foul drain beneath the railway line. By the time they walked along the railway line, turned at the rail siding and reached the timber yard, Dada had descended into the lake, carrying the injured fellow on his back. And he swam directly to this bank. He then put him on a rickshaw, and I don't know where he took him after that.'

Ganesh now asked the stranger, 'Where did you take him, Dada?'

The question was a very simple one, and so the stranger had no trouble answering it. 'Where can one take a person with a bullet injury? To get him treated.'

Ganesh said, 'I didn't know you before that day. I had heard about you though. The porters who carried basketloads of vegetables to Palpara Bazaar knew you, they spoke a lot about you.'

He paused for a while, wrung his gamchcha, and as he wiped himself, he said, 'I never met you after that. But how could we, after all we had stopped coming to these parts out of fear. And if it was not for fear of the police, your party was engaged in bomb battles, day and night, with the party from Loharpara. That had gone on for about two years, isn't it, Dada? After that, Ashu-da died, and Bor-da, Tulsi-da and so many others! Silence descended everywhere. Who knows where the Naxals disappeared to after they left Palpara, Salampur and Santoshpur. I saw you sitting in our station one day sometime after that. And then I began to see you every day.'

Finding a cue, the stranger said, 'I got acquainted with you people after that, and we became friends. Isn't that right? If I hadn't made the station my den, would I have found you? I don't know if there are friends like you all anywhere else.'

Jalil said, 'Wherever you go, Dada, people will embrace you. Won't people love the man whose days and nights are always devoted to others, who has nothing to call his own other than the clothes on his body and the friends by his side? People are not so dishonest. It wasn't you who found us, we were fortunate to have found you.'

Jalil's voice was tearful. He said, 'Dada, don't ever leave us and go away again. We don't have anyone but you.'

4

Jatadhari Guru

All the hawkers, porters and rickshaw riders who lived in the railway station, and for that matter, the daily passengers here, knew Jatadhari Guru. He was dark-skinned, with a Mahishasura-like appearance, the thick moustache and beard on his face forming a veritable jungle of black and grey, with a knot of matted hair on his head, and his eyes red as hibiscus under the influence of ganja; that was more or less his description. But despite the man's frightening appearance, like an Aghori tantrik clad in crimson, actually he was not like that. In fact, he was of a quiet, calm and benevolent disposition, although there was always an unresolved debate among scholarly folk about whether his acts were beneficial or harmful. But that was a different subject.

Jatadhari Guru sat at his shop in front of the stairs of the overbridge on Platform No. 2, and sold various kinds of roots, herbs, amulets and talismans. He also read palms. Apparently, he could infallibly tell you all about your past and future, on the basis of oceanic or some such calculations.

Another man in this railway station sold similar amulets. His name was Golam Gazi. He sat at the eastern end of the platform.

Jatadhari Guru had been here for many years. Observing this railway station on his way back from the Gangasagar Mela, he had suddenly got off one day. He did not leave after that. And Golam Gazi had arrived here only a few months ago. Like Jatadhari said that all his amulets, talismans and spells were obtained from Kamakhya, in Kamrup, Golam Gazi claimed that everything of his had been brought from the mazaar of Khwaja Baba.

Conflict was inevitable when there were two bulls in the same field. But what if one was a bull, and the other a buffalo! In this regard, it was difficult to discern who was the bull, and who the buffalo. But the truth was that no clash had taken place yet. It was also true that Jatadhari Guru could not stand the sight of Golam Gazi. According to him, the man was not just a thug and a cheat, but a murderer as well.

It was a lazy afternoon now. The stranger was walking along the platform, wondering what he ought to and ought not to do. Jatadhari raised his eyes and glanced at him. He hurriedly called out to him in a grave voice, 'Hey, listen!'

Both the platforms of the railway station were relatively vacant. If one looked around a bit, one would observe that various spots in this secluded station were being merrily used by different people for various purposes. Some womenfolk—who washed utensils and clothes, and mopped the floors in babu homes, who were, in short, maidservants—were sitting here after having completed their work, waiting for a train to return to their homes in the village. They sat in twos on the steps of the overbridge, one behind the other, plucking out hair lice. If one eavesdropped on their conversation, one obtained a glimpse of the ugly and deformed mental makeup of a class of educated and affluent people living in the city. 'Oh dear Didi, what can I tell you, I was absent for two days last month. I didn't do it just like that, my younger daughter had diarrhoea, that's why. The wretch deducted the amount from my salary! Whether you're sick, or the train's not running, she doesn't listen to any of that. She says, where's the question of wages when you didn't work?

Achcha, tell me, they too have jobs working for someone. Are they never absent? Is their salary deducted then?'

One observed a few people belonging to the labouring class, who had arrived here with basket, spade, axe, rope and suchlike, in the hope of finding some work somewhere. They did not get work today—because in this unfortunate country, the number of jobs available was always much lower than the number of candidates. But they couldn't return now to the places they had come from. They got the news that there was stringent checking going on in the next station. As soon as ticketless travellers were apprehended, they were put inside a cage. Who knows whether they would be released today, or tomorrow!

Some porters of the railway station had spread out a gamchcha and sat down to play cards. They quarrelled among themselves from time to time. It could also eventually lead to fisticuffs. But one could be certain that the police, or the police station, would not be involved. If all these people ever went anywhere near a police station or a court, that was as accused persons. They did not possess the qualifications to be plaintiffs.

A dark-skinned and thin woman. Her clothes were dirty, she had dust and grime on her body. She had quite a few glass bangles on the wrist of her right hand, which sparkled and clinked. By clinking her bangles, and through her movements and gestures, she sought to convey, 'I am cheap, and easily available. I need a bit of money badly. Which was too little to buy even a kilo of chicken meat from the market. She was eating muri-chhola now, leaning on a railing. She would drink water next, and then move from this railing to another, and from this platform to the other—she would keep trying, so as to get a few rupees. If she got the money, she could buy rice.

⚬

As the stranger walked up and down the station in this lazy time, wondering what he ought to do, it occurred to him to visit the sick girl by the name of Kushi, in the No. 2 railside squatter settlement. Kushi's Ma had wept and informed him in the morning, 'Unless you see it with your own eyes, Jibon, you won't believe how badly the girl's burnt. Oh God, how can a person do this to another!'

The stranger was looking for Ganesh, or Gopal, or Amal, or Bimal to accompany him. But it wouldn't be difficult for him to find Kushi's place. Or else he would have had to grope around like a blind man.

The cheap eatery run by Chhechan Sahu of Arrah district in Bihar was right where the line of rickshaws from the base of the banyan tree ended. It was the only appropriate place for all the poor and destitute folk of the locality to eat in so that they could stay alive. The item that was prepared here by adding some salt and turmeric to rice foam was called 'dal'. He picked things up from all the unsold vegetables and greens that the vendors in Sandhya Bazaar threw away or sold at throwaway prices and prepared his vegetable curry. And the rice came from a ration shop near the rail gate. Rotten rice, crawling with insects, which the babus of the city considered to be inedible. Kushi's Ma stood waiting at the ration shop. The moment someone declined to take rice, she pleaded, 'Babu, please let me take your rice.' The babus didn't object to that, they let her have it. She sold the rice to Chhechan at a slight profit. Ghoti Narayan had gone to Chhechan's eatery to eat. He had said to the stranger before going, 'If you don't find Ganesh, or anyone else, I'll come along with you. I'd like to visit Kushi too. I stand by my words. Whether she's burnt, or whatever, she'll be the one I marry, if she survives. After two years.'

'Why after two years?'

Narayan firmly believed that by then, he would be able to save money from his earnings driving a rickshaw, deposit the money at the Bhagwan Das Motor Training School and become a driver of private vehicles. He would then be able to earn enough to provide for his family.

As he was walking towards Chhechan's eatery, the stranger was stunned to hear Jatadhari's roar. He thought that the man wanted to do with him what such fraudulent sadhus, tantriks and astrologers did with simple and foolish folk, spinning a web of words to cheat them. He got angry. I've travelled to many states, and seen many sadhus and pilgrimage sites. It won't be easy to make a fool of me. He retorted sharply, 'Why are you calling me? I'm not interested in showing my hand, or buying any amulets or talismans. I don't believe the slightest bit in all that.'

Jatadhari Guru laughed, exposing his stained, yellow teeth, 'You don't believe? Fine, don't believe it! No one asked you to swear that you'll believe!' He then lowered his voice a few rungs, and said, 'You should know that I don't either!'

The stranger said in a sarcastic voice, 'You say you don't believe it, but here you are selling all these things.'

'That's my business. I sell roots, herbs and amulets.'

'This is no business, it's a scam to cheat people.'

Jatadhari impatiently retorted, 'Tell me which business doesn't involve cheating people. Can there be business without cheating people? It's because they are blinded by superstitions that I can run my business, and feed myself. Wouldn't I starve otherwise?'

'Very strange!'

'What's strange? What I said, or my business?'

'Both. You spin a web of words and make people believe what you yourself don't believe in! Doesn't it prick your conscience?'

Jatadhari's eyes turned as sharp as a knife, and as poisonous as a snake's fangs. 'Who on earth told you that people say or do what they believe? Do the political leaders who stand before people and speak, really believe that to be true? Can they fulfil the promises they make? They can't, yet they make them. They need to. Or else their political shopkeeping won't succeed. Do the brahmins believe that the *ong-bong* mantras that they chant bring to life a clay idol? That the gods are pleased, and grant them wishes? Fill their lives with happiness and wealth? They don't believe that. Yet they need to carry on doing that, or else their capital-less business will be done for.'

The stranger said, 'All the people you compare yourself to are the same in my eyes, simply thugs and cheats.'

He glanced at the stranger, as if sizing him up, and then asked him, 'What about Anjali?'

'What about her?'

'Is she a thug, or a cheat, or a businesswoman?'

'Why should she be a thug or a cheat? Whatever she does is simply business.'

'Doesn't Anjali know what she's selling? It's poison. Pure poison. She knows that people die when they consume it. The one who ought to live to sixty is finished at thirty. Yet she sells it, because people pay money to buy and drink the poison. If she shuts the shop, the drunkards will go to another shop, won't they? If I folded up my business, everyone would go to Golam Gazi, won't they?'

The stranger didn't have the answer to Jatadhari's question.

A man was sitting inside a *jhanka*, or large basket, counting money. He sold green coconuts. He had brought the coconuts from his village in the basket. He came every day, and sat in front of the main entrance of the TB Hospital. Opposite the gate, across the road, was the entrance of Jadavpur University. The patients, doctors and nurses, from this side, and the teachers and students from across, were his customers. Before returning home after selling his wares, the green coconut seller was calculating the profit he had made. The money too had to be bundled and tied up and kept properly, or else someone might filch the money in the crowded train. The pickpockets had their lairs in Park Circus, Bondel Gate, in Ballygunge, Mallikpur, Ghutiari Sharif, and in this station; their job was to carry out 'dor' in the 'iron wheel'. Iron wheel meant a train, while rubber wheel meant a bus. Carrying out 'dor' meant travelling on, or investigating, and pouncing on and taking what belonged to others the moment an opportunity arose. Their handiwork was so deft that although it took place before thousands of eyes, no one caught on. The coconut seller, who commuted daily, knew all this, which was why he was being cautious.

A man came and stood in front of the green coconut seller sitting in his jhanka. He was wearing a shirt and a pair of trousers that were caked in dust and mud, a pair of spectacles, a faded, old attache case in his hand. He opened his attache case, took out a bunch of lottery tickets, and held it out in front of the coconut seller. 'Bhutan lottery—the first prize is a hundred-thousand rupees. The draw is tomorrow, the ticket price is a rupee. Shall I give you one?'

Pointing in that direction, Jatadhari asked the stranger, 'What is the man selling? Look properly, and tell me.'

'A lottery ticket.'

'Look properly. I know that you'll never spot it.'

'I'm looking properly, it's a lottery ticket.'

Jatadhari laughed, shook his head, and then looking the stranger in the eye, he asked, 'How many eyes does a person have?'

The stranger thought Jatadhari was talking rubbish in his state of intoxication with ganja or bhang. In an annoyed voice, he gave an oblique answer. 'Some have two, some one, and some none.'

Swaying this way and that, Jatadhari said, 'And do you know that some have three! That third eye of some people is so powerful that they can see what will happen a year from today, ten years later, and a hundred years later. They are called seers of the future.'

'Do you have the third eye?'

'Or else how do I read people's palms? Why do seven or eight of the ten things I tell a customer turn out to be correct?'

In a sarcastic tone, the stranger said, 'Then look through that eye of yours, and tell me what precious thing the man with the attache case is selling.'

His eyes were bloodshot and his demeanour was like he was the Budhha sitting under the wisdom tree, explaining to his principal student, Ananda, about progressing along the path to knowledge. Jatadhari said, 'The man is selling hope. A person buys a lottery ticket for a rupee, and from then on, until the draw, night and day, with the ticket in his hand, he is taken over by a state like that of a traveller, who, lost in a field enveloped in darkness, sees the light from a faraway hut, and walks ahead. In this way, he can go through one day after another in the hope of good times. One can't say, maybe the ticket is fake. Why should one be surprised if lottery tickets are fake in a country where currency notes and university degrees are being counterfeited? Even if the ticket number matches the winning number, the person won't really gain anything. His only gain is the prop he gets, thanks to the lottery ticket, that enables him to be like the camel that fearlessly buries its face in the sand during a storm and survives.'

Jatadhari paused awhile, and then continued. 'Man is a terribly weak creature. He cannot survive without some prop. So they seek refuge either under some political leader's umbrella, or at the feet of some guru, or come to astrologers like us. What do we give them? Nothing at all. We boost their morale, hope and faith with mere words, assurances and exhortations to be fearless.'

'But as a result, even if they stay the way they are, no matter what happens to anybody else, you people can live in great comfort. Isn't that so?'

The stranger's jibe made Jatadhari Guru very angry. And when he got angry, profanities emitted his mouth like a fountain. He shouted, 'Look, there are all kinds of people in the world. There's one kind who enjoy screwing others. That's bad, it's condemnable, but people do it, don't they? If you go to a neighbourhood of drunkards, and open a shop selling milk there, no one will buy it. If you go to sell mirrors in a place where blind folk live, you won't find customers. That's why you ought to sell lathis in a neighbourhood of drunkards. Then you will be a successful shopkeeper. Do you get anything? *Arrey*, if you are content to lie on your back, why do I need to turn you over into a prone position! After all, man is not a tortoise, who can't turn over on his back, man is like a compass needle, no matter which way you turn him, the fucker will still turn and face northwards.'

White foam was visible on the two sides of Jatadhari's mouth, since he had blabbered so long without let-up. He wiped the foam, the perspiration on his forehead and the corners of his eyes with his gamchcha. He looked the stranger in the eye once again, and slowly said, 'It's not that I don't know, it's not that I don't understand, but at the same time, I also realise that one has to flow with the current. There's no problem in becoming one with that, there's no risk involved. It requires a lot of courage to go against the current, one needs a spine for that, and the ability to accept loss. But I don't have that.'

Jatadhari had calmed down by now. He continued, 'Although I don't have it, I'm not saying that no one else has that. They do. They are different from others. One in every hundred- or two-hundred-thousand still has a spine. They have the guts to call a spade a spade. They don't walk on the path made by others, they make their own path in the course of their journey. They have the deep confidence and determination required for that. Which makes them dependable, both to themselves and to many other people.'

The stranger now looked at Jatadhari Guru in astonishment. He hadn't realised earlier that the man possessed such profound wisdom. He was like the fabled stone that lay neglected on one's path. No one could imagine, seeing it, that it possessed fire inside. The fire would emerge when the stone was struck by another stone.

He had once encountered a youth on the pavement of the city of Calcutta, of the same age as himself, and as poor and dressed in similar dirty, tattered clothes. He had watched in amazement as the youth explained in fluent English to an Englishman who had lost his way, how he could reach Park Street. The youth had told him that he was completely illiterate. He used to work earlier as a porter in the Khidirpur docks. He had mastered the language through long association with foreigners. The stranger had heard that Sri Ramakrishna too was illiterate. But he could amaze great scholars with his words. People like Vivekananda too had been overwhelmed by him.

After a while, Jatadhari said, 'Arguments and counter-arguments are pointless. Nothing is gained through that. But you will gain when you actively pursue what you think. All talk and argument is like the nor'wester storm in the month of Boishakh, like leaves and torn bits of paper flying in the wind. Neither the one who speaks, nor the one who hears benefit from that. But if you can build yourself up in accordance with your own thinking, that would be meaningful. Although it's extremely difficult.'

The stranger had been standing at a bit of a distance for so long, as he was speaking. He now went up to Jatadhari Guru and sat down on the plastic sheet he had spread on the ground. But was it he who sat down? Or had Jatadhari pulled him there with invisible strings? Pulled him like a powerful magnet which drew the tiny pins and clips lying around it. Jatadhari now suddenly grabbed the stranger's hand, examined it and then pushed it away. The stranger eagerly asked him, 'What did you see?'

'I saw your hand.'

'But that was my left hand. Don't astrologers look at the right hand of men?'

'What I was looking at is supposed to be in the left hand. It wasn't there.'

'Can you tell me what you were looking for?'

'But you don't believe in palmistry, astrology and suchlike. Why do you need to know?'

'Forget about whether I believe it or not. You tell me what you saw and what you didn't. Let me also see how seven or eight of the ten things you say turn out to be correct.'

'Do you really want to know?'

'Yes.'

'You'll be shocked!'

'I won't.'

Jatadhari laughed. And then he said, 'You told me that I cheat people. But you cheat people too, make fools of them. You claim to be someone you are not. You are not Jibon. Isn't that true?'

After he said that Jatadhari looked at the stranger with his intense, piercing eyes. The man pretending to be Jibon seemed to shrink before his gaze. He felt terribly helpless. Jatadhari suddenly seemed very cruel now. The stranger was scared.

Jatadhari spoke again after a while. 'I got the news a few days ago. Someone or the other told me, "Jibon has returned!" But that was quite a few days back. I was quite surprised that he had returned, but hadn't come to meet me yet! That shouldn't have happened if he had really returned. How could it be that Vivekananda visited Dakshineshwar but didn't meet Sri Ramakrishna? That's when I became suspicious. And when you walked past me now, I called out to you. But now I realise you are someone else. Not Jibon.'

The stranger now had the look of someone who had been caught stealing. He sat with his head bent. He seemed to lack the words to say anything. Nor did he have the mental fortitude to get up and leave. He felt like a genie that had emerged from a bottle being made tiny and stuffed back into the bottle again.

Jatadhari said, 'Do you know why I didn't get cheated, although you managed to fool everyone else? It's because of these eyes of mine. I had observed Jibon very closely. He had a scar on his left wrist. Your hand didn't have the scar. Once when Jibon was very small, he was playing "goat sacrifice" with his brother. The trunk of the banana palm was the goat. Jibon was holding that, while his brother, Jatan, was meant to strike that with a chopper. But the blow had landed on Jibon's wrist instead. He had another identification mark as well. He had a small lump near his left earlobe which was almost invisible. But you don't have any of those marks! If you had them, I would have accepted you as Jibon, even if you were not speaking in the Bangaal language. Tell me the truth now, aren't you someone else?'

The stranger realised that it was pointless to lie to him any longer. As if he was surrendering to some authority, the stranger admitted, 'No, I'm not him.'

'Who are you then?'

'I don't know who I am, or why I'm here.' The stranger inwardly thought the game was over. He ought to jump into the next train. He ought to go where he had been headed—to a purposeless, uncertain destination, which lacked any address.

Jatadhari now seemed to be submerged in a deep sea that was free of all care.

After quite some time went by this way, Jatadhari opened his eyes, and said, 'People come to me when they are in trouble. I prepare an amulet, and tie it around the neck, or wrist, or waist, or wherever, and say, "There's nothing to fear, go now. All your troubles will pass." I know that the amulet has no power, and yet I say that. Because people feel strengthened by what I say. You have become like an amulet to Ganesh, Gopal, and why only them, to many others too. They are not like Jatadhari, they are ordinary folk. Their eyes can't distinguish between what's true and what's false. They think you are the same old Jibon. These people were in great difficulty, they were like orphans, to tell the truth, they had come down to the plight of the dogs on the street, whom anyone could kick and go away. Your return has given them back their morale, because Jibon would protect them all like his own children. After Jibon went away, their plight was like that of tiny saplings on dry, cracked soil in drought-ridden, rainless days, which somehow, with great difficulty, managed to survive. After your arrival, it's as if there's been a shower of rain on these dying saplings. They have glimpsed hope of survival. But if they find out that you are not their Jibon, but someone else, all their hope and joy will be finished.'

Anjali had said something like this, Jatadhari was saying it now. All the salutations and praises were being showered upon a person about whom the stranger knew absolutely nothing. His head throbbed. There was darkness in front of his eyes. There was no sign of light anywhere on the vast dark ocean. Jibon had built a massive family with all these people who lacked any resource or kin, who were beset with hundreds of problems. Where did the stranger have the ability to raise such a family? After all, he had failed in looking after even himself. He spent days after days consuming merely water, air, and sunlight.

The stranger sheepishly mumbled to Jatadhari, 'So what should I do now?'

'Become Jibon.'

'How is that possible?'

'Through the power of your will. The way a caterpillar becomes a butterfly.'

After a while, the stranger asked, 'What did Jibon do?'

'What do you mean?'

'Where did he find the means to attend to so many problems of so many people? He must surely have had to do something, which provided a lot of money!'

Lice dwelt on the knot of matted hair on Jatadhari's head. They bit his scalp all day. Even the anti-lice medicine seemed to be adulterated. It wasn't as effective as before. Scratching his head, Jatadhari said, 'It's difficult to say what exactly he did. To tell the truth, he did next to nothing. But again, he did everything on earth when required. A king never does anything unjust or illegal. Because it is he who decides what is just and legal. Similarly, Jibon had defined for himself what was right and what was wrong. Whenever it was required, he also did what ordinary folk often considered to be wrong.'

Jatadhari's eyes rose from above the stranger and gazed at the sky in the north-west. He heaved a deep sigh and added to what he had last said: 'Jibon was the king of this locality.'

A king! Didn't the cowherds too have a king? He was the king of all these starving, abused and beaten folk. That's what the stranger now thought. The responsibility of this kingdom had now fallen on his shoulders.

The sun had slanted a bit by now. But it wasn't any less hot. It was as if the sunlight of late afternoon had sharper teeth. People felt they were dying in the heat. The stranger had forgotten that he wanted to visit Kushi. Where had Ghoti Narayan vanished?

Soldiers of a defeated army went down on their knees, and bowed their heads before the general of the victorious army. The stranger knelt down before Jatadhari in such a gesture of surrender, and said, 'You are my guru from today. Teach me how I can become exactly like Jibon. I can't even think where to start.'

In the manner of someone throwing a life-saving coil of rope to a person fallen into a well, Jatadhari said, 'Can you act? Have you ever acted? Poran Dolui sits with a bonti in Sandhya Bazaar, removing the scales of fish. He plays the part of king in jatra performances. When he gets on stage, no one's dad has the temerity to declare that Poran isn't Nawab Sirajuddowla, or Shah Jahan!'

Jatadhari paused, and then, in the manner of a judge in court sentencing to death a prisoner standing in the dock, he said, 'You have to play the role of Jibon now. That's as important for you, as it is vital for some unfortunate, vulnerable folk. I don't see any other way out.'

5

The Nocturnal Operation

A railway line runs straight from the heart of Calcutta city to the very tip of southern Bengal. A stranger had arrived one day, with no prior plan, at the railway station by the name of Jadavpur that was on this railway line. Although that was not so long ago, it wasn't so recent either.

What the time on a watch was, what the date on the page of a calendar was, or what the day, month or year was, were all very important to some people. But the stranger's life was not so calibrated. He seemed to be lying like an unclaimed corpse on flowing time. Lashed by waves, the corpse either floated to Platform No. 1, or to Platform No. 2, to Anjali's shanty, or to Nadu's liquor den; such was his daily routine. And at night, one found him sprawled either beneath the stairs of the overbridge, or on one of the locked-up rickshaws in the rickshaw stand.

The sun rose every morning, and set in the evening. Night arrived, and then passed. Something good or bad happened every day on this fringe of the city. Which caused a stir in the entire locality. This station and the adjoining area too were no exception.

The impact was felt there as well. There was a stir in the station area a few days ago over an incident.

Kumir Mari was the name of a small island in the Sundarbans region. A girl from there had been enticed and brought to the city by a middleman in the women-trafficking racket. He had planned to entice her with the promise of a good job in Delhi, take her there and sell her off. But he was apprehended by Ganesh and Gopal. He was handed over to the outpost of the GRP. The girl was brought to court the next day. She complained to the judge there that four constables in the GRP outpost raped her at night. After much deliberation, when the girl was finally examined medically, the complaint of rape was proved to be true, but who the rapists were, was not established. The girl was now sheltered in a government home.

Another incident had taken place a few days before that. A girl had arrived from somewhere. No one knew whether she had intentionally thrown herself in front of a Diamond Harbour Up-train at dawn, or whether she had stumbled and fallen while attempting to cross the rail track. Her right arm, on which she had worn a gold bangle, had been severed from the shoulder. And her right leg, broken and crushed, looked like a coiled rope. That time, too, Ganesh and Gopal had brought her on a stretcher from the railway line to the station master's office. The girl was unconscious as she was being brought. But she had been fully conscious before that. Even in that terribly wounded state, she was aware that she was a woman. She possessed certain bodily assets that set the eyes of these youths aflame. The body awakened desire. With great difficulty, she had pulled the anchal of her sari with her left hand and covered her exposed, bulging breasts. There was a discussion in the station about this stinginess on the part of women even while dying.

Clicking his tongue, a man with a freshly groomed moustache had castigated her for the wasted opportunity, saying, '*Eesh*, how unfortunate she was, she'll have to rot in the autopsy room now.'

The latest incident of this week involved a fifteen- or sixteen-year-old girl named Kushi from the railside squatter colony. There were some fifteen or sixteen small shanties on the far end of the foul, blue-black pond laden with hyacinth that lay to the right of the eastern end of the platform. There were a few shops in front of these shanties, that is to say, facing the railway line, which sold tea, paan, cigarettes, and so on. Kushi and her parents lived in one of the shanties in the rear of the cluster. Kushi was dark-skinned and of a tall and thin build. But the hair on her head—it wasn't hair but a black python which flowed from her head to her knees. Kushi's Ma had taken her along to a two-storeyed house at the intersection of Kali Krishna Road and got her a job there. She would be provided food and clothes by her employer and a meagre salary at the end of the month. The people in the household were a bad-tempered lot. Kushi would sometimes come and tell her Ma that if she made any mistake in the work, they would beat her badly. She showed her bruises as well. Kushi's Ma had decided that she would bring Kushi away as soon as the month was over. She had found another job for her as well. But before that could happen, Kushi got badly burnt.

Kushi had, of course, stated that she had been burnt by a daughter-in-law of the household. Apparently Kushi had put milk to boil on the stove and then forgotten about it when she got occupied with some other task. The people of the household complained that she was standing at the door of the adjacent room and watching television. That she often did that. And that she had dropped the work at hand and rushed to watch television. As a result of which, milk had boiled and spilt over twice in the past.

Television sets had arrived in the homes of well-to-do people. Black & white. Apparently colour television was coming soon.

The hot-tempered daughter-in-law of the house discovered the boiling milk spilling over. Kushi came running when she screamed. The woman poured the remaining milk on Kushi in rage. Their contention in this matter was that the utensil fell. The accident had happened when she hurriedly sought to remove the hot utensil with her bare hands.

This locality was home to educated folk. They had a huge number of complaints about maidservants skiving work. Only the bhadralok understood the language of the bhadralok. They immediately accepted that it was simply an accident, and nothing else.

But the lowly folk believed what the little girl said. That it was a deliberate act. Or else, why would Kushi alone have got hurt, some of the milk should have splashed on the woman too.

All the rickshaw-drivers, porters, labourers and maidservants in babu households, in short, all the lowly folk, knew from their own gruelling life experience what such bhadralok were really like. They could even go so far as to remove a kidney from poor, destitute and vulnerable people.

The sturdily built Gadai Mondol lived near Rambabu Bazar, and used to ride a rickshaw at the stand in front of Palpara Bazaar. A babu took him along to Hyderabad. Why was that? Oh, he'd get him a good job there. After reaching there, he was lying in bed after having had his dinner. But he could not get up the next morning. He had a terrible ache in his abdomen. The babu was compassionate, he took Gadai and got him admitted in a nursing home. After various kinds of tests, the doctor concluded that he had gallstones. There was no option but to get it operated. But that was an expensive affair. The babu was only too willing. He said, 'Let's get the operation done first. Once you've recovered, work hard and pay me back little by little. Or else you'll die.' Gadai did not really have to do much after that. It was the babu who did whatever was necessary. Gadai only put his signature on some papers.

The operation was done in a few days. Gadai was discharged from the nursing home within a month. He was very weak then. The compassionate babu told him, 'You won't recover well if you stay here. I'll give you some more money, take it and return home. Come back again when you are well.'

Gadai returned home. He lay in bed all day. Instead of getting better, he got worse by the day. But there was no news of the babu after that. Gadai was compelled to visit a local doctor. That's how it was discovered that a kidney had been removed.

All the shanty folk, who harboured great ire against bhadralok, went in procession with Kushi to the police station. But they refused to file the complaint. They advised that the matter ought to be settled mutually. The officer-in-charge of the police station also added that he personally knew everyone in the Sengupta family. They were very nice people. If such nice people were blamed, it was them that he would lock up in custody.

The babus had confined Kushi to the house after she got burnt. They had fetched Burnol and some medicine, and attended to her too. But Kushi escaped from the house when she got a chance. They got very angry when she was taken in procession to the police station. They said, 'Oh, so you've jumped the gun, have you! Now that you've gone to the police station, and I've already been disgraced in the Jadavpur locality, we have nothing more to do with you.'

After that, the shanty folk took Kushi to the hospital. Public hospitals did not provide any treatment. They either gave the address of a nursing home, or handed over a prescription. Poor Kushi was unable to buy the required treatment. Her burn wounds were not healing.

Kushi needed a good doctor and proper medical treatment now. That was expensive. Ganesh arrived and said, 'I have some information. There's a place where money is available. It's lying there, only needs to be picked up.'

'Money lying there? Where's that?'

'Why don't you come along, you'll see what I mean. You don't have to do anything. It's a minor thing, all you need to do is stand there. We'll do whatever needs to be done.'

The stranger replied fearfully, 'What are you going to do, Ganesh? A robbery?'

Hanging out almost his entire tongue in mock shock, Ganesh exclaimed, '*Chhee* Dada! Will we steal! Am I a thief, or what? After all, you know me from childhood. Even if I'm starving to death, I'll never steal. If required, I'll thrash someone and take what I have to.'

After a pause, Ganesh continued, 'It would be good if we could carry some knives, or swords, and a couple of country bombs. I don't think we'll need them, but we'll feel braver if we have them. Nanu-da has some of them. He won't refuse if you ask him. Once the job is over, we'll return them.'

The stranger was at a complete loss. He had no idea where Ganesh and company would take him, and maybe abandon him! Would that be at the final floor of seventh hell, or the first step to reach heaven? After all, the stranger did not know the Jibon that Ganesh and his group were familiar with. So he knew nothing about what he would have done in such a situation, whether he would go ahead, or whether he would turn back. Which was why he didn't think he could simply say, 'I won't go, you people go.' The stranger realised that he was now seated in the chariot in which Jibon had been seated earlier. And the reins of the chariot were held by Ganesh, Gopal and Kaliya. If they went to commit suicide, he would have to accompany them too. He could not say 'no' because if he did that, he would be caught. The real Jibon was no longer there. He had to go on proving now that he was indeed Jibon.

The stranger asked, 'So who all are going, besides you and me?'

'Everyone,' Ganesh replied. 'Not a single person will be excluded. Everyone's terribly excited to be going out on a hunt after a long time.'

He was being asked to get the weapons from Nanu. And there would be a whole gang of youths accompanying them. So had Ganesh hatched a plan to commit a major robbery? The stranger didn't feel brave enough to ask. Let them do what they plan. If they are ready to die, so am I. If they survive, so will I. After all, that's what a shared life means.

'When do we go?'

'Today.'

'At what time?'

'At exactly twelve at night.'

'Where should I be?'

'Wait beneath the water tank. Everyone will arrive there.'

They reached there a bit before twelve at night. There were seven people. All were clad in battlegear, some had cycle chains, while others carried the rickshaw axle. Bachcha Amal was the youngest, but he couldn't stay away today. He had stuffed 'Bengal bombs' into a bag, meaning, large stones from the railway track. They had walked cautiously but with determination, and assembled at the designated spot. But Ganesh, who was supposed to be there first, had not yet come.

He came half-an-hour later. He was carrying a pipe gun. He said, 'I got delayed a bit in fetching this. We are going quite prepared now, we'll cut them to pieces if they make too much trouble. Dada, are you people ready?'

Like cats, one by one, they silently and stealthily jumped across the broken part of the wall of the hospital on the railway station side, and entered the hospital compound. The grounds were completely desolate now, not a single person in sight. A large field lay ahead of them. The children of the hospital staff played football in this field in the evenings. The squad crossed the field and walked briskly down the straight road that ran from the main gate of the hospital, through the hospital compound, over the city's large drainage channel in the east, past the sweepers' quarters, and reached the culvert at Lohar Para. A narrow lane branched out from this road and wound its way to Raja Subodh Chandra Mullick Road. Since there was a gate of the hospital there, there was supposed to be a watchman there. But there wasn't. He had locked the gate at ten o'clock and gone off to sleep. But there was no problem on that account. Garbage used to be thrown earlier on the left side of the gate. Grass had now grown over the garbage heap. Those who wanted to go across, climbed atop the mound, and then jumped over the wall. They went across the wall like that, crossed Raja S.C. Mullick Road, and entered the narrow lane in front. Ganesh walked ahead, while the others followed him. It was evident from their gait that everyone knew where they had to go. The narrow lane was completely dark. After going a little distance, the lane turned, and at a short distance, on the left side, was the house in question, on Kali Krishna Road. Where Kushi had been burnt. And at some distance on the right side was the supermarket in front of the timber yard behind the bus-stand intersection. One could reach there in a minute from the hospital gate, by turning left and walking down Raja S.C. Mullick Road. But there was the possibility of being spotted by someone or the other, especially by those in Jhantu-da's shop, which sold tea, green coconut, Coca Cola, cholai, i.e., illicit liquor and English liquor. Which was why they wanted to go to the place by a roundabout road. Of course, the stranger was still unaware of where they were headed.

The stranger had not asked Ganesh anything. Neither had Ganesh elaborated. He didn't think that was necessary. Or who knows, maybe he had forgotten to. But he now thought that since this was a nocturnal campaign of the enraged miscreant youths from the station, in response to the scorching of Kushi, the mission of vengeance must be headed towards the house on Kali Krishna Road. But his presumption turned out to be wrong when the procession turned to the right.

The stranger asked, 'Where are we going?'

'Didn't I tell you?' Ganesh was shocked.

'When did you tell me?'

'Damn! I completely forgot!'

'We are heading for the timber yard,' Ganesh said. 'The gamblers are in action. They have been sitting almost every day for the last few months. Some fuckers have ill-gotten money in their hands, they can't figure out what to do with all that money. So what else can they do but blow it up drinking alcohol, going to whores and gambling it away.' Ganesh paused, and then said, 'No one ever wins in gambling. If someone loses, then obviously, he's lost. But even if he wins, he'll blow it up on something nefarious. That's also like losing, isn't it! Come, let's lighten their pockets today. Let them lose, we'll be the winners. Let the money be spent for two good causes.'

'Which two good causes?'

'One is Kushi's treatment. That comes first. Whatever's left after that will go towards helping orphans. You didn't get that, did you? Do any of us have parents? We don't, isn't it? So the rest will be used to help us.'

After walking westwards stealthily along the lane for about two minutes, they reached the timber yard. It was shut now. The monster-like mechanical saw was at rest after having rattled and rumbled all day. Some Bihari labourers were lying on string-cots here and there in the timber yard. Didn't mosquitoes bite them! Or could they not afford to buy mosquito nets?

And the gambling session was going on at one end of the timber yard, in a hut made with bits of wood. The players included some building contractors with freshly acquired wealth, mini-bus owners and suppliers of building materials. There were ten or twelve people playing. The game they were playing was called 'andar bahar'. It required playing cards. Everyone was unperturbed. There were disorderly piles of five- and ten-rupee notes in front of each player. Ganesh and Gopal's gang now walked stealthily and silently, and came and stood in front of the timber yard. The gamblers could not make anything out because it was dark there. All of them were breathing heavily now. Their heartbeats were like the banging of hammers. It was Ganesh who had been directing them so far. Moments before their operation commenced, it occurred to the stranger that he ought to assume leadership now. After all, this was the moment when it was imperative to establish himself at the top of everyone.

Like a military general, he now ordered everyone in a gruff voice, 'Cover your faces with the gamchchas you are carrying. No one should be able to recognise us. Ganesh, you stand here, fire only if I tell you to. Make sure you don't hit anyone. It's just for the sound. Kaliya, stand next to Ganesh with the country bombs. Hurl them when I tell you to. You two Gopals, Narayan, Shibu and Bhola, pounce on them suddenly, and start thrashing them up before they can react. So that they scatter. Amal, you'll break the lights. I'll pick up the money amidst all the pandemonium. Is everyone ready? Come, let's go!'

Those who were gambling outnumbered them. But they were entirely unprepared for an attack like this. And they were unarmed, while the attackers were fully armed. As if they were all robbers. Everything happened so quickly that the attackers took away all the money on the counter even before the gamblers knew what was happening or why.

As soon as lathis descended on them out of the blue, the gamblers ran hither and thither for fear of their lives. Once they overcame their fear and were able to band together again, they thought of resisting the money-snatchers. Since it was a timber yard, there was no shortage of lathis and suchlike. As soon as they advanced two steps with that, they heard someone yelling, 'Fire!' A bullet flew over someone's head. A bomb was hurled. The gamblers were compelled to halt.

The gang of snatchers returned by the same route they had come. After coming quite a distance, the stranger said, 'Stop. Everyone stand in a line.' And then he counted them. There were nine of them. No one had been left behind, everyone was there. He then said, 'Let's go. No one should jump across the hospital wall. People will identify who we are. Walk straight down the main road, and then take the canalside road behind the hospital.'

As they walked, the stranger observed that Shibu was limping. He asked, 'What happened to you?' Shibu replied, 'I cut my leg.'

'Here, hold my hand,' said the stranger.

They walked along the canalside road and reached Nanu's liquor den. The funny thing was that even the violent dogs belonging to the sweepers didn't bark at them, or chase them with bared teeth. They shrank back in fear. When they reached the water tank, the money was counted. They had got seventeen-hundred-twenty-two rupees in all. That was a lot of money to them.

The stranger said, 'Call Jalil, and keep this in his shop for now. We'll do the rest tomorrow.'

6

Surabala

It was an evening about a month later. The stranger had crossed the broken wall, and was going to Nanu's vend. He went there at this time on most days. After crossing the field, as he turned right on the road, he spotted a girl advancing towards him, almost in a run, from the direction of the No. 2 gate of the hospital. She called out, not so loudly, but nonetheless intensely, 'Hey Jibon-da, just wait for me!'

Stunned by that, the stranger stopped and saw a girl, no, not exactly a girl, but a woman, and it was him that she was calling. She had red sindoor on her forehead, and a pair of cheap white bangles on her wrist, instead of the customary ones of conch shell, iron and coral. Cheap earrings too. Her clothes were not so neat either. She was very dark-skinned, a bit tall, and with unkempt hair. Altogether, an unattractive figure.

The stranger had become acquainted with her only five or six days ago. She had come to meet 'Jibon', together with an aunty from her village, who was of roughly the same age. The aunty had come with a complaint. She explained that there was a man who worked as a painter in this locality, who came on the same train, and the same compartment, as the one she boarded every morning from her station, to come to Jadavpur to work in babu houses.

The aunty said, 'So you know, Dada, whatever happens when you travel together, and laugh and make jokes! The mind is weak, as they say. I suffered a lapse of judgement. His name is Subol Naskar. He said he'll marry me. When ghee is kept close to fire, it melts. I melted too. After all, I'm a woman, aren't I? Tell me, what option do I have, but to agree to marry him? Subol then told me that he would marry me after two months. Apparently, he was due seven-hundred rupees from some contractor. He said he would set up home with me as soon as he got the money, and that the two months would be over before one knew it.'

The stranger had guessed what she was going to say next. Subol Naskar had taken her here and there over those two months, had slept with her. But now he didn't want to marry her. This wasn't just Aunty's problem. Many of the women coming to work in babu households faced the same problem. But the stranger didn't interrupt her. He allowed her to continue. 'What happened after that?'

'I believed him. A good groom had been found for me, from Kedra, from the same village as my aunt's in-laws. I didn't marry him. Now Subol, the son of a slut, doesn't want to marry me. He's found another girl. You tell me now, Dada, what am I to do? The only way out for me is to take poison. Subol's baby is growing by the day in my belly.'

The stranger asked her in a distraught voice, 'If I explain your situation to him, will he agree?'

'Explain to him! He won't agree if you merely explain. If you catch Subol, give a few solid blows, and tell him that if he doesn't marry me you won't let him into Jadavpur, that will do the trick. How will he survive if he doesn't come here? Is there any work back in the village? Tell me, Dada, will you do me this favour? If you do it, I'll do anything you say. If you go knee-deep for me, I'll go neck-deep for you.'

Receiving people's love in one's lifetime was a great achievement. The stranger was receiving that after arriving here. The womenfolk from poor households who arrived by train every day from rural Bengal were very fond of him, they trusted him. After all, a train journey now meant an uncertain journey. No one knew whether you would be able to return after having arrived, or whether you would be able to go again after you returned. The electric railway cables could get stolen, the rail tracks could get submerged after heavy rain. Some mechanical failure could crop up in the train. Some political party could block the railway line to press for some demand. Cowherd boys could think of it as a game and throw a banana stem atop the overhead cables. The inevitable result of all such incidents was—no trains. Can't return home. In that frightening time, when spending the night in the railway station could mean loss of dignity and honour, and rape, for any young woman, by a miscreant, or by a policeman on night duty, the women looked for Jibon-da. Chandal Jibon, who had a party. The party that stood beside imperilled folk, protected them from danger. The women slept in peace all night long while they stayed awake and kept watch.

The stranger had never seen Chandal Jibon before. But he could not help being amazed at how his strange companionship had made a group of people so humanely sensitive. People like Ganesh and Kaliya were all like wild buffaloes, so to speak. Taming them, and turning them into such compassionate people was not a simple matter. As if they were responsible for everyone who was sick, or needed blood, for every unfortunate person who was starving. Kushi, the poor girl, would have gone without treatment for want of twenty rupees, she would have died. It gave one gooseflesh to think about how bravely they had risked everything for her. You are blessed, Chandal Jibon. May you always be victorious, the stranger thought.

And now, Dulali Mashi's niece, Surabala, had come to Chandal Jibon for something. She was from a remote village called Begumpur.

She worked in Nabanagar, in Anandapur, in two or three houses in the housing estates there. She was a part-time maidservant. Besides her monthly salary, she got stale rutis and torn clothes. She had come with her Mashi who had been betrayed by Subol Naskar, but narrated her own life's tale as well. Her father tapped toddy.

She came up to the stranger and asked, 'Where are you going?'

'Oh, in that direction, I have some work.'

'There's something I want to tell you.'

Although the stranger was busy, he still asked, 'What?'

'Let's go and sit somewhere. It'll take some time to tell you everything. I can't stand here and tell you.'

If one took the road to the left, and walked a few minutes, one came upon the Hundred-Bed Ward. These parts were quite desolate. There was place to sit as well. The stranger went there and sat down. Surabala sat down next to him and began speaking in a soft voice. 'Shall I tell you something? It's been on my mind for the last few days. Shall I tell you?'

The stranger gave her his assent. 'Tell me.'

'I hope you won't mind.'

The stranger smiled, and said, 'I won't mind. So many people tell me so many good and bad things, I never take offence at anything people tell me.'

But Surabala wasn't forthcoming. She was hesitant, as if in some deep crisis. The stranger said, 'Then let it be for today. Tell me some other day.'

'No, no, sit down. I'll tell you.' She moved closer to the stranger, bent her head down, and slowly said in a most embarrassed tone, 'I've decided to have a love marriage. All the girls of my age whom I know are doing that. I want to do that too.'

The stranger was astonished. He said, 'But you're already married!'

Surabala felt hurt at the stranger's response. In a voice full of anguish, she said, 'Shall I spend my whole life like this, simply by holding on to something that happened ages ago? Don't I have wishes and desires? Do all one's desires come to an end with this conch shell bangle and sindoor?'

'Isn't your husband here? Are you separated?'

After a pause, Surabala said, 'How old was I then? I hadn't even had my period. My breasts were just this tiny.' She gestured with her fingers. 'So my drunkard father brought a middle-aged man and married me off. It was a meaningless marriage, but I was no longer considered unmarried. He didn't stay with me for more than three or four months. I can't even remember the man's face properly now. I had no idea what marriage was, whether it was something to eat, or something to wear on the head. I'm grown up now. I know and understand everything. That's why I want to do it. Tell me, am I doing something wrong?'

If what Surabala said was true, her desire to get married was not wrong by any standards. After all, women could get married even after their husbands died. Present-day society and law had accepted widow remarriage. Since her husband was absent, and she had both the urge and the age, she could certainly get married. Who had the right to say anything in that regard!

But the stranger was a bit confused now. People had all kinds of problems. A lot of people came to him all the time with a lot of problems. And the most surprising thing was that the problems included finding a groom. He and his station boys had already undertaken two jobs of that nature. A girl had run away from North 24-Parganas after she was fed up with her stepmother's oppressive behaviour. And she had taken shelter in this station. Who knows how it happened, but the girl caught the attention of Sadhan-da, the former mastaan, and presently local leader of the party with the cow-and-calf symbol. After hearing about everything from the girl, he couldn't send her back to her stepmother. He roused Ganesh and Gopal. 'You have only seven days. You've got to find the girl a suitable groom by then.' He would bear all the marriage-related expenses. The groom was found within not seven but just two days.

Bijoy, a rickshaw-driver from the station, had agreed to marry her. That young woman was raising a family now, she was happy.

Similarly, Amulya, who had arrived from Medinipur, used to ride a rickshaw here. He used to hang out with the oldest and most respected man in the rickshaw trade, Haren Ghosh, who loved him like his own son.

Haren Ghosh decided one day to get the youth married. He would get him married, and then rent a house and go and live there. It wasn't much of a problem living in the station at other times, but he found it very difficult in winter and during the rainy season. He had put up with the difficulty for almost twenty-five years, because who knows why, people did not want to rent out rooms to rickshaw-drivers, especially to those without a family.

So he began looking for a bride, and he found one too, a girl from Lakshmikantapur, who was suitable in every way for Amulya. Haren Ghosh himself went to the village to confirm the match.

This business had been going on for about a month. Meanwhile, people from the village had arrived here, people from here had gone there. But Amulya had not said a word. Seeing his enthusiasm, it seemed he wanted to get married. After viewing the girl, and confirming his decision, he had also paid a five-rupee advance towards the rent for a room at twenty-five rupees a month. But all of a sudden, who knows what happened to him, just twenty-four hours before the wedding, Amulya vanished. Everyone had their hands on their heads, what would happen now! The girl's Mama, who bought and sold old newspapers, bottles and cans in this city, had wept and declared that all the arrangements had been made, all their family members and in-laws had been invited. If the marriage did not take place now, they would have no face left. He also said that if Amulya was not found, some boy or the other had to be found and brought to the village on the specified day, at the specified time. Let whatever happens later, happen, but let the marriage take place now.'

Reduced to helplessness, Haren Ghosh had then sought the assistance of Ganesh and Gopal. 'Do something. You people will surely be able to do it.' They had then pressured Hari, the one who had set up a shop behind the line of rickshaws, selling rice and rutis. 'Hari-da, save a poor girl. Otherwise we won't be able to save you in times of danger.' So Hari agreed to the proposal. There was no reason for him to disagree. He could see from the photograph that the girl wasn't ugly. So Hari too was happily married. Both of them ran the rice and ruti shop now. Thanks to the culinary skills of Hari's wife, there were more customers than before.

That's why the stranger's head was in a whirl—would Surabala ask him to find a groom for her now! Play matchmaker! Things were not normal now. Especially after the raid on the gamblers. They were influential people, and were asking around everywhere. If they found out about those who were involved, there would be trouble. Was there any time now to look for a groom!

Before arriving at the main point, Surabala spent a long time narrating in detail the story of how she lost her 'unmarried' status. Next to their village, Begumpur, was the village of Bakultala. Many well-to-do, high-caste householders lived there, who possessed a lot of land, and various other kinds of businesses. They required day labourers almost throughout the year to cultivate their lands. The paddy cultivating season was when they needed the most people. The babus then employed poor folk belonging to the Keora and Bagdi castes, as well as Muslims, to work their fields.

Golok Sardar, who lived across the river, in the Golabari area, was a salaried employee at the famous household of the Purkait babus. Surabala's father was called 'Pagla' or 'lunatic' by people because he sometimes acted a bit crazy. He too worked in the fields belonging to the Purkait babus, to pay off a loan he had taken. Although there was a difference of ten or twelve years between them, Surabala's father and Golok became friends. At the end of a long day of work one day, as the two of them were sitting and drinking toddy, they turned emotional and decided that since their friendship would end once the farm work for the Purkait babus was over, it had to be secured through an extraordinary familial bond, which would remain unbroken all their lives. And it would not be some trivial relationship but a full-blown son-in-law and father-in-law tie.

If nothing else, most importantly, Pagla Sardar would be spared the burden of getting his daughter married. His only daughter wouldn't die a spinster. Apparently when such women died, they didn't find a place even in hell. It was out of that fear that a girl's parents got her married off to whoever they could find, and if no one was found, they married her off to a palmyra tree, or a banana tree. Apparently, that was permitted according to the shastras.

Golok Sardar had been high on toddy then. What if he changed his mind once he turned sober! So Pagla Sardar got together a few people from the hamlet, blew the conch shell, and had Golok apply sindoor on the parting of Surabala's hair. It was very late at night then. Eleven-year-old Surabala had been asleep. She had no idea what went on after she was woken up. She went back to sleep after that.

Golok remained in the village of Begumpur for three or four months, staying in the house of Pagla Sardar as his *ghar jamai*. When the farm work of the Purkait babus got over, he returned to his village in Golabari. Before he left, he promised to come back for his wife three months later, for the harvesting season. But he never returned.

All this had happened some eight or ten years ago. Surabala had grown up since then. Getting together with some Keora and Bagdi girls from the neighbourhood, who too were poor and unfortunate wretches like her, she had begun going to work in babu homes in the city of Calcutta to make ends meet. After all, no worthwhile jobs were available in the village.

After arriving in the city and then becoming used to the ways of the city, and after watching a couple of movies, she learnt a lot about things she never knew about. In keeping with her age, her body and mind now yearned for a strong, virile male body. She had sexual experience. But that was when both her body and mind had not yet matured. She used to think of it as a kind of torture inflicted upon her. She had once bitten Golok on his arm in a moment of agony, and run out of the room.

But Surabala was an adult now. Just as the anguish of having lost a partner pecked at her all the time, the intoxicating feeling of delightful pleasure too excited her constantly. She yearned for the thrilling nights to return, when she would be full to the brim. But there was only one problem. Surabala was not good looking. She had a tall body that lacked flesh. She was black as coal, with a coarse complexion. She had so much hair on her head it couldn't be arranged in a bun. She had to use a rubber band and knot it crudely on top of her head. None of the female assets that enticed men were evident or pronounced in Surabala. So no one even looked at her, which was why, even after many attempts, nothing much besides emptiness had come her way.

Surabala's father, Pagla Sardar, was an impoverished man. Where did he have the means to get his bad-looking, once-married daughter remarried! He could have, if he had lots of money. Couldn't he have done it? Even such girls could get married, why once, even five times! If the required money was there!

A girl is usually accustomed to seeing the male species, and their aggressive attitude, with great fear. But if she somehow fell into a man's company, she found out that a man was not a fearsome creature. His wildness was an expression of liking something, a natural active expression. One could plunge into this stream of recklessness, and reach the mythic abyss of the sensation of intimacy.

Surabala's father was crazy. She too had inherited, via blood, some signs of craziness from her father. And so, she could never become submissive, humble and shy like other girls. She leaned forward, and almost fell over, when she talked to someone. When she was happy, she laughed loudly. And when it came to swearing, screaming and quarrelling, after all she had been nourished and nurtured in all that from the moment she was born, thanks to the munificent bounty of her environment and circumstances.

Ever since the stranger first met Surabala, he had spoken to her everyday about something or the other. That was how he learnt all this. Perhaps Surabala too had found out what this man was like. That was why she declared, with firm conviction in her voice, 'I'm going to have a love marriage now.'

The stranger didn't give much importance to what she said. He casually said, 'Do it. There's nothing preventing you from doing it.'

'But there's a slight difficulty.'

The stranger was on his way to Nanu's vend, but that was only to while away the time. It was only the stranger who did not do any particular job. He had not yet found any job that was apt for him. That's why he was idle the whole day. All the other youths in the station either rode rickshaws, or collected waste paper, or were porters, or removed scales off fish in a big shop in the market. They almost never saw one another the whole day. And if they did, they hardly spoke. It was only at ten or eleven at night that they all got together. That's why the stranger was going to Nanu's place. Only he was available at this time.

He didn't dislike spending time with Surabala now. He laughed, and said, 'If it's a problem getting married, then where's the need for that! Why not simply forget about it?'

'Then what shall I do?'

'There's so much you can do besides getting married. Do that.'

The stranger wanted to say that marriage was not the only major achievement in a person's life. There were a lot of things that were bigger, greater and more valuable than that. But Surabala thought he was referring to the illicit relations between man and woman outside of marriage. She grimaced and wrinkled her nose, '*Chhee!* I'll never do that. I'll just get married.'

'Do that then.'

'But if I have to get married, I need a man.'

'Yes, that's needed,' the stranger replied. 'You can do without other things, but you do need that. A man for a woman, or a woman for a man.'

Surabala asked in an anxious voice, 'I can't find anyone I like.'

The stranger consoled Surabala, 'Just be patient, and you'll surely find someone you like one day.'

The stranger paused a while, and then he said, 'Keep a watch everywhere. You'll discover that just like you're searching for someone, somebody is looking for someone like you. All that remains is for you to meet.'

'You talk so nicely.'

'I learn from my guru.'

'Your guru! Who's that?'

'Jatadhari Guru. He sits on Platform No. 2.' After another pause, the stranger continued. 'My guru told me that if a person wants something with his heart and soul, every force in the world strives to get that to him.'

'I want something with my heart and soul.'

'What?'

'You!'

The sun had set now. Its red glow remained in the sky. Dusk gradually turned into evening. An ashen semi-darkness descended upon the city. A flock of birds twittered away on the kadam tree in front of them. Tree-felling by the destroyers of everything green had not really happened in this hospital. So there were still many trees and plants all around. A krishnachura tree was so full of red flowers that it looked as if its canopy was aflame. The stranger was gazing at that. When he suddenly heard what Surabala said, he was stunned. 'What are you saying!'

'I'm saying, please have a love marriage with me.'

'Are you out of your mind or what! What's all this crazy talk?'

'Why? Aren't you old enough for that? I want you with my heart and soul. I can swear about that on anyone you ask me to.'

'Do you think marriage is child's play! It takes a lot to get married. Do you know that?'

'It doesn't take anything.' Surabala said emphatically. 'I'm telling you, you don't need anything. All it requires is will. So many blind and lame people get married. And you're a fine young man. Just say yes, and then everything will be settled.'

The stranger wanted to get up now. What would she do when she heard that he did not have the slightest desire to hear such rubbish! He felt sorry for the girl, he felt compassion, but her touch brought him no arousal. He had heard many times, and from many people, that a woman was like an electric current, whose slightest touch caused a volcanic eruption in every nerve of a man. But not even a particle of that was present at this girl's touch. She had moved closer, little by little, and her body was almost touching the stranger's now.

Seeing the stranger rising, she held his arm firmly, and said, 'What happened, are you leaving?'

'I have some work.'

'But you didn't reply. Tell me, what do you say?'

'What can I say to such things! You've taken a liking to an incapable man! I spend my nights on a rickshaw, or under the railway overbridge, or on the roof of the morgue. Where shall I keep you if I marry you?'

'Wherever you may be, I'll be able to squeeze in beside you.'

'And what will you eat! How will I feed you?'

'Am I starving now?' Surabala shot back. When there was no reply, she said, 'You don't have to worry about feeding me. I can't even finish the food that I get from the four houses I work in.'

'Maybe you can carry on like that now, but what will you do once you have a baby, and so on?'

'I will think about that when it happens. Why should I worry about that now? There are borers inside wood, God didn't deny sustenance even to them. The one who'll come will bring along all the arrangements too. Basona, from our village, got pregnant before she was married. She tried so much to abort the baby. But once her boy was born, fate brought happiness into her life. Now she has a nose ring and earrings of gold. All because of that boy's fate.'

Surabala was saying everything so simply. But nothing she said to tempt him could allure him. He was nothing but a redundant man. He knew the pain and humiliation suffered by a redundant man. He simply did not have it in him to knowingly pave the way for the arrival of another redundant person.

'After all we are human, intelligent creatures. But actually, even a small forest bird is more intelligent than us. It builds a nest with straw and twigs first, before thinking about laying eggs. And you're saying ...'

Surabala interrupted him. 'Then let me do something, shall I rent a room? The kind of room that rents for fifteen rupees. I get sixty-six rupees at the end of the month. I'll be able to pay fifteen rupees out of that.'

The stranger realised that gentle words wouldn't do. The girl was in a frenzy. No gentle words would get into her head now. He said, a bit harshly, 'As long as I don't get a roof over my head, and a regular means of income, I won't think about things like marriage. Don't pin your hopes on me. I'm unsuitable. I can't bring another person into my life, and then let her drown in hell.'

The stranger got up and left. Without looking back even once, he kept walking straight ahead briskly. And in the melancholy, dim light, a failed, defeated maiden devoid of beauty sat weeping.

$$7$$

Gurjol Rambles, Nanu Counsels

'Hey, what took you so long today?'

It had become dark by the time the stranger reached Nanu's liquor vend. To the extent that one could barely make out people's faces. Nanu was there, as was Bachcha Dilip. There were also some people whom the stranger did not know. They were drinking. But he did know one person, whose name was Gurjol, or molasses-water. No one knew what his real name was. He drove a rickshaw, and drank alcohol. He returned to the stand and took a swig after every couple of trips. It was because of his love of alcohol that everyone called him Gurjol. Those were the two substances required to prepare cholai, or illicit liquor.

Gurjol was sitting on spread out newspapers at quite a distance from Nanu's vend. He had in front of him a paper packet with muri, chhola sheddho, salt and green chillies. Beside him was a bundle of bidis, matches, a bottle of alcohol and a glass. Observing the paraphernalia, it was clear that he would not leave before ten at night. He might also stay there all night long. Gurjol had a favourite poem in Hindi, which he recited from time to time. *Piyega nahi to jiyega kaise! Jo piya, woh hi jiya, jo nahi piya, ma ka bhog mein gaya.*

How will you live if you don't drink! Only the one who drinks truly lives, the one who doesn't goes to hell.'

The stranger observed him as he suddenly began laughing loudly. *'Bach gaya sala. Yeh bhi bach gaya.* The fucker survived. He too survived.' And then he lowered his voice and asked, 'Has she left you?' He stuffed a handful of muri-chhola into his mouth, dipped a chilli in salt and chewed it, and continued, 'The way she trapped you, I was reminded of how a python winds itself around a calf and then swallows it. She won't spare you until she has swallowed you.'

The stranger immediately responded, asking, 'Who? Who are you talking about? Are you talking about me?'

'Who else?' Gurjol laughed again. 'Yes, I'm talking about you. Hadn't Kali caught hold of you! I saw that on the way here, she was sitting with you. She catches whoever she finds. But tell me, who on earth will have her? She's just a bunch of bones and nothing else.'

Nanu walked towards the stranger now. He had a steel glass and a clay cup in his hands. He poured tea from the glass into the clay cup, and gave it to the stranger. 'Is it still hot? I got it a while back. And then he asked Gurjol, 'Who has nothing?'

'Why do you ask?' Gurjol cleared his throat, and began. 'A girl, it's better to call her a stick rather than a girl. You don't know her, but all the rickshaw-drivers know her. She works in the Nabanagar locality. She has grabbed Jibon. She's always after someone or the other. I saw her chatting with Jibon on my way here. You can ask Jibon whether what I'm saying is true.'

Gurjol was tanked up with strong liquor. A great quality of alcohol was that it made timid folk brave, and the brave even more daring. It made a mute person speak. Gurjol was now loquacious under the influence of an intoxicant.

Nanu stared wide-eyed at the stranger. 'What's the matter, Jibon? Is all this true?'

Gurjol said, 'I'm telling Jibon, and I don't care what you think about me for that. I always give sound advice. Don't pay any attention to such girls. If you give her the slightest chance, she'll simply climb over your head. She'll stick to you like hair lice. And then you won't be able to get rid of her. Thank God I was saved! My wife sat on my head for five long years. Made my life hell. But I didn't have to do anything. She left on her own. Bongshi will face the music now. Let him live with her for a couple of years. I bet you he'll send Rani packing after that. I told Bongshi that I wasn't angry with him. Why would I be angry! Hey, you're the one who gave me freedom. You must surely have been my brother in your last life. I don't want Rani any longer, I don't, I don't! But she took seven-hundred rupees that I had saved with a lot of difficulty. Just return that.'

Gurjol had started weeping now. The stranger took Nanu away from there, and explained to him all that had happened, and finally said, 'So that's what actually happened. It's no big deal.'

Once the stranger finished, Nanu almost dragged him eastwards. The garbage incinerator on the right-hand side was operational now. Thick white smoke billowed in all directions. The smoke had an acrid smell, which made one's eyes and nostrils burn. They moved away from there, and took a narrow T-shaped path, which had a pool on either side. Some people called them ponds. The far end of one of them touched Raja S.C. Mullick Road, while the other one extended past Loharpara, and ended at the railway line. Arriving at the spot between the two pools, Nanu said, 'Here's the spot. Do you remember, we were sitting here and eating muri one day? Babua, you, and me.'

'When was that? I can't exactly remember! I'm forgetting a lot of things these days.'

Nanu said, 'It was the day Babua was shot. The fucking bastard Pal, the officer-in-charge of the police station, shot him.'

The stranger hurriedly said, 'Oh yes. We ate muri here.'

'Do you remember what Babua said before he died?'

'What did he say?'

'As he ate the muri, he became kind of sad, and said, "I'm a grown man, but I'm yet to know the taste of a woman's body." He

had said, "If a bullet hits me on the chest now, I'll never know that."
What a fate! Almost as soon as he said that, the bullet hit his chest.
Do you remember?'

'I do, I do.'

Nanu's face was not visible in the darkness. His voice sounded
like a sorrowful dirge. 'Nowadays, I don't know why, I too think
that because of the path we chose, we won't get a lot of things that
others normally get. We'll be dead before that. Don't you think that
way?'

'What will I think!' The stranger was philosophical. 'One has
to be alive to die. I've been dead for ages. Tell me, who can live as I
have all these years? No one. Only a ghost can survive such a life. If
there is a life after this ghostly existence, if I am born as a man this
time, I too shall aspire to all that is worth aspiring to in a life.'

There was a pause, and then Nanu said, 'The lifetime of a
mosquito is two-and-a-half days, the life of a mastaan is two-and-
a-half years. Have you seen a drop of water on a lotus leaf? Our
life wobbles like that. You won't even know when you fall off. I
think that in such a situation, one should pick up whatever fate
gives you. You should never forsake hot food and fresh clothes. If
you kick what Ma Lakshmi offers, you'll eventually have to regret
that. I don't know who the girl is. But she's a girl! Whether a
sugarcane is straight or crooked, it's sweet when you chew it. What
was that thing Ram Chowdhury used to say? If another life is not
attached to a life, the life is a failure. So when this girl, after learning
everything about your situation, wants to attach her life to yours
without being a burden on you, when she wants to give you what
you never got—I'm telling you, don't turn the girl away.'

The stranger now asked him in a displeased tone, 'Are you
drunk or what! You're talking a load of nonsense! You've lost your
head altogether. Hey, she's a wife, her husband has left her. She's no
virginal girl!'

Nanu was in the liquor business. He drank alcohol all day.
People could tell him whatever they liked, but his own thinking was

that he never said anything that could be called rubbish. Whatever he said was irrefutable. He said, 'What's called roasted rice is also called muri. Tell me, isn't that true? Hey, what the hell's a virgin or a wife? They're all the same. It's just a matter of a spot of sindoor, isn't it! What was that girl's name again? Golapi. She's still not married. Can you tell me how many guys she has screwed until now! I'm a man of the red party, brother. That's what I am now, and what I shall remain. I won't change as long as the colour of my blood is red. You used to be red too after all. Tell me, weren't you? You were more red than me. I haven't been able to commit any murders yet. But you bloodied your hands way back when you were thirteen- or fourteen-years-old. We should not hold on to such superstitions. Someone put a bit of sindoor on her forehead long ago, so does that mean she has become rotten? Hey, don't look at the body, look at her mind, her mind!'

Nanu paused to get his breath back. He then continued, 'If you are murdered, it's not so bad. You'll be gone without much pain. But suppose you have some major charges slapped on you, and you are sent to prison for ten or twenty years—what happens then? You would have lost your teeth, your hair and beard would have turned white, and when you get out of prison you'll be bent with age. And you'll tear your hair out in despair thinking about today. *Eesh*! There was a well at my doorstep, I had a bucket tied to a rope in my hand, and yet I couldn't get a sip of water!'

The stranger responded saying, 'All right, so you gave me such a long sermon, but your situation is a hundred times better than mine. Your liquor vend is running fine, the hospital has given you quarters to live in, your father has a job, and when he dies, you'll get the job. So why don't you get married? You get married first, and then tell others. Don't they say, practise what you preach. Do that.'

'I will.'

'When will that be?'

'Pretty soon. You'll see. You know the girl as well.'

'Really?'

'Hey, what would I gain by lying?'

After a while, Nanu again said, 'Poor Babua got killed. His parents are old. Two unmarried sisters at home. How better can I help! I'm thinking of marrying his younger sister.'

'Have you discussed it?'

'With whom?'

'With Babua's parents.'

'No, not yet. But I told Moyna.'

'Who's Moyna?'

'It seems you can't remember anything. Moyna is Babua's younger sister. If she agrees, then I'll talk to her parents. I think she'll agree.'

They returned to the liquor den. Gurjol was emptying the first glass of his second pint of booze down his throat. He remarked, *Dilli ka laddu, jo khaya voh pachhtaya, jo nahi khaya woh bhi pachtaya.'* And then he began rambling on about something or the other.

Nanu admonished him. 'Be quiet. No shouting here. This is a hospital. It's not a liquor den beside the rail line.'

'Okay, okay. I won't speak, and I won't sing either. I won't listen to anyone's admonition either. Why should I listen to anyone when I'm drinking with my own money!' Gurjol went on blabbering. Addressing his employee Bachcha Dilip, Nanu said, 'Don't give him any more booze. He won't be able to return home.' And then they sat down in the middle of the field, a little distance away.

The two of them sat there for quite some time. Neither of them said a word. They could think of nothing to say. Both of them were worried about their respective futures. Dense darkness descended everywhere. There were lights in the hospital. That was unavoidable. But those lights hardly reached here.

After a while, the stranger observed Rakhal Das, the teacher who lived in the railside squatter colony, standing in front of him. He was soaked in perspiration, and he had an anxious look on his face. He said, 'Jibon, my son, I've been looking for you all evening.'

Rakhal Das was from East Bengal. His speech had the distinctive pronunciation and cadence of the other Bengal, the one across the border. Jibon, whose replica the stranger was, was also from East Bengal. The same Bangaal speech emitted from his mouth too. Nowadays the stranger sometimes tried to speak to some people in Jibon's lingo. He asked Rakhal Das, 'What's happened? Why were you looking for me?'

Rakhal Das replied, 'We can't find Yadav anywhere.'

'He must be somewhere. Have you looked everywhere?'

'Everyone in the station is looking for him. No one can find him. I believe no one's seen him since afternoon.'

'Really? Where's the boy gone? Come, let's go and look for him.' Addressing Nanu, the stranger said, 'I'm going to the station. I'll be back.'

'Come soon.'

8

The Missing Child

Yadav was missing. No one could find him. All those whose lives revolved around the railway station, all the porters, hawkers and rickshaw-drivers, searched frantically for him all day. The sweet little boy who used to roam around there on his tiny feet was gone. So everyone was sad. It wasn't because of Yadav only, quite a few children had gone missing from here earlier.

This was a time when the means for birth control were not yet so easily available in the country. The product called 'Nirodh' was still only the stuff of jokes. The ordinary folk, who had little education, had not yet gained the confidence to walk into a medical store and buy Mala-D. So a large number of illegitimate children were born. Some poor people were also incapable of raising their children. This was why a lot of abandoned bastard boys and girls used to roam around in this railway station, who had no one to look for them if they got lost, no one to weep for them if they died. Some of them went missing from time to time. But that didn't really cause anyone any headache.

The latest addition to the list of those who had gone missing was Yadav. That wasn't the name his parents had given him. It had been given by the wretched folk whose lives revolved around the station. Who knows why they had done that.

Way back in 1971, when East Pakistan was being ravaged by the cruel atrocities inflicted by the Pakistani army, his Ma had crossed the border all by herself and arrived in West Bengal with him in her arms. No one asked her why she was all alone, or where her husband was, or whether he was alive or dead. Neither had she told anyone about all that. Many people now believed that her husband was one of the countless people whose corpses had floated down the Padma and Meghna rivers.

Be that as it may, after having gone from one place to another since crossing the border, the woman finally arrived at this station one day. And she came down with dysentery one day after drinking contaminated water, and died. But although she was dead, her child was alive. The responsibility for raising the child fell upon the denizens of the station. All the porters and labourers, rickshaw-drivers and handcart-pullers, hawkers and shopkeepers, thieves and pickpockets, whores and their pimps and customers, drunkards and alcohol vendors, gamblers and priests, together with Chhechan from the cheap eatery, kept him alive. They were the ones who gave the bubbling, radiant, irreproachable child the name Yadav.

Who had taken Yadav away now? And why? Raghu, a porter in the railway station, said, 'I last saw him at ten or ten-thirty in the morning. He was playing here when I carried Manik's basket of coconuts to the university gate. I didn't see him after that.'

Rakhal Das, the teacher, said, 'When I went looking for the children of the second batch, after finishing with the first batch of children, I found all of them. Only Yadav wasn't there.'

The story that Rakhal Das then narrated made the stranger's heart tremble. It was as if someone was howling away inside him in grief at the terrible plight of an unfortunate boy. No one had any doubts that Yadav had been kidnapped. And everyone was also certain that he would never return, because none of the children who went missing before had returned. Almost everyone here kept tabs, to a greater or lesser extent, on the activities of the underworld. They knew that there was a child kidnapping and women trafficking racket that was active in the region. When it came to trafficking women, they were taken essentially to various brothels in Delhi, Bombay and Calcutta. And the children were taken via the Bondel Gate station to places like Delhi and Meerut. Some went to Arab countries.

It was rumoured that there was a settlement of hijras somewhere near the Bondel Gate station. Apparently, they severed the male organs of such children, gave them some kind of hormonal injections, and made them into hijras, and groomed them in singing, dancing and feminine graces, to be part of their band.

Every country had its own favourite sport. Like it was football in Brazil, table tennis in China, and cricket in the West Indies, camel racing was what the wealthy oil barons of the Arab nations loved to watch. But in this camel race, a child was tied to the camel's neck or back. Once the camels began running, the more the children screamed in fear and pain, the faster they ran. Those who didn't die were maimed and crippled for life. These children with broken limbs were then made to beg on the streets of Mecca. Zakat, or charity, was an obligatory duty for devout Muslims who performed Haj. A sixth of the wealth accumulated in one's lifetimes must be given away there, in accordance with the Koran.

These unfortunate boys were forced to beg for alms and then deposit their collections at a specified place, or else starvation and thrashing was their fate. A helpless, innocent child separated from his parents and taken to a faraway country had to experience the hellish agony of being consigned to spending the rest of his life in slavery.

Of course, it wasn't only abroad; factories that blinded and crippled poor children were to be found in many parts of this country too.

Everyone was worried now. Where was Yadav? Who took him away?

No one would ever have had the slightest inkling about that unless Aadhuli, the *kamake khanewali* girl, or whore, from the No. 1 railside squatter colony, had been present today in a pilgrim site called Ghutiari Sharif with a babu to exchange hot cash for love in a ramshackle hut that rented for ten rupees every four hours. She had entered the hut at twelve noon, and she would emerge at four in the afternoon. That was the understanding. Only then would she get twenty-five rupees in cash, and a meal of mutton curry and rice.

After entering the room and latching the door, the babu had removed all the clothes from Aadhuli's body like a butcher skinning a goat. He didn't leave even a stitch on her. He had removed the bangles on her wrist, her earrings, and even undone the chignon on her head. And then she was on her back, on her tummy, on her side, sitting, and standing. Simply following what the babu said, what he wanted. He would pay twenty-five rupees. That wasn't a small amount. It was a month's pay if one washed utensils in a babu's house. After all, when he was paying so much money, he would surely recoup that.

Around two in the afternoon, when Aadhuli rose from bed, that was when she spotted Yadav through the gap between the window shutters.

As soon as she returned to Jadavpur and alighted from the train, she ran to give everyone the news.

'Who was with Yadav?' 'Who took him so far away?' 'Was he alone?'

Aadhuli said, 'Golam Gazi. He was holding Yadav by the hand.'

'You should have caught him right then. What if he denies that now?'

'How could I have caught him?'

Aadhuli had felt a kind of unease as soon as she spotted Yadav with Golam Gazi there. There was definitely something fishy about it. But the babu had her in an octopus's bind right then. And after all, she couldn't run out of the room as soon as she was freed from the bind. She had to put on her clothes and so on. And then she had to collect her dues from the babu. Or else, if the babu fled without paying, where would Aadhuli find him among the teeming masses of the city?

However, from the moment Aadhuli was free, she had searched the lanes and alleys, and the station of the pilgrim site. But she did not find either Yadav or Golam Gazi.

The stranger said to Raghu, 'Go right now and see if Golam Gazi is sitting at his spot! If he's there, call him here.'

Raghu ran there, and returned running. 'He's not there.'

Aadhuli insisted, 'But I told you. Don't you believe me? If you want to find him, someone should go to Ghutiari Sharif right now. If at all you find him, that's where he'll be.'

The stranger said, 'Don't tell anyone what we know. He has to return here tomorrow, or the day after. We'll catch him then.'

Who knows why, but the next day, Golam Gazi did not come with his bundle to sit at his daily spot. Gopal and Ganesh now left to search in Ghutiari Sharif first, and then all the possible places in Mallikpur, where Golam lived.

It was not so long ago, only about six months back, that Golam had arrived at this railway station, and laid out his bundle of wares near the sign board on Platform No. 2 with the name of the station. He used to sell gemstones of various colours, rings, amulets, talismans and massage oils. He claimed that through the use of herbs he could straighten a crooked penis, and make small organs big and thick. His medicines could cure venereal diseases like gonorrhoea and syphilis. He could enhance men's sexual prowess. He could cure arthritis and asthma.

Actually, that was a front. He was in fact the ringleader of a child trafficking racket. On the pretext of selling the medicines, he used to wander around looking for children he could separate from their mothers' bosoms.

No one suspected Golam Gazi when he first arrived at this station. When he used to seat the orphaned Yadav beside, and buy him this and that to eat, people were impressed by his kindness.

How would a child who had no one be able to survive unless he received love? The treasure of everyone's love, Yadav, had disappeared. When a dirty, naked child with mucus running down his nose disappeared, his absence wasn't supposed to be noticed so quickly. But Yadav was the apple of everyone's eye. That's why they were looking for him. They had realised within a few hours that the naughty, sweet, little rascal was missing. As was Golam Gazi.

After spending the whole day searching in Ghutiari Sharif and Mallikpur, Ganesh and Gopal returned with the news that there was no trace of either of them.

Golam Gazi was found ten days later. He was sitting with his hands covering his face in the darkness of the vendors' compartment in the Diamond Harbour local train as it arrived at Jadavpur. He was truly unlucky. Of all the people, it was Raghu who entered and spotted him. He recognised Golam at once, although his face was concealed. Others came running hearing his cries. All of them dragged him off the train.

'Tell us where Yadav is?'

'How do I know where he is?'

'Yadav went missing, and you stopped coming here. You took him away. We have a witness. Tell us where Yadav is and we'll spare you.'

'I swear on Allah I don't know! I was down with a fever, that's why I couldn't come. You people are unnecessarily suspecting me.'

Golam had been apprehended around seven in the evening. The stranger got the news about an hour later. He went running to the station. Golam was handed over to him. Raghu informed him, 'We have been questioning him for an hour. But he's simply not telling the truth.' Ganesh and Gopal too arrived there now. Gopal said, 'Asking him nicely won't work, Dada.'

There was a green turban on Golam Gazi's head. The turban was removed and his hands were tied behind him with that. After that he was made to walk down to the railway siding, behind the heap of stone chips concealed by the goods train standing there.

'Tell me where you took Yadav, Golam. Tell me the truth, and I give you my word, no one will do anything to you.'

'I swear on my mother, Dada, I'm telling you the truth, I don't know anything.'

The stranger realised that something that had never happened to him was happening now. He was losing control over himself. A destructive, demonic force was gradually awakening inside him, which did not know forgiving, which had no compassion or kindness. He said to Jalil, who was standing beside him, 'Bring me the pliers.'

When Jalil arrived with the pair of pliers, the stranger gripped one of his fingers with it, and asked, 'Where's Yadav? If you want to live, tell us now.' One finger was twisted, and then another, and in this way, all his ten fingers were twisted. When the ring finger of his left hand was being twisted, the ring on it cut into the flesh, and blood dripped. There were ten toes on his feet to be attended to now. But by then Golam had reached the limits of his endurance. He admitted to what he had done.

'I don't know about the children who went missing earlier. I swear on Allah. I didn't take them. But yes, I did take this boy.'

'Why did you do that?'

'He doesn't have parents, he suffers a lot here. After all, I'm human. I too have children. I felt very sad for him, so I took him away, and left him at Brindaban Babu's house.'

'Who's Brindaban? Where does he live?'

'Brindaban Naskar, haven't you heard his name? He lives in Hotor. He owns at least eight or ten large fish ponds, and has two- or three-hundred bighas of agricultural land. But although Allah granted him everything, He denied him something. His wife is infertile. He's been married for twelve years but doesn't have any children. Believe me, the boy will grow up like a prince there. But if you don't want that, I'll go and bring him back tomorrow morning.'

'Ganesh!'

'Yes, Dada!'

'The fucker is lying to us, he's not telling the truth. Break his hand.'

The fingers were already done for. Now the crushing of the hand began. But Golam could no longer harbour any secrets in his doomed, monstrous being. He spilt everything out. It was learnt that there was no Brindaban Babu in Hotor, but Sulaiman from Ghutiari Sharif, who had already reached Bombay by now. There had been six children in the shipment. There were means to take them via sea from Bombay to an Arab country. Sulaiman knew how to take the children via that route. Arrangements with the police had also been made.

So what would happen now? Everyone looked anxiously at the stranger. His eyes blazed like those of an enraged wolf. He knew that there was no way of getting Yadav back. If he was killed now during a camel race, he would get away cheaply. And if he didn't die at once, he would spend the rest of his life as a cripple in that faraway country, dying little by little.

'What should we do with Golam now?'

Chewing his words, the stranger replied, 'I don't believe in caste, or fate, or in God. But Golam does. He is a genuine Muslim who prays five times a day. He has the mark on his forehead, he wears prayer beads on his neck, and keeps the fast too. Am I right?'

Golam nodded his head, and said, 'Yes.'

His eyes blazing, the stranger said, 'I think it wouldn't be right to do anything to him which is not sanctioned by Islam. Isn't that so Golam, you tell me!'

Before the slaughter, a camel is asked whether it is willing to be ritually slaughtered. It's only if it nods its head in consent that the knife is then run on its throat. In the same way, did he know that by trapping him in a spider's web of words, arrangements were being made to kill him too? Trembling with fear, Golam said, 'Hand me over to the police. Let me be judged for the crime I have committed.'

The stranger responded, 'You can't be handed over to the police. They will accept a bribe and release you. So it's better that we ourselves release you. But that will take a while.'

The stranger now looked at the crowd of people there, and said, 'I believe there are clear instructions in the Shariat about the punishments for various crimes. Jalil! Where's Jalil? I believe the Shariat calls for an eye for an eye, and a tooth for a tooth. So if we assume that Yadav doesn't die, I would like what he will go through to be done to Golam. What do you people say?'

None of the people assembled here were vegetarian in their diets. After suffering continuous thrashing at the hands of fate, the state, society and people, these people were now in a dire plight. Their blind rage and fury taught them to distrust and deny all the prevailing laws and customs. And they were in favour of judging all the wrongs inflicted upon them, and then punishing the responsible criminals themselves. They were simply unable to forget about the innocent child Yadav. Full of rage, they said, 'Let Golam be beaten and made lame. That would be the most appropriate punishment for him. He should be paid in the same coin.'

'Jalil, go and fetch the axle rod. Ganesh-da, get a couple of bricks from somewhere.'

Golam was now made to lie on his back, and his legs were raised and placed over the bricks. A crowbar descended upon his exposed legs. His two legs were thus broken into four parts. Golam's screams shattered the stillness and silence of the dark night. But no one came running to protect him. The times were most frightening. No one wanted to invite dangers upon themselves by being concerned about the plight of others. But the police did arrive a long time after the incident. They were the ones who took Golam to hospital.

9

The Pack of Scoundrels

It was almost midnight, on this night of Shiva Chaturdashi. There was silence all around. And it was a bit cold. The stranger was about to fall asleep, covering his body and head with a black-coloured sheet. A supermarket was being constructed behind the bus-stand intersection. Its roof was a safe place. Some rickshaw-drivers and Bihari labourers slept there at night. None of them were the stranger's enemies.

It was almost a year now since the stranger's arrival in Jadavpur. He had certainly made some enemies in this time. Nothing had been found out regarding the raid on the gamblers. The blame for that had been attributed to a gang of snatchers from near the glass factory. Or else it would have been difficult for the stranger to move around freely. However, the responsibility for the Golam Gazi matter lay entirely upon him. He no longer slept under the rail overbridge, or on the roof of the morgue, because the police were looking for him. If someone informed on him, he could be picked up all of a sudden. That's why he came here to sleep. He would have to find another place after a few days.

There was none of the evening's titter of young women's laughter, the clinking of bangles, the delightful rustle of freshly starched saris, the fragrance in the air, or the wave of entrancement prompted by tresses flying in the breeze. All that was only till about ten or ten-thirty at night.

At this time, the black metalled road looked like a prehistoric, long, black python, lying lifeless. Looking at the road now, one would never imagine how many people had gathered there from late afternoon until late in the evening. The whole locality had resounded with a delightful uproar and clamour, full of joyful laughter. Everyone was inside the four walls of their locked houses now, gone to wander the land of silent slumber. Come night, this most crowded road in the city fringe was taken over by cud-chewing cows, mange-covered street dogs, drunkards returning home on tottering legs, and a few antisocial elements.

Like every year, this year, too, a round-the-clock recitation of Hari's name had been organised in front of the market behind the bus-stand intersection, under the aegis of the traders' association. Some people were staying up, listening to the kirtans, *Bhajo Shri Krishna, Chaitanya Prabhu Nityananda, Hare Krishna Hare Ram, Shri Radha Gobindo.*

There was a big crowd here in the evening. People left, one by one, as the night advanced. Only about twenty or twenty-two devotees, all old, were there now. Most of them were old women who had shed all responsibilities and were free of all preoccupations. The only refrain in their lives now was *Hari din toh gelo, sondhya holo, paar koro amare,* Lord, the day is over, it's dusk, take me across.

Also present together with the old folk, and utterly out of place among them, was a girl. Youthfulness had stealthily crept into her body, but she still had something of the air of a tender teenager about her. She was lying on the thin, dust-filled carpet on the kirtan dais, fast asleep, insensate. The sizeable chignon of her shampooed hair had come apart and lay swirling in the dust. A particular kind of change had taken place during this period as far as women's clothing was concerned. At the age when Bengali girls conventionally stopped wearing frocks and began donning saris, they had now started wearing churidar-kameez. Some of them went a step further, and wore trousers.

This girl was wearing a pair of red trousers and a half-sleeved shirt with a printed design of green vines and leaves. She had a small red dot on her forehead, and a pair of thin gold rings on her ears. The stranger had advanced a few steps after going past the No. 8B bus-stand on the left side of the road, and the name-recitation dais on the right side, when he noticed the girl in the blink of an eye. That was when someone called out to him sharply, 'Hey Jibon dear!' Who could be calling him like this at this time! Turning his head to look, he saw it was Basu Das.

There was a high wall surrounding the No. 8B bus-stand. Basu Das' shop, whose rear grazed the wall, faced the main road. Although it was known as a tea-shop, it was well stocked with every kind of thirst-quencher; there was tea, of course, but also green coconut, Coca Cola, as well as alcohol of both the country and foreign varieties. Another special feature of Basu Das' shop was that it stayed open all night. He couldn't shut it, even if he wanted to. Given the ramshackle door flap of the shop, men, dogs and bulls could enter even after it was shut. So Basu Das had decided to keep the shop open all night. And he sat on a broken chair and slept inside that shop.

Basu Das' shop, eight feet by ten feet, had no electricity connection. Once it got dark in the evening, it was lit up for some time with a kerosene lamp. But that too was off now. The only light was what came from the lamp post on the road.

Basu Das had left his home across the border. He lived in a rented house in Katju Nagar now. He was married and had a son and a daughter. The son sat in the shop during the day. The girl was in school. She was in Class Nine now.

Hearing Basu Das' call, the stranger turned around and went up to the shop. 'What's the matter? Why were you calling me?'

Sitting in semi-darkness in the ramshackle shop, like a watchman in a graveyard, the man cried out, as if grieving for a beloved who had departed. 'My dear Jibon! A poor girl is on the verge of ruin. Please save her if you can, Jibon!'

'Which girl are you talking about?'

Basu replied, 'The one sleeping there. She's in deep trouble.' After a pause, he said empathetically, 'All of us share the same scorched fate. I came to this place because of Partition. How can I let the life of a girl from the land of my birth be destroyed in front of my eyes! That's why I'm telling you. You can do it, it's only you who can do it, please save her!'

'Who's the girl? Is she related to you?'

'I told you, she's a girl from our country, just like you!' Basu Das then cried out again, 'I too have a daughter like her. I can't see any difference between them. You've done so many misdeeds in your life, who knows how many more you'll do. But please do a good deed today, be a true human for once.'

The stranger had no clue about the reason for Basu Das's tears. He looked in the direction of the girl sleeping on the dais. Where was she in danger! There were so many girls like her, who spent the whole night in railway stations, or here and there. It wasn't that all of them had left or lost their homes, or been compelled to be on the streets; some of them had a roof to lay their heads under, in some squatter settlement beside the rail line, or a canal. They spent the night out in the open for various reasons, and to various ends.

Basu Das said, 'This girl belongs to a respectable family. She's there because she is in trouble, not out of any fancy or ploy. They were from the village next to ours. I knew her father.' He paused, and then continued, 'The girl's name is Anita, from the Dutt family. There used to be a Durga Puja in their village house. We had gone there many times to have the prasad. Her father was a very fine man.'

'What do you mean "was"? Isn't he a fine man now?'

'He is no longer alive,' Basu Das said. 'Yahya Khan's army shot and killed him back in 1971, during the Liberation War.'

'Eesh!' the stranger couldn't help saying.

'That's how her misfortune began. Her Ma fled with her and another older daughter. They crossed the border and came to West Bengal. They did not really have any close relatives here. They had not been able to carry much money with them either. All they had was some ornaments. They arrived with that, and stayed first with a distant cousin in North 24-Parganas. Some of the ornaments were grabbed by the cousin, and some were sold and the money from that was paid in lieu of the expenses on their food. When the money ran out, the cousin kicked them out of the house. What could they do after that, they went here and there, and finally arrived in Jadavpur. The Ghost Colony had just come up then. *Arrey,* Azad Nagar colony was called Ghost Colony. That's what people used to call it. The railside settlement where the people earlier lived, was full of thieves, crooks, drunkards, gamblers and whoremongers, but it wasn't that there weren't a few decent households. You know how horrible those people are. What else could they be called but ghosts? Don't they say that the black of coal can't be washed away, and a person's nature doesn't change! So what if they pulled down their shanties from the railside and occupied the zamindar's land overnight, and thus established a refugee colony! Their character was still the same.'

Who knows on whose advice Anita's Ma then rented a cheap room in that Ghost Colony in the middle of the vast field, and began living there. There's a saying that even a pitcher full of water eventually empties out. The money from the sale of the few remaining ornaments ran out one day.

'What can I tell you, Jibon! How cruelly fate throws a person from one situation to another. That very morning, the daughter-in-law of that famous Dutt household was compelled, entirely for survival, to work as an ayah in Dr Chakraborty's nursing home on

North Road. And she was compelled to put her elder daughter, Putul, to work as a cook in a household.

'The people of that family loved the educated girl like a daughter. They had also arranged for Putul's marriage to a boy they knew. The engagement ceremony had taken place too. But Putul burned to death just twenty-three days before the marriage. Women consider the hair on their head to be a symbol of beauty. The length of women's hair is a matter of pride. But it was Putul's hair that was the reason for her death. While doing something with her back to the lit stove, the fire had risen through her hair and seized her.'

Basu Das continued, 'The mother and the younger daughter somehow endured all the grief and hardship. But as soon as Anita grew up a bit, a new danger presented itself at their doorstep. Some scoundrels from the Ghost Colony were after her. Her Ma left home at seven in the morning, and returned only at nine or ten at night. Her duty hours at the nursing home were from eight in the morning to eight at night. So during that time, and especially at night, finding her alone at home, they made various kinds of indecent proposals to her, they offered her money.'

'But what about the landlord? Doesn't the landlord do anything?'

'Oh, he is an even greater scoundrel. A worthless animal. He has a wife and two daughters. The elder one is at least ten years old. He wants to marry Anita. Apparently, he told Anita's Ma one time, "Mashi, I fancy having a baby. I hadn't realised it then, but Khuki's mother got the operation done. Marry Anita to me." But she didn't agree. Would anyone agree? Who knows whether it wasn't the enraged landlord himself who set the scoundrels upon her!'

'After that?'

'What can happen after that! When the rascal youths were unable to seduce the girl after trying in various ways, they began threatening her. That if she didn't agree of her own volition, they would break down the door and carry her away. It's pitch dark after sunset, and not a single decent person is to be found in the colony.

Ghost Colony is surrounded by open fields, hogla-reed thickets and fisheries. You tell me, won't the mother and daughter be fearful! What would the woman do if Anita was really taken away? They are poor, they are no one in the colony, and have no one to speak for them. And the scoundrels have the party leaders behind them.'

'Which party?'

'Why do you need to know that! They're all the same, only the names are different. Whether the goat is black or white, once you remove the skin, they're all the same.'

'Hmm. So then?'

'So Anita's Ma told her daughter that until they found a new house, Anita should lock up and leave for Jadavpur before it gets dark. And she should sit where there are lots of people around, whether at the bus-stand intersection, or the railway station. Once she finished her work, they would return home together. She warned her never to be alone at home. So that's what the girl has been doing for the last ten or twelve days. She comes here while it's still daylight. She walks around here and there to while away the time. When her Ma finishes her duty at 8 or 8.30, the two of them leave together. But I don't know why her Ma hasn't returned today. Who knows, maybe some serious patient arrived just before she finished. After all, it's a nursing home. Or maybe the ayah who is on duty at night didn't come, and so Anita's Ma is stuck there, and can't leave.'

Basu Das said, 'That's what I think. Tell me, what else could it be? When a woman's young daughter is waiting for her on the streets, what reason could there be, other than the fear of losing her job, for her to still be at her workplace?'

Basu Das did not have to explain any more, the stranger got the picture. The girl was observing the fast for Lord Shiva today, and had not eaten all day. That was a ritual girls of her age practised. She had been running and revelling around all evening with the girls of the neighbourhood. Her friends had returned to their respective homes, and she had then come here. She was very tired after all the running around, and hungry. So she had come and sat in the kirtan pandal, as she waited for her Ma, with her eyes on the road. It had become very late. At some point, she had dozed off, because of which she was lying on the carpet that was grey with dust.

The place was noisy, full of mosquitoes, and cold as well. And it was full of dust. That had to be there. After all, it was this dust that was considered to be the dust of the Lord's feet. This was a most sacred substance. But where was the danger in that? The fear of which made Basu Das tremble and weep?

After a while, Basu Das said, 'Those people got word that the girl is lying here like this, or else what was there to be afraid of. I think they'll come in a taxi when it gets a bit quiet, and take the girl away. Don't they say, the snake charmer knows the snake's sneeze. The moment I saw them, I knew what they were up to. Please save her, dear Jibon!'

It was midnight now. A girl in the darkness of night. Not at all bad to look at, and of a tender age. She was lying all alone by the roadside, entirely unprotected. If this news reached the ears of those who were on the prowl for such women, they would certainly be excited. Their intoxicated blood would raise a storm.

The funny thing was that all these scoundrels could not be recognised properly in the light of day. They were party workers then, under the patronage of some political party. Once night descended, this identity of theirs was concealed. As the night advanced, their sharp fangs and claws were bared. Those claws tore out someone's heart, and someone else's throat, or somebody's modesty.

Such a dead body of an unclothed young woman had been found in the infamous playfield a few days back. She had been ravaged by a group of barbaric rapists whom the police had not caught to date. It seemed unlikely that they would ever be caught.

Basu Das knew Jibon. He knew that Jibon had committed many crimes. He was compelled to do them. But he had never, by any means, attacked a woman's modesty. He hated that act. Hated it acutely. The very mention of the word 'rape' was enough to set fire to the gunpowder of his rage. And even if he pardoned every kind of crime, he could never pardon a rapist under any circumstance. Jibon had grown up in front of Basu Das' own eyes. On some occasions, he himself had been a witness to some incidents. Everyone knew how severely he had thrashed the university employee who had raped the poor lunatic Mankhushi in front of the urinal in the No. 8B bus-stand. That was why Basu Das had immense confidence in Jibon. He had assumed the stranger was Jibon and appealed to him to protect the girl.

'Jibon, my dear, the girl is in terrible distress. She has no one now.' Basu Das then thought for a while, and said, 'When someone falls sick, all doctors can cure her. But the real doctor is the one who prevents the sickness. Please don't let the poor girl be ruined.'

This was not the time of the Partition, that lawless era of riots. This was no faraway, inaccessible field or forest of rural Bengal, devoid of people or light. This was the city of Calcutta, the hub of Bengal's culture, the centre of pride—and arrogance—of all of Bengal. And it was here that a girl was in peril once it got dark. A few soldiers of the Indian Army raped a girl in the Victoria Memorial grounds at 9 p.m. one night. It was truly an amazing country, where the protector became the ravager. Who would people turn to!

The stranger could not handle the situation all by himself. But neither Ganesh or Gopal were nearby. What was he to do! He already had plenty to worry about. He was in deep trouble following the Golam Gazi case. Besides, he was surrounded by the countless enemies that he had inherited via Jibon. Protecting oneself from all the known and unknown enemies was indeed a difficult task. And now this new bunch of people who would become his enemies. Would he be able to continue living in Jadavpur!

By way of inciting the stranger, Basu Das said, 'If I was your age, Jibon, I wouldn't have wasted any time talking to you. I would have taken the chopper used to cut green coconuts and set out on my own. Let's see who has the balls to touch the girl! I did it, I did all that at one time. But what can I do now? I'm too old.'

Basu Das' apprehension about the miscreants arriving by taxi turned out to be true. One was going around the spot time and again. And then it went and stopped in the darkness behind the rear wall of the No. 8B bus-stand. In front of them was the urinal, where, who knows why, one observed condoms lying on the ground.

Five or six youths got out of the taxi. Everyone in the locality knew that they were Bannerjee Babu's boys. He was a local leader of a political party. The party Nanu was with had had to flee the neighbourhood because of them.

The eyes of all those who got out of the car were bloodshot. They were drunk. Their eyes gleamed like sharp knives, with greed and lust. An absolutely fresh virgin was lying all alone by the roadside. Unclaimed. If only she could be lifted up and carried to the car, the cold night would be transformed into a warm and colourful one.

There were six of them. The stranger muttered, 'I'm all alone.'

Basu Das replied, softly but firmly, 'Like a tiger before a flock of sheep. What can the sheep do to the tiger? It's the tiger that will do whatever's done.'

'Are they sheep?'

'Weaker than that.' Basu Das said, 'If a single good man defies a hundred scoundrels, all of them will flee. Injustice cannot raise its head before justice.'

He paused, and then continued, 'You have proof of that. Isn't it? How many people were there at the time of the trouble in Laskarpara? The moment you hit one of them, didn't all the others run away with their tails between their legs? But seeing you and hearing you now, I'm beginning to wonder, is it the same Jibon? Or is it someone else?'

The youths who got out of the car knew Basu Das by name, as a middle-aged tea seller. But they could not make out who exactly the stranger with a shawl around him was. Maybe he was some rickshaw-driver. They didn't accord any importance to the two of them. And there were some half-dead Hari devotees. How could they fend them off at this time of the night! What would they fend them off with? Each of them had a weapon with which someone could be murdered with ease. The very sight of which was enough to shock them out of their wits.

The shastras referred to sound as 'brahma'. It was sound that was turned into a mantra. A mantra was supposed to be so powerful that it could instil life in a clay idol. Basu Das resorted to that now. 'People say that if Jibon has a shot of liquor in his belly, and a lathi in hand, he can stand up to even a hundred people.'

The right arm of one of the youths was severed near the wrist. His arm had been blown off when he had stumbled while running with country bombs one evening in 1971. His left hand was inside his trouser pocket. It shouldn't have been difficult for anyone to figure out that he was holding a weapon. Probably a one-shotter.

And across Raja S.C. Mullick Road was the TB Hospital, on the right side of which was Loharpara. And across the station and the railway line was Palpara. The former was a bastion of the reds, and the latter that of the ultra-reds. These two areas had not fully been taken over by the Congress party. But here, people belonging to any party had blended among the general public in such a way that it wasn't easy to identify them. With their faces and heads covered, they could suddenly attack, using what was called 'guerilla tactics'.

It was just a few days ago, one evening, that someone, or some people, stabbed a worthy of the sun of liberation—who had only recently started romping around—in his belly and thus liberated him. This was in Palpara, near the No. 9 bus-stand. In such a situation, it was a grave error to be incautious. There was another person standing next to the one with the severed arm. He was short, sturdy and snub-nosed, with a round scar on the parting of his hair. He had two balls wrapped in twine in his hands. Although they looked harmless, they were country bombs. These could be exploded to create panic among the public. It could also take lives.

Long ago, in another era, such bombs had made life difficult for the British rulers, but although they had left, the bombs remained till date. The same bombs, handmade by Bengalis, were now used to teach a lesson to fellow citizens.

Observing the girl in her stupor of deep sleep, Severed Hand and Shorty whispered something to each other. The stranger knew that they were drooling at the prospect now, like a fox that had spotted a chicken. The two of them then called another one. He was a bit tall, with a mop of curly hair. Who knows why, but he was wearing dark glasses even though it was night. Was he blind in one eye? Was he the one called Blind Kanai? It was clear that they were ready for the operation now.

Someone who had made his lair in the stranger's chest had woken up now. He asked, 'Am I dead or what? Am I dead, and rotting on a pile of bodies? Are you too dead and rotting with me? If that's not the case, hold my hand and stand up. Whether you like it or not, your fate has now joined you to the girl's fate. If you don't save her now, and the goondas carry her away, they won't stop at just that. Tomorrow morning, everyone will say, 'Jibon was there. The goondas carried the girl away right in front of him. Jibon couldn't touch even a hair of theirs. Will you be able to show your face in public then! You'll drown, but I, Jibon the Naxal, Chandal Jibon, will go down with you! Cast away all fear and move ahead. An honourable life, or an honourable death is ahead of you.

One day, in the course of conversation, the stranger had said, 'It won't do to have differences with the crocodile when you live in water.' In reply to that, Jatadhari Guru had said, 'If you have to live in water, you will have differences with the crocodile.' Another time, the stranger had said, 'There's no real harm in mistaking a rope for a snake, but it's extremely dangerous to mistake a snake for a rope.' And in response to that, Jatadhari had said, 'If you think a rope is a snake, you'll see that it turns into a hissing snake. And if you step on it, thinking it's a rope, the snake will turn into a harmless rope in fear.' It was these two things that the stranger remembered now.

He began to walk ahead with determination and confidence. There was a chopper, used for cutting green coconuts, lying on the large basket in front of Basu Das. He picked it up. He ran the thumb of his right hand on its blade to test it. It was sharp. The green coconut could not be sliced unless the chopper was very sharp, or else the chopper would simply slide away. The street light fell on the sharp edge of the chopper, making it flash. His breathing became faster. The heft of the chopper held in his fist turned wet in his sweaty palm.

Across the main road was Jadavpur University. There was a row of many tall trees inside. Who knows why, but an owl sitting on the hollow of some tree shrieked hideously just then. The lunatic who was sleeping under the shed of the bus-stand suddenly awoke, sat up, and began screaming, 'Devour them, devour the fuckers!'

Chopper in hand, the stranger gave Basu Das a meaningful look. After that, he walked ahead bravely in the direction of the kirtan stage, where the girl was lying. All those who were singing and hearing the kirtans were elderly folk. Their eyes were seasoned with experience. Seeing a goonda-like youth advancing towards them with a chopper in hand, they lost their rhythm out of fear. They could not render the sweet name of Hari in melody. The kirtan eventually came to an end.

The stranger made his way through the listeners and climbed up to the dais, like the king in a jatra performance. A microphone hung above his head. Turning his face in that direction, he said, 'A kirtan in the Lord's name is going on here. Those who want to listen to the kirtan can do that, there's no problem. But if someone so much as tries to touch the sleeping girl, I'll cut his hand off right here. My name is Chandal Jibon. All those who know me, know that I do what I say.'

After that, he went towards the girl, and stood at a small distance from her head. She was still fast asleep. The sleep of the unperturbed.

The people sitting on the dais had all stood up, out of fear. There was a circle of people around the stranger now. They could not throw a bomb at him, or shoot at him, from afar, and injure him even if they wanted to. No such intention was visible either on the part of Severed Hand and company. They had come to pluck and take the girl away, like one would use a fruit-picker to pluck a ripe fruit from a tree. There was likely to be a little bit of a commotion. But that was no big deal.

But a mountainous hurdle stood before them now. They could definitely kill. They had the capability. But that would take away the fun altogether. Which was what they wanted tonight. Deferring the violence for later, they decided to dock the boat of the present on another shore. *Tum nahi toh koi aur sahi.* If not you, then someone else. When nothing was available here, they would get it in the red-light district.

Dejected, Severed Hand returned and sat in the front seat of the taxi, and told the driver, 'Let's go to Watgunge.' And then he stuck his head out of the moving taxi, and hurled a flying threat to the stranger, 'You're going to die, you son of a swine!'

The fear and confusion among the group of devotees was dispelled. Only a moaning sound had left their throats, but now they could speak. A man with a chopper in his hand—it wasn't the chopper that was of any significance, but the man. When a knife was in the hand of a murderer, people lost their lives, but when it was in the hands of a doctor, lives were saved. Everyone realised that the man with his face and head covered like a dacoit was no dacoit, he was not a goonda or scoundrel, he was the protector of a vulnerable girl.

The girl woke up now. As she opened her eyes, she observed a man standing near her. With a shiny chopper. She shut her eyes again in panic. Her whole body trembled in fear.

The taxi had left. After its tail lights disappeared at the faraway intersection, Basu Das heaved a sigh of relief. He emerged now from the dark interior of the shop into the light outside. And then, overcome by emotion, he held the stranger's hand firmly, and said, 'Nothing can be greater than what you did today!'

10

Towards Safety

Every night comes to a close. However long it might be, it has to end at some point or the other. An unbearable night had ended for Shefali Dutt today. The night that had begun about two months ago.

She was headed homewards one morning, after completing a double shift. She was consumed by anxiety regarding her daughter. Where was she? What was she doing now? Was she all right? Had something untoward happened?

It took about fifteen minutes to walk from her nursing home on North Road to the bus-stand intersection. As she walked, her eyes scanned the roadsides. She had to return to duty again. But this was her own duty. What she had done last night was overtime. She had to do that because Ashtami's Ma couldn't come. That wouldn't have been much of a problem. She would have got off duty at the usual time if not for an urgent delivery case. She also happened to be a relative of Dr Chakraborty. His wife's cousin. Dr Chakraborty's wife was also a doctor. She had attended to the delivery, but the ayah Shefali Dutt had to stay back to clean up. She had taken some time off now to look for her daughter. She had fasted all day yesterday, who knows whether she had eaten anything after that. Once she met her, she would make all the arrangements before returning to the nursing home.

Another person was keeping watch over the route that Shefali Dutt took. That was Basu Das. He knew her very well. She had to come to Basu Das's shop from time to time to buy green coconut for patients.

The person Basu Das knew as Jibon was a creature of darkness. As soon as daylight broke, he left for his secret cave. He had done whatever needed to be done. Someone else would do whatever needed to be done next. It was in regard to this subsequent responsibility that Basu Das was waiting for Shefali Dutt.

As soon as Basu Das spotted her, he reported what had happened the previous night. 'The girl was saved from terrible danger. She was saved this time, but that may not be the case the next time. Jibon or someone else won't come and stand guard every night. You can't ask Anita to be on the street when you are uncertain about when you'll be back.'

Tears streamed down from Shefali Dutt's eyes. Did anyone stay on the street out of choice! After all, when someone doesn't feel safe at home, they have to go out in search of a safe shelter. A hunter stalked a deer for its delectable flesh, and so its own flesh was hostile to it. Even the streets have become terribly dangerous now. What will she do? Where will she go? Where can I hide the girl so that the talons of the scoundrels lusting for flesh can't reach her?'

'May I tell you something?'

'What?'

'What does your daughter do?'

'I don't understand?'

'I mean, does she go to school?'

'She studies in Rishi Aurobindo School. She is in Class Five now.'

'Oh, that's inconvenient. Or else I would have asked you to put her to work somewhere. She would have been safe then.'

Shefali Dutt said, 'No, even if she doesn't go to school, I won't put her to work. My older daughter died of burns. Do you think I want the one remaining to die as well!'

'Then think about what's best. But I would say she shouldn't come here. The times are not good.'

This was a great irony. The fathers, uncles, brothers and relatives of all these youths abandoned the homesteads of their forefathers one day in order to protect the honour and chastity of their womenfolk, and were compelled to cross over from East Pakistan to West Bengal like fugitives. They did not have to seek shelter in any dole-providing refugee camp, like those belonging to the lower castes. They did not have to venture to places far away from Bengal, like Dandakaranya, or to some desolate island in the Andamans. Thanks to the patronage of influential politicians belonging to their own caste, they were able to occupy valuable land, settlements and houses in the heart of the city of Calcutta. But after having found a firm footing here, they had forgotten all about the past and were now pouncing like violent hyenas once it was night on an uprooted, impoverished, helpless person. Thanks to favourable times and opportunities, those who had been oppressed at one time had risen to occupy the seat of the oppressor. How students of the social sciences would find a solution to this classism, and its resulting psychological perversions, was anyone's guess.

Anita's Ma Shefali Dutt felt somewhat relieved when she heard that her daughter was safe. Henceforth Anita would wait for her at the station itself. Shefali Dutt then returned to her workplace.

⌘

The Chakraborty couple's nursing home was called 'Lifecare'. The couple lived on the top floor of the four-storeyed building. They had a son, who was a doctor too. He was in Canada at present. He would return to the country after a year. Finding a suitable moment, Shefali Dutt broke down and explained everything to

Dr Chakraborty. 'Tell me, what can I do now? My eyes see only darkness everywhere.'

Dr Chakraborty was a good physician. Many important and powerful members of society were among his patients. Right now, around the end of 1972, his fee was fifty rupees. And he never saw more than twenty patients a day. He was acquainted with a former major in the Indian Army. After his retirement, the major, who was childless, had established an orphanage in the village of Shimurali, in Nadia district. Dr Chakraborty knew that this gentleman would definitely respond to his request. So he said, 'You should have told me your problem earlier. Wait for a day or two. Let me see what I can do.'

He called Shefali Dutt three or four days later, and told her, 'Take a day's leave and go and drop your daughter at the Bhagirathi Shilpa Ashram in Nadia. She'll stay there, be fed there, continue her schooling there, and also learn a skill. Tell me, are you happy?'

Anita's Ma's eyes had brimmed with tears in gratitude. What could be a better arrangement for her unfortunate daughter!

Shefali Dutt had dropped her daughter there today. The girl had been roaming the streets like a crazed soul for almost two months. That problem had come to an end now. She sighed in relief at having been able to arrange for her daughter's transfer to a safe place. There were almost five hundred orphans, both boys and girls, in Bhagirathi Shilpa Ashram. Anita would stay with them, and Shefali would visit her every month, and drop off essential items, odds and ends.

After returning from Shimurali, she gave the news to Basu Das first. 'Finally my anxieties are gone. You saved me from a terrible calamity. I don't have words to thank you.'

Basu Das replied, 'I didn't do anything. It was Jibon who did all that was needed. If you must thank anyone, thank him.'

'When can you take me to him? I can take time off from work if required.'

Scratching his head, Basu Das said, 'I don't know what to tell you! It's very difficult to meet him. It was sheer luck that I found him that day. I have no idea when I'll see him next. One has to look for him, you know!'

'Why's that? Are the police looking for him? What did he do?'

'Oh, he's a goonda. Don't they say, it takes iron to cut iron. It was because Jibon was a goonda that he went and confronted those goondas. Decent folks are of no use in times of danger. They sit at home behind shut doors. Didn't you see it during the time of the riots? It was goondas like Jibon who stepped out to protect people. So Jibon is that kind of goonda.'

Shefali was a bit disheartened. 'Maybe he's a goonda, but I do want to meet the person who helped us.'

Basu Das said, 'I'll try, let's see if I can. But ...'

'But what?'

Basu Das smiled, 'Since we live under the same sky, and on the same soil, I'll certainly see him today, or tomorrow, or the day after. Be on the lookout on the streets, you'll find him.'

11

Gupi's Folly

The Jadavpur locality had been reasonably peaceful and amicable for quite a few days now. Something relating to a girl had taken place a long time back at the bus-stand intersection, and after that everything had been quiet. No bombs had exploded anywhere, nor bullets been fired, and no girl had been abducted. No dead bodies had been found either, in any foul pool. Such times were rare in the fate of this locality. This was unprecedented, at least in the last three years. So what happened all of a sudden! Such a vegetarian existence went against the nature of the locality. Something or the other would happen everyday, crowds would gather at every street intersection, people would be bubbling with excitement. How else would anyone know that people and their very souls resided here?

All the apprehensions finally came to an end today. It became clear that the peace was actually a preview of a preparation. The city returned to its usual rhythm. The news came wafting with the breeze that just a little while back, Galkata Gupi, the aspiring mastaan of Mistripara with a scar on his cheek, had been killed.

There are some people who die while trying to survive. And there were some mastaans who were born only to be killed. Gupi was a creature that belonged to that rare latter species. It is said that in the Ramayana, King Ravana had made his deathly arrow himself, and had kept it in his custody, but only to die by it. Similarly, Gupi had bought a knife with his own money, sharpened it himself, and he used to carry it along wherever he went, but only to die by it. He had not killed even a chicken with the knife, and the people of the locality still had doubts about whether he had the capability to do that. But he had handed the knife to the killer out of a death wish. If he hadn't done that, the bird of his life would not have exited his lungs and flown away. Perhaps he would have suffered some thrashing but still been alive today. And he would still be standing at the tea-shop in the intersection, wearing a checkered shirt and white trousers, trying to catch the attention of girls returning from school. Just like a writer was very fond of his pen, and people had no doubts in their minds as regards his literacy, an aspiring mastaan was very fond of his rampuri knife. The weapon helped to give him the identity that he was no ordinary youth.

As soon as Gupi began his career as a mastaan, he had secretly pilfered some money from his Ma's piggy bank and bought a full-size rampuri from Bowbazar, or Burrabazar, or who knows where. It made a clicking sound, which startled those who had never heard it before. Whenever he left home and went out, he always had that at his waist. And whenever he felt like it, he used it to frighten people who were already half-dead in fear. That included vulnerable folk like itinerant vendors who tramped through one neighbourhood after another, cart-pullers, rickshaw-drivers, and waste-pickers. Just like Gupi had heard that people grew into armed robbers in the course of cutting taro stems, he hoped that by terrifying all these people he would be transformed one day. And that one day, at an opportune moment, he would be able to stab someone with it. He would be elevated that day, and be counted as an aristocrat in the world of mastaans.

Every morning and evening, he sharpened the rampuri, stuffed it inside his waistband, and went and sat at Amasha Mamu's tea-shop at the Mistripara intersection. He had no real work other than gossiping all day. He used to take out the knife on some ploy or pretext and bare it in public. 'Oh, I can't sit properly, it's hurting me!' And the knife was suddenly laid on the table. The times were such that the public was scared of anyone who had a weapon. They regarded him with some awe and respect. Gupi truly enjoyed that.

Gupi, who was dark-skinned and a bit tall, and had left his studies after failing twice in Class Eight, was earlier with the red party. The red leader of Mistripara was Pinaki Sen, and it was under his leadership that the reds had a stronghold in Mistripara. It was this Pinaki Sen who had inducted Babua, Amar, Jhantu and Gupi into the party. Later the leader Pinaki Sen had fled the locality out of fear of the police and the Congress party youths. It was heard that he was in Guwahati, in Assam. He would not return to West Bengal unless there was a change in the political scenario. There were quite a few cases of murder that he had been charged with.

Pinaki Sen had money in his pocket, so he could flee to a safe place. But the others could not. Babua and Amar fell to police bullets within a few days. Amar was killed first, right in front of Amasha Mamu's eyes, in front of his tea-shop. After that, Babua went and hid himself in the hospital compound. But he couldn't survive. Officer-in-charge Pal Babu went right in, killed him, and then left. And Jhantu was shot and killed by Congress youths.

Observing all this, Gupi had realised that if he didn't quit the red party, the prognosis wasn't good for him either. Of course, he hadn't really done anything. But what of that? After all, he too used to swagger around with a thick lathi on his shoulder behind those who had really done something and then died. He too had pranced around, chanting the slogan, *'Maar ka badla khoon hai,* murder is the revenge for a thrashing'. So everyone noticed him too. That was justification enough to slit his throat.

Just like Loharpara was the biggest and strongest bastion of the red party in this part of the city, and Palpara was that of the ultra-reds, Bijoygarh was the big bastion of the Congress party. Gupi's elder brother had a tailoring shop in the Bijoygarh market. So Gupi got in touch with the 'dadas' of Bijoygarh through his brother, who accompanied him to Jagarani Club, where he surrendered before the Congress. 'Whatever I did was wrong. I give you my word, I'll never make the same mistake again.'

Nakul Mitra's house was near Jagarani Club. He was currently the president of the rickshaw union of Bijoygarh. He said to Gupi, 'You were with the reds earlier. Who knows how many of our boys you murdered! How can I believe that you have left that party! You need to take a test! Or else, remain in that party. We won't accept you.'

Nakul Babu was in his forties. He had big eyes. His head was three-fourths bald. He had a drinking habit. Once he had had a few drinks, he set out to look for rickshaw-drivers who were gambling, or rickshaw-drivers who misbehaved with passengers, or charged higher fares. If he found them, he gave them a terrible thrashing. If a man was on fire, he would run and jump into a pond, whether or not he knew how to swim, whether or not there were crocodiles in the water. Gupi was in that plight now.

Not far from where Gupi had been made to sit was Lalu Kaka's field. This was the field where many youths were sleeping beneath the soil. Akhil, Nitin and Nakul had put them to sleep for ever. There was no one in the huge field surrounded by walls. There was only Gupi, who was surrounded by Akhil, Nikhil and Blind Kalu. A signal from Nakul Mitra was enough for them to riddle Gupi's chest with bullets.

Gupi was afraid. He said, 'I'll take the test.'

'What test?'

'Whatever you say.'

'Bring one of your red leaders. Is there anyone in your neighbourhood? I'll send four boys with you. Can you do that?' A cunning smile appeared on Nakul Mitra's face. He continued, 'Remember, this will be your final test. If you pass, you will become one of us. You can stay in your neighbourhood without any fear.

No one will say a thing to you. Or else, you will have to leave the locality and flee.'

Gupi remembered Bimal Deb Sen, the poet. He was a teacher in the Ramakrishnapur Primary School. He was in the neighbourhood. A harmless soul. All he did was teach his students and write poetry. It was in one of his poems that he had written, 'Our struggle shall continue, the mountain of endless conflict and exploitation shall totter!' Picking him up was an easy matter.

After completing this easy task, Gupi became a trusted entity for the Bijoygarh boys. And he was at the centre of a rip-roaring adda session that took place one day at Amasha Mamu's shop at the intersection of the red bastion, Mistripara. Jogai, of Bijoygarh, had been given the responsibility to look after this bastion. For Bijoygarh, Mistripara was a lot like Pakistan was to the United States of America. If a military campaign against India was ever required, that could be achieved by using that country. Although the reds had vacated Loharpara, if they ever returned, launching an attack on them from the Naxalite Mistripara, or resisting an attack there, would both take far less time than it would for the Congress boys to come running there from Bijoygarh.

❦

Babua was a Mistripara boy. He was a friend and comrade of Nanu. He was killed by the police one evening in front of the hospital's waste incinerator. Moyna was a sister of Babua. Nanu was previously acquainted with Moyna. The acquaintance turned into love afterwards. Lured by his love for the short, fair-complexioned and shapely Moyna, Nanu used to leave his safe cave in the hospital and go to Moyna's house in Mistripara.

Love was a journey of solitude. Although one could fight, or create a riot-like situation with a group, when it came to love, no group had any place. It was love so long as it was a secret. All the sweetness and joy lay in that. Nanu was not an ordinary person, and so the routes ordinary people frequented were not the ones he used either. The route that he took departed from the direct one; he walked along the canal in the hospital premises, crossed Raja S.C. Mullick Road, went down the lane in Shyamnagar for a good distance, and then turned right to go all the way around Mistripara. Although one could reach there in ten minutes, it took Nanu half-an-hour. So what of that! After all, people knew that a roundabout route was best if it was safe.

Gupi had been a comrade of Nanu. They were very fond of each other. Because Gupi was neither very brave nor bloodthirsty, Nanu did not fear him despite his switching over to the Congress party. He was sure that even if they ever encountered one another, Gupi wouldn't lay hands on him. He was sure Gupi knew the difference between the poet Bimal Deb Sen and Nanu.

But Nanu was completely wrong. Times had changed. What Gupi sought, almost like an addiction, was to become a notorious mastaan like Balak Das of Loharpara, or Jogai and Blind Kanai of Bijoygarh.

It was only poor and destitute folk who lived in Mistripara earlier. They were all basically grease monkeys, mechanics, fitters, repairmen and suchlike. Subsequently some people of the babu class arrived there. They constructed single- and double-storey pukka houses. Thanks to the contemptuous misbehaviour of the people from the pukka houses, the dwellers in the original huts turned towards the red party, although, quite a number of the party members had either been killed, or fled the neighbourhood. Only Gupi remained. Like a solitary tiger in a forest.

Gupi ran into Nanu one day. While Nanu was alone, Gupi was with a group of four or five people. And he forgot all about his former identity and thrashed Nanu. After all, how could an aspiring mastaan give up such a perfect opportunity to display his heroism. Nanu was beaten up right in front of Moyna's house. 'Fucker, you dare come to our neighbourhood for womanising!' That hurt Nanu much more than the beating did. All the honour and heroism in Moyna's image of him was crushed to bits.

This incident took place a few days ago. Nanu had somehow managed to extricate himself from Gupi and his gang after the thrashing, and run away. There was the terrible danger of him being dragged to Bijoygarh for punishment.

Returning to his own locality following the thrashing, Nanu began thinking about how he might recover the honour that he had been robbed of. After taking the advice of several people, he arrived at the decision that Gupi ought to be beaten up in public in his own neighbourhood, and that word of this should reach Moyna's ears, so that she would realise that Nanu was no ordinary sort, he was nothing short of a tiger's offspring. And a tiger was still a tiger even when it got old, it didn't turn into a sheep.

The success of an operation depended upon opportune timing. Through personal investigation and experience, Nanu realised that the most weak and disorganised time of the enemy was between six and half-past-six in the evening. Gupi was alone in the tea-shop at this time. None of his friends were able to be at this den then.

A team of at least five or six people was required to carry out this task. But where did Nanu have any associates now! All of them had left the neighbourhood. So how would Nanu be able to handle such a big thing all by himself!

Bachcha Dilip was the one Nanu trusted the most. Although he was a kid, he was intelligent. He said, 'Nanu-da, why don't you talk to Jibon-da. He can ask Ganesh, Gopal and others to join.' But after listening to everything, Jibon said, 'No, Nanu, it won't be right to involve them in this. After all, whatever they might be, they aren't hired goondas that they'll just go around being violent. They are all poor, labouring boys. And it's not that things will come to an end with this thrashing, its impact will continue to be felt for a long time. They are already in a bit of trouble on account of the Golam Gazi matter. But the saving grace is that Golam Gazi was an outsider. The police too knew what he was up to. That's why they are going slow on that. I will go wherever you ask me to. I'm ready for whatever happens to me. But I can't involve them.'

So what was the option? Nanu had Jibon and Dilip. At least two or three more people were needed. After getting Jibon on his side, Nanu started thinking about who he could get. That was when he remembered Chhotka. This strong fellow, who was very dark-skinned and had frizzy hair, was not very intelligent. He had never been involved with any party. He had not engaged in any violence or murder. But he had courage like a wild buffalo did. His monster-like appearance terrified everyone.

When Nanu went to him, even before he could say anything, Chhotka said, 'I believe Gupi beat you up?'

Nanu nodded. 'Yes, man. I got thrashed.'

'Aren't you going to take revenge? Come, let's go and beat up the fucker!'

'Will you come along?'

'Of course, I'll go. Bulu will also come with me. We are also furious with that fucker Gupi. Didn't he take away our teacher? We'll settle all the dues now. When do you want to go?'

Today was the day selected. One by one, four of them arrived at the specified spot, in front of Nanu's liquor den. Chhotka and Bulu were carrying metal rods. And Nanu had a chopper-knife. It was not really needed, but still, he had carried it. But where was Jibon, on whom Nanu relied the most? There was no sign of him.

Meanwhile, the stranger was in a sad state with travel fatigue, hunger and thirst. Evening had turned to night, a night that made your very bones shiver. He came running to the river jetty. He would find food, shelter and rest only if he could get to the other side of the river. Arriving at the jetty, he saw that the last boat of the day was already full of passengers, and it was about to leave. The stranger told the boatman, 'Take me too, bhai. There's no other boat to go across on. If I'm stuck here all alone, I'll die of hunger, thirst and cold.' The boatman told him, 'The boat is full already. If I take you now, it will be overcrowded. If the boat capsizes, all of us will die. It's best for everyone that it's you alone who dies.'

So the stranger remained on this bank. And the boat set off towards the other bank. The stranger felt like weeping at his misfortune. If only I could have reached a bit earlier! Before just one person. I would then have got food and a warm shelter. I wouldn't have had to suffer this hardship. The stranger gazed at the departing boat in despair. But what's this! The boat capsized when it was mid-river. It sank into the river bit by bit. Those who could swim began swimming desperately towards the shore. And all those who couldn't, drowned in the unfathomable depths.

It then struck the stranger, but for the grace of God, I too could have been aboard the boat. And I too don't know how to swim. The one who had considered himself unfortunate a few moments ago now thought he was most fortunate.

The stranger had been mentally prepared to accompany Nanu. After having his lunch in the afternoon, he went to the university grounds to rest for a while. A lot of people dozed there at this time. There was no risk in sleeping there.

He left the place after a nap, had a free cup of tea at Basu Das's shop, and thought it was time and that he ought to set out. But as he was crossing the road, he was hit by a motorcycle. Who knows whether he ran into it, or the motorcycle ran into him! Whether a vegetable fell on the blade of a knife, or the blade fell on the vegetable, it was the vegetable that got cut. The stranger's toe was badly injured as a result.

By the time he could get his foot bandaged, and limp to Nanu's den, Nanu, crazy for vengeance, had already left with his gang after waiting impatiently for a while. They went towards Mistripara. After all they were going to thrash an arsehole like Gupi, the four of them were enough!

After finding out from someone about the direction they had taken, the stranger ran along to join them. It took him quite a while to reach, as he dragged his injured foot along. When he reached Raja S.C. Mullick Road and looked westwards, he saw Nanu and his associates returning. What was the matter? How come they were back so soon?

They were running. As they ran past him and moved ahead, Chhotka shouted out, 'Gupi's gone. To the lap of God. He's lying on the road with his mouth gaping!'

There was no need to go ahead now. There was fire there. The stranger too ran behind Nanu's group. But who knows where Nanu, Chhotka and Bulu disappeared in a trice. Only Bachcha Dilip was there. Dilip, the son of a sweeper, had entered his hut there, and was trembling in fear. Oh, what a calamity had befallen him! Nothing short of a case of murder. The punishment for which was the noose, or life imprisonment.

The stranger heard from Dilip about what exactly had transpired.

Gupi had just reached Amasha Mamu's shop, got a glass of tea and taken a couple of sips, with his other hand placed stylishly at his waist when the group suddenly appeared there and surrounded him. Before he could realise anything, or try to run, someone grabbed him by the collar of his shirt. He was wearing the same checkered shirt and pair of white trousers. Nanu punched him on his chest at once—to avenge the other day's thrashing. The glass of tea went flying out of Gupi's hand, and the tea splashed on his white trouser.

Gupi then pulled out the shiny, sharpened knife from his waist. All those who were acquainted with him knew about him, they all knew he did not have what it took to stab anyone with it. He had bared the knife like this many times, and then folded it and put it back at his waist. A knife was a weapon which frightened people—and so they would run when they saw it. That's what he had thought.

But how would the thick-headed Chhotka know that! He saw a knife in Gupi's hand. He pounced on Gupi at once. He twisted his arm and snatched the knife away. And he stabbed Gupi on the chest with the same knife. The knife went directly into his heart and punctured it. Blood gushed out of the wound, and Gupi died.

Nanu had said that he would never flee his neighbourhood. A fish out of water, and a man away from his neighbourhood, were in the same plight. But he had no option now but to run. It wasn't a chicken that had been slaughtered, a man had died. So Nanu fled. But the police picked him up from his sister's house in Medinipur. The names of those who were with him were revealed during the police investigation.

After that Bachcha Dilip too was picked up by the police. And Chhotka and Bulu surrendered in the court.

12

Shiba

Shiba returned to his neighbourhood after he obtained bail, having been in jail for almost a year-and-a-half. 'Shiba', meaning fox, wasn't his real name. It had been given to him by the people of the locality. Because he was apparently as cunning as a fox, and a skillful hunter. He could pick up and bring his prey just like a fox picked up a householder's chicken or duck. He hunted people. That was the only thing that gave him joy.

If one walked eastwards a bit from the Jadavpur railway station, took the lane on the right and advanced some distance, one arrived at Loharpara. The lanes and alleys of this locality were impenetrable and inaccessible.

Until about a year-and-a-half back, Loharpara was an indomitable stronghold of the red party. Workers of that party from various regions—whom people would later know as 'harmad' —used to take shelter here after fleeing from their own localities following some operation there. There were arrangements to provide food and shelter for as many as a thousand, or twelve-hundred party workers. Meat and rice were cooked in large pots. These party workers were sent all over southern Bengal to eliminate those opposed to the party. Sometimes a group of them, armed with guns and country bombs, used to attack Palpara, the stronghold of the Naxalites, or Bijoygarh, the stronghold of the Congress. They used to bring back their victim, whose body was then disposed of in a foul pool beside some railway line, or in the garbage dump in Dhapa, or the hogla jungle in Hussainpur.

This was why there was a saying about Loharpara, that no one who entered the locality left the place alive. They had invented several gruesome methods of killing people. Some were killed with a blow to the head with a crowbar, some were put into a sack and their head smashed with bricks, while others were simply stabbed in the belly with a pair of scissors.

The name of the lord of the sanctuary called Loharpara was Balak Das. He was away from the locality at present out of fear of the police. No one knew where he was. It was said that Balak Das had supposedly killed at least twenty people. And nothing other than murder seemed to please him. Balak Das had several hands. He had as many as three right-hand men. They were Chandu Bhaiya, Bishu and Kartick.

Shiba's big grouse was that although he was in no way inferior to them, he hadn't been accorded the honour of being a right-hand man. But Balak Das was absent now, and none of his right-hand men were present either. Now he would show what he was capable of.

Shiba secretly raised his own army in Loharpara to fill the void. There were only three members at present, but the numbers would gradually grow. This was the time when no organised political party existed in a large area around the Jadavpur railway station. The Congress boys from Bijoygarh no longer crossed Raja S.C. Mullick Road to try and enter this place. And the police, weary after having killed lots and lots of Naxalites, were resting a bit. Their earlier activities, like regular patrols and search operations, had ceased for the time being.

Although Shiba had formed a group at this time, he was short of money. After all, who would accord any worth to a group that lacked money and arms. For some reason, all the illicit liquor dens, *kamake khanewali* women, thieves and pickpockets, who made offerings of obeisance earlier were tight-fisted now. Mastaans and goondas shared a natural similarity with leaders, actors, sportsmen and writers. They did their work with unceasing devotion so that their names remained in the limelight. If there was the slightest pause or laxity, all their reputations sank into oblivion. Leaders like Lenin, actors like Chaplin, sportsmen like Bradman, writers like Shakespeare, and hoodlums like Gopal Patha had only been born once in the world. Their names were immortal. But that didn't apply to others. They had to be on the job every single day.

After Shiba went to jail, the people of the locality somehow got the idea that he was no longer the Shiba of old. That one could get by without being scared of, or making offerings to, him. It was vital to demolish that notion.

Shiba was sitting on the culvert at Loharpara one morning and sipping lemon tea, wondering what he ought to do to make a big bang and restore his reputation. A man riding a handicapped person's hand-pedalled tricycle arrived and stopped in front of him. He was bearded and dressed in a long robe, with a green turban on his head. It turned out that Baghai, who ran the tea-shop, knew him well. Baghai said to Shiba, 'Golam Gazi wants to speak to you about a problem of his. I told him you would be able to sort it out. He will take care of any expenses.'

Golam Gazi had not met Shiba earlier, but he had heard about his activities from Baghai. He had also heard that Shiba had just returned from jail. That he was empty-handed. If Shiba was paid now, he would surely get his job done.

Golam said, 'Dear Dada, I did nothing wrong. But they made me lame for no fault of mine. If I don't avenge the one who did this to me, I'll go to hell when I die. Please do this for me. Even if I have to sell off ten katthas of land for this, I'm willing to do that.'

'Who did this to you?'

'The fucker Jibon.'

'Which Jibon? The one who lives in the station? Chandal Jibon?'

'Yes, it's that chandal who is responsible for this.'

'What about the police? Did you file a complaint?'

'Oh, the police won't do anything. If they wanted to, they could have acted long back. After all, he didn't flee from Jadavpur. He roams around here all day and night. They could have caught him. This happened during the summer last year. Another summer has gone by since then.'

Shiba took another sip from the glass of tea, put it down, and said, 'I can only do what you ask me to do. The more jaggery you provide, the sweeter it will be. Do you understand what I say?'

Golam nodded his head. 'I got it.'

The shastras say that the call of Shiba the fox during the daytime was always inauspicious. But the stranger was unaware that the call of a person by the name of Shiba could be ominous too.

Shiba was standing with his associates Shankar and Dhani in front of Madan Ghosh's tea-shop at the very end of the eastern side of the platform at Jadavpur station. That was when he called out, 'Hey Jibon, there's something I need to tell you.'

The stranger had gone to Kushi's house. Ghoti Narayan had entrusted him with the responsibility of matchmaking. He too thought that wouldn't be a bad idea. Just as he had left after completing the discussion, he encountered danger.

The stranger went up to Shiba, and asked, 'What is it?'

'Come with me to Loharpara.'

The stranger was taken by surprise. In the past year, or year-and-a-half, he had never heard anyone ordering him like this. He asked, 'Why? What do you want?'

'There's something I need to tell you.'

'Tell me here then.'

'If I could tell it to you here, I would have done that. I can't tell you here.'

Meanwhile, two of Shiba's protégés, Dhani and Shankar, had come and stood behind the stranger. The stranger was hesitant. He wasn't able to decide whether to advance or to retreat.

'Hey, are you afraid to go with us or what!'

'Why should I be afraid? Do I have any enmity or any quarrel or dispute with you people!'

'Then come along.'

'But I have some work now.'

'It won't take much time. I want to show you something, you can leave immediately after that.'

This was a perfect Boishakh noon. The sun was burning in fury directly overhead.

The stranger was here a year ago, but now the heat was fiercer in comparison. For some reason, he got the feeling that life was pushing him towards one more test today. That was the message the secret radar of his sixth sense was conveying. How would he escape from this predicament? Ought he to run? But then he would have no way of knowing what he had left behind. Why did they want to take him to Loharpara? What was waiting for him there? Who would tell him that? Maybe a hearty welcome awaited him there. The warm embrace of friends. That could be. How would he know it wasn't unless he went there!

'What happened? Come!'

'I'm coming.'

The three men had an eye-to-eye exchange. The stranger could not figure out the meaning of that. He walked ahead with an unanswered question in his head. Shiba was in front, the stranger behind him, with Dhani and Shankar walking side by side behind him. Everyone's eyes were red and puffy. Their breaths were hot and deep. Their bodies were sweaty and flaccid. A hammering in their chests.

They walked eastwards along the railway line. Suddenly Shiba came to a halt. He felt his legs trembling, as if he had somehow become heavier. As if they just didn't want to move. Such things happened. It wasn't anything new. That's why people said that knowledge diminished with lack of practice. After all that he had done in the past with great ease, why else would his limbs be so stiff after returning from a brief spell in jail! Why would his heart thump? Why would his throat turn dry?

One could say that this man by the name of Jibon was an extremely harmless victim. One rarely found someone in his circumstances. He had no parents, siblings, or any relatives. He had his meals in Chhechan's cheap eatery, and slept in the railway station. He did not have the patronage of any political party either. He was a criminal in the eyes of the police and a goonda in the eyes of the public. There was not much of a difference between such a man and a street dog. Anyone could kill them. No one would weep for them if they were killed, and no one would search for them if they went missing. So why was Shiba's heart thumping!

No, he ought to gather his courage. Who would provide that? It was to be found in a liquid beverage called alcohol. Alcohol was a substance that made the timid brave and the brave daring. There was no act of bravery in the world that was beyond a drunkard.

On the right-hand side of the railway line were rows of countless tiny shanties made of discarded tin sheets, hogla and bamboo-matting. There were several illicit liquor dens here. Those who ran these dens knew Shiba. They didn't dare to ask Dada for the payment after providing him liquor, they sought his favour. 'Dada, keep me in mind! If the business runs well, I'll be able to keep my children in good health.'

Shiba went and stood in front of an illicit liquor den. He wanted to moisten his dry throat. He wanted to drive away the limpness he felt in his legs, and to charge the battery of his depleted courage.

'Hey Kalo, dear Kalo-da, get me a pint!'

A dark head emerged from a shanty. 'Who's that? Oh, Shiba bhai! Are you going to stand outside and drink? Don't you want to sit inside? I've got a nice snack to go with it. A fish chochchori.'

'No time to sit. Bring it here. I'll come later and have the chochchori. Let me finish my work first. Just bring me a pinch of salt for now. Shiba began to feel somewhat at ease. One felt light-headed in an instant. The second glass boosted his courage. And with the third one, the conviction grew in him—I am the one. I can do whatever I want. There's no one or nothing that's bigger or stronger than me.

A pint measure yielded three glasses of liquor. Observing Shiba gulp down three glasses in succession all by himself, a sea of grief seemed to pour out of his protégé Shankar's voice. 'Wow! Guru, wow! I'm waiting expectantly here, and you polished it off all by yourself! You didn't spare even a drop. Is this your socialism? *Chhee!*'

'You guys are drunkards, that's why I didn't give you any. If you booze and pass out, everything will be ruined. You've already downed a pint each.'

'But that was a long while back. I pissed twice after that. All the booze is gone. Just look at my tummy, it's completely empty.' Shankar pulled up his shirt to show Shiba his belly. There was a rampuri knife tucked into the edge of his trouser at his waist.'

'Hide it. People are looking.'

'Fuck the people's mother! Order some booze first.'

'Don't have too much!'

'Where's it too much! There's only three glasses in a pint. We'll have only a glass each. Order it, hurry up.'

Shiba got another pint. But this time he paid the price. They were poor folk, with children. How would the poor man survive if they had everything for free! After that he sipped from the glass, to the accompaniment of slices of ginger dipped in salt. 'Ah! Kalo-da's booze is really strong. Whatever else the fucker might do, he doesn't add water to the booze.' An absolute epitome of honesty. After all, the real capital of a businessman was honesty. The one who was honest never starved to death. God sent customers crawling to Kalo's door under the cover of the darkness of night.

After they finished drinking, they lit Charminar cigarettes and began walking along the railway line again. They walked for quite a distance before turning right at the rugged stony road. Although this was where Loharpara began, they had to go past the culvert, and then some more. Right to the middle of Loharpara. But there were no more liquor vends there. You couldn't get alcohol even if you banged your head to death. However, a bit more was needed. A little bit.

This wasn't their fault, it was the fault of alcohol. The more you had, the more you wanted to have. And this would go on until you threw up and toppled over. The three of them therefore stopped in front of the last cholai den on the way to Loharpara, and another person was also certainly with them. But he was as good as 'absent' in their view.

Once again, a pint was divided into three parts, which went down their gullets. '*Ab thik hai! Ab bilkul thik hai. Ekdum full tight!* This will do.' The stranger remembered what Jatadhari Guru had said. 'If you drink a glass of liquor, you have consumed that. If you have another glass after that, the liquor consumes the liquor. But if you have yet another glass after that, you should know that the liquor has consumed you. I won't ask you not to drink, but just one glass.' True to his words, the three people had been consumed by alcohol.

The sun in the sky above seemed to be pouring down in fury and rage on the earth, people and their homes. It was extremely difficult to stand outside. There wasn't the slightest breeze. Not a single leaf stirred. A street dog lay panting with its body submerged in the drain along the road. The road beneath one's soles was a red-hot iron sheet in a blacksmith's furnace. The stranger had no slippers on his feet, the strap on one of them had snapped a little while back. His feet were burning now, his whole body seemed to be aflame.

Three pairs of wobbly feet walked along the twelve-foot-wide lane of Loharpara. As if a stumble would land them in the open drain beside. Dhani suddenly stopped, squatted beside the drain and vomited noisily.

'What happened man?' Shiba asked. Dhani replied, 'It's nothing. Everything's all right. Let's go. I felt a bit nauseous. I'm fine now.'

'Didn't I tell you earlier? Do you want to wash your head?'

'No, no, let's go. I'll be fine now.'

There was an old house in front of them. Behind that was a pond, a bamboo grove, a jungle of weeds and undergrowth, a field and a few empty sheds. The house was a three-storeyed one. There were no windows or doors in any of the rooms. In some parts of the building, the inner brick lay exposed. Who knows why, long ago, the construction stopped while the building was coming up. Bricks, sand and stones lay scattered here and there. Arriving there, Shiba pointed with his finger, and said, 'Come inside.' Without saying a word, the stranger entered the house.

Tired from the noontime heat, the people of this area had fallen immobile and silent with their doors and windows shut. There wasn't really anyone on the streets to speak of.

The stranger went in like a loyal servant following his master's instructions, and saw that the design of the house was a lot like that of the burnt house he had once seen in a cinema, where bodiless, unsatisfied souls wept as they hovered around dark rooms. There were many rooms on the ground floor, all without doors or windows. They had been there earlier, but it seemed someone, or some people, had removed and taken them away. Needless to say, there was no furniture in any room. The whole place was laden with dust. And in that lay cigarette butts, empty matchboxes, packets, old newspapers, a collar torn off a shirt.

It was the stranger's first time here. But many people had come before this, they had been brought from various places, in various ways. Who knows whether or not it was their souls that hovered inside the dilapidated house.

Shankar had assumed the role of sentry and stood in front of the entrance to the house. He knew that given what was going to take place now, some screams, moans, cries of *Baba go! Ma go!*, and words like 'Help!' were natural. Let it happen. That was not a problem. Such sounds always emanated from this house. People had grown accustomed to hearing it from the time of Balak-da. They were not perturbed any more, no one came running. People were very intelligent, clever, astute and aware now. They did not waste any more time on others' matters. The police might arrive. Someone may have made a phone call or something. They never used to come earlier. They were scared. But of late, they came sometimes. After all, they had to do something when they were idle. They did a round of the place from time to time.

That's why some caution was appropriate. If they did arrive, he would spot them from afar and inform his friends inside the house, 'The cops are coming, run!' There was no difficulty in running away. Once one escaped from the rear of the house through the narrow lanes shrouded by undergrowth, and went past Rajpur, and hid in the hogla jungle in Hussainpur, no one, or their dad, would ever be able to find them.

They were all veteran fighters of many battles, surgeons of many successful operations. They knew what each one's role was. Once Shankar stood guard at the entrance, Dhani walked ahead beside Shiba. There was a large, doorless bathroom. Shiba pointed to that and told the stranger, 'Go in there.'

The stranger thought it was all a bit strange. But then he entered the bathroom. Shiba followed him. And Dhani stood in the doorway. He was now Dr Shiba's personal assistant in the operation. The nurse who was beside the surgeon during an operation played no minor role. Dhani knew that.

Shiba now extended his hand towards Dhani, and said, 'Give me the *kaniya*.' Dhani extended his hand likewise towards Shankar, and shouted out, '*Kaniya*.' Shankar pulled out an eighteen-inch knife from his waist, and went and handed it to Dhani, who opened it and gave it to Shiba. The knife was truly something to gape at. Some artisan had crafted it with great devotion.

The brass butt of the dagger in Shiba's hand was shaped like a fish. Its scales too had been inscribed on it. Vines with leaves and flowers were drawn opposite the sharp edge, right from the butt to its pointed end. A beautiful eye had also been drawn in its right place. The blade was long and thin. That was absolutely shining. It looked as if it had just been brought from the knife-sharpener and not been inaugurated yet. Its sharp edge of hard steel looked like the flicking tongue of a snake. It drooled in expectation of blood.

But the stranger was startled to see the dagger. What's this? What crime did I commit? There had never been any dispute or discord with them. So why the dagger?

The stranger thought that perhaps they were playing the fool. Frightening him for a bit of fun. There were terms in mastaan lingo for this, like *chomkani deowa*, *ketri khaowano*, or *horkhani deowa*, meaning, to shock and horrify. Doing that was some people's whimsy.

Once, on a Kali Puja night, a few wicked boys with freshly sprouted moustaches were going around dragging a plastic snake tied to a string on the road, in order to shock pedestrians. The most effective way of spoiling the fun in such instances was not getting scared. That's what a girl did then. She just trampled on the head of the snake and walked away giggling.

The stranger realised that he ought not to be afraid. I am representing Jibon. I may be a coward, but Jibon was unmatched in courage. In a voice that was fearless for that reason, the stranger said, 'You've had a lot of booze, you might cut yourself! Put the toy away and tell me what you have to say. I have some work, I need to leave.'

The answer to the stranger could have been provided in spoken words. But that did not happen. It was 'word' which was the reason for that. Shiba had given his word to Golam Gazi. Besides, if this job went down well, his name would be proclaimed in victory chants. The rust that had grown on his reputation in the last one or one-and-a-half years would be wiped clean.

That's why Shiba's jaws were clenched now. Fatal intention flashed in his eyes. Without wasting any time, he let the dagger do the talking. He said nothing. He didn't think that was even necessary. Work more, talk less was his motto. Before the stranger knew it, the dagger went in, *snip*, into the flesh on his shoulder. Blood flowed down. With Shiba's speedy dagger landing on target, death was knocking on Jibon's door.

Shiba's knife flashed again, this time diagonally. The target was the throat. That was also a vulnerable spot in the body. Perhaps the weakest one. One could be killed with a single swipe. But the very same instant, the stranger moved his head to one side and somehow managed to save his throat. The dagger sped again, once again the target was the throat. But there was no place to move this time. A solid cement wall beside and behind him, and in front was the drunken Shiba, standing like a wall. The stranger was compelled to raise his left arm and shield his neck. The dagger pierced him just above the elbow. Hot blood spurted out and splattered on the dust and sand on the floor.

Shiba was fuming in rage after having failed as many as three times. He wouldn't fail any more now. He was going to deliver the final blow. A perfect one. He stepped back a little. The way a bull in battle did. And then came running at twice the speed, raising the dagger once again.

'Are you going to die?' The stranger asked himself. 'Are you going to be butchered like a goat? He was seized by mortal terror, and like a cornered rat, an indomitable desire to survive reared its head. 'No, no, no!' I'm not going to die like this. There was time. There was still time. He could still turn around, and live.

Waves of thought lashed his brain like flashes of lightning. Shiba might be a notorious mastaan who had committed many murders. But he was not superhuman. He was a man like everybody else. He too had only one life beating inside his chest. From where, if there was a six-inch hole made by the stab of a dagger, the bird of life could suddenly flutter its wings and fly away.

It took a second for the stranger to realise that Shiba was hardly ahead of him when it came to bodily strength. If they fought with bare hands, he could thrash him to bits. He had a bit of an advantage only because of the weapon in his hand. But the cholai in his belly had made him quite wobbly and unrestrained. If he could snatch away the dagger in a sudden motion, certain defeat could be transformed into honourable victory.

The dagger was advancing rapidly. Aimed not at his chest, but his abdomen.The distance between life and death was only a foot or two now. The bathroom was walled on three sides. Shiba stood in front with the dagger in his hand. And Dhani was standing in the doorway of the bathroom. There was no way of running in any direction. This was like the boy Abhimanyu trapped in the maze formation. There was only one option now. Do or die!

Resting his back against the rear wall, the stranger prepared for battle. Come, death! But know this, that I am not dying like a coward. I will fight till my last breath. Come!

Shiba, drunk and blinded by the arrogance of power, could not really see this great explosion of energy coming. He came running and thrust the dagger towards the stranger's belly. And at once the stranger swung to the left with the speed of lightning. The dagger missed the target. There was only a long cut on the thin skin of the abdomen made by the base of the dagger before it swung to his right side. Here was the opportunity! Without wasting a moment, he gathered all his strength in his right arm and pounced upon the dagger. In one fell swoop, the dagger changed hands, from Shiba's to the stranger's.

A great warrior had said long ago that keeping a killer alive meant death. The stranger remembered that inexorable, infallible statement now. And then he turned the face of the dagger and thrust it directly and with full force into Shiba's lower abdomen. It was as soft as flour dough. Where the dagger met no resistance. It went right in. A mixture of blood and cholai spurted out like a sprinkler on the stranger's hand.

'Baba go!' Shiba's eyes seemed to bulge out of their sockets in severe agony at being stabbed suddenly. A stream of salty water rolled down from his eyes. They fell in drops on the floor of the bathroom, where he had trampled on the tears of many others. His eyes certainly saw the dense darkness of his impending death. He flailed his arm and grabbed the stranger. He gripped him firmly in an embrace with both arms. It was no embrace of love, but the coil of a python. The cunning Shiba was playing for time. So that his friends could come to help him. But he couldn't be given the time. Or else it could prove fatal.

Shiba was hugging the stranger, who now held Shiba's neck in the crook of his arm, and with his right hand he thrust the dagger repeatedly all over Shiba's back. But none of the stabs were powerful ones. Shiba did not release his grip even after eight or ten stabs. One had to grant that he was powerful. He had several lives in the single body. Perhaps this was called the life of a tortoise. Even after three-fourths of the body was cut off, the remaining part moved.

The tables had turned. The sudden happenings left the sentry Dhani bewildered. In his drunken state, he couldn't exactly figure out what needed to be done. Leaving his guru behind when he was in serious danger was not right. But how would he go near the mobile and aggressive dagger! Money, a wife and a sharp dagger, were never one's own. They belonged to whoever happened to possess it.

The house had been constructed in the old style. The bathroom with the commode was outside the building. With a water tap in front of it. A few bricks had been laid on the muddy slime in front of the bathroom door. The bricks had been pressed into the soil by the pressure of feet. Dhani cleverly picked up a brick, and aiming it at the stranger, he screamed out, 'Let him go, fucker! Let him go, or I'll smash your head. Let him go, I tell you!'

The stranger did not desire the embrace. He wanted to let go of Shiba. But where was Shiba letting go of him? He was putting up a fierce fight. He would see it to the end, and then let go. Finally, the impatient Dhani hurled the brick. He had aimed it at the stranger's head, but it didn't touch his head. Because Shiba was standing in front of him like a shield. The brick hit him behind his head. As a result, there was a *fotash* sound, like a coconut cracking open. Shiba emitted a groan and dropped down to the floor like a severed palm tree. A friend had done to him what an enemy would have. With friends like that, one didn't need enemies.

The first brick missed the target. Now there was nobody in front of the stranger. Shiba, who had been standing like a wall, was gone. If another brick was flung at him, it would hit him. Dhani had bent down to pick up another brick, but he couldn't. Before that the stranger had pounced on him like a tiger, and plunged the dagger into his back with all his strength. A single plunge. But a perfect one. Dhani slumped face down to the ground.

The maze formation had been shattered. The fortress that had seemed impregnable had been penetrated. Now he had to flee. A successful retreat was also part of battle strategy. As the stranger ran out of the house, he saw Shankar running for his life, screaming, 'Hey, whoever's here, come at once! He has killed Shiba-da!'

But who would come! Whoever could have, had left the locality long ago. The lane was completely deserted. The stranger chased Shankar, with his dagger bared. He wasn't actually chasing him. He wanted to get out of this zone of death at once. Who on earth would he chase and kill! He was being chased now by Shiba and Dhani. Two men. Two corpses.

There was a culvert ahead. A man was standing there. It was Ramdeo, the old milkman from Bihar, who owned a cattle-shed. He was a long-time resident of the place. Through all his years there, he had seen that the people who were brought here on foot left on a bier. This was the first time someone was walking back. And that too after laying others down.

There was a foul pool beside the culvert. Ramdeo's buffalo-shed was on its far side. All the refuse washed away from the cattle-shed flowed into the pool. Shankar jumped into the pool to save his life. But the stranger did not enter the pool. He ran along the bank of the pool, in the direction of the TB Hospital.

The stranger was fleeing in search of a hiding place.

13

An Act of Expediency

Evening was turning to night. A terrifying, endless night descended upon the fringe of the city. It was one of those black nights of the 1970s, riddled with police and C.R.P. bullets. Hidden away in the night was a brutal and cruel hand that craved blood. There was a tiger claw on each of its five fingers. No one knew when those claws would tear someone's heart out, so once it turned dark everyone trembled in fear. Their throats turned dry. In their distraught hearts they prayed to the god of good fortune to protect them from danger, so that the night passed well.

It did for some, but not for others. Some people read the newspaper the next morning, while some made the news in the paper. The pages of newspapers nowadays were stained with blood, with their grand descriptions of orgies of death.

It was a murderous time indeed. The exultation of killers everywhere, the whole country seemed to be a land where murderers roamed free. There seemed to be no way for people to survive now. You could survive only if you were able to snatch the weapon away from the killer's hand. You would survive if you knew the art of killing the killer. There was no other alternative.

And not with any compassion, or kindness, or forgiving, or remorse; the hairy hand had to be rendered useless by ruthless blows. Its right to kill had to be snatched away. It had to be violently taught to be human.

Jatadhari Guru had once said, 'Just think about the gigantic creatures that once existed on earth, whose footsteps made the earth tremble. They were wiped off the face of the earth because they were unable to adapt themselves to changing nature, and had failed to acquire the experience of surviving by launching a counter-assault.'

Jatadhari had said, 'The elephant is so huge, but it does not know how to be unchained and free. That's why a chit of a mahout sits with his foot on its head. A cow has two sharp horns, but it has forgotten how they could maul someone. That's why people could thrash it and make it pull carts and ploughs under sun and rain. Whether it's an elephant or a cow, its meek nature is its greatest enemy, and the reason for all its troubles.

'But observe the ant, the bee, and the beetle. How tiny they are. But no one has ever been able to bring them under their control. Or even kill them. They are free and independent. Why is that? Because if anyone harms them, they know how to hit back. That's why they still exist today, with their courage intact. Do you know what a bee sting is called? The sting of death. It knows that it will die once it uses its sting. But it does not shirk that; it delivers the sting and dies. That's why even an elephant flees the moment it spots one.'

Having concealed himself in the semi-darkness of the morgue, behind the refuse heap of discarded, unusable, torn blankets, mattresses, broken cots and suchlike, the stranger was reflecting on what Jatadhari had told him.

His left arm was almost paralysed now. Terrible pain radiated from near his shoulder and elbow, where the dagger had pierced him, to every part of the body. He did not have much time. The toxic pain would devour him altogether. He was feeling cold, and the pulsating veins on his temples signalled a fever's arrival, which would consume him. There was a hint of warmth in his breath. There was already a slight trembling in his arms and legs. As the night advanced, symptoms would emerge from all parts of his body. He would suffer stomach cramps from hunger. He had not eaten anything since morning. He had gone off to Loharpara before he could eat at Chhechan's eatery. And then he had had to hide himself in this rat burrow. Fortunately, Nanu's liquor den was closed now. Or else he would have never been able to use this hiding place. Perhaps this was an instance of sport for a cat being death for a rat.

But for how long could he hide here like this! There was no one outside because of the fierce afternoon sun. That was why the stranger had been able to run along the canalside and enter the dense jungle of morning glory without being spotted by anyone. After that he had almost crawled here and hidden himself behind the refuse heap. A day had gone by without anyone coming here. But that didn't mean that someone wouldn't come tomorrow. Everyone knew him. News of his derring-do would have reached not only this hospital, but spread throughout Jadavpur. And it was to be expected that the police were already looking for him. But he had not been caught yet, perhaps because the police never imagined the offender to be sitting so close to the site of the incident.

It had turned dark. He ought to do something now. And it had to be done before the terrifying time set in, when his body turned weak and immobile. He ought to have visited a doctor by now. The wounds needed to be dressed, and he had to take a tetanus shot. He would need at least thirty or forty rupees for that. But where would he get so much money right now?

The stranger pondered: so would the wounds get infected, full of pus, before he arched in agony and died? Was there no means of survival? The stranger tried to recall, one by one, the faces of those who could possibly aid him in this moment of crisis. No, they were all so poor that they themselves went for days without food. And it was difficult to find Ganesh and Gopal now. He would be spotted if he went out in the open now in his present condition to look for them in the station.

And the stranger also realised that he was no longer who he had been until just a few hours ago. He was now a criminal who was eligible to receive the highest punishment under the Indian Penal Code. If someone provided him help, the police could haul him up for that very reason. It would not be right to do anything that might get a band of poor youths who loved him into trouble. It would be better to suffer alone.

The wounds had stopped bleeding. There were red-black clots over them. He had looked for cotton and bandage material among the refuse, and bandaged his elbow. He couldn't do anything on his shoulder. From time to time, there were lightning bolts of pain from the spot. The cut on his abdomen was also turning very painful. But neither of the wounds were of a fatal kind. However, if the wounds were not treated in time they could become life-threatening.

He lay immobile like a corpse in the dark room where corpses were brought at one time, counting the seconds. After a while, everything turned silent and still. A clock rang somewhere, intimating it was midnight. But that was clock time. Actually, it was midnight in this locality in the city fringe even before a quarter of the night was past. That was because of fear! Terror, which lay coiled like a serpent in everyone's mind. Of what was coming the next moment! No one ventured out unless it was absolutely urgent.

The stranger slowly raised himself. He prepared himself to take another risk. There was no option besides that. He tucked the fish-shaped dagger with the brass butt into his waist fold. There was no greater friend than that right now. He emerged from the morgue like a nocturnal creature now. Looking all around and confirming that no one was watching him, he walked through the jungle of akanda and morning glory shrubs behind the morgue, skirting the human and pig excreta that littered the place, and arrived at the edge of the foul sewage drain. He glanced westwards, towards Loharpara, which began past the sweepers' quarters, where he had ignited a conflagration which was going to last for a long time.

He considered himself extremely fortunate. Not because he was still alive, but because he was free although he was only about three kilometres away from the spot. That was only possible if one was extremely brave, or enjoyed political patronage, which wasn't the case. That meant that he was either a great fool, or that there was no other place for him on Indian soil.

There were no lights here on the canalside. The only light came from the lamp posts on Raja S.C. Mullick Road and from the hospital. But they were very dim here, and the stranger thus had an incorporeal appearance, of someone, who had died long ago, and was therefore no longer worried about dying.

Every action has an equal and opposite reaction. When someone murdered somebody, he killed himself in a sense. He had to spend his entire life standing over his own corpse. He found no release from that. The stranger walked along the canalside and came to a stop at the intersection of Raja S.C. Mullick Road. There was a tea-shop on the right-hand side and a provisions store on the left side, while across the road was Jadu Babu's bamboo yard and Mahalakshmi Sweets. All were shut. The stranger looked leftwards and rightwards along Raja S.C. Mullick Road. The 8B bus-stand intersection was a kilometre away on the right and the Jadavpur police station another kilometre from there. On the left side, Baghajatin Mor was a kilometre-and-a-half away. The whole road looked like a long black tape laid over the earth.

After a little while, a police van with its powerful headlights blazing like hyenas' eyes came speeding from the direction of Jadavpur police station. Eight or ten policemen were packed tightly inside the anti-riot vehicle with a protective mesh. Their eyes were alert, as were their fingers on the triggers of their rifles. Looking at them, it seemed they would not let go of the slightest opportunity to kill people, as if they were thirsty for blood now after many days of rest, their fingers itching.

The stranger slipped underneath the machan of the provisions store where dogs usually slept in the afternoon to escape the sun.

People now feared the police much more than they did goondas, scoundrels and mastaans. The more decent a person was, the more he feared them. They could enter any place or premise, at any time, on the pretext of a search. They could thrash anyone they wanted and break their bones; lock someone up for as long as they wanted in the station lock-up. They could shoot someone too, if they fancied doing that. The police minister, Manu Ray, had given them carte blanche to do whatever they liked.

The stranger emerged from his hiding place a long time after the police van went by. Standing in the darkness of the lane, he looked to the left and the right. What was he looking for? He was looking for prey. This ominous time had made him go beyond all the boundaries of distinction and analyses regarding right and wrong, and moral and immoral, and brought him face to face with a difficult situation. He had no way of turning back. He could only move ahead now. What happened after that depended entirely on his fate.

A lot of time went by as he sat waiting in the darkness of the lane like a tiger on a hunt. Nowadays nights were terribly dark, and smeared with terror. He couldn't spot a single passerby who could appear as a saviour to the stranger in his moment of peril. The one or two people around were taxi and vehicle drivers. But they were anxious about how quickly they could speed away and reach a safe destination.

The stranger himself was unaware of how long he eventually sat there, staring at the road. Nor was there any accounting for the amount of his remaining blood after the injury that went into the bellies of mosquitoes. Suddenly he spotted a rickshaw coming very slowly from the east. There was a passenger seated in the rickshaw. From his appearance, it was clear the rickshaw-driver was drunk, as was the passenger.

The passenger was someone everyone in this locality knew and was fond of. He was Anadi Das, a singer of revolutionary songs. He lived near the Satyananda Thakur Ashram, in Jadavpur. His wife had left him, and out of anguish at that he drank to his gills. Although, strictly speaking, he belonged to the anti-Congress camp, they paid him no attention because they thought he was harmless. He sang and so on. They let him do that, as long as he didn't hurl any bombs at them.

The stranger now emerged from the darkness of the lane and went and stood in the rickshaw's way—'Stop!' Seeing the bared dagger in his hand, the rickshaw-driver stopped his rickshaw in fear. But the man seated in the rickshaw was someone the stranger was very fond of. He was a much-respected and loved person.

Why, it was only the other day that he had heard him singing the hypnotic song, 'Runner', full-throatedly, in Viveknagar, about the jingle of the runner's anklet bells ringing through the night as he ran carrying a load of messages. He seemed to be asking people, the society and the present times, the question: *how long would the runner continue running? When would the night end, and the sun rise?*

The stranger did not know who wrote the lyrics, or who first set it to melody and made it into a song. But that night the anguished question came alive in Anadi Das's voice, the melody had touched the unknown stranger. And right then his face had become imprinted in his mind. This man is one of us.

He hesitated for a moment. What a day of cruel irony it was today. After that, brandishing the dagger at his own man, he said, 'Give whatever you have quickly. If you shout, I'll kill you. I already killed two. They can hang me only once even if I kill another.'

The rickshaw-driver's name was Lohar Kartick. But not because he lived in Loharpara. Actually, Kartick's rickshaw moved so fast that none of the other rickshaw-drivers could keep up with it. Anadi Das had taken Kartick along to Boral for some work. Liquor was a bit cheaper there. That's why the two of them had had a bit before returning. And now this threat had arisen!

Kartick said, 'Anadi-da, do what Jibon says. Give him whatever you have. Or else he'll really kill you.'

Anadi Das realised that there was no use resisting. One only had to skim through the daily newspaper to know about what befell those who did not fear such people. Anadi Das softly said, 'I have only twenty-two rupees in my pocket. After paying you four rupees, I'll have eighteen left.'

Kartick said, 'You don't have to pay me. You treated me to booze and snacks, I won't take the fare from you. Give all the money to him.'

Anadi Das was an empathic man. The famous song of his, which he had sung after the brutal mass murder in Srinath Colony, *'They didn't let my Khokon live'*, had moved a thousand people to tears. But the stranger could not show any compassion or kindness to that man now. He had to survive. Someone had told him once that whatever one did for the sake of survival was not wrong. And if at all it was wrong, that could be rectified.

In a grave voice, the stranger said, 'Give me your watch too.'

The much-respected artist removed his watch and held it out towards the stranger, together with the twenty-two rupees.

The stranger didn't know until tonight that an occasion would arise when a person he was genuinely fond of would be trampled under his feet. A man who went around with a torch from door to door, singing songs of awakening. *'Awaken O proletarians, O starving slaves!'*, who believed that people would certainly awaken one day. That would be the day the country would attain freedom and an egalitarian society would be built.

But Anadi Das's belief had been shattered tonight. Would words ever be able to blossom again from his mouth as flowers, as dreams and love, and as fire? Or would they be jaded and out of tune in contrarian rage?

The stranger did not know what exactly he would do. For now, he only said to himself, 'Dear one, please forgive me. I am an unfortunate wretch, captive to circumstances now. See how my hands are stained with blood. I didn't smear that on myself voluntarily. I can't wash it off if I want to. I can never make an auspicious beginning with these hands. Forgive me.'

14

Satish

Beyond Nanu's liquor den, to the west, was a small field. Next to that was a long hospital ward, two actually, wards No. 30 and 35. Satish was the name of a ward boy in these two wards. He was the father of a son and daughter, and lived in Rajpur. He used to cross the railway line, go through Loharpara, and then take the path in front of the culvert to reach his workplace. His duty hours were from 2 p.m. to 10 p.m. When he went through Loharpara yesterday, whatever happened there had already taken place a little while earlier. So he did not take the usual route when he was returning home. He left via the main gate of the hospital, walking along Station Road and going a long way after crossing the railway line.

But he took his usual route on the way to work today. Observing the 'grieving' Loharpara, he actually felt a secret sense of delight. Ever since people from Loharpara had driven a spike through the head of a youth named Tapas from Rajpur, the locality had assumed a toxic nature in Satish's eyes. He couldn't stand the place, but he couldn't say anything either. Oppressed folk had to erase their inner rage themselves.

Was Tapas related to Satish? It wasn't Tapas alone, after all so many like him had been devoured by Loharpara. So why was Satish so troubled by that? Tapas was a nobody. He was just a decent youth. He stood beside people in their joys and sorrows the way Jibon did. Jibon did not tolerate any injustice, and neither did Tapas.

Satish had not really heard the subject being discussed anywhere yesterday. Who knows why people's lips seemed to be sealed! But they were speaking a bit today. In the tea-shop, at the rickshaw stand—wherever a group of lowly folk gathered—they whispered, 'The son of a bitch died like a dog as he deserved to. That's what happens when you go too far. The fucker used to smuggle rice earlier, and then he started riding a rickshaw. It was after he joined the red party that he turned arrogant. But he's finished now. Tigers kill buffaloes everyday, but yesterday a buffalo's horn was thrust up a tiger's arse.'

Someone quoted the Bengali proverb about the impoverished weaver who bought a male calf, thinking he would improve his plight by ploughing the field, but only failed in both weaving and farming.

All these points of view were about Shiba. And as regards Dhani, the son of Harinath Moyra, owner of Sri Hari Sweets, they said, 'The boy was a decent sort earlier, he got ruined once he started associating with Shiba. He'll be bloody lucky if he survives now.'

The fact that they had hauled up Jibon and taken him in order to kill him was no longer unknown to anyone. Many people had observed him being taken by them. For instance, the cholai seller Kalo, who was still owed three- or four-hundred rupees by Shiba. Gesticulating with his hands, he said, 'I'm telling the truth, so what's there to be afraid of! He took Jibon along right in front of me.'

Basudeb used to work in a tea-shop in front of the Jadavpur police station, and then he got a chance to get into the Home Guard. He said, 'The fewer the criminals, the better. What good would he have done by staying alive! Only killed more people. Rather, with him gone, a bloody nuisance has come to an end!'

Satish was a timid sort. He was especially afraid of ghosts. Back in his childhood, he claimed to have seen a ghost and then come down with a fever. An amulet brought the fever down, but the fear still remained. Because of his fear of ghosts, he never ventured towards the old morgue. That place, surrounded by a jungle of shrubs, took on a desolate appearance once darkness descended. It seemed like some people were tramping through the darkness. Earlier, when Nanu's den was running, some people frequented the place. But that was no longer the case.

Just before Satish walked through Loharpara yesterday, he had seen a man running along the canalside. Satish had got just a brief glance of him, before he disappeared in the dense jungle of morning glory. Shortly after that, he had spotted Sompal and his wife, whose face was entirely veiled by her ghomta, coming walking from the direction of Raja S.C. Mullick Road. They worked near Baghajatin Mor, in a number of houses, as well as a school. They were laughing as they walked, carrying their buckets and brooms. If the man who had been running had gone in the direction of Raja S.C. Mullick Road, he should have encountered Sompal and his wife on the way. But would they have been laughing in that case? Wouldn't they have been a bit scared?

Satish had asked him, 'Coming now, Sompal?'

Nodding his head, Sompal had replied, 'It's my usual time.'

'Did you see anything on the way?'

'What do you mean?'

'Did you see someone running?'

'No! Why, did something happen?'

'I heard something happened in Loharpara.' After Satish said that, he thought he had left out something. So he asked again, 'Did you see Jibon? Did you meet him on the way?'

'No!'

There was a foul sewage canal on the right side, across which was Ramakrishnapur. And on the left was the thick jungle of morning glory, next to which was the large pool. Insects swarmed over the pool covered with hogla reed. Next to that was a vacant plot of land, which was also full of weeds, and littered with human and pig excreta. The old morgue was situated to the right of that. There was a wall behind the morgue, beyond which was a field, which was referred to as 'Mosque'. Perhaps there used to be a mosque there in the past. But it was no longer there. This field too was covered in a jungle of shrubs. But of late, wealthy people had started clearing the jungle and building their houses there. A curving road went directly from here to Raja S.C. Mullick Road. Nanu had once jumped down from the roof of the morgue and fled down this road while being chased by the police. The hospital on one side, and the field called 'Mosque' on the other. It was as if there were two different countries on the two sides of the wall. Hardly any news from the other side reached this side, and hardly anyone from this side was interested in news from the other.

Satish pondered, so Jibon had not gone towards Raja S.C. Mullick Road. Maybe he had realised that if he headed in that direction, he wouldn't get a hiding place. That he would get into trouble. Then where would he go?

Where would he think of hiding? Something inside him told him that he had to be hiding in this jungle of hogla reeds, morning glory and akanda shrubs. If this entire wooded stretch had to be surrounded in order to catch him, that would require a lot of people. There weren't enough people in Loharpara for that, and especially those who would stand by Shiba.

And even if two or ten such people did come, or if the police did, they would have to come via Loharpara, or along the canalside from Raja S.C. Mullick Road. In that event, he could escape by jumping over the wall and running through the Mosque field.

Satish didn't know whether the stranger had made such calculations before coming here, but his own calculations pointed to this hideout. So he kept peeping in the direction of the thicket in between his chores in the ward. After a long time, he thought he saw some movement there. Pigs foraged for food in this jungle. So if their bodies grazed against some shrub, it moved. But that movement was of a haphazard kind, whereas this was like a long scar being made through the shrubs, ending at the rear of the morgue. It had then occurred to him—if it's really Jibon, and not pigs, he might go across the wall to the other side. But if he did that, the construction workers and masons on some plot in the Mosque field would spot him. Or else he could enter the disused morgue through a broken window.

From where Satish was, the eastern and southern sides of the morgue were not visible. So he couldn't figure out what exactly might have happened. But he was a lot less afraid today than he had been yesterday. He supposed that even if Jibon had hidden there yesterday, a whole night had gone by since then; he must certainly have left at night and gone to some safe place.

It was afternoon now. It was desolate all around. A crow sat on a roof cornice and cawed hoarsely. A mother sow with piglets in tow was grunting in the sweepers' pig sty. A dog sat panting with its tongue hanging out.

Once Satish's duty hours were over, he tiptoed across to the doorless morgue. He looked this way and that, and slipped inside. There was a room within the large room, with a heap of torn blankets, mattresses, and assorted discarded items. It was like a small hillock. He heard someone calling him by his name from behind the refuse-heap. 'Hey Satish-da, I'm here. The timid Satish began to tremble all over, and in a trembling voice, he asked, 'Is it you, Jibon?'

'Yes, it's me.'

Satish took a few steps forward. Putting his hand against the wall to keep his balance, he asked, 'Have you been here since yesterday? Why didn't you go somewhere far away?'

The stranger replied in a voice full of fatigue and pain, 'I couldn't do that.' After that he emerged from behind the heap. 'Who else besides you knows that I'm here?'

'I don't know. But I don't think anyone knows. Or else wouldn't someone or the other have come by now? Why are you here? I don't know what's happening. Run, or else there's trouble coming.'

The stranger said, 'How will I go? You can see my clothes are full of bloodstains. If I step outside like this, anyone will figure things out. I'll get caught.'

'Don't you have anything else to wear?'

'I do. But that's in Anjali's place.'

'Who's Anjali?'

'Oh, she runs a liquor den. She lives in the shanty settlement past Platform No. 2.' After a pause, the stranger continued. 'Can you do me a favour, Satish-da?'

'What?'

'Can you get me a set of clothes from Anjali's place?'

'But I don't know who Anjali is.'

'Whoever you ask there will show you the way. All right, forget about Anjali, you know Jatadhari Guru, don't you? Or Ganesh and Gopal? Whoever you find, ask him discreetly to get a set of clothes from Anjali's house and give it to you. If they ask about me, tell them to come to the Kalighat crematorium at eight. I'll meet them there. Once it's dark, I'll get out of here somehow or the other.'

'Let's see what can be done.' Satish was thoughtful for a while. And then he said, 'It looks like you haven't eaten since yesterday! I have a rice meal, do you want to have that?'

'Where did you get rice?'

Satish replied somewhat hesitantly. 'Almost all the patients in my ward are in a critical condition. Some can move, and some can't. But I bring the meals of all the patients from the kitchen. A lot of that remains uneaten. I put that into my bag. Everyone does. Rice is the grain granted by Ma Lakshmi, if it's not eaten, the pigs will eat it. If I take it, my children will survive. Do you want to eat?'

Whatever the rice was like, after all it was rice! The stranger could not refuse. Satish spread out a newspaper, and laid the rice, a boiled egg, and some alu bhaja on it, which he took out from his bag. There was no water to wash his hands. He rubbed his hand on the lungi he was wearing to clean it as much as possible, and put the first handful of rice into his mouth. He realised that the human blood on his hand still had a strong stench.

Blood did have a strong stench. Police dogs followed this smell to find culprits. Since the culprit's identity was not unknown in this case, the police did not have to take the assistance of the dogs. Or else, the stranger would have been in the police lock-up by now.

The stranger had assumed that Dhani too had died. He learnt from Satish now that he was in hospital. He was being treated there. It looked like he would survive, but he would suffer.

Life was really strange. A series of unimaginable and incredible incidents and accidents. Just like someone you had no discord with could suddenly attack you, similarly, someone who wasn't a close friend could stand by you during an emergency, and render unsolicited favours that are hard to imagine.

That's what happened in the stanger's life today. Satish, who the stranger had always thought to be soft and weak-minded, had appeared as a saviour.

The stranger thought to himself, I don't know what will happen tomorrow. But if I stay alive, I'll never forget you, Satish-da.

15

Haran Sardar's House

The whole day went by somehow. Hopes of getting something, anguish over not getting something, the pain of losing something after getting it—nothing really worried her very much. But once the sun set and it got dark, or the moon rose in the sky, Surabala's heart seemed to wail and cry out. She felt a terrible void inside her, as if an endless emptiness from all around was gripping her. I don't belong to anyone in this vast universe, no one belongs to me, no one whose hand I can hold and walk a few steps, on whose shoulder I can lay my head and weep in times of grief. What an unfortunate wretch I am!

Surabala was already twenty-three or twenty-four years old. This was the age when women laughed wildly. A time to cock a snook at sorrow and poverty and sing and dance, when one had the opportunity to wring every last bit of joy from life and drink it to one's gills. She could do that. She could have enjoyed everything if she hadn't been so skinny, dark-skinned and unattractive. If her appearance had been of a passable type, some man would surely have nestled her in a corner of his heart. A woman's life and youth without a man's love were like a tree that could not bear fruit, or a lake without water.

The life of the unsatisfied and incomplete twenty-three or twenty-four-year-old wept sorrowfully now under the pain of an old memory. It was a memory of the time when she had no awareness or understanding of anything. It seemed to Surabala now that she was then a naive girl who came upon a thousand-rupee note while walking on a desolate road. The note was a bit torn and soiled. But after all it was money! But she could not figure out what she would do with the money. The immature village girl had no idea that she ought to keep it carefully somewhere, and that by using it at an opportune moment and place, she could buy necessary goods, as well as a lot of joy and pleasure. She had mistakenly thrown it away, unaware.

She wore frocks then, not saris. If she had been of sari-wearing age, she would have acted like a mature woman and knotted it in the fold of her anchal and kept it to make her future joyful. She regretted not having thought of that then. The naive girl was made to take off her frock one night and wear a sari. She wasn't comfortable in that. She had thought that it was a burden, a bother, a torment imposed on her. That's why even before she reached the age by which one knew and understood everything, she had lost the currency note due to her own fault.

She felt very distraught now when she remembered that. More so, when she observed some girl of her age buying bangles, earrings, alta and face snow from the market or mela. Her wretchedness became ever more acute. An inevitable pain writhed inside her chest then. It poisoned every part of her mind, as if a snake had suddenly thrust its fangs into her.

Sonka Sardar was the same age as Surabala. She had been married earlier. Her husband used to drink and beat her up a lot. She left him after she had a child. What would Sonka do then, after all she had to do something to feed herself. She had to save her child as well. She returned to her father's house and began selling toddy. She went with her mother to Park Circus, carrying a pitcher of toddy. That resulted in her 'love marriage' with a Bihari worker in a shoe factory. He had come to drink toddy, and was entranced by Sonka. She lived with him now in a rented place in Bondel Gate. She was quite happy. She had another child. Her Bihari husband returned to his village once a year to visit his first wife.

When Sonka's husband went to his village, she left for her father's house in the village. She had four or five saris, all of an expensive kind. Apparently, the price of one such sari was twice what Surabala earned each month.

The train that left Sealdah at 4.10 p.m. in the afternoon had arrived at Champadali station after an hour-and-a-half's run. Carrying a big earthen pitcher on her shoulder, Surabala had got off the train and advanced just a few steps on the platform when she suddenly spotted a familiar face, a man she liked. He was standing next to the signboard bearing the station's name. But why was this man here?

This man was none other than the one whom fate had turned into a villain, the fugitive whom we referred to as a stranger, and people knew as Jibon. The day he met Satish, and asked him to get him a shirt and a pair of trousers from Anjali's house, Satish's duty hours were from 2 p.m. to 10 p.m. So it wasn't possible for him to do that in the afternoon. He went there at night, after finishing work. But he didn't go to Anjali's place, nor to Ganesh or Gopal, or even to Jatadhari's spot. He went directly to his own house, and picked up a set of his own clothes. He also took some antiseptic to apply on the wounds. Returning to the morgue, he told the stranger, 'I don't have anywhere to hide you, or else I would surely have arranged that. But you know so many people. Go away somewhere tonight itself. Don't stay here any longer. Nothing happened for two days, but who knows what will happen on the third day! Someone is bound to spot you.'

It was Jibon who knew lots of people. How did that help the stranger! After all, he wasn't Jibon, but only his replica. Where was he to go in this moment of peril! But he had to go somewhere. He couldn't remain forever in the morgue, like a corpse. So he had left his hiding place in the middle of the night. And after going around continuously from one place to another, he had reached here today. Out of the same plan of aimless peregrination.

He knew that there was a pawn shop here, run by the Gyne family. He had heard from someone that apparently one could pawn anything from pots and pans to gold and silver in the shop. But he hadn't remembered that. It was only after arriving here randomly that he remembered. His pockets were empty, the twenty-two rupees he had obtained had been spent. So he went to the pawn shop with the watch. He didn't want to sell it off, he would only pawn it for now. If he ever happened to have some money, he would redeem the watch and keep it with him. After that, he would drop it in the letter box of the singer's house at an opportune moment.

He got forty rupees from pawning the watch. The interest was five rupees a month. After a month's interest was deducted in advance, he received thirty-five rupees. If the watch wasn't redeemed within three months, it would be 'forfeited'. After spending two rupees on lunch at an eatery, the stranger had come here to the station. He was wondering where he could go. He had spent a night at the Kalighat crematorium, and another on the pavement in front of Kolay Market. Night was approaching again. Where would he hide?

Surabala, who was seated on a cemented bench a little distance away from the signboard, had been observing the stranger fixedly, and once she was certain it was him, she went up to him. 'Hey, do you recognise me?' She smiled, and said, 'How come you're here? Don't you live in Jadavpur any more?'

Surabala had asked several questions at once. Although the stranger had initially been alarmed when he saw her, he steadied himself and said, 'I'm waiting to meet a person here.'

'Who's that? A girl?'

'No, no, not a girl, a man.'

'What's his name?'

'You wouldn't know him. So what brings you here?'

Surabala pointed southwards, and said, 'If you go down this way for two miles, you'll come to a canal. My village is about a mile away along the canalside. One can also reach the village from Baruipur station, via Phultala. But since that's a longer route, we commute from this station.'

The stranger thought he shouldn't be silent. Who knows what the girl knew or didn't know about him. In order to appear normal, the stranger said, 'I love the countryside. The openness here. I feel suffocated in the congested city. If I get a place to stay in these parts, I'll come here.'

Surabala said, 'I don't like the city either. But there's no means of livelihood in the village. So I have to endure the pushing and shoving on the train and go to the city.'

'Isn't there any work here? I mean, for me. As long as I can feed myself.'

'Only during the cultivation season. But that's three months away.'

The two of them were conversing. Inquisitive eyes were watching them from all around. Their gazes frightened the stranger a bit. He wanted to be far away from any inquiring eyes. But if Surabala was in front of him, it was inevitable. So he felt uncomfortable. People would want to look. And they would look again if they liked her face. They would stare for a long time. If they didn't like her face, they would turn their face away and move on.

The place where they were standing was dimly lit. After sunset, the rural darkness set in slowly. The darkness in which Surabala's skin colour, her psoriatic fingers and toes, her nails full of grime and the mop of lice-infested straggly hair on her head were not visible. All one could see was a female body. A body which had some riches that satisfied the needs of men.

The stranger said, 'Everyone is watching us.'

'Let them!' Surabala said with a flourish. 'So what if they look? We are only talking, not doing anything else! Their looks can't harm us.'

The stranger was silent for a while, and then he asked her, 'Why is there a pitcher on your shoulder? What's in it?'

Slanting the pitcher to show him, Surabala said, 'It's empty, there's nothing in it. I had taken toddy in it. I run a toddy business here. I stopped going to Jadavpur. There's money in the toddy business. I make a profit of three or four rupees a day. How much would I get if I worked as a maidservant in a babu household! Tell me, didn't I do well by giving that up?'

'Where do you sell the stuff?'

'Do you know where Majerhat is? There are hundreds of factories in the area. The factory workers drink it. I'm not the only one, lots of people go there to sell toddy. They carry large drums on their shoulders. They make ten to twenty rupees' profit a day.'

Now that it was getting dark, the stranger thought that Surabala would leave. But she didn't. She put down the pitcher and sat next to the stranger on the cemented seat. For some reason, she bit her lip, and tried to dig the earth with her big toe. But as the ground was paved, that failed. Finally she said, 'Do you remember I told you something one day? Did you think about that?'

'Think about what?'

'Don't you remember?'

The stranger did remember. He couldn't help remembering. But he didn't want to bring that up right now. And what was the point in remembering that? When someone was headed either to prison or to the crematorium, he didn't want to remember anything other than what concerned him. He didn't think it was even necessary. Even though his eyes were ashen, and he couldn't spot any shore or bank, all he desired now was to swim in the sea of danger he was in and somehow reach some shore.

After a while, the stranger looked directly into Surabala's eyes, and asked her, 'Do you know why I'm here?'

'To meet someone.'

'No, that's not true. I made it up.'

'Then what are you doing here?'

'I've run away from Jadavpur. The police are looking for me. If they catch me, they will throw me in jail. Who knows how long it will be before I'm released.'

'Why are the police looking for you?'

'Because I attacked someone.' As the stranger said that, he thought he had said too much. There was no need to say that. So by way of explaining what he had just said, he then added, 'Do you remember the incident involving Golam Gazi kidnapping a child? I had beaten him up. It's because of that. That's why I'm running around. Can a man think about marriage, family and all that in such a situation? What can anyone who joins me now get other than danger and suffering?'

Surabala's eyes gleamed. The light of hope awakened in her. That light was visible even in semi-darkness. Someone had said that if someone desired something with their heart and soul, God would certainly provide it one day. Surabala had certainly desired it heart and soul. She saw herself as a pumpkin or gourd creeper, which couldn't survive and grow if there was no roof or support to hold on to, and couldn't bear fruit. A plant that didn't flower or bear fruit had no value. It was like a weed.

Surabala asked, 'Since you can't be in Jadavpur, where are you staying now?'

'I'm just going around from here to there. Sleeping in a field, or the pavement, or the crematorium.'

It was a very bad time for Jibon. There was also a terrible rule of God. A person couldn't be favoured without another person suffering. When an egg was broken, a life was lost, and someone else got an omelette on his plate.

Surabala's dad was half-crazy. She carried his craziness in her genes. Those genes pranced. She said, 'Will you come with me?'

'Where?'

'Wherever I take you!' And to allay the stranger's anxieties, she added in a stage whisper, 'I won't take you somewhere and kill you! You're sleeping in fields and so on, I'll take you to a better place than that. Do you know Bodra? My uncle lives there. Come, let's go there.'

'Fine, I can go there. But when they ask you who I am, what will you say?'

'Oh, I'll tell them something. After all, it's my uncle's house! You don't have to worry about that. '

'Still, tell me.'

'You don't have to be afraid, I won't get you into any trouble. My uncle's family is very nice.'

Overcome by a sense of ultimate attainment, Surabala's voice now trembled. Waves of joy arose within her being. She said, 'After a few days' outing at my uncle's place, we'll take a small room for rent in China Mor. Rooms are available at a low rent there. Didn't you say you like being in a village! So go and live there. I can feed you two handfuls of rice twice a day with what I earn. When it's not safe for you in Jadavpur, there's no reason to be there. Don't you agree with me?'

Surabala didn't want to think about the future now. She wanted to enjoy the present to the fullest. What might the future bring? Nothing at all. If everything slipped out of her hands, and all that she had attained lay in the dust on the street, she would go through her days in the same way as she was doing now. After all, nothing could be worse than it was now! Why should I worry about some problem arising in the future and thus forsake today's happiness ?

'Aren't you afraid of me?'

'Why should I be afraid of you? Are you a tiger or bear!'

'People call me a goonda. And that's what I am.'

'Even if you're a goonda, aren't you a human being! So what if you're a goonda? Rajnath, in our village, was such a big goonda that he killed his uncle. He was sentenced to life imprisonment. He was released from prison after fourteen years and got married after that.

Doesn't he love his wife! Or else how does she produce babies every year! Does a thief steal from his own house, or a tiger eat its own cubs? So you're a goonda, and someone else is a sadhu, but that's for people at large. What does that matter to people at home? You are still the same to them.'

Surabala finished speaking and sat quietly. The stranger couldn't figure out what to say. Night was descending upon the rural railway station. Meanwhile a train arrived. Two women alighted from the train. They were from Surabala's village. One of them called out, 'Hey Suro, aren't you going home?' The other woman replied, 'When he lets her go!' After that the two women giggled. As they walked past them, one of them flung a jibe at her in jest. 'Swallow it whole, Suro, no need to chew it.'

Surabala again said, 'If you're coming, let's go. People are looking at us and thinking all kinds of things. Who knows what gossip the sluts will spread.'

The stranger repeated Surabala's own words to her. 'After all, we are not doing anything. We are just sitting. What does it matter what people say!'

'That's what I'm saying. We didn't do anything at all, and yet we are shamed. Listen, when I get into a pond because there are fish there, and if my feet get dirty with slime and silt, you know what, I just wash it off with soap!'

The stranger stood up now and said, 'Let's go.'

'Where?'

'Wherever you want to take me! As long as it isn't inconvenient for you. Don't blame me later.'

Surabala bravely replied, 'Let's go first, we'll see to the rest later.' And then she walked ahead of the stranger, thinking to herself. The thought of her unfulfilled life burned her up again. I was lost, directionless, in a vast sea. But I will plunge underwater now. As I keep plunging deeper, if I reach the seabed, I'll touch soil again.

Champadali was a bustling mofussil town. There were lots of fireworks factories here. Chinese folk used to live here at one time, which was why an intersection there was called China Mor. They were possibly the ones who developed the fireworks industry in its early days. A major part of the fireworks that locked people's ears on the night of Kali Puja with their explosive sound, which was enough to make the earth and the sky above quake, went from here to the markets and shops in Calcutta.

Walking slowly, they exited the station and went and stood at the main road. Surabala bought some jilapis from a sweetmeat shop. After all, she was visiting a relative. One shouldn't go empty-handed. The bus arrived half an hour later. Surabala boarded the bus, almost pulling the stranger along with her.

Once the bus went past the urban area, they saw meadows, paddy fields and different kinds of greenery, within which lay small, impoverished villages. There was no question of electricity, there were kerosene lamps in the shops at the intersection. One saw the melancholy, bleak faces of a few people in that light, faces that had no smiles. There was no light in their eyes, and no dream of a future possibility in them. Those people seemed to have died a long time ago. They were a collection of dead folk.

'What are you thinking about?'

The stranger looked at Surabala. Women were compared to rivers. The river in Surabala's mind was in full flow and susurrating now as its waves lapped the banks. A feeling of celestial love spread to every part of her being like a sweet melody.

'Hey, tell me what you're thinking.'

'I'm wondering where we're going.'

'You're going with me.'

'That's right. I'm wondering where I'm going with you.'

These words resonated in the stranger's mind for a long while. Where are we going? How far away is it? Are we there yet? Would he ever return? To his former location? And his former situation?

The bus finally came to a halt at a triangular junction. They got off. It was pitch dark outside. One couldn't see beyond one's hands.

There was a shop at the intersection, lit up with a petromax lamp. The whole world beyond the area lit by that seemed to be covered in tar. A broad, dusty, rugged pathway ran through a field. Surabala held the stranger's hand and took him along the path.

A couple of other people besides them had also got off the bus. One of them asked, 'Hey, where do you live?'

Surabala did the answering. She said, 'I live in Begumpur. I'm going to Haran Sardar's house. He's my uncle.'

'Oh my! Are you Sannabala's daughter Suro?'

'Yes, that's me, dear.'

'I couldn't recognise you after all these years. I am Balai Nayak's mother. Do you recognise me? Who's with you? Your husband?'

Surabala laughed heartily and said, 'Although you couldn't recognise me, you recognised him perfectly! It's exactly as you said. So what do you think?'

The old woman widened her eyes and peered in the darkness. And then she said, 'It's a man. That's all that matters. You have to make a few adjustments, here and there. If I were to tell you that it would have been nice if he was a bit taller, or that he looks younger than you, that would be pointless. Don't they say that you ought to knot a torn string on a garment, and not tear it off! I'm saying the same thing. One shouldn't say anything that hurts others. After all, how long is this life of ours? All I want is to spend my remaining days with the little bit that I got in life.'

Surabala didn't say anything, and the old woman too walked silently along the path. The stranger suddenly noticed that the pitcher was not on Surabala's shoulder. He asked her, 'What happened to the pitcher?'

Shocked, Surabala said, 'Oh no! I think I must have left it where we were waiting for the bus. No, I think I had it with me when we got into the bus. I forgot to pick it up when we got down.'

The old woman now said, 'So how come you are suddenly visiting your uncle at this time of night? You won't find your uncle at home. They've all left for Arda to sing kirtans at the shraddha ceremony of Kali Naskar's father. They took Balai along to play the kansi-drum.'

'I didn't plan to come here. We came here suddenly after a problem came up. And just see, I forgot my toddy pitcher on the way.'

The stranger panicked now. There was no certainty regarding what this girl of limited intelligence and indiscreet speech might reveal. But Surabala handled the situation. 'I was returning home from Calcutta. Someone told me that my grandmother was very unwell. So I thought I should come and visit her. '

Those who had got off the bus and were walking ahead of and behind them took roads on the left and right sides and went away. Only the two of them remained on the pathway. An empty field lay on the left side. Paddy would be planted here during the rainy season. There were various kinds of trees and shrubs on the right side. Orchards of mango, blackberry, palm, coconut and banana and clumps of bamboo, interspersed with a few huts, ponds, cattle sheds and piles of paddy straw. The stranger asked, 'How much further?'

'Are you scared?' Surabala laughed, and then almost wrapping herself around the stranger, she said, 'Don't be scared. When I'm with you, what's there to be scared of?'

'No, it's not that. I was just asking how much more we have to walk. I'll have to come this way if I have to return for some reason.'

'Why would you need to return?'

'In case I'm not allowed to stay.'

'Why won't you be allowed to stay? I'm his niece. He's my Ma's only brother.'

'That may be so. But who am I?'

'Didn't you hear what I told the old woman? That's what you are. His niece's husband.'

'But why will your uncle accept that? After all, he knows your husband. Doesn't he?'

Without the least disconcertion, Surabala said, 'You are my second husband. I got married again. Who's to say anything?'

They walked in silence for a while, and then glancing at the stranger, Surabala said with a tone of determination in her voice, 'It's not as if you are visiting the red-light district—what's there to be worried about?'

She held the stranger's hand and gave a tug. 'I hope you don't mind that I was married earlier. If you have no objections then I have no more worries. Don't they say that if you are with the man of your heart, even living in a forest is joyful. Don't say anything before them. If they aren't hospitable to you, we'll leave. There are so many trees in the fields, we'll spend the night under some trees. And then we'll see what happens tomorrow. Won't you be able to stay the night?'

They were silent again for a while. And then Surabala began. 'Anga Pishi in our village says that women are like the brass and bell-metal plates in a babu's house. Whether it's a Kaora, or a Bagdi, or a Pode, or a Muslim—no matter who eats from them, nothing happens to the plates. Once they're washed with soap and ash, they are clean and shiny again. What happened? Why aren't you saying anything?'

'What will I say? You're talking and I'm listening. If both of us talk, who'll listen? Someone has to listen, isn't it? Carry on, I'm listening.'

'I've talked for a long time. Now you say something.'

'What shall I say?'

'Whatever you like! Good or bad. There's no one else here, just you and I. I'll listen to whatever you say.'

'I have nothing to say.'

'Nothing to say! I'm so close to you now, and yet you don't feel like saying anything to me. What kind of man are you!'

'There's a big danger hanging over my head.'

'That's why I'm with you. You helped me when I was in trouble, so I'm helping you now. I'll keep you in a place where no one will ever find you.'

Haran Sardar's house was at the very end of the village. He was a man of repute in this Kaora hamlet. He possessed something which no one else did. Two bighas of paddy land, a fish pond and a bamboo clump. He also had a kirtan-singing group. For all these reasons, he was a man of special esteem for the thirty or thirty-five Kaora households in the hamlet. The Kaoras were fishermen by caste, who caught and sold fish. They played drums in festivals and ceremonies, carried palanquins, worked as day labourers and prepared toddy. But times had changed and most people could not stick to their caste occupations. Every household was engaged in beedi-making. There were mahajans or middlemen, who weighed out and gave the leaves and tobacco, paid wages of twenty rupees for a thousand beedis and collected the goods.

By the time the two of them reached Haran Sardar's house, the people there had finished their dinner and were getting ready to go to bed. Surabala called out twice to her uncle from the courtyard, then climbed up to the verandah and called out to her aunt. An old woman came out with a kerosene lamp in her hand. 'Who's that?' she asked in a rasping voice, holding the lamp up to Surabala's face.

'It's me, Didima, Surabala. Sanno's daughter, your granddaughter—don't you recognise me?' Surabala hugged the old woman. 'I haven't come alone, I've dragged your grandson-in-law along. I heard that Mama has gone to sing kirtans. I need a verdict from him. He pronounces judgement on right and wrong for the whole village, let him judge on my matter now, and say who is at fault.'

The old lady was beside herself with joy. She said, 'Your uncle has gone on a four-day job. He'll only be back on Friday night.'

Friday! That meant three days. Surabala's face was clouded with worry. Unless she met her uncle, her problem wouldn't be solved. And it was a complex problem. She said, 'It's difficult for your grandson-in-law to be absent from work for three days. But let that be. There's no way he can leave until the matter is settled. He'll stay on even if Mama returns after four days.'

Surabala turned to the stranger, who was still standing in the courtyard, and roared out, 'Why are you standing so meekly there?

She's my grandmother, come and pay your respects. I suppose your parents didn't teach you that one ought to respect elders. How much can I teach you!'

The stranger stepped up to the verandah, and as he bent down to touch the old woman's feet, she moved back a few steps and said, 'Let it be.' She spread out a torn mat. 'Sit here.'

Surabala's aunt had joined them in the meanwhile. She was fair-skinned and, by rural standards, she had once been quite a beautiful woman. But after bearing three children, very little of her beauty had remained. After the stranger sat down on the mat, she peeped at him sideways through the gap in her ghomta. She asked, 'Where's the boy from?'

'He's Bangaal, dear!' Surabala said, and before the stranger could say anything, she added with a flourish, 'Don't they say, a Bangaal who's a beggar for prawns? He's a perfect Bangaal like that. His parents lived in a rented house in Jadavpur.'

After that, in the manner of narrating her complaints against the stranger before a judge, she said to her aunt and grandmother, 'Tell me, Didima, didn't we belong to a high caste earlier? Didn't the king turn us Kaoras into a low caste in rage after some of them entered the king's court once in a state of intoxication, with their bodies covered in mud and slime? Mama knows everything. But this man's father says that we are lower than the Bangaals. You tell me, Mami, is Kaora lower or Bangaal? It's been ten or twelve days since we secretly got married. But his father is so stubborn that he simply won't let me into the house. And this man says, I'm the only son of my parents, I can't hurt them, I'll do whatever they say. If you can't hurt them, then why did you do love marriage with me? When you took me to Kalighat and put sindoor on my forehead in front of Ma Kali, I became your wife, didn't I? No one may know, but Ma Kali is a witness. So what are you going to do with me now? The one who has to get married, gets married one time. And the one who can't get married, fails even after a thousand attempts. And what will you do when someone comes into my womb? I want this matter to be decided upon. That's why I've dragged him here. Let him state in front of Mama whether he will leave his parents and stay with me, or not. If he doesn't, I'll go to the police station and file a case.'

Both her grandmother and aunt realised it was a serious problem, which was too difficult for them to solve. But Haran Sardar could do that. He had settled matters in an instant on innumerable occasions. Let him return, whatever had to happen would happen then. Surabala's problem was also a problem of theirs. After all, she wasn't an outsider, but their own kin.

The girl was born with a scorched fate. Her first husband left her and ran away. Be that as it may, she had found a husband now but he did not belong to their caste—he was a Bangaal. What was she to do if he also left her? Haran Sardar was the only one who could counsel her, and so there was nothing to be done until he returned.

Surabala's aunt said, 'Suro, take your husband to the pond, so he can take a bath. We finished eating, soaked the leftover rice in water, and were about to go to bed. Have something to eat, and go and lie down in the verandah on the side. We can get fish and prawns tomorrow morning. I'm going to bed now. I can hardly keep my eyes open after working all day.'

Surabala's Didima served the rice. Just watered rice, without any curry to go with it, only some salt and a green chilli. The times were bad, and for most of the people in rural Bengal, even this was something valuable. Haran Sardar was fortunate, whatever happened, and however things were, food was cooked twice in his house. A preparation with chuno, or small fish, was served for lunch. When guests or in-laws visited, they never left without a meal. Not many people here were so fortunate.

After they had eaten, the old woman prepared a bed for them in the verandah on one side. She herself went to sleep in the verandah on the other side. The house had three verandahs. And the large room was occupied by Haran Sardar's wife and her three children.

The stranger was lying on his back now and trying to review whatever had happened in the last few days and today. Everything unfolded like a play—it occurred to him that some playwright who was sitting out of sight had cast him and made him act in a role that he had never imagined. One could say he lay immobile on the stage, in the role of a dead soldier. The principal actors did whatever had to be done with him. Shiba, Satish and Surabala. A dead soldier! Who had no chance to move or speak. Whether he was turned over, or made to sit, he simply had to comply. Time had consigned him to silence and immobility. After all, what else could he do now, other than to surrender himself to fate, to the future!

He was lying on the mat made of date-palm leaves spread out on the floor. A thorn pierced his back through the thin sheet. And crawling through the darkness of the house came a fierce hunger. Which would grasp the stranger in its long arms and demand its right. Which would fill this darkness with its emptiness. Moaning with the thirst of long years of unfulfillment, it pounced upon the stranger. A pack of jackals howled somewhere far away.

16

A Domestic Arrangement

If one walked three or four miles southwards from Baghajatin Mor along the rugged road, the huge field one came upon on the left side was known as Lalu Kakar Math, or Uncle Lalu's field. Ward No. 3 of the Bijoygarh refugee colony touched the north-eastern corner of the field. If one went past the field known as Layelkar Math, as Lalu Kakar Math was pronounced in the area, and advanced southwards some more, one came upon another field on the left side. This was called Barobhuter Math or the field of twelve ghosts. This was not full of pits and bushes like Layelkar Math, it was quite bare and even. There was a temple on one side of the field. A large number of sadhus gathered here at the time of the Gangasagar Mela in mid-January. The mela, or fair, ran for a week. The sadhus lit sacred fires, and there was a ferris wheel. The refugee colony adjoining this field was called Srinath Colony. A man by the name of Abhay Pandit lived here, although he was known now not by his name, but his surname. He was Pandit-da to the youths of the locality.

He had been a brilliant student of Jadavpur University at one time. The university had been a major stronghold of the ultra-red party then, whose leader's name was Majumdar. He was killed in an encounter on the day of the state assembly elections in 1972. Under his leadership, almost the entire population of youths in Srinath Colony had swung in that direction.

This was a time before the election of 1972. The Congress party too was not so strong in this locality then. It hardly had any workers apart from a handful of khadi-clad leaders belonging to the Jagaran Club. All the violence and murders in the entire Jadavpur locality was limited to that between the two red parties. As casualties mounted on both sides, the reds were getting weaker fighting among themselves, and seizing that opportunity the Congress was expanding its organisation. And that had the tacit support of senior officials in the police administration.

But all that came later. So when the hostilities between the two red parties were at their peak, a murder squad from one of the red parties attacked Srinath Colony from three sides one night. It had rained heavily that night. A group of youths were sleeping in a room. Perhaps they were dreaming of the possibility of a beautiful new morning, when there would be a smile on every face, joy in every life and hundreds of fragrant flowers in every garden.

Armed murderers banged on the door, thus putting an end to the dreams of potential joy. A band of sleepy-eyed youths who had not yet entered their twenties were dragged as their parents watched. The next morning, people of the locality saw with tears in their eyes five mutilated bodies floating in the muddy rainwater in Layelkar Math. Some had their eyes gouged out, the intestines of some others were exposed. Some were holding their own decapitated heads. A writer by the name of Mahasweta Devi had written a story about the horrifying murders and the singer Anadi Das composed a song on it. *'Amaar Khokonke owra banchte dilo na. Banchar boro shadh chhilo owr, sheitai oporadh chhilo owr. Notun diner aagomoni gaan gaite dilo na.'* They didn't let my boy live. He loved life, and that was his crime. They didn't let him sing about the arrival of a new dawn.

It was Abhay Pandit that the murderers were after the most. But they couldn't catch him. He managed to escape somehow. Within a few days of the incident, following a joint operation by the red party and the police, the ultra-reds had no organisation left in the Jadavpur area. By then the Congress party too had grown in strength. They entered the stage now to wipe out the battle-weary reds. They too took over the area with country bombs and pipe guns, in the same way that the red party had once done.

Abhay Pandit was forced to go underground then. The fire of revenge smouldered like burning chaff within his breast. The faces of his five friends floated constantly before his eyes. Revenge was called for. Nothing else but revenge would do. Ideals and policies could be thought about later. Marx, Lenin and Mao could be attended to later. All he yearned for now was the death of the murderers. The people who had killed Bubai, Poltu and Bapan had to be punished. They did not have the right to live in this world. Even if he had to join hands with the devil for this end, he would do that. 'I'll kill the butchers with my own hands.'

Abhay met with Bhajan Gupta, a leader of the Congress party in Bijoygarh. He expressed his wish to join the party. Bhajan Gupta wasted no time, and he made Abhay a member. And one day Abhay, now with arms and money, returned to his locality, treading over blood. The hand that once held a pen now spread fire via a 9 mm pistol.

Abhay had once spent a few days in Palpara. It was still an impenetrable stronghold of the ultra-reds then. That was when he became acquainted with a youth by the name of Jibon. For some reason, he took a liking to the poor but honest boy, who was simple-natured and extremely brave. Abhay left the shelter in Palpara a few days later for some other place. He lost contact with Jibon. The police then launched a fierce assault. Some youths in Palpara died as a result, while some others were arrested and put in jail. The whereabouts of the rest was unknown.

Abhay had almost forgotten the name of Jibon because he had not seen him in a long while. He thought that perhaps he was dead. But now he found out that he was still alive. Very much alive. Although Loharpara was five or six kilometres away, Abhay Pandit got the news of happenings there. The rickshaw-driver Balai had brought him the news. 'Pandit-da, he's been killed!'

'What happened?'

'Shiba of Loharpara is dead.'

'Who killed him?'

'Jibon. Chandal Jibon. One of our rickshaw-drivers.' He laid emphasis on the word 'rickshaw-driver'.

Riding a rickshaw was a lowly occupation in society. Despite being human, they worked like the bullocks and donkeys who pulled carts, because of which they lacked dignity or respect in society. Anyone could thrash them at the drop of a hat. Someone could address a rickshaw-driver disrespectfully as '*tui*' despite the latter being as old as his father. Balai was elated that such a rickshaw-driver had killed a leading mastaan. The resounding tone of his voice seemed to suggest that this achievement was not his alone but that of the entire rickshaw-driver community. Jibon had been a rickshaw-driver for a few days many years ago. Balai knew that. That's why he was so delighted. But he didn't know that Shiba too had been a rickshaw-driver at one time.

Abhay Pandit gradually remembered Jibon. He then asked, 'Where is Jibon now? Have the police caught him, or was he able to flee?'

'I heard that he fled.'

Rabi-das had a tea shop on one side of Barobhuter Math. That's where Abhay Pandit camped. Quite a few youths arrived there, one by one. Their confabulations would continue until late at night. Much of the discussions today were centred around Shiba. And Jibon's name too came up in that connection. Someone said, 'I knew him when he lived near the ink factory.' Someone else said, 'He had come to our house to cook when my brother got married.'

A third person said, 'Sen Babu had beaten him up very badly.' But everyone concurred that he had done something tremendous—to go to Loharpara and do that required real guts.

Someone had once said that one never found what one was looking for in Calcutta. If one was looking for a barber, it would be the man who chipped the grinding-stone who would appear. If one happened to be looking for, say, Ram Babu, one would reach Rahim Chacha's eatery instead.

Balai rode a rickshaw. He had been in prison for a long time, he was shrunken after much suffering. That is to say, he used to drink earlier, but he gave that up and took to smoking ganja. Consequently, he spent much less on that. He had come to the Pir Baba mela today looking to buy a tiny packet of ganja, but to no avail. An officer had been posted in the local police station, he was a 'rascal'. Those who sold ganja and illicit liquor, as well as those who rented rooms by the hour, were all exasperated with him. No one knew when or where the next raid would take place. And when someone was caught, he thrashed them badly. You couldn't get intoxicants at ease like before. If Balai had known about this situation, he would have bought a couple of packets of ganja from Jadavpur itself. After all, could one invoke Pir Baba, or Baba Bholenath, without imbibing something, and even if one did so, would a sense of devotion awaken! How could there be liberation unless there was devotion? There was such anguish in human life. Who could liberate you from that? Pir Baba could, as could Baba Bholenath.

Balai made a pilgrimage to Tarakeshwar once a year, carrying the lath with two pots hanging from it on his shoulder. And he came to this Pir Baba's mazar at least once a month. But he had never imagined that something like this would happen in Baba's place.

A man said, 'Walk eastwards along the railway line. You'll see a large banyan tree on the left side. You could try there. I'm not sure, but you might get a little bit from the sadhu who sits there.'

It was an addiction after all! The banyan tree was about a mile away. There was a level-crossing there. The road on the northern side went via Naranpur to Bodra, and on the other side it went to Kudali, where it curved westwards and ran along the canal to Begumpur. Arriving at the banyan tree, Balai saw a man walking behind a bamboo-laden bullock cart on the dusty road, who looked just like Jibon. He looked again, and was certain that it was Jibon. The same face, the same gait. He could recognise him even though he had tied a gamchha over his head.

Balai ran up to him. 'Hey Jibon! Do you recognise me?'

Jibon, that is to say the stranger, had an axe in his hand. He gripped the handle firmly with both hands and squinted at him enquiringly. 'No, I don't? Who are you?'

'I'm Balai, I drive a rickshaw at the stand near Barobhuter Math. Can't you recognise me! We used to go to booze at Anjali's den. You used to be there, don't you remember?'

'Don't you go there now?'

'I don't drink anymore.'

'Oh! How come you're here?'

'I've come for Baba's mela.'

'Okay, go to the mela.' And saying so, the stranger walked ahead briskly. Balai followed behind him, and said, 'I have something to tell you.' The stranger continued walking, and said, 'I don't have time now, the bullock-cart is moving ahead.' But Balai continued behind him, and said, 'It's good news.'

He eased the grip on the axe and suddenly came to a stop. 'Good news? What's that?'

'Pandit-da was talking about you. Pandit-da from Srinath Colony.'

'What did he say?'

'That he knows you! You don't have to run around. I think you should meet Pandit-da. He hangs out at Robi-da's shop all day. Once it's night, go via Ranir Mor and meet him. You have guts.

Pandit-da needs guys like you. I'm sure he'll arrange something for you if you speak to him.'

'What will he arrange ?'

'A place to stay, and food. And not being caught by the police. Pandit-da is now Pankaj-da's right hand. Once he speaks, why Pal Babu, even his dad won't harm a hair on your head. After all, what did you do? You killed one of the reds. But that's considered a good job these days. Listen to me, just go and meet Pandit-da.'

The incident in Jadavpur was stale news now. Two or three months had gone by. Dead bodies were strewn all across West Bengal, and yet there were dozens of goondas around in the city's localities. Jadavpur was no exception. How could one blame the police! How much could they keep track of, and how many criminals would they search for? There was no more space in the prisons. It was natural for Shiba's case file to get buried under hundreds of other files. And Shiba was no eminent citizen. He was a criminal and an ex-convict. Why would the police toil on his behalf?

The stranger thought that it wouldn't be a bad idea to meet Pandit-da, if that meant being able to return to Jadavpur.

The day Surabala had reached her uncle's house in Bodra with the stranger, her half-crazy mother went out to look for her when she hadn't returned home at night. Selling toddy was an illegal trade. The excise police arrested you if you encountered them. But that was if you were a man. With womenfolk, they only smashed the pitcher. So why hadn't her daughter returned home? Some mishap on the way? An accident?

Surabala's Ma made and sold dung-cakes. She wandered around fields collecting dung, prepared the dung cakes, and went to the tea shops and eateries near Champadali station to sell them—a hundred dung-cakes for a rupee, with two more thrown in free. Although she was worried about her daughter, she still had to walk to the station with the sack of dung-cakes on her head. How would she buy rice if she sat at home and grieved! She laid down the sack in a shop, and rushed to the station platform. And she asked everyone she knew whether they had seen Surabala. Finally, Shashticharan from Bodra—her father's village—gave the news. 'Suro? Oh, she's gone to Haran Sardar's house. I saw her brushing her teeth at the pondside in the morning. Your son-in-law was with her.'

Son-in-law! Which son-in-law? Was it a secret marriage then? But in that case, why would she go to Bodra with him? What was wrong with her own house! With various questions like these vexing her, Surabala's Ma simply boarded a bus, without any clear plan, and bought a twenty-five paisa ticket. So let me go to my father's house. Let me find out for myself what the matter is. And after reaching there, what she saw, and what she made of that, filled her with joy and pain, light and shadow, hope and apprehension. What had the girl gone and done! But what other option did she have? The two thoughts lashed at each other.

Haran Sardar was not at home then. But other people of the village were around. They too had a point of view. Surabala was a woman, and since she had done something awkward, what else could one do but deal with it. She called some wise men like Nede, Pulin and Khagesh to Haran Sardar's courtyard and said to them, 'You people need to make a ruling. So that my daughter isn't ruined.'

Nede and Pulin were high on toddy then. Khagesh had not yet drunk any toddy, so he was sober. The three of them, and Surabala's Ma, grandmother and aunt, surrounded the new son-in-law. Like they were six charioteers surrounding the solitary Abhimanyu. There was no escape today. Nede was puffing a beedi. He let out a lungful of smoke, glared at the stranger with fiery eyes and shot a question at him like an arrow. 'Whom does your life belong to? You, or your father? If it belongs to you, it's your right to decide how you wish to spend it. You are the one who decides what you like and what you don't. How much longer will your parents be around? They'll be gone pretty soon! You have to decide whether you want to set up home with this girl, or not. If you decide to do that, then there will be one outcome, and if you decide not to, the outcome will be different.'

Surabala's Ma said, 'Think carefully before you say anything.'

Surabala's aunt said, 'If either of your hands are cut off, it's painful. If you want to be with your parents, you can't get your love. And if you want to keep your love, you won't have your parents. Since a doubt has entered your mind, it won't go away so easily. So tell us now whether you want to be with Surabala or not.'

Surabala thumped the stranger on his back. 'What's this? Why are your lips sealed like a shy bride? Say whether you want to start a family with me or not? Are you prepared to leave your parents?'

The stranger nodded his head. 'Yes, I am.'

'No, no, you don't have to tell us so quickly, ' Pulin said loudly. 'Think about it, think ten times. Think for ten days. A spoken word and a gun's bullet can never be retracted. If you give your word, you should know that. You can't go back on your word later, I warn you.'

Sober Khagesh got annoyed with the intoxicated Pulin now. 'He has given his word. He said he's willing. So why are you asking him to think about it? What should he think about? Can he say that he won't stay with Suro? He should have thought about such things before getting married. There's only one conclusion here, since you got married, you have to live with her.'

Fearing the exacerbation of the quarrel, the stranger said, 'Let my parents go to hell, I only want my wife.' He then looked all around, and continued. 'But starting a new family is not a simple matter. We need pots and pans, mats, bedding and mosquito nets. Given the mosquitoes in Jadavpur, you can't sleep without a mosquito net. We have to rent a room. Or else make a shanty beside the railway line. I need some time for all that.'

'How much time?'

'I need at least a month or a month-and-a-half.'

'All right.'

'What is all right?' Surabala said, as if pouncing on Khagesh.

'Didn't he say that he would rent a room, or make a shanty, within a month or so, and keep you there? You can stay with your father until then.'

Surabala said, 'So you're saying that I will stay with my father, and he will stay with his father. You don't know his father, Mama. Mark my words, once Jibon returns to him, he will get him married to someone else. He can't say "no" to his father. He will go meekly and sit down before the priest.'

'So what do you want then?'

'I won't let him leave. I won't let him go to Jadavpur. Let's see what that old rascal does. I'll keep him here.'

Discussions between mother and daughter, and between the mother and others, carried on for sometime after that. No part of the creature known as son-in-law was involved in the discussion. He was a wrongdoer on account of his father. So he was being judged for an appropriate form of punishment. He had no say in this matter, it was the jury and judge who would decide. Surabala's Ma expressed her position after a long time. 'If Suro and her husband want to stay here for a couple of days, have a holiday, that's fine. There are fish in her mama's pond, there's rice from the harvest at home, so let them eat and enjoy themselves. They can come to Begumpur after that. I know there's only one room and a verandah there, but what else can one do? Since it's my daughter and her husband, I can't send them away. We can all eat together for now. And when they have bought their own pots and pans, they can start a new household. There's a canal beside Begumpur. There's vacant land at the canalside. There are bamboos in the clump there. They can make a hut and live there for the rest of their lives. If his parents return to their senses one day, they can meet them. Otherwise, they can live happily in Begumpur. Surabala will sell toddy, and her husband can play the drum, or make beedis, or learn some other trade. He will carry on just like everyone else.'

The stranger was now a captive of time, or else he would have to submit to being thrown into a river with a strong current. So two days later, he followed Surabala to her house in the village of Begumpur. Their hamlet was at a distance from the main village, on the other side of a field. Thirty or forty families lived there. All the houses had earthen walls and roofs of thatch. Every one of them was below the poverty line, and they led lives of utter deprivation. No one possessed any land, or held a secure job. But the people were mostly simple and honest folk. Radhanath was honest too. He had an old feud with his uncle. He had struck him on the neck with an axe in a fit of rage. He had had to go to prison for that. But notwithstanding that, he did not have a bad reputation. So Surabala and the stranger spent quite some time here, with a semblance of safety.

Surabala would leave in the morning to sell toddy. She would return late in the evening and cook after that. The kitchen fire was lit at least once a day in every household here. If something was left over after dinner, that was eaten for lunch the next day. Men, women, old people and children—everyone was involved in some kind of work or the other. It was only the stranger who had nothing to do. He could not figure out what exactly he would do.

One side of Pagla Sardar's verandah was partitioned with a sheet of cloth, and Surabala and the stranger spent the night in the bit of space behind that. Irrespective of whether she got enough to eat or not, Surabala was very happy now. But despite that, a thought pricked her like a thorn. She told the stranger about what was on her mind one night.

'We are getting by somehow here, but what comes next? How much longer will we continue like this? The rains will be here soon. How can we remain in this place?' And then she herself advised him. 'Let us go and build a shanty of our own at the canalside.' Haran Sardar had inherited a bit of land, a pond and a bamboo clump from his father. There was a law now that a daughter was supposed to get a share of her father's property. So Surabala's Ma too had a right to all that. But she never claimed her right. She only took a couple of bamboo poles, or some bundles of paddy straw, or a maund or two of paddy, in times of acute need.

After discussing the matter with her Ma, Surabala asked her uncle for a dozen poles of bamboo and a kahon-and-a-half of straw. 'Mama, there's just one room and a verandah in the house. Tell me, how can we survive there? Don't we need some privacy? Please do something. It's not as if I am some outsider, after all I'm your own niece. A niece is like a daughter, isn't it?'

After a few days of procrastination, Haran Sardar finally gave the bamboo and straw. That was what the stranger was taking back on a bullock-cart now.

The best way to get to the Champadali railway station from the village near Bodra was to walk a bit and then take a bus. And from Begumpur, too, it made sense to walk a bit and then take a bus. But if one had to go from Bodra to Begumpur, and especially to the Kaora hamlet there, taking the bus meant making a significant detour. The easiest way was to go along the canalside, along the unpaved road that was as straight as a bowstring. But the stranger had not imagined that he would encounter someone he knew on that path.

But after the stranger met Balai and talked to him, a thought kept swirling around in his head. 'The enemy of an enemy is a friend.' Following that principle, Abhay Pandit could well give him a place to stay. There was no work for him in the village. People were running from the village to the city like crazed souls on account of poverty. The stranger needed a bit of money now. As he sat idly in the village, he thought it was unfair and immoral to feed off the hard-earned income of a woman. He was also worried about her getting pregnant because of their free association. She wouldn't be able to go to sell toddy then. How would they get by in that case?

He needed money because the arms of the law were very long. No one could flee and survive forever by evading the law. If the police swooped down on him like a hawk and picked him up some day, at an inattentive moment, money was the only thing that could protect him. Repentance or tears were of no avail then. Recognising the right to self-defence as a fundamental right, the Constitution of

India included some clauses and sub-clauses in this regard. But who would stand in court and state that this was an act of self-defence? Money would. If money was spent and some eminent lawyer was engaged. Or else the lawyer for the prosecution would scan the history sheet of the creature by the name of Jibon and prove beyond doubt that he was a habitual criminal. He couldn't be saved then.

In the guise of chatting with 'twenty-year' ex-convict Radhanath one day, he learnt that criminal cases never ended, unless they were killed. A dust-covered file could rise from the bottom to the top even after ten or twenty years. Fresh investigations and court proceedings could begin. But there was one way of finishing the case now—going directly to the court and surrendering, and coming out on bail to fight the case. And to keep fighting, from the lower court to the High Court, and then the Supreme Court. Fuck, some court or the other would surely rule in his favour. But that required hundreds of thousands of rupees. That was possible for people with millions of rupees. It was beyond poor folk. Did one ever hear about rich folk going to prison?

The stranger's days here passed without any trouble. The people of the village were so anxious about their own food and clothing that they hadn't found the time to engage in any revelry with Surabala's Bangaal husband. Womenfolk from a couple of neighbouring households had visited a few times in the initial days, and giggled a bit with Surabala, that was all. Everyone knew this was Surabala's second husband. But that did not seem to matter. There were several second and even third husbands in this hamlet. It was as if some God-like man had written down the rule of Kaora and Bagdi girls changing spouses repeatedly.

Ninety per cent of the people belonging to the Kaora community had no land to speak of. Their earlier occupations were carrying palanquins, playing drums, fishing and so on. But rivers and streams had dried up now. There was no sign today of what had earlier been a river flowing with a powerful current. How would they catch fish if the rivers had ceased to exist! The cycle-van, rickshaw and car had replaced the palanquin. The microphone and loudspeaker had replaced the drum in pujas and festivals. So how did this community feed themselves? They couldn't, nobody could.

Surabala was happy despite her acute poverty. She wanted to enjoy him fully. She did not want him to be out of her sight for even a moment. She wanted to hold him with a grip like that of a leech, or of a blind man on his staff. So she shut down her business, and stayed at home. As a result, they became poorer.

So one day the stranger decided that he had to leave the place now. He would go to Srinath Colony. He would see if something came of that.

17

Shelter in Srinath Colony

Standing atop the roof of the house, Bhajan Gupta cast his eyes in all directions. Everyone regarded him as the undeclared proprietor of this vast area which stretched as far as one could see. He had acquired this wealth after two years of untiring effort, and after much bloodshed. There was a time when he was unable to live in his own house, in his own neighbourhood. He had fled, and then taken shelter in the headquarters of the Congress party. After much discussion with senior leaders, a plan was hatched for takeover of the area. And acting according to the plan, he returned to the neighbourhood in the dead of night with a CRPF contingent, in their vehicle. A police camp was established at Jagaran Club, in front of his own house. After that he organised the youth of the locality, and armed them. And then he kept organising attacks on the reds who had taken over the locality. His party received the full support of the police administration.

It was Bijoygarh that they took over first, after two or three months of effort, involving a lot of killing and destruction, bloodshed and tears. Bhajan Gupta did not count the number of those belonging to the rival party who were killed. But the number of youths from his own party who were killed was substantial. This locality was home to some forty- or forty-five thousand households, and divided into thirteen municipal wards. After declaring the locality 'CPI(M)-free', he directed his attention to bringing the entire Jadavpur area under his control. Srinath Colony in the east, Padmapukur and Katju Nagar in the west, Azadgarh and Netaji Nagar in the south, and Mistripara, beyond Nabapalli and Narkelbagan, in the north—the immediate goal was to establish his leadership and authority in this vast stretch.

When he was engrossed in the efforts to take over Jadavpur, he needed the help of Abhay Pandit and all the other youths in his party. So the day the fleeing Abhay came and requested to join the party, he happily agreed. He remembered a famous piece of dialogue from a well-known film of the time—*Loha lohe ko kaat-ta hai*, it is iron that cuts iron. It wouldn't be bad if the red strongholds of Anandapur and Nabapalli were smashed with the help of the ultra-red Abhay.

That is what he did. And Abhay Pandit accomplished what he had desperately wanted by relying on the former's strength.

That was the period of war. Things were fine until then. But now it was a period of peace, which some referred to as the peace of the graveyard, and some others viewed as the temporary calm before a fierce storm that was imminent. Having arrived at this juncture, he was compelled to think afresh as regards Abhay Pandit. The man had been entrusted with so much power, and yet he did not abuse that to earn a bit of money, he wasn't drowning himself in wine and women, he always rushed to stand beside people when they were in danger—after all, these were not good signs. He was gaining in popularity by the day as a result, and what would one do if he demanded a party ticket in the next elections to the state assembly? It was he who had given a new life to Abhay Pandit! Where would he go then!

Politics was the name of a double-edged sword, with which you slayed your opponents, and when required wiped out one-time companions and colleagues within your own party who were vying to be your equal. There was no place for ethics or morality here. If one did that, one was bound to perish. And the people behind him would tread over his body and move ahead and rise upwards. So Abhay Pandit had to be ruthlessly put down without the slightest feeling of remorse or guilt. Just like he had opened the lid of a bottle one day and let out the genie, Bhajan Gupta would put it back there now. There was no other option now. He might not get the opportunity later if he did not do this right away. He could only tear out his hair in despair then.

But what exactly should he do, and how? At first, Bhajan thought he would have him murdered. Thereafter he realised that was not possible. There were at least twenty youths surrounding him at all times. No one could push their way through that cordon and reach Abhay. And if at all someone did, they wouldn't return alive. If they got caught, it was highly likely that the conspiracy would be revealed.

But just after that he got the idea of getting him arrested for one or two murders. If he spent some time in jail on a non-bailable charge, and thus left the locality, he would be on shaky ground after that. Before the thought slipped out of his mind, and he came down from the roof. After that he picked up the phone and called Pal Babu, the officer in charge of Jadavpur police station. 'I have something very important to discuss with you. Can you please come to my house? Or should I come to the police station?'

Only he knew what reply came from the other side, but seeing Bhajan's face it was evident that he was pleased. Light and shadow played over his entire face now. He drank a glass of water, put the glass down, and gazed at the image of Kali hanging on the wall. And then he inwardly said, 'You are wish-fulfilling, Tara. You do your work, Ma, and people say I do it.'

Jatadhari Guru had set out today to meet a young man who was a replica of Jibon. He had got the news many days ago. The man had returned to Jadavpur again after being in flight for quite a few months.

Each one of the trains that arrived in the morning at Jadavpur station had a different name. Like *shobjir train, jhiyer train, maachher train*—vegetable train, maidservant train, fish train—and so on. So the rickshaw-driver Ghoti Narayan had arrived at the market in Srinath Colony with a large basket of fish unloaded from the fish train. He did that every day. The fish seller 'Dandimara Kamaal' was his pre-arranged passenger. Narayan could have left after the basket was taken down. But he didn't. He was standing out of greed for a couple of damaged fish. But he would get that only after the market closed.

A long time ago, when the large wooden weighing scales were in use, which no one really uses now except for dealers in old newspapers, there was a word which was used extensively by fish sellers, 'Dandimara'. Thanks to those wooden scales, they could make one seer of fish one-and-a-half seers with their deft hands. So Kamaal had become such an expert in that job that the appellation 'Dandimara' came to be applied before his name, meaning cheating on the wooden scales. Of course, it was not everyone who called him that, but only his fellow traders and friends. And Kamaal used to say that his name wasn't Kamaal but 'Kamal'. He had adopted the other in order to bag a Muslim girl. He had started wearing checked lungis purchased from Basirhat. He couldn't bag the girl, but the ignominious name remained. The wooden scales had also gone out of use. But the name 'Dandimara Kamaal' stuck.

But whatever his disgrace, the fish he sold were fresh. This was why there was a queue of customers as soon as he arrived in the market. All the fish he brought was sold out in an hour, or an hour-and-a-half. If Narayan stood around for that bit of time, he could get two things; one was the damaged fish, and the other was taking Kamaal back on his rickshaw. While returning with Kamaal and two of his small fish with tears on their bellies, he spotted Jibon in the Barobhuter Math field. He braked his rickshaw at once. His feet seemed to forget how to pedal. He got off the rickshaw and almost sprinted up to him. 'When did you come here? I didn't see you earlier!'

Weariness was writ large on the stranger's face. 'I came a few days back. How are you people? Is everything alright?'

Narayan said, 'I heard that Shiba's brothers, Bocha and Shankar, are going around saying that if they find you, they'll shoot you.'

'They'll shoot me? Do they even have a gun?'

'I think they do, or else why would they say that? Maybe they managed to get one.'

The stranger's eyes seemed to blaze with rage. 'Then ask them to come here. They'll find me every evening in this field. Or ask them where I can meet them.' After a pause, he continued. 'That day, I was alone. That's why I got injured. If they are their father's sons, then instead of going around declaring what they'll do, let them do something. I'll give them a sound thrashing.'

There was a passenger in the rickshaw. And he had a train to catch. He couldn't be there for long. So Narayan had to leave. He said, 'I'll come and meet you, and talk to you later.'

The stranger had returned here a week ago. He was familiar with the name of Abhay Pandit, but he had never met him. But perhaps Jibon had. And he was Jibon's replica, and an actor performing the role of Jibon. But he was now so absorbed in that, and had penetrated so deep into the character, that the acting element could not be discerned. He had perfected being Jibon over time.

It was almost night. Gathering courage, he walked cautiously and arrived at Barobhuter Math, and after pacing this way and that aimlessly, he went and stood in front of the Robi Cabin, the only tea shop there. Beside which stood a line of rickshaws. There were four or five rickshaws parked there. The drivers were sitting on them. The stranger was scanning their faces, looking for someone. Unless he found him, he might not be able to reach Pandit. So he asked one of them, 'I can't see Balai. Hasn't he come today?' A rickshaw-driver replied, 'He has taken a passenger.' Balai returned some twenty minutes later in his empty rickshaw. After he parked his rickshaw in the line, he spotted the stranger. He came up to him and said in a whisper, 'Why are you standing here?' The stranger replied, 'I need to meet Pandit-da. Come along with me. I don't feel comfortable going by myself.'

'You don't need to go to his house. Just sit, have some tea. Pandit-da will be here very soon.'

'You'll have to introduce me to Pandit-da.'

'Let him come. I'll introduce you.'

Almost half-an-hour later, Balai said excitedly, 'Pandit-da's coming!' Following his line of sight, the stranger observed six or seven youths walking in his direction along the narrow road from the eastern side of Barobhuter Math that ran till the bus-stand. Which one among them was Abhay Pandit? How would he recognise him?

The stranger said, 'Go, Balai, and tell Pandit-da that I want to speak with him. There are other people with him, it wouldn't be appropriate for me to go. If he calls me, I'll go.'

Balai got the substance of what the stranger was saying. It was true, some things could not be said in front of others. And it wasn't right for everyone to know who was acquainted with whom. So he went alone to Robi Cabin. He took Abhay Pandit aside and said something to him. Abhay Pandit himself came out of the shop, and signalled to the stranger to come. It was a tricky situation. Wasn't the stranger consumed by hesitation? Was it fear? He didn't really know Balai properly, nor Abhay Pandit. He had taken such a big risk merely on the basis of a blind notion. A wise man had said a long time ago that your enemy's enemy is your friend. That was all he had relied upon. Even if he didn't help him, perhaps he wouldn't want to harm him. Even fools didn't seek to do someone any harm if they gained nothing from that; and so, the stranger walked ahead towards the man who had called him. The slim young man of thirty-five, whose face seemed to be unfailingly lit with a glow of light, smiled so warmly when he saw the stranger that it seemed he had known and loved him for a long time. As if he was meeting him after a long time in some unknown city.

Pandit said, 'What do you have in mind? Do you want to stay here?'

'That's what I was thinking,' the stranger said. 'If a place to live can be arranged, I'll stay here.'

'There are arrangements. There are a few more people who have fled their neighbourhoods. If you can stay together with them, there shouldn't be a problem.'

'What about the police?'

'Oh, I'll take care of that. Nothing will happen.' Pandit paused, smiled sardonically and continued. 'I never imagined that I would become like this. How things have turned out. Which camp was I supposed to be in, and where have I landed up! I feel terrible. But there was no other option.'

As they spoke, Abhay Pandit took the stranger to a vacant spot. And then he said in a low voice, 'Don't tell anyone, but I'm telling you. You should know that I am still what I was. I shall take on my real persona at the appropriate time. I'm only waiting for the right time. After all, we have to bring about a revolution. We were all born for the revolution, and we shall die for the revolution.'

The stranger realised that Abhay Pandit was saying all this thinking him to be Jibon. And he was saying it because deep down he felt uncomfortable for having switched camps. He wanted to conceal that.

After that he said a lot more, he talked until late at night. And then he sent the stranger off to the Naba Jubok Sangha stronghold. This youth association in Srinath Colony ran with Pandit's assistance. Eight or ten youths who had fled several localities were staying there now, who would be sent back to their own places very soon. Plans were being made for that. The stranger was accommodated there for the time being.

A few days later, the stranger left for Begumpur. He found that a date palm thorn had pierced Surabala's father's foot, and it had swollen up very badly. And he wasn't able to walk. He would either sit or lie down, moaning in pain. The few rupees he earned doing odd jobs was gone now. Surabala too had stopped her toddy business. So how would he get treated? There was fear of the wound becoming gangrenous if left untreated. And that meant death. But the stranger didn't have the means to stand by the imperilled family, and provide them some financial assistance. Abhay Pandit had arranged a place to stay for him, and food, which was a huge thing for a fugitive criminal. But he didn't give him any money. He couldn't ask for it either. So he felt terribly destitute now. By way of saying something, he said, 'Let me see if I can raise some money, I'll be back in a couple of days.' And he went away. But neither could he raise any money, nor could the stranger go back to Begumpur.

A few more weeks went by. He spent the whole day roaming around here and there, engaging in idle talk, and from time to time going in a group and making a round of all four directions. And when it was night, he went to the club to sleep.

Then one day, the officer in charge of the police station called Abhay Pandit to the police station for something important. After he went there, the police arrested him in connection with some cases. It was evident that there was a deep conspiracy behind the arrest. But it wasn't clear how extensive the web of conspiracy was. However, given the nature of the cases and the sections and subsections of the Indian Penal Code they fell under, it was highly unlikely that he would be released before ninety days.

Whatever had to happen would happen. What was the stranger to do now? It was as if he had taken shelter under a tree on a night of heavy rain, and the tree itself now lay uprooted. Where would he stand now? He couldn't show his face in Begumpur. The family was mired in poverty, starvation and sickness. He hadn't been able to help them in their time of distress. How could he go there now, and add to their burden?

It occurred to him that he could take the advice of someone at this time. That was none other than Jatadhari Guru. Perhaps he might suggest some way out. There wasn't much time, he had to leave this place. But he ought to meet Jatadhari Guru before that. So he sent Balai to the station. 'It's very urgent. Ask him to come and meet me. You know I can't go to the station.' After Balai complied and delivered the message, Jatadhari Guru did not tarry. He arrived with Ghoti Narayan to meet the stranger.

Jatadhari felt a secret pride regarding this youth. The kind of pride that a blacksmith, or potter, or carpenter felt. A piece of iron, or a lump of clay, or a block of wood, was generally considered to be of little value. Through their labour and skill, these people turned these ordinary materials into expensive and useful products. Something of little value was transformed into something expensive. That was not because of the iron, or clay, or wood. It was entirely the achievement of the creator-artist.

Jatadhari reflected. A youth, without a name or identity, had suddenly arrived at Jadavpur station one day and become famous. But that success was not of his own making. Jatadhari Guru's power of management was constantly at work behind the scenes. He had transformed him bit by bit, towards becoming stronger and more capable. It was too early yet to say whether what he had become was good or bad. After all, good and bad were relative concepts, which were never permanent. These concepts were re-evaluated and analysed over time. *However, he may be judged by time, whether as humane or a monster, I, Jatadhari, am certainly the creator of that.* Just like Swami Vivekananda's guru was Sri Ramakrishna, and Shivaji's guru was Ramdas, Jibon was Jatadhari Guru's disciple. The moon had no light of its own, it was lit up by the light of the sun. A guru attained merit and glory through the attainments of the disciple.

Jatadhari Guru found a somewhat concealed spot in a corner of Barobhuter Math. He was sitting face-to-face with the stranger after a long time. He looked at him fixedly for quite a while. The poor boy seemed to have become a hard lump with the torment of sorrow, hardship, anguish and danger. Clay was something extremely soft and supple. It dissolved in water. But once the clay was fired and made into a brick, it never dissolved.

Jatadhari was silent for a long time. Then he said to the stranger, 'Say something. Why did you call me? How will I understand if you remain silent?' The stranger then slowly narrated all that had happened from the time of the incident with Shiba until now. And then, with a cheerless smile he said, 'You look at people's palms and tell them everything about their past and future. So tell me what my future is. Will I live or die?' Jatadhari narrowed his eyes and said, 'I am a vendor of words. I sell words and survive. I'm telling you, you won't die. Mark my words.' He then looked at the stranger from head to toe, and continued, 'But anyone can say that, he doesn't have to be an astrologer for that. Because if you do die, will you be able to come back and tell me that I was wrong! That's why I am not thinking about your death at all. If you die, then you die. But I'm thinking about your survival. About where and how that's possible. People survive in prison too. Is that how you'll survive?'

A few people were walking here and there in the field. The evening arati had commenced in the temple. Some devotees had gathered there for prayer and blessings. Abhay Pandit's arrest had not caused any disruption in the daily life here.

After a while, Jatadhari said, 'The person you trusted and moved here for is no longer around. You can't be certain about your safety either. Someone could inform the police, and the police could swoop down and pick you up. When it's cold, people cover themselves with a shawl. But when the sun is up, the shawl becomes a burden. There's no longer a war taking place between the Congress and the CPI(M). So why should they support you? Isn't there a saying that when an idol worth a hundred-thousand rupees has been immersed in the river, where's the need for a two-rupee drummer, let him perish too! Do you think the people who pushed Pandit behind bars will spare you? I can't believe that.'

'So what should I do?'

'You have to leave this place as soon as possible. Today itself, if possible. Right now. Who knows what conspiracies are being hatched even as we speak.'

'But where shall I go?'

'Why, isn't there Begumpur?'

'Those people are terribly poor themselves. How can they feed me?'

'But you must still go there.'

After some thought, Jatadhari said, 'Try to bury yourself there somehow for ten days or so. I've considered all the aspects. I will think about what can be done. Something or the other will come up.'

'Do you think so?'

'Absolutely.'

'You seem to be certain.'

'I'm an astrologer. I can see the distant future.'

18

The Quest for Gold

Man was after all only human. Just like he could never become God, becoming a monster or Satan was also beyond him. Neither of them ever erred. Whatever they did was flawless. But man made mistakes at every step. One foot and then the other got caught in the trap of error. Some were able to pull the foot out and return to the correct path, while others could not. The one who couldn't do that got caught in deep slime and drowned.

Jatadhari Guru was an astrologer, he knew about the position of the stars and planets, and their influence. He could tell one's fortune by looking at the palm. But just like a doctor can't treat himself, an astrologer can't read his own palm to know his destiny. So he made an error.

Angulimal, the son of Bhargav, the priest of the king of Kosala, desired education, in order to attain fame and success. But one little mistake led him to the horrifying path of killing a thousand men. His revered guru had pushed him to that act.

Whether in Bengal or in Bihar, it seemed that every railway station had been cursed by God. And so, wherever there was a railway station, there would be some shanties and shops, and just as illicit liquor dens would come up, so would an anti-social underworld. Like lice in hair, a hidden subterranean tributary of a band of creatures of darkness flowed within the mainstream there.

There was a youth who ran a small cholai den beside the Jadavpur railway station. He had a unique name—Mahadeb Molla. It was impossible to distinguish him from any set of ordinary youths. Thirty-year-old Mahadeb was not really a mastaan, or goonda, because his name had not entered the police register until then, he had not been in jail. But he kept track of a lot of things in the sphere of darkness.

Mahadeb Mollah presented himself before Jatadhari Guru one day. 'Guru, I have some fabulous news. What should I do?'

A large number of biscuits, of course, of the 'golden' variety, bearing a Hong Kong imprint, were secretly smuggled from Bangladesh via river, and arrived at places like Kakdwip, Namkhana and Diamond Harbour. This wasn't some cock-and-bull story, it was a hundred per cent true. It could be verified from police reports too. The gold made its way by bus or train to the major jewellery shops in the city of Calcutta. It was then melted and made into ornaments in the dead of night, behind closed shutters.

Mahadeb said, 'I have a confirmed tip. A large shipment will be moved on the Diamond Harbour local within a few days, either on the 12.30 p.m. train or on the 2.10 p.m. one. It's a solid tip. I'm in a tizzy!'

'Why? Why are you in a tizzy?'

Mahadeb said, 'Just think about it, Guru, some village man, he doesn't even know what's in the gunny sack, someone tells him I'll pay you a wage, deliver the sack at this address in Bowbazar. And so, he does that. He'll be passing through our station. There's nothing wrong in robbing a thief. Just think about it, Guru, if we can snatch that sack, we'll be settled for life. I'll go from a beggar to a bhadralok in one go. I'll never be in need again. Fuck, if I get a license for an English liquor shop, I can live in comfort for the rest of my life!'

Mahadeb paused, and then continued enthusiastically, 'Do you know why I'm so keen on doing this job? Because there'll be no fucking police involved! Those moving the gold are criminals themselves, the consigner himself is a thief. If he goes to the police station and tells the truth, the police will lock him up in jail first. Isn't it? So how can he go to the police!'

If what Mahadeb said was true, and one assumed that the man was only a deliverer, who didn't know what the sack contained, and his job was only to deliver the sack at a particular address in return for some wage, a doubt still remained. Were those who were in this trade such amateurs? There would certainly be one or two people to keep an eye on the man, and to keep watch over him. They could well be armed. They would watch from a distance, to see whether the delivery man and the goods encountered any danger, or if he tried to slip away with the goods, and take necessary action. Jatadhari expressed this doubt to Mahadeb. 'How do you know he's alone? Isn't there anyone to help him?'

'There is.' And then Mahadeb blurted out, 'But he won't be able to do anything. If we go and stand in front of him, he'll be the first one to flee.'

'Did he tell you that?'

'Yes.'

'What do you mean?'

'Why do you want to know the meaning, Guru!' Mahadeb turned towards Jatadhari, and said, 'Who do you think tips off the police about counterfeit currency, or gun factories, or a major robbery? It's one of the gang members who does that. The watchman himself is my informant!'

'Does he know what's in the sack?'

'He didn't know that initially. He found out a few days ago. He's been in a tizzy since then. He said, "I'm like a fucking bullock carting sugar. I just carry the load, without getting even a lick of the sugar. I deliver gold worth a hundred-thousand rupees, and get paid twenty-five or fifty rupees. There isn't another bullock like me on Indian soil. "'

'Now that he knows what's in the sack, why did he tell you? Why doesn't he run off with the sack?'

'He's scared. Just like he's keeping watch on the delivery man, perhaps there'll be someone there keeping watch over him as well. That's why he gave me the tip. He said, "Do it if you can. But you must give me a share. Don't try to double-cross me." I really want to do the job. You're the one who said that it's not wrong to do something wrong once, in order to be able to do well and do good deeds all one's life. You said that even God forgives that one fault.'

Jatadhari Guru was caught in his own net. He said various things in various contexts. When times changed, the meaning of what he said also changed. He no longer remembered when or why he had said that. But right now, he thought Mahadeb was not saying anything wrong. What was the point in sticking to the honest path? He knew the fate of honest folk. Honesty meant acute poverty. Poverty meant living a dog's life. Whoever wants to, kicks you. It was better to be dead than to lead such a life.

'So what do you think, Guru?'

'What do you want me to say?'

'Shall I do the job?'

Jatadhari thought for a while, and then said, 'I know that all the tips you get are correct. But do think about all aspects before you decide. After all, I won't be in any danger if something goes wrong, you're the one who'll die. Don't they say, "Look before you leap"? Not leap and then look! If you bite into a brick when you're starving, it won't ease your hunger, you'll only break your teeth. Is the tip you got correct? Think about it.'

'Shall I bring him to you? Will you speak to him?'

'No, no, not at all!' Jatadhari said in alarm. 'Don't bring him to me. Don't even mention me to him. If you make a couple of rupees, you can give me a paisa if you feel like, or nothing if you don't feel like. I have no qualms about that. But don't mention my name even by mistake.'

They were silent for a long time after that. The two of them drifted along opposite banks of the same river, with different streams of thought.

After a while Jatadhari asked, 'What are you thinking about?' And then, observing that Mahadeb wasn't being able to answer him, Jatadhari now asked him, 'Do you know about the Mahabharata? The Pandavas wandered through forests and mountains for twelve years, and they spent that time thinking about what they would do, and how. That's why they won the war in just eighteen days. After all, how much time does it take to do the real job? It's the planning that takes time. Have you thought about how you'll do the job? Or are you simply floating in the air? Whether the job you do is a small one or a big one, it's still like a battle. So tell me what your plan is.'

'Some of us will board the train two or three stations earlier.'

'Okay.'

'The one who'll keep watch on the passenger will signal us from afar about the wagon and the seat the man with the sack is sitting on. We'll board the wagon and get into position. The moment the train moves from Jadavpur station, we'll pounce on him and snatch the sack. You know there's track maintenance work going on near the railway gate at Khalaspur. The train moves very slowly on that stretch. We'll get off there. That's what I had in mind.'

'Who else will be with you?'

'You wouldn't know them! There's Gobindo from Anandapur, Haru from Narkelbagan, Aurobindo from Rajpur, and me. All of them are brave boys. They won't slip up. They'll give their lives if need be. They have only one thing in mind—no more of this dog's life. We'll take a chance, and then whatever has to happen will happen. There's only one man, won't the four of us be able to handle him?'

'There may be just one man, but there are hundreds of people in the wagon.'

'What are you saying, Guru! The public is extremely wary nowadays. No one wants to poke their nose into other people's business. Look out for yourself first is the motto. And the people on the trains are even more cautious. It's not his father who's in trouble that someone will risk his life to stand by him. They'll run away as soon as they see the weapon in my hand.'

'What weapon will you be carrying?'

'A single-shot gun, two khukris and a rampuri. That's more than enough to scare everyone. Don't you agree?'

That was when Jatadhari Guru remembered the youth whom everyone called Jibon now. He was strong and brave, and he needed a lot of money. A major police case was hanging over his head like a hangman's noose. Also hanging over his head was his duty towards the one he was now sheltering with. What would happen to her if "Jibon" got caught today? If she was pregnant by now, what would happen to that child! Who would feed it? How would it survive? Jibon had to be told about this opportunity.

Jatadhari said, 'An even number is not auspicious in such jobs. Either get rid of one person, or add another one.'

Mahadeb said, 'I can't get rid of anyone now. Or else they'll spread the word. The police will get to know about us. That's how the police track criminals.'

'Then take another person.'

'Whom can I get? Who'll go? Is it a picnic, that I'll find someone or the other as soon as I mention it!'

'Shall I try to find someone?'

'Do that. But he shouldn't be a coward. Or it'll be a disaster.'

'He won't be a coward. If I find someone, it'll be a son of a tiger!'

'Whom do you have in mind, Guru?'

'Jibon.'

'Oh Jibon! Do you know his whereabouts?'

'I mean, if I find him, will he do? If I find him, that is.'

'If you can get him, nothing like it. He is indeed a son of a tiger. To go into Loharpara, and then exit flashing a dagger! Only he can do that.'

⁂

One evening, a few days later, Jatadhari told Mahadeb, 'Come along somewhere with me.' And thus, the two of them arrived at the overbridge at the Champadali railway station. After a few minutes, they saw Jibon approaching. Mahadeb burst out ecstatically, 'Guru! You're in touch with him!'

'No one must know that.'

When the stranger joined them, Jatadhari said, 'Tell him everything about your plan. He can decide after that whether he'll join you or not.'

Mahadeb told the stranger exactly what he had told Jatadhari. After hearing everything attentively, the stranger looked at Jatadhari in astonishment. After he had left Srinath Colony and come to Begumpur, Jatadhari had visited him a few times. Sometimes he had given him five or ten rupees. On those occasions, he had told him, 'Be brave, everything will turn out fine. Let me see what I can arrange for you.' What arrangement had he brought now! Which direction did he want to push him towards! The question flew about in his mind like a bird that wouldn't stop fluttering its wings.

Jatadhari had his face turned away, and was looking at the sky. When he looked the stranger in the eye now, he felt embarrassed. He said, 'When Mahadeb told me about the plan, I thought of you. Because I know you are in dire straits.' He paused a while and then asked the stranger a question. 'Let's say someone is in prison. He has been sentenced to death. The date of the execution has also been decided. What will he do then?'

'What will he do? He'll try to escape if possible.'

'If possible. Will those who hold him in custody make it possible? All right, if he can escape, that's good. But if he can't, what will he do so that he can live?'

'I don't know, I have no idea.'

'He'll kill some Ram or Shyam.'

'What will that achieve? Will he live?'

'He won't be hanged until the verdict on the new crime is pronounced. At least he will live a few more days. Your situation now is like that. You have to take a risk now. There's no other option. If you come back a winner, it solves all your problems. And if you don't, after all you can't be hanged twice! Only once.'

Jatadhari paused and then continued, 'Once the poison of cancer has entered someone's body, why should he be afraid of a common cold, or a fever? Don't they say, one poison counters another? You have a boil somewhere on your body, it's throbbing with pain. Press down on it. Give yourself some more pain. But once the puss and blood come out, you'll feel better. Or if a rusty nail pricks your foot. Singe the spot, apply a burning wick on it. These are the home remedies of poor folk. I only told you how I see things. The rest is up to you.'

There was a foam of saliva on the corner of his lips. He wanted to smoke ganja now. But he deferred that desire and lit a beedi instead. He took a deep puff and blew out the smoke, and said, 'It's not my thinking, great souls have said that when man falls to the earth, he holds the very same earth to stand up again. That's the rule.'

The stranger thought for a while and then said in a tone of uncertainty, 'I understand. But I fled from the Jadavpur locality to survive. To go there again, that too in broad daylight—what if I get into trouble?'

Mahadeb answered him now. 'You're not going to Jadavpur, you'll be going to a station that's one or two stops before that. You'll be inside the train compartment after that. Nobody will know that you are there. And even if someone suddenly boards that wagon, what can he do? Aren't we with you? If something like that happens, we'll take care of two jobs at the same time. If he acts too smart, we'll finish the bastard. Right there. It makes no difference. So what are you going to do now? Join us?'

'It's a big thing. Let me think about it a little bit.'

'There's no time for thinking too much. We have five or seven days in hand. If you say "no" at the last minute, we'll have a problem. Say what you have to right now. After all, if you're not going, we have to find someone else. Such things take time.'

The stranger could not figure out what he ought to do. Whether to advance or to retreat. Behind him lay a bottomless abyss, eternal darkness, coming to devour him with gaping maws. In front of him was a very faint ray of light, although it was a long distance away. The path was rugged and full of thorny bushes. There were snakes, tigers and scorpions.

'You're scared. If you're scared, forget about it. Jatadhari Guru once said that the warrior who is afraid can never win a battle.'

'No, no, I'm not afraid.'

'Then why are you dithering?'

Jatadhari quieted Mahadeb, and said with a philosophical air, 'The amount of fire required to light a beedi can ignite a conflagration. I know you. Sure, you have the fire. But you'll squander that. If the fire is extinguished some day—you'll tear your hair out in despair. Your time has come. My advice is, jump in.'

'You're telling me this, Guru?'

'Of course, it's me telling you! Is it my ghost!?'

'This is wrong.'

'There's no time now to think about what's right and what's wrong. You'll have lots of time for that later. You have to survive now. Survival comes first, and then everything else. People all over the world are engaged in wrongdoing, it's not as if you alone have been contracted to do the right thing.'

It seemed Jatadhari was annoyed at missing his dose of ganja. He said, 'Think about that night, when you snatched Anadi Das's watch. Why did you do that? Because you had no other option then, you needed treatment. Did questions of right or wrong enter your head then? Anandi Das is a good man. But these people are smugglers.'

Mahadeb said, 'Bhai, the essence of what I've gathered is that I won't lay a hand on any small folk. I thrash goondas and loot treasures. I'm going to take a chance, and if I die, then I die, and if I live, I'll live like a human being.'

Jatadhari's voice now took on a harsh tone. 'If you go to a coal mine, you'll see each of the workers descend a thousand feet below the earth. Doesn't he know that he won't survive if the mine collapses? But he still goes because he has loved ones at home. If he doesn't do the work, everyone will starve. You're living off a poor girl and getting a handful of rice to eat everyday. That's why you have all these thoughts in your head. What will you do when you have none of that tomorrow?'

Jatadhari turned grave after he finished speaking. He then remembered the life story of the youth whose name was Jibon. Shortly after the partition of the country, like hundreds of thousands of refugees, nestled in his Ma's arms, the infant Jibon was compelled to leave East Pakistan for West Bengal. They were put up in a refugee camp. That was a harsh life, almost like a prison. Everything was measured out—rice and a few rupees. The money was so meagre that it was difficult to buy vegetables and greens with that, and the amount of dust and stones in the rice was so much that it made chewing difficult.

After suffering that imprisonment, albeit without labour, for six or seven years, one day the government sent a lorry to the refugee camp. Everyone had to leave. Where were they to go? To Dandakaranya, the forest where Ram was exiled to by his stepmother Kaikeyi. Like all the others, Jibon's father too was stubborn. 'I won't go to Dandakaranya.' So the dole was discontinued, and their names were struck off the camp register.

And thanks to that, the family descended to a life of daily starvation. As a small boy, Jibon witnessed a horrifying form of naked poverty. When a child cried out in hunger, his helpless father hit him, and his Ma cursed him, 'Die! I'll be spared then!'

Once, when Jibon was eight or nine years old, he was compelled to go to work in a house in a faraway village, in exchange for food and clothes, and nothing else, when he couldn't bear the pangs of hunger. It was winter time, when cauliflowers and cabbages were cultivated. He was woken up when it was still dark, and given a pole with two small buckets tied at its ends. He had to fetch water from a pond that was almost a mile away, and water the one-and-a-half kattha vegetable garden. After that, he would eat some muri, and take thirteen goats and four cows to the fields to graze. He took a short break in the afternoon for lunch. He returned at dusk, put the animals in the cowshed and gave them their fodder, before he was done for the day. Even after all this toil, if he made the slightest mistake, he got a sound thrashing. No one showed any kindness or affection to the miserable, weak boy.

After that, Jibon's father left the refugee camp and went to another camp where his brothers were staying.

There was a saying that when one went to Bengal, one's destiny too went along. Although they changed their location, their plight did not change. Jibon's father fell ill, he came down with a stomach ulcer. He lay in bed, writhing like a slaughtered goat. He did not receive any treatment for lack of money. A sister of Jibon withered away and died of starvation. Lacking clothes, his Ma covered herself with a torn mosquito net and hid herself indoors. She couldn't step outside in daylight, come what may.

Jibon ran away from home in those terrifying times and set out on the road. He was about thirteen years old then. He had heard that humans were supposed to possess humanity and altruism, that is to say, kindness and compassion. He had wandered around the whole country in search of one such person who would understand the sorrows of an impoverished boy. Grazing cattle, washing cups and plates in a tea shop until his hands and feet turned pruritic, carrying loads, and snatching a ruti from a dog's mouth when he didn't find any work and was dying of hunger. But despite all that, he hoped that one day or the other he would find the person.

He didn't. How would he, when he did not know the whereabouts of such a person. It could well be that he had died before even Jibon's father was born. The only people Jibon had encountered were of a cruel, merciless, ruthless, brutal, unkind, heartless, wicked, malicious, barbaric and ghoulish nature. It was only they who roamed the land. Their lives of opulence, luxury, joy and dissipation were enabled by the blood, sweat and tears of the poor.

In the household in south Bengal where he worked as a cowherd, they didn't let his shadow fall on them because he was an untouchable, they despised him as they would a mangy street dog. He was served food on a broken plate. He had to sleep atop the sacks of dung-cakes in the cattleshed. For no fault of his, the mistress of the house had flung a cooking ladle at him and dented his head. And her husband had hit him on his back with the bamboo cattle prod till the lath broke.

An employer in Siliguri had made him work for eight months without paying him a single paisa. Another man in Assam stole the money paid to Jibon as salary. A man befriended him in a train compartment, declared him to be his spiritual son, and then left him in a garments shop saying 'He's my son, I'll just be back', and vanished with some clothes. People from the traders' association labelled him a thief and thrashed him. A police havildar in Lucknow put him to work in the locomotive workshop and then took away a month's wages for clearing ash.

He had to return home empty-handed after roaming around various parts of the country for a few years, suffering endless humiliation, contempt and torments. But by then his father had moved to the city of Calcutta. His Ma washed utensils in a babu household, and a brother of his worked in a tea shop. His father lay half-dead like before, full of rage and grief. When he felt well, he worked as a day labourer.

Once again, they had to suffer various kinds of torments because they were poor and belonged to a low caste. That was a long story.

A local leader once tied Jibon to a lamp post and thrashed him as if he was an animal, all for no fault of his. He suspected that Jibon was a Naxalite, and therefore felt it necessary to send a message to the youths of the locality, in order to terrify them. By making an example of Jibon—this is what would happen to anyone doing that brand of politics. Beware! Don't tread that path even by mistake!

After that, Jibon moved to the Naxalite stronghold of Palpara. He began giving back as good as he got, and walking down that slippery bloody path. His name did enter the police diary, as a Naxalite. The people of the locality drove away his father. Jatadhari did not know where Jibon went after that. Jibon had told him a lot of things, but not that. When the Naxalite movement was smashed, he made Jadavpur station his stronghold. A group developed around him. Who were half-Naxalite, and half-criminals. None of them had read the Red Book, or the *Deshabrati* paper, and they didn't know which country Mao Tse Tung belonged to, or what the meaning of revolution was. All they knew was that whatever Jibon-da said and did was true and right.

This stranger youth was not Jibon, only his replica. How could he become like the real Jibon? He was not supposed to experience his anguished life. Why would he harbour feelings of affection for people like himself, and fierce hatred for the enemies of the people? That was still fine, but he surely ought to have some love and affection for himself. Some thought about the future.

Jatadhari said, 'I have to leave now. Come, Mahadeb. If we miss this train, we'll have to wait another hour.'

They stood up and were about to move towards the stairs, when the stranger asked, 'How will I know when I need to go?'

'So, you're in?'

'Yes, I am.'

'Are you sure? You won't change your mind later, will you?'

'No.'

19

The Misadventure

A band of youths who were as effulgent as the morning sun had declared that they would completely transform the system. The Himalayan gap between the rich and the poor in the country would be eliminated. Caste and untouchability would be wiped out. People would no longer lack food and shelter. Everyone would get the same opportunity as regards food, clothing, housing, education, healthcare and employment. In a word, they would carry out a 'revolution'.

Now one realises that there will never be a revolution in this country. Who would bring it about? Those who wanted to do that had all become brick-and-cement memorials at street corners. Through a massive counter-revolutionary conspiracy, carried out at every level, all the possibilities were erased. So that no seed of revolution remained anywhere.

How could a tree grow without a seed? The young generation wanted to become building promoters, or building materials suppliers, middlemen or slaves of the powerful. They did not have any love lost for the people or the country. Each one of them had become a self-gratifying mechanical dog that sat at the feet of the party in power and wagged its tail. And in return for such fealty, they would get the licence to do whatever they wanted.

The stranger reflected: no one promised me anything, nor did I promise anyone anything. So why should I wander about here and there? Why not sink deeper into the depths and see whether my feet touch the earth? Jatadhari Guru was a wise man, and he had said that there was actually no such thing as justice or injustice, sin or virtue, right or wrong, legal or illegal. What was seen as just today could become unjust later, once times changed. And what was seen as wrong today could become right. Everything was the play of time.

The stranger went and stood at the instructed spot. Mahadeb, Aurobindo, Haru and Gobindo arrived one by one. As if they had been drawn there magnetically by unknown destiny. All their hearts were thumping, dread was writ large on their faces. They had to jump into danger in a little while.

The stranger asked, 'What weapons are we carrying?'

Mahadeb said, 'I've brought a khukri.'

'And you all? Someone was supposed to bring a single-shot gun. Did you get it?'

Mahadeb said, 'No, he couldn't get it finally. You have a dagger, don't you? That'll be enough.'

The stranger became quite dejected hearing that. Some people were very reckless nowadays. Nothing scared them. There was no way of knowing what someone might suddenly do. If he was of a nervous nature, he would think a rope to be a snake and run. But if he was brave, he would trample the snake as if it was only a rope, and thus turn it as passive as a rope.

The stranger said, 'It's become very risky now.'

'I'm telling you, nothing will happen.'

But Mahadeb's words didn't allay the stranger's apprehensions. How did he know that nothing would happen? It was good to be confident, but overconfidence was another name for foolishness. I won't go, he decided. He was on the verge of saying it. But just then, Aurobindo said, in a voice laden with sarcasm, 'Mahadeb, are you sure this is Jibon? Is Jibon such a scaredy-cat! Hey, either we'll all die, or we'll all survive. So why are you scared? Come, don't be petty-minded before an auspicious job.'

So the stranger did not turn back. 'Fine. If you people jump into the fire, so can I. Let's go. Let's see what fate has in store for us.' He wiped the sweat on his brow with his left hand, and felt the dagger tucked at his waist. This was his greatest friend right now. It had saved his life once, and ever since then it was his constant companion. Let's see how it performed today.

After a while, they spotted a train far in the distance, coming down the railway line. It was the train five inveterate heretics were waiting for. The stranger realised his heart was thumping in excitement, his palms were sweaty. The train arrived at this station after a while, and halted. Because it was an afternoon train, it was not as crowded as it was at other times. There was a man waving his hand at the door of the third wagon from the rear of the eight-wagon train. Mahadeb advanced in his direction.

The man told Mahadeb, 'It's the wagon after the vendor's wagon. A window seat on the left side. He's wearing dhuti-punjabi. The punjabi is brown in colour. Go ahead. I'll be behind you, in the next wagon. If you have a problem identifying the man, signal me.'

The train stopped at the subsequent stations. And they moved from one wagon to the next, till they arrived at the specified wagon. They identified their prey. There was no question of not being able to do that. There was no one else in the wagon who was clad in dhuti-punjabi. A couple of people were in lungis. Standing at the door, Mahadeb leaned out a bit and waved to signal to the wagon behind that everything was fine. Having ascertained what he had to do, the man got off at the next station.

The five of them were ready now. As the train got closer to Jadavpur, it gradually got more crowded. All the seats that were empty earlier were full now. People were standing in front of the seats and at the doors.

The train finally reached Jadavpur. A large number of people boarded the train, most of whom were women. Not finding any seats, they sat down near the door. The stranger whispered, 'What do we do now?'

Mahadeb was surprised, he asked, 'What do you mean?'

'It's so crowded now.'

'So what? How does it matter? Since we're in this now, we'll see it to the end.'

When the train began to move, and their wagon left the platform, Mahadeb clenched his jaws. His eyes blazed. Win or lose—let the game begin! He had waited for such an opportunity all his life. It had finally come today. Having come so far, he couldn't go back empty-handed now.

Mahadeb's family had been quite a well-to-do household of the locality at one time. As long as his father was alive, they did not lack for anything. That began once he died. They lost some of his property through others' designs, and his Ma sold off the rest bit by bit to run the household. But Mahadeb was immersed in a happy dream now. He would get lots of money today. He would get a licence for a foreign liquor off-shop. He would live the rest of his life in comfort.

Gobindo was a boy from a refugee family that had arrived from East Pakistan. He lived in the railside shanty settlement. His father had been a worker in a glass factory. The owner of the factory had shut it down seven or eight years ago. Almost two thousand workers had been rendered jobless. At present, Gobindo's father sat in front of a table with some jars, on the street in front of his house. There was also a tea kettle. If he sold some cups of tea, the household ran. Gobindo had an elder sister. She was unmarried. A few strands of grey had begun to appear on her hair. She made paper bags. Their mother suffered from painful arthritis. Gobindo hoped to mitigate all their hardship now. His sister would get married. He would be able to repair their broken shanty too.

Aurobindo had lost both his parents at an early age. An aunt of his had raised him like a son. Her husband drove a rickshaw. He was over sixty now. He couldn't work as hard as he could before. His body was run down out of excessive labour. Aurobindo's aunt worked as a cook in a babu house. They had two daughters. One of them was married. Her husband too drove a rickshaw. He was supposed to be given a rickshaw as dowry. Because he hadn't been given that yet, he drank and then beat his wife badly. Aurobindo felt he had a responsibility and duty towards them. That's why he had taken up this job. He had joined a motor driving school, and learnt driving. But he couldn't get a driving licence because he did not have the money to pay the agent. He would get that now. A driving licence, and who knows, maybe a second-hand car as well.

It was Aurobindo who was supposed to bring the single-shot gun. A youth from his locality, who was associated with the red party, and had run away to Assam fearing the Congress toughs and the police, had given it to him in a cloth bag before he left. 'Hide it in a proper place. I'll take it back when I return.' There was a single-shot gun and five bullets in the bag. Aurobindo had hidden that among some bushes near the bank of a pond. But when he went to fetch it, he didn't find it there.

Haru did not have a father. His stepfather, whom his Ma subsequently married, was in the fish trade. They were more-or-less well-to-do. But for some reason, the stepfather could not stand Haru. As early as when he was ten or twelve years old, his stepfather beat him badly for the smallest mistake. And his Ma, in all her kindness, sided with her husband. Was Haru to blame for the fact that he was unemployed now? Thousands of youths were unemployed in the country. They were all educated. And Haru had failed in Class Eight after two attempts. What job would he get with that education? His stepfather beat him for that. He kicked his food plate. Nobody in the world understood Haru's grief. Only Kalyani did. She too didn't have a mother of her own, only a stepmother. If money could be arranged, Haru would run away somewhere with Kalyani. He would start a small business. He was quite keen to set up a provisions store.

Tucked into the stranger's waist was the sharp dagger with a brass handle that he had snatched from Shiba. Anyone would be terrified seeing the dagger. A single stab could free the bird of life from its cage. Would he be able to change his fate today with the help of this dagger? If he could, he would no longer be poor, or starve. And if he failed, he would lie in the morgue, among the pile of unclaimed bodies. There was nothing worse than being beaten by a mob.

The wagon was a bit crowded before it arrived at Jadavpur station. But once the train began moving again, a group of youths got into the running train and stood right at the door. They wanted to savour the breeze. The stranger thought they couldn't go ahead now. The crowd could not be controlled with the ordinary weapons they possessed. But neither Mahadeb, nor the others, were afraid. 'Do or die' was the credo they stubbornly held on to. Rather than die bit by bit every day, they would either win today, or die.

The train left Jadavpur station, and once the driver's cabin passed the signal post, Mahadeb pulled out the knife from his waist and flashed it, and headed towards the man in question. There was no more time to turn back, or to be afraid, or ask questions. The battlefield was in front of them, with the enemy troops lined up. War had been declared. There was only one thing to do now: self-defence. One had to survive, or die. The word 'public' referred to a large number of people. They were powerful. Once one was in their hands, they would beat you to death, like a snake.

The stranger took out his dagger and held it in his fist, and roared out, 'Remain seated as you are, no one should move. If anyone comes in our way he'll die!'

Mahadeb brought down the gunny sack on the bunk above the dhuti-punjabi-clad man's head. But it wasn't very heavy. Why was it so light? But there wasn't any time to think about such things now. Flashing his knife, he pushed through the crowd, making his way towards the door. Mahadeb was in front, and the stranger at the rear. The train slowed down on account of the repair work on the rail track between the two stations, but not so slow as to be able to get off easily. Besides, the train had already started accelerating after the brief slowdown.

Mahadeb jumped off first, and then ran as fast as he could. Haru and then Gobindo followed him, and also ran. All of them had jumped out of the door on the right- hand side, crossed the rail track on that side, and headed towards Salampur and Vivek Nagar. But where was Aurobindo? He had tried to be smart. Even before the operation commenced, when he saw Mahadeb and the stranger advancing towards the prey, he had moved towards the door on the left-hand side. He stood there, amidst the crowd, with his hand over his face. Once the job was done, and his companions had got off, he got off too. The people on that left side did not notice him. Nor were they supposed to. All their eyes were trained on the two men flashing knives, who had roared out a dire warning.

All of them had got off the train and landed safely. The stranger was the last one to get off. Since he had stood guard until all of them got off, there was quite a delay. The train had gained speed by then. It wasn't easy for him to get off. He fell down on the stone chips on the rail track and cut himself on his kneecap. His leg turned numb with pain. His companions were running for their lives. None of them looked back to see whether anyone had fallen down.

The man whose sack had been snatched was at first stunned by the suddenness of the incident, but then recovered his senses, as well as his speech, soon after, and screamed out, 'Robbers! Robbers! They're running away with my things! Catch them!'

A passenger was intelligent enough to pull the chain. The injured stranger had hardly taken a few steps before the train came to a halt. And hearing the cries of the robbed man, hundreds of passengers got off the train. All of them chased the fleeing robbers. Hearing the screams of the people—'Catch them, they're running away'—two G.R.P. constables too came running from somewhere.

Those who were chasing the thieves picked up large stones from the rail track and flung them in their direction.

The people of Bengal had given such stones a name—*banglabom*, or Bengali bomb. These could be more powerful than a real bomb at times. If a banglabom was thrown correctly, and hit the right place, a single blow could kill. Mahadeb did not have any shield to protect himself against the countless Bengali bombs raining down on him. They were in peril, and helpless, in the face of such an unanticipated counter-offensive. They only had two knives, which were of no use in combating enemies who were afar.

Life was the name of a battle, and of a warrior. Jibon had been in many battlefields. He had learnt from experience that if two people stood one behind the other, and turned around bravely, they were as good as eleven. With each man baring a weapon. These eleven could put eleven-hundred to shame. He had done that too on many occasions. But the stranger was not Jibon.

There was also a big difference between the situation now, and anything in the past. A warrior without a weapon in the battlefield was like a goat on a butcher's block. Mahadeb and his companions were aware of that. Meaning, they were made aware of that now. They were running to save their lives, hoping to reach some safe spot. They were not in a mental frame to look behind to see who had fallen. The stranger with the injured leg trailed behind them.

None of them belonged to the party where people were prepared to lay down their lives for their ideals, who disregarded their own lives, and stood beside their colleagues and friends. In the face of heavy gunfire, Jibon had once swum across a lake with a friend whose hand had been blown away by a country bomb. But for these people, nothing was dearer than their own lives.

The stranger realised that given the speed at which they were running, he would not be able to catch up with them with his injured leg. They were already about a hundred yards ahead of him. And the mob chasing them was now only about twenty yards away. The stranger had no option but to enter a narrow lane on the right-hand side. But once he was there, he realised it was a blind alley. There was no exit route. A two-storeyed building blocked the way. The building had high walls on all four sides.

Jibon had stayed in this locality for a few days following a battle. He had climbed over many such walls when he was being chased by the police. Perhaps this one as well. He was well versed in that. The spirit of Jibon seemed to permeate into the mind and body of the stranger playing Jibon's role now. He climbed over the wall in a single leap. The chasing mob fell into confusion and came to a halt in front of the wall. And the stranger screamed out from the other side, 'I'll kill the first person who comes here! I'll cut his belly open! Let's see who dares to come!' The bewildered crowd stood on the other side of the wall for a while, out of fear of their innards springing out. They could not decide who would give up his life first. That lasted for thirty or forty seconds at most. That little bit of time proved most valuable now, it was enough to save a life. Without wasting a moment, he crossed over another wall on the opposite side. And then another. After crossing over a few walls, he reached a lane. The lane wound this way and that until it reached the lake in Palpara, and the timber yard.

There were hardly any people in this lane now. After running a bit, the stranger slowed down to a walk, like an ordinary pedestrian walking on the street. Although he was still firmly gripping the handle of the dagger tucked behind his shirt, his only friend now.

The stranger had survived a terrible calamity today. But Mahadeb, Gobindo and Haru could not. They were running, and chasing them was an enraged, belligerent mob. The screams of the mob, 'Catch him!', drew more people from all around. They picked up whatever they could find, bamboo sticks, bricks, stones. People surrounded them from all directions, like trapping an animal. The three men were caught by the pursuing mob. And within merely ten minutes, the mob beat the three bodies into three lumps of flesh. The two police constables were powerless to protect them from public outrage. Haru died on the spot. Gobindo survived, but his legs were broken so badly from blows with a crowbar that they never healed. He remained twisted for the rest of his life. Mahadeb was in hospital for a few days with a broken hip.

Then came their court trial. There was evidence, and there were witnesses. Both of them were sentenced to seven years' imprisonment. But all that came much later.

⌘

Those who have never toured rural Bengal, mixed with the people there, and known them, and have only seen trees and greenery, rivers and streams, and small earthen huts, and tearful, bare-bodied men while travelling on a train, can never imagine that the same villages are inhabited by some people of such rare cunning and intelligence that they could sell a knowledgeable city dweller four times over in four different markets before the other has a clue. The impression someone gave earlier, of being a fool, an idiot, or a simpleton, was not him at all. Actually, he was a skilled actor. His face was all makeup.

The truth emerged after Mahadeb's court trial began—once one reviewed the summaries of the police's presumptive reports. It turned out that the story of the gold smuggling ring was purely a piece of fiction, which was composed through the artfulness of the brain of a rustic man of great expertise for the strategic purpose of eliminating the enemies of the nation, while himself remaining at a safe distance.

There was a long-standing conflict between two brothers, relating to land and property. In a scuffle resulting from that, one brother struck the other and split his head. A complaint was registered with the police. So the person in question had to go to prison. Once in prison, through association with thieves, robbers, murderers and smugglers, the doors of evil-mindedness opened in his brain. He realised—I can be far away from the site of action, so that no one can touch me, let alone catch me, and yet remove a thorn with another thorn, or break a stone with another stone.

He made up the story of the gold smuggling ring. He said that first to one person. Before a writer sends a story that he has written for publication, he reads it out in some literary gathering, and uses the criticism to rewrite it, removing the flaws and weak parts. So after our man told the story of the gold smuggling ring to one person after another, it acquired an air of credibility.

Once he was out of prison, driven by a desire for revenge, he searched around in every station between Diamond Harbour and Sealdah for someone through whom he could actualise his plan perfectly. He knew that God cast a poisonous gaze at each and every railway station in India. There were shanties there, some shanty-like shops, illicit liquor vends, the flesh trade, gambling, thieves, and so on—in sum, a world of darkness. Whether it was in West Bengal or Bihar, Assam or Uttar Pradesh, there was no freedom from that.

So one day, the man got terribly drunk in Mahadeb Mollah's cholai den and divulged his secret. 'I'm a fucking bullock carting sugar. I'm an arsehole, I live a dog's life. I fucking guard and smuggle gold worth hundreds of thousands of rupees. And what do I get in return? A hundred or two hundred rupees. They get rich, and I remain the beggar I was.' Tears streamed down from the man's eyes as he spoke. 'Fuck, sometimes I think I should grab the stuff and run away. What can a middle-aged man do to me? But I lack the courage. They will burn my house, kill my wife and children. I'm telling you the truth, I swear on Ma Kali—if someone gives me a one-eighth share, I won't resist. Let him take away all the gold. What do I care! I can live in comfort with my share of the gold.'

The story attracted Mahadeb. To the extent that even Jatadhari Guru was fooled. After that, Mahadeb made all the arrangements. A hair-raising incident of robbery came to be organised, which happened in public view, in broad daylight, right in front of thousands of train passengers, and despite the G.R.P. patrol.

There's a story about a man who got a boil on his neck. So he went to see a doctor. He said, 'Make an incision.' The doctor, who had an MBBS degree, examined it, pressed it, and said, 'The boil can't be incised now. I'll give you a medicine, have that, and come after two days. I'll see how it is then.'

After that, the man went to a barber, to get a shave. The barber was absent-minded. He had no clue when a swipe of his razor cut the boil along with the stubble. The man screamed out in alarm, 'What have you done?' The barber realised he had made a terrible mistake. Whatever had happened had happened, he had to handle the situation now. He said in an unperturbed tone, 'What happened? The boil looked bad. I cut it.'

'But the doctor said it can't be incised now, only after two days.'

'What do you mean "can't be incised"? Didn't I just do it?'

'What if something happens to me?'

'Nothing will happen. Just see, it will heal. I cut such boils everyday.'

The man's boil really healed. As a result, word spread in all quarters that a barber who charged two annas had done what even a doctor charging two rupees a visit couldn't. He incised boils too for the price of a shave. People now ran to the barber's door when they wanted their boils incised. His fame spread everywhere, as did the doctor's infamy.

The angry and deprived doctor presented himself at the barber shop one day. After talking about this and that, he said, 'You don't even know how to spell "doctor", but you have such deft hands. I tell you, if you knew a little bit, I mean, if you had read a book or two of medicine, you could have become the top surgeon in the country. And then you wouldn't have had to give shaves for two-annas. You would have had a house and a car by now. If you want, I can help you out by giving you the books.'

Enticed by the doctor's words, the barber got some books from the doctor. And then he read them with full concentration. He learnt about the human body. He learnt about the location of veins and arteries. A few days later, another patient visited him, with a similar boil on his neck. 'Please incise this, bhai.' But the barber didn't pick up the razor that day. He observed that the boil was directly above the respiratory tract. If that got cut somehow, or if the boil didn't heal after the incision and turned septic, the man wouldn't survive.

Mahadeb and his companions were all like the barber. None of them had done a job like this before. They had heard stories, read in the newspaper, and seen in the cinema, how easily everything happened. They were unaware about how dire the consequences could be. Like with the barber, it was ignorance that was the source of their courage.

Three snatchers had boarded a train at Sealdah. It was 11.30 p.m. It was the last Down-train. As soon as the train began moving, they began. 'Hand over whatever you have!' Money, watches, women's bangles and earrings. One of the snatchers had a loaded revolver. Made in China. The passengers were quaking in fear.

The snatchers began their operation from one end of the wagon and reached the door at the far end. No one offered any resistance. No one screamed. They all handed over their belongings silently. It was a day of weddings. The pickings were not bad at all. A green coconut seller who sold his wares in front of Kolay Market was sitting on his empty basket in front of the door. He was the final victim. Once what this man had was collected, the snatchers would flee as soon as the train stopped. The man with the revolver advanced towards him. 'Out with whatever you have!'

There were almost thirty or forty passengers in the train wagon. The green coconut seller was actually quite enjoying watching everyone being robbed. He was laughing away inwardly. Observing the loaded revolver being pointed at him, he burst out in rage, 'I'm returning home with a few rupees after toiling the whole day, so why on earth should I give that to you? Who the hell do you think you are!' The man with the revolver roared out, 'Give it, or else I'll shoot you!'

'Shoot me? Go on, let's see you shooting me!' the coconut seller roared back. 'Don't frighten me with that toy. Do that with babus. I have two of those at home. My son plays with them. It's sold on the pavement in front of Sealdah station. We are farmers, we know about guns. Get lost!'

The urban snatcher did not get startled at the coconut seller's retort. He forcibly took away the man's money pouch. The coconut seller at once brandished the chopper he used to slice open the green coconuts. He brought it down on the arm holding the revolver, which sprang out of his hand. The snatcher's arm hung limply from his shoulder. But before that, sensing danger, he had pulled the trigger, but who knows why, the revolver did not fire. Perhaps the bullet was very old, and had become damp. Maybe the coconut seller survived because he was very strong.

Meanwhile the train had reached the platform. The coconut seller had pushed the wounded snatcher and thrown him out of the train. The other two snatchers had jumped off the train, and fallen and hurt themselves. All of them were now at the mercy of the public. But ultimately here too it was not courage, but the coconut seller's ignorance, his stupidity, his foolishness. No person of intelligence would have taken such a big risk for a mere fifteen or twenty rupees.

Distinguishing courage from stupidity was not only difficult, it was quite impossible. The same act which once made someone a hero among hundreds of thousands of people could fell him to the ground on another occasion. This had happened in many instances.

Chandan Chakravarty was twenty-six years old, and lived in the railside settlement known as Rail Colony No. 1 in Jadavpur. He was once a mastaan who made the people of the locality tremble in terror. He had stood on the railway line one day to stop a train. And surprisingly the train stopped too that day. People had praised him for his daring. Hailed him.

The same Chandan, aka Chandu stood on the rail track on another day to stop a train. But the train did not stop. And that day people called him thick-headed, an idiot, a donkey.

All that he had done on both the occasions was undertaken in a state of intoxication.

There was a difference of opinion now among people about whether Mahadeb and his companions were brave or downright stupid. Nor could anyone figure out the true extent of the courage or stupidity. This was like knowingly hurtling towards one's death for no rhyme or reason.

Jagannath Mondol apparently lived in a village somewhere near Diamond Harbour. He ran a provisions store. He visited Burrabazar, in Calcutta, every month to pick up supplies for his shop. He went by train, and returned with the goods in a lorry. He did the same on this occasion. He had about twenty-five thousand rupees on him. This was a meagre amount. At least in relation to the hullabaloo the robbers made, and the tremendous risk they took. After all, how many rupees would each one get as his share? After all that daring? What dunces they were!

No one actually knew, except for one very clever man. Robbers would snatch away his brother's money. If his brother resisted, they would certainly stab him or something like that. If he didn't resist, he would lose the money. The provisions store would go to hell. All the might that some money endowed him with would vanish. Come what may, I shall be far away from the action, where no one can touch me, let alone catch me. But he made a mistake in his calculations. However, that made no difference to him.

20

Pancha's Ploy

This was a small railway station in rural Bengal. It had started getting dark. A dense, eerie darkness. People were gradually turning into hazy, unrecognisable phantoms.

A large pond covered with water hyacinth fringed the iron railing near the station. The pond was ringed by a jungle of weeds. Somewhere among those weeds, a snake had grabbed a huge toad's leg in its fangs. The toad croaked plaintively in agony and terror. Initially, after the toad's leg was caught in the snake's fangs, it jumped up and down for quite a while. But soon it got exhausted with all the jumping, and couldn't free itself. That wasn't possible. Once something was caught in a snake's fangs, it was done for. The more it tried to pull itself out, the tighter the clasp became.

A snake could not see as clearly as all other creatures. It got some idea about things, partly through smell, and partly through a hazy vision of the pattern of movement, which was useful for its purposes. Through the ways of life, through habits and knowledge based on inference, having hazily glimpsed something moving, it sensed that this was food, and struck at the frog's leg. It wanted to swallow up the whole toad bit by bit, beginning at the leg. But once its fangs were planted on the leg, it realised it had made a terrible mistake. The prey was much larger than the size of its mouth, and while it was easy to digest, it was difficult to swallow. When the frog jumped high in pain and fear, the snake too rose into emptiness and then fell to the earth. In those moments, it thought that it would perhaps lose its life. It was willing to let the toad go, it was prepared to tear off some of its skin and escape. It wanted to be free of the danger, even if it meant losing one or two of its fangs.

Weakened by falling again and again, many times over, it sensed that the frog had become feeble. It had realised that death was near. There was nothing to be gained by any movement. It may even be delayed. The agony of death would be prolonged. It lay as if it was dead next to the snake's fangs. It awaited death.

After getting a bit of rest, the snake recovered some of its strength. It then started swallowing the toad bit by bit. After all, it had no other option but to swallow it now. The prey it had caught was lifeless. The more the slumped creature entered its mouth, the bigger the snake's mouth became. Snakes had this amazing capability. At particular times, they could somehow swallow a prey much larger than themselves. It took them a long time, and various contortions, to swallow it, and then they lay silently among the weeds, gasping after their exertions.

The stranger could not figure out right now exactly which creature his plight was like. Whether he should compare himself to the snake or the frog. Maybe he was both snake and frog. Because he was blind and ignorant like the snake, he had unwittingly attacked a creature which was impossible for him to swallow. But his plight was also like the frog's. The snake now was python-like Time in whose coils he had been caught. He wanted to get away like the frog by jumping, and leaping, and slipping out of the snake's grasp. The more he tried to escape, the tighter the snake's coils got to squeeze the life out of him into unfathomable darkness. There was no escape now. Python Time would finally swallow him entirely.

Time luxuriated in murder now, it was prone to destruction, and bloodthirsty. The time was friendless and unfriendly. It was indeed an accursed time. No one was intimate with anyone at this time, they did not want to be intimate. And so, the stranger was sitting and wondering what he ought to do, where he ought to go, and how he would protect himself from the fangs of time.

Today the stranger had run along the bank of the lake and turned left when he arrived at Palpara Bazaar. And then he had walked down one lane after another and reached Budher Haat. He sat there for a long time, concealing himself behind the jungle of hogla reeds. And then he went to the Baghajatin railway station. This was just one station away from Jadavpur. Staying here too long could be dangerous. So without a second thought, he boarded the first Down-train that arrived there. Once he was on the train, he realised it was a Diamond Harbour local. Some of the vendors who were on this train now had been on that afternoon train. They were discussing the incident that took place. The situation in the country, the condition of the railways and the question of passenger safety all came up in the discussion. That was when the stranger learnt that the three robbers had been caught.

It was said that if a deer that was caught in a tiger's jaws somehow managed to free itself, it apparently returned to the same tiger's jaws because it had lost its sense of direction in terror and panic.

Is that what had happened to the stranger? Or else why would he have got into this particular train, the Diamond Harbour local, rather than all the others? What if someone recognised him?

They hadn't recognised him yet. Just as a single glimpse of a face during that disruption, a time of fear, anguish and danger, was not supposed to be remembered by anyone, it could also remain imprinted like a picture in the minds of some, which they could never forget all their lives. After all, such things happened in life. One person's face, among a hundred-thousand, made its way into one's mind so powerfully that it could never be forgotten.

The stranger was scared. That was natural. What would happen if someone recognised him! He was also seized by another fear—those who had got caught were certainly not accorded the loving treatment reserved for a son-in-law. People had been beaten to death when there was the slightest suspicion that someone was a child-snatcher. And these were robbers who had been caught with the loot. Who knows what they spilt out after a severe thrashing. If they had mentioned his name and the village where he was putting up, a police squad should have arrived there by now, or at least be on their way there.

He couldn't return there. He ought to wait until he ascertained the full details. He realised that he ought to go and hide in a place where no one read the newspaper. Where no one knew his face, or his name. But before that, he had to get off this train. That was absolutely vital now. And thus his sudden unplanned arrival at this station. Where he was sitting and thinking now.

Perhaps the snake had recovered a bit by now from its exertions for the giant meal. It slithered slowly and entered the hyacinth-covered pond. As the stranger turned his eyes away from his ophidian observation, he noticed someone standing near him. He was thin, dark-skinned, wearing dirty clothes, and stinking of sweat. And his eyes had a cold, gleaming look, like a snake's. The man smiled, and said, 'I couldn't recognise you when I saw you from afar.' The stranger's hand automatically went to the handle of the dagger at his waist. His breathing became faster. An electric current seemed to course through his chest.

The man smiled slyly through his teeth. 'Could you recognise me, Dada? I'm Pancha. I ride a rickshaw at the 8B bus stand. I remember you made all the arrangements for me.'

The stranger could not remember. How could he remember such trifles when his present time was so intensely eventful. He had done countless favours like this. How many people could he remember!

The man said, 'I always speak about you to Shyamali's Ma. I tell her that the little that we get to eat now is because of Jibon-da. I've been wanting to bring you to my house for a long time. But I didn't ask you since I wasn't sure whether you would be able to come. But now that you're here today, you must come along with me.'

Night was descending. A night of darkness and danger. The stranger was amazed that such an unanticipated offer of hospitality had come up. 'Do you want to take me to your place?'

'It'll be great if you come. Will you come?'

Did Pancha not know about today's incident? Had he not gone to Jadavpur today to ply his rickshaw? The whole locality was abuzz today. It was being discussed in every street corner. But why was Pancha silent about that? If he hadn't heard about it, it could only mean that he hadn't gone to Jadavpur today. The stranger moved his hand away from the dagger. There was nothing to fear. Pancha was not an enemy.

The stranger said, 'I have some urgent work. I need to return to Jadavpur. But since you're insisting, come, let me visit your house. Who knows when I'll be in these parts again. I'll stay with you tonight.'

They descended from the platform to the rail track, walked about a mile-and-a-half in the northward direction, and then walked for about twenty minutes along a muddy road on the left side. Pancha's village lay on their right. The village looked isolated in the pitch darkness. There were vast tracts of land and paddy fields all around that spread to the horizon. When these lay submerged under water during the rainy season, the area took on the appearance of a real island.

It was probably only about 9 p.m. now, but the village had already turned still. Crickets chirped in the bamboo grove. Fireflies glowed in the darkness. The moon in the sky resembled a thin slice of coconut.

As they walked, Pancha said, 'Looks like everyone is asleep. But one can't be sure. If someone asks you anything, don't tell them your real name, or where you stay. There are a couple of households in our village with radios. They listen to that. Who knows whether you were mentioned in the news. An uncle of mine happens to be a security guard. Who can say what might happen!'

The stranger had assumed that Pancha had not heard anything about him. But now it appeared that he knew everything. And yet he was taking such a person to his own house. It didn't make sense. It was customary for people to avoid someone who had such a reputation. No one wanted to invite trouble upon themselves nowadays. So was Pancha an exception? Or was he an idiot?

The stranger felt overwhelmed. He would never forget this man who was offering him help when he was in danger. He would remember this favour all his life.

Pancha entered his house silently with the stranger. As if he was entering someone else's house for some misdeed. He called out, almost in a whisper, 'Hey Shyamali's Ma, open the door! It's me.'

The house was in a dire state. It was an earthen hut with a thatched roof. But owing to lack of maintenance, it was in a shambles. Pancha's wife was awake, waiting for her husband to return. He had gone to the city to drive a rickshaw. When she opened the door and emerged, Pancha said, 'Take Dada quietly to the side verandah. Bring whatever food is there.' He then said to the stranger, 'Wash your hands and face in the pond. You can take a bath if you want.' The stranger washed his hands, and ate the meal served by Pancha's wife. After that, when he lay down on the mat made of hogla in the side verandah, he heaved a sigh of relief. He was fortunate to have found a safe place for at least one night.

After a little while, Pancha lit a beedi and came and sat next to the stranger. There was a mysterious air about him, like some co-conspirator. He didn't say anything, he sat there puffing his beedi for a while. His eyes gleamed in the glow of the beedi like those of a cat hunting a mouse. He stubbed out the beedi, threw the butt into a corner, and said, 'Mahadeb and Gobindo entered a house when they were being chased by the mob. Did you hear about what happened after that?'

Pancha knew everything. He had found out. The stranger realised there was no point in concealing anything from him. He had gathered from snippets of the conversation among the passengers on the train—that what had happened to them was truly heart-rending. But in order to find out the details, he said, 'No, I don't know.'

'The mob surrounded the house, and then caught them. And then they were beaten up very badly. They blurted out the names of all those who were with them to save their lives. That's how everyone came to know your name. I went there after I heard about the incident. That's when I learnt that you had escaped in another direction.'

The stranger was silent. For some reason, he felt a bit scared of the harmless Pancha. 'I never imagined that you would be here, in our place. I recognised you as soon as I spotted you. Anyway, so where's the bag?'

The stranger was shocked. 'Which bag?'

'The one with the money. Which you ran away with.' Pancha continued, 'The man said that he was carrying money in two bags. The one which Mahadeb snatched was found. Where's yours?'

It was a kind of eternal truth that when people reported their profit, they reduced the amount. But when they spoke about losses, they exaggerated. So the man in question may have simply been acting on the same tendency, and cooked up the tale of two bags of money. And even if he hadn't, some people—those who did not like Jibon—could have spread such a rumour. But whatever the case might be, that was what Pancha had heard and believed, and was telling him now. There seemed to be an air of mystery in the way he said it.

The stranger thought for a while, and then said, 'Since you've found out everything, I won't lie to you. You must have heard about our plight, with hundreds of people chasing us. They ran ahead, but I entered a lane on the right. I was scared to death. What if they caught me? So I hid the bag in the timber yard, and once I was empty-handed, I blended in like a decent man among decent folks. Would I have been able to escape otherwise? I have no idea what was in the bag, or how much. I thought I would go and retrieve the bag once the locality cooled down. But from what I hear, it seems Jadavpur is boiling! I don't know what to do.'

Pancha contorted his face in disbelief, although that was concealed by the darkness. The stranger did not know, nor was he supposed to know, that Pancha had only very recently started driving a rickshaw in Jadavpur. He had been a house-breaking burglar before that. He had been to prison twice. So he knew the truth about the members of the criminal underworld. How could he believe that once Jibon got the money that he had risked his life to get, he would simply leave it somewhere, under God's protection!

After sitting quietly for a while, Pancha said in a somewhat disgruntled tone, 'Look, Jibon, the fact that you came to my house, and I fed you, will never remain a secret. The police will surely find out about that. Nor can one be sure that you won't talk if the police catch you and give you a thrashing. I will become an accomplice in your crime. And I already have a criminal stamp.'

Pancha lit another beedi. 'I'm not asking you to give me all the money you have. I am not going to inform the security guard. You are the one who did the hard work, you should keep the major share. There's no compulsion, I'll be happy with whatever you give me. You can see the condition of the house. It might collapse on our heads at any time. If I could repair the house. That, and whatever the price of a rickshaw is. I don't need any more than that. You know very well what remains in the hands of a rickshaw-driver from his daily earnings after he pays the rickshaw rent to the owner. Tell me, can one survive on that? I helped you when you were in danger, please help me in my time of need. You can hide in my house for as long as you like. I'll tell people that you are a distant cousin of my wife. They won't have anything to tell my security guard uncle.'

The stranger realised that he had set foot in a snare laid by a cunning man whom he had taken to be a simple, hospitable person.

The real face hidden behind the rustic appearance was gradually becoming evident. Pancha's volcano of greed had erupted. He had forgotten about the favour he had received in the past. He had figured out that this man would not be able to return to Jadavpur and reclaim his position there. He would have to keep running for his life. He was already involved in an earlier crime, and this was another one now. He was like a fish outside water now, a bull without horns, a toothless tiger, a gun without bullets. He was powerless to do anything. Why should he be feared! But he had money in his possession, which had been obtained wrongfully. If he took a part of that, he could never be blamed for that.

It did not take the stranger long to be seized of the reality of his predicament. It was an unfavourable moment. He could not afford to do anything foolish. He had to find a way of escape from this difficult situation by staying calm and using his intelligence. He could not anger the nasty man called Pancha.

After some more thought, the stranger said, 'I would have given you that amount even if you hadn't asked me. But you can search me, I'm not carrying any money. I can't go to the place where I've hidden the money during the daytime. I'll fetch the money tomorrow night. Can you come along with me? Or are you scared?'

There was no question of saying "no" to such a proposal. Pancha nodded his head, and said, 'I'll go.'

By way of offering some more reassurance to Pancha, the stranger said, 'We have to take the roundabout way, and go via Rambabu Bazaar. We'll take the last train of the night, get into the last wagon, get off at Baghajatin, and walk from there with our faces concealed. Once we reach the timber yard, will you go in and get the bag if I show you the spot?'

'Sure.' Pancha said, 'Just show me where it is.'

'Will it be a problem if I hide the whole day in your house?'

'No, not at all. No one will know.'

The stranger said no more, he shut his eyes. Pancha too lay down on the mat spread on the floor, his mind at ease now. His wife, son and daughter were sleeping in the room inside, he would sleep here today. He had to keep an eye on Jibon, so that he did not flee. This goose would lay a golden egg tomorrow. The question of who got the bigger share could be decided once he got his hands on the bag of money.

After lying with his eyes shut for about an hour, the stranger called out to Pancha, 'Hey, please wake up!'

Twisting himself lazily, Pancha asked, 'Why?'

'I need to piss.'

Pancha had returned after driving his rickshaw all day. His body was weary, and eyes full of sleep. He unwittingly made a mistake. A very big mistake. From the depths of his sleep, he blurted, 'Go down to the courtyard, and do it there.'

The stranger crossed over Pancha, and stepped down into the courtyard. He retraced his steps while coming into the house, and stopped at the far end of the courtyard. Ahead of him lay an all-enveloping darkness stretching to the horizon. As if it were not fields but a sea of tar, with no visible shore. The stranger went to the bamboo clump beside the spot and urinated there. The dry leaves made a rustling sound, like a baby crying in some distant house. A dog was howling after seeing something disagreeable. After he finished urinating, the stranger cast a glance in Pancha's direction. Pancha lay unmoving. The stranger did not waste another moment. He ran into the sea of darkness. And he kept running.

21

Badal

A man was running. He was being chased by the present time. By his fate. He did not exactly know who the author of his destiny was. At times he thought he was merely a puppet on a string. Some skilled artist was sitting unseen and pulling the string according to a pre-written script, and staging some drama by making him dance. All that had transpired, and all that would happen in future, was only a prelude to the main drama.

When he thought about the events over the last few days, he found it incredible. Where had he been? Where was he going? When there were so many cities, towns and settlements all around, why had his feet got stuck in a station like Jadavpur? And then the role that he had played for a long time was way beyond his imagination. How did he do that? How was he able to? He wasn't supposed to walk this difficult path. Who made him do the walking?

In the course of his peregrinations one day, the stranger had arrived at the Kultala intersection. The place was full of guava orchards. So if the name had been Peyaratala, or guava-region, that would have done justice to the place. Who would explain why that was not so, and it was Kultala, or jujube-region, instead, when there wasn't the slightest trace of jujube here!

The Kultala intersection was always very crowded. There was a marketplace, and quite a few shops there, as well as a cinema hall. The nearest railway station was about eight or ten miles away. One had to commute from here either by bus, or van-rickshaw. One couldn't exactly figure out the socio-economic explanation behind such an affluent region coming up so far away from modern transport, and business and commercial establishments.

It wouldn't be wrong to say that there were almost no mud houses with thatched roofs, or any poor people's houses. Just a few. All the rest of the houses were old, and made of brick and concrete. There were trees of mango, blackberry, coconut and various other kinds, and greenery everywhere. Although it wasn't congested, nonetheless it was a crowded place. Metalled roads from the directions of Matla, Ghatakpukur, and Baruipur converged at Kultala. This small region was full of paddy fields and guava orchards. As always, there was no specific plan behind coming here. As if it was the same fate that had impelled him so far that drew him here.

The stranger was standing at the Kultala intersection, looking this way and that. His eyes suddenly fell on the tea shop across the road. He spotted four people whom he knew. They too were staring at the young man in astonishment. The stranger was wondering, why are they here, journeying in a reverse direction?

One of the four was Bhim Paramanik, who lived in the canalside shanty settlement past Rambabur Bazaar. Another was Kalachand Shikari, who lived in Boral, near Garia. The third person was Sona Haldar, who lived in the settlement on the bank of the Matla river that was known as Dighirpar Colony No. 1. And the fourth man was Badal Naskar, who lived in Sangrampur, near Diamond Harbour. All of them drove rickshaws in Jadavpur. But the stranger knew that although they drove rickshaws, none of them were ordinary rickshaw-drivers, each one of them had a criminal past.

They had spent time in prison too on a couple of occasions. Badal was the dare-devil in the group, reckless and fearless. Looking at the lean, slender-limbed, thirty-five-year-old Badal, no one would have a clue about what a deadly person he was. Rickshaw-driver Sanatan Bag of Kalikapur had told the stranger a story of Badal's daring. 'Dada, you won't believe me if I tell you! If I hadn't seen it with my own eyes, I too wouldn't have believed it either. About three months back, Badal-da told me one day, "Come to my house, Sanatan. We'll go there together. My Ma is unwell, I'll look her up, and we'll return by the first train in the morning." But I couldn't go with Badal. I had to go to Bangur Hospital with a patient, and one of the tyres of my rickshaw burst on the way back. No repair shops were open at that time of night. By the time I wheeled my rickshaw back, it was too late to join Badal. I would have to spend the night in the station. I would not be able to sleep either, thanks to the mosquitoes. And there was the police, if they hauled me up, I would be in big trouble. So I decided to join Badal-da, stay the night with him.

'So, bhai, I took the last train to Lakshmikantpur, and got off at Sangrampur, and the two of us began walking. There was a narrow, metalled road going through the village. Van-rickshaws and suchlike ply on it during the day. But there was none of that at that time of night. We walked down that road for quite a distance, and then descended to a muddy path on the right-hand side that fringed a marsh. It was a full moon night. It was as clear as daylight. But everything was silent. Not a stir anywhere.

'We walked for quite a while, bhai, and when we reached a tree near the middle of the marsh—I thought they were ghosts, but they weren't, they were men. All of them were sitting atop the tree. They clambered down when they spotted us. There were five of them. The fuckers were waiting to attack us.

'What can I tell you, Jibon! The fuckers were carrying big choppers, like the ones used to cut trees. I almost soiled my clothes in terror when I saw that. One of them brandished his chopper and threatened us, "Hand over whatever you have, quickly!" I had driven the rickshaw all day, earning seventeen rupees. I don't know how much Badal-da had on him, but he was wearing a watch, whose value wouldn't be less than seventy or eighty rupees.

'I put my hand into my pocket at once, bhai. Let the money go, let me save my life at least, I thought. But just then—what was this I was seeing! Reaching for his waist, Badal-da pulled out a revolver, just like the one the police carry. It was gleaming in the moonlight. Badal-da pointed it towards one man's chest, and said, 'I'll shoot you if you come any closer. If you want to live, throw those choppers and axes down. Do you have any idea who you dared to attack tonight? Do you know my name? I am Badal Naskar.'

'What can I tell you, Jibon bhai, the moment they heard Badal-da, they scooted with their tails between their legs, and that was the last of them. But one of them, the one who was in front, threw down his chopper, and suddenly fell at Badal-da's feet. He said, "I've heard your name, but never seen you, that's why I made a mistake. Forgive me, dada." So I learnt that day what Badal-da—who everyone makes fun of in Jadavpur—is made of. A great robber. I heard later that apparently his father was a robber too. He was murdered. I believe Badal-da was in prison in connection with some case, and was released after four years. He hardly visits his village. He lives in a rented room in Jadavpur. But if he sat idly, and didn't do any work, people would suspect something. So he drives a rickshaw to put on an appearance. But actually, they are quite well off at home. Their house has a tiled roof, they have a fish-pond, about two bighas of paddy land, and his wife has a business selling fresh vegetables. She took that up when Badal-da was in prison, but is still continuing with that. Because who knows when Badal-da might get killed, or go to prison again. Badal-da goes secretly to meet her from time to time.'

The stranger knew their names from before, and knew their faces, but he never mixed with them. He knew something about them, and so he kept his distance.

But there was a big difference between those times and now. Things had changed very rapidly. Jibon was no longer someone who fought injustice without making any compromises. He was a heinous criminal as far as the country, the time, people and the law were concerned. He was their kin.

The four men smiled in acknowledgement, and one of them waved his hand and signalled the stranger to join them. 'What brings you here? Have you come to see a film?' Although they knew that Jibon went through periods when he had no interest in jatra, cinema, songs and suchlike. It was such a time for him now.

The stranger walked across with slow, measured steps, looking at the four men watchfully. He placed his right hand at the appropriate place, and answered with his own question, 'You people here! What's up?'

The four men exchanged sly glances. Sona Haldar said, 'We've come to the cinema.'

The four of them were from four corners of the countryside, and it was in the Jadavpur locality that they were brought together through their work. For the stranger, the fact that the four of them had left the city of Calcutta, where there were plenty of fine cinema halls, and come to another region—entirely in a reverse direction, as it were—to a rundown cinema hall in an agricultural area, had a strong whiff of mystery.

They had ordered tea for themselves. They asked for another cup for the stranger now. It was time for the evening show to start at the cinema hall, Neela. This was the time of the day when the place was most crowded. Observing the crowd in front of the cinema hall, it was natural to think that there was a class of people here who certainly had some extra money to spend after buying rice, oil, potatoes and salt.

At a slight distance from the cinema hall, under an aswath tree beside a field, was a gambling wheel. There was a crowd there as well. They seemed to be in very high spirits.

Although the stranger couldn't now remember exactly where, but he recalled he had once seen a man in a railway station. The singlet and lungi he was wearing were dirty, and he had a gamchha wound around his head, but it seemed to be a kingly crown rather than a gamchha. He had a sack on his shoulder, and he had descended to the rail track and was collecting waste paper. The sun in the sky was impaling him like the point of a spear. A salty river flowed down his dusty, muddy body. But the stranger had been astonished seeing his face. Although his clothes and appearance conveyed the image of acute poverty, he was chewing a paan. He had a joyful air about him, as he walked ahead, artfully let out a stream of paan spittle, and picked up and put things into his sack— as if they were precious gems. He had seemed to be very happy. No one chews paan on an empty stomach. It was unpalatable. Although he looked poor, he was not starving. That unknown man seemed to be wealthier than him. As if he was spitting out all the distress of deprivation in his life with the paan spittle.

Someone had said, if I find a penny, I will buy bread. If I find two pennies, I will buy bread with a penny, and a flower with the other. The stranger had longed for bread all his life. The one who couldn't afford to buy bread wouldn't even dream about flowers. A flower was a symbol of beauty. But it was also a sign of the comfort and luxury of happiness. Like the paan in the mouth of the waste paper collector and the paan spittle.

The stranger had heard that some great person had apparently said that if someone doesn't love flowers, one should hit him on the head. And then he remembered that in some faded past, a flower was very dear to him. Someone had made him bora, or fritters, with pumpkin flowers. Pumpkin flowers ... lovely! He loved the hot fritters.

The stranger's throat was dry. And when he got a cup of tea in his hand, without bothering about etiquette, he slurped the tea noisily. He sensed four pairs of eyes looking at him pointedly. Without saying a word, they were saying a lot through their eyes. After finishing his tea, Badal put the cup down, tapped the stranger's shoulder, and then said almost in a whisper, 'People say, when you're going to die, you might as well have the medicine given by a proper physician first. Why should you die with some quack's medicine! That's your plight now. If you're going to get into the trade, you should have gone along with those who are experienced, who have done a few jobs, and gone to prison a couple of times. Don't they say, *khaya piya kuchh nahi, gilas toda, barah anna*, the food's free, but it's twelve annas for the glass you broke. Isn't that what happened when you went along with useless people? You didn't get any money, and now there's a police case against you.'

Badal paused to light a beedi, and then he continued, 'That fucker Mahadeb doesn't know a thing, and he went to do a job. As if I lie next to my wife, and at once a son is born, or I sow a seed, and at once a plant appears. If it was so easy to do a job, everyone would have gotten into the trade. A fine mess the idiot made, what else can one say! He was caught red-handed. Whatever had to happen naturally happened. The one who died was saved, it's the ones who survived who're in trouble. They can't evade a long prison sentence now. The same will happen to you if you're caught.'

The stranger replied in a low voice, 'I know that very well!'

'You know it!'

'I said I do!'

'Aren't you doing anything about it?'

'What can I do?'

'You're simply running around. Here today, there tomorrow.'

'Exactly.'

'How are you feeding yourself?'

'I'm not. I go through the days without food. I live on air and water.'

'And the police are after you.'

The matinee show at Leela Cinema had concluded. The bustle for the evening show now began. There was a queue of people entering the cinema hall. But these people did not move. The bell signalling the commencement of the show rang after a while. The stranger asked, 'You people said you've come for the cinema, aren't you going? The show is about to start. '

Badal retorted, 'Why should we come here to see a cinema! Are you out of your mind? We've come here to study things for a job. We saw what the scene on the street is like when the matinee show gets over, and how dark it is. One needs to study things ten times over before doing a job. If someone tells me something, and I just jump into it, I am bound to fail.'

They paid for the tea, emerged from the shop, and went and stood in a vacant spot. The other three were silent. It was only Badal who did the talking. He said, 'Look, Jibon, whatever you may or may not have been in the past, you are in the same trade as us now. I don't mind telling you. But you're not a member of our gang, so I won't tell you everything, I'll conceal some things, leave certain things out. Come, let's go and sit in the corner of the field. Or else, who knows what someone might overhear.'

They crossed the road, went past the cinema hall and walked towards the large field on the right-hand side of a pond. There was fair on this field once a year, at the time of Rathyatra. They went and sat down in a corner of the field. Badal then said, 'There's a job here. A household with old wealth. They have a gun at home too. And the main door is locked after dusk. So it's difficult to do the job at night. We have to do it just before dusk, before the door is locked.'

Turning his head to look all around, Badal said, 'The matinee show gets over at this time every day. And when the show is over a few days later, it'll be a bit darker than it is today.'

'What? How's that?' The stranger was astonished.

'Don't you know that the days are shorter in winter, and the nights longer.'

'I don't know.'

'One needs to know that for such jobs. You have to keep track of the new moon, and the full moon.'

'All right. So tell me.'

'So let's say that each one of us who is there buys a ticket and gets into the cinema hall. The show gets over, everyone leaves and so do we. And then we suddenly storm into the house together. The main door is open then, and the menfolk aren't at home. There'll only be some women and children there.'

'Why aren't any menfolk around?'

'Does any man stay at home at dusk? Doesn't he have his job, or business, or gambling, or gossip? So we'll get hold of the women, lock them all up in a room, and take what we get from the safe. The gun as well. And then we'll exit through the guava orchard next to the house. And go from one orchard to another, and then there's the vast open field.' Badal paused, looked at the stranger, and asked him, 'Would you like to join us? There's no compulsion, bhai. You can come along if you want. We need someone.'

The stranger said, 'I just can't figure out what I ought to do, or ought not to do. I escaped a big danger just the other day.'

'You haven't escaped yet.' Badal said, 'Your name's in the red register of the police now, there's no way that you can return, and lead a proper life. Just like if a girl does something with somebody, people call her a slut, and that mark can't be washed off even with a hundred cakes of soap, once a man's name enters the police books, he becomes a wanted criminal. He can't live in society like others.'

'Lots of people have told me all this before.'

'Of course, they will. Only those who know will tell you.'

Badal lit another beedi. It was dark all around. His eyes gleamed in the flame of the matchstick like those of a cat on the prowl.

The stranger said, 'Give me a beedi.' Holding out a beedi towards him, Badal said, 'How long will you go on running like this? However much you run, you're not safe. After all, you're human, not a fox which can hide in its burrow. You have to go out when necessary, out on the street, to the market, and so on. Just like we found you, so will the police. You're bound to be caught. The only thing that can help you then is money. Make sure you don't get caught on the spot, and then if you get a good lawyer, you'll get bail. Join my gang, the money will be arranged.'

He paused, put his hand over the stranger's shoulder, and said in an intimate tone, 'Bhai Jibon, when a man's alone, he's no better than a fool. He can't do anything. Don't they say, strength lies in numbers? That's why I'm asking you to join our gang. I'm forming a new one. And we'll get down to jobs. I badly need a brave man like you. Someone who can stand in front of five hundred people with a dagger in his hand during the day can handle five thousand at night if he has a gun in his hand.'

Badal was now like a leader seated on a dais, making a speech. He rambled on. 'So many political parties have come and gone in our country. But there has been no improvement in the lives of the people, they have only become poorer by the day. Only the leaders have swelled up and become fat.'

The stranger hesitantly mumbled, 'But the Naxalites were different from all that.'

'It's because you were different that all the bastards killed and wiped out all of you. These scoundrels don't let good people survive. Now that they're gone, there's no one to stand beside the poor. So what will the poor do now?'

'What will they do?'

'They had said, finish off the exploiters, meaning the landlords, the wealthy folk. There will no longer be any wealth or poverty in the country. They had said they would uproot the tree of inequality, whose roots had sunk very deep. But the tree remains. So come, let's form a gang and cut off a couple of its branches. We'll survive on the fruits that those couple of branches fetch us. If we sit waiting for those who are in prison now to be released, so that they will then uproot the tree, we would be dead, and have turned into ghosts by then.' The stranger gazed at Badal's face in amazement. This wasn't the man he knew earlier, who drove a rickshaw with his face covered. It was as if someone else was sitting inside him and speaking.

'I've met Naxalites while in prison, spoken with them. They said that a man becomes wealthy only by exploiting a lot of people and appropriating the value created by them. There's nothing wrong if we take away some of the ill-gotten gains of those who exploit many and drive them to penury, and thrive on that.'

The stranger nodded his head now. But whether it was he who did the nodding, or his present situation that made him nod could be a matter for psychological research. The Gayen household in Hatkhola was like any other wealthy landowning family. And the people of the Gayen household were also like other wealthy folk, in terms of their qualities and faults. Such people were living in insecurity everywhere, and not just in places like Naxalbari, Kharibari and Phansidewa. Whether they were in the house, or outside, they were hounded by abject fear. While the daytime went by somehow, the nights never seemed to pass. They were afraid that someone might attack them the very next moment. Nine-feet-tall walls had been erected on all four sides of the house. Sharp nails were embedded in the tops of the walls, and the door of the main entrance was made of strong wood.

It was a two-storey house. Most of the affluent people in rural Bengal preferred two-storey houses. With those, they could think of themselves as creatures who lived a bit higher than the soil. As a result, they got the opportunity for some elevated thinking. They got a lot of light and air. And they could keep a watch over a vast terrain. They had less mosquitoes, they were less troubled by floods, and of course, it provided them added security against thieves and robbers.

Bhuban Gayen was in his seventies. He had four sons, seven grandsons and a granddaughter. It was a large household. One son worked in Calcutta. Another one was a schoolteacher here. One looked after the land and fishery. And the last one was studying. A close family. Bhuban Gayen was the eternal master of the family. A brother of Bhuban Gayen's was the pradhan, or chief of the panchayat, while another was a clerk in the court.

Bhuban Gayen was a powerful man. Like in the village, everyone in the family had to abide by his orders. He had instructed that the main door ought to be locked as soon as the sun set. No one could leave the house after that, nor could any outsider enter. All the work outside would be attended to before the main door was locked. It would be opened, if at all, only after verification of the particulars. Robberies were taking place everywhere nowadays, one had no option but to be alert in such bad times.

Meanwhile, there had been a few robbery attempts at Bhuban Gayen's house. But they were thwarted. Once it was at 10 p.m. at night. It was a very dark new moon night, and Bhuban Gayen's son who worked in Calcutta was returning home like he did every day. After taking the path to the right from the road on which the bus plied, and advancing a bit, when he reached the sirish tree—at the base of which Bipadtaran Dolui had been beaten to death on the instructions of Bhuban Gayen's younger brother, back during the time of the first United Front government—a group of dark-skinned men, with their faces covered, had surrounded him. They had told him, 'We are robbers. If you shout, we'll shoot you dead. Go quietly and call the people at home, tell them to open the door. Or else you'll die.'

The times were very bad. Political party workers no longer had only party flags in their hands, they carried country bombs and revolvers too. Those who bore the identity of party workers during the day were criminals at night. People from the hammer-and-sickle party went to loot some hammer-and-sickle house. Because Bhuban Gayen was a hammer party man, he suspected that those who attempted the robberies belonged to the paddy-and-hammer-and-sickle party. There was a fierce battle going on between these two red parties at the time regarding control of the region, and about who would get the paddy, land and fisheries. So what was poor Amiya Gayen to do! After all, everyone feared for their lives. It was said, let one's wealth be lost if it means saving one's life. He went up to the house and called out to the people inside in a trembling voice. 'Who's there? Open the door. I'm back.' Gadai, the old family retainer, was about to open the door, when it struck Amiya's elder brother Bhajan Gayen that his brother's voice sounded different from other days. 'Gadai! You fucker Gada! Where the hell are you? Will your dad come and open the door!' Suspecting something, Bhajan shouted and called his brothers, and went up to the roof with a double-barrelled gun in one hand and a powerful flashlight in the other. Once he was on the roof, he fired at the sky twice in succession.

The whole thing had happened because of a suspicion and immense fear, a bit like throwing a stone into the darkness, which was quite likely to become an amusing matter for people to discuss the following day. But that didn't happen. The stone flung at random into the darkness had hit the target. It was probably a group of novice robbers, who got scared hearing the sound of gunfire, and released Amiya and fled the place. But before fleeing, they took away the twelve-hundred rupees of his salary, his watch worth three-hundred-seventy rupees, and his gold ring.

Amiya no longer returned home now if he was delayed. And when it was a new moon night, he stayed at lodgings in Calcutta. Because the times were very bad. People in the countryside lived in terror of what someone might do at any moment. Until things changed, one could not be in peace even while living in comfort. That's why one had to be a bit cautious, there was no other option! Ajoy, the schoolteacher son of Bhuban Gayen, was fond of playing *pasha*, a game played with dice. He sat at the homoeopath Dr Purkayet's chamber every evening earlier. They played until late at night. But nowadays he returned home by half-past-seven. He listened to Vividh Bharati on the radio, with the gun within reach.

Was the job carried out even after such caution? How did that happen? Who knew that the proverb about slipping through the loophole would turn out to be true like this! If something like this happened, nothing called safety remained as far as the wealthy folk in the countryside were concerned. So how were these people to survive?

It was the day of the weekly market in Hatkhola Bazaar. People from almost sixty or seventy nearby villages came to the market to buy and sell. Rice, dal, vegetables, as well as ducks, chickens, cows and goats were sold here. The market ran from afternoon to evening. Thousands of people gathered there. Quite a number of people used the road in front of Bhuban Gayen's house. Bicycles, cycle-rickshaws, cycle-vans and bullock-carts plied on the road. That did not really cause any problem, except for the dust in the air. But there was muddy slime on the road during the rains. The road was supposed to be metalled in a few months' time. It took the menfolk of the households a while to return home on the day of the weekly market. They only got back at about 9 p.m. There were only the womenfolk, children and the aged Bhuban Gayen at home until then. It was clear that the robbers knew that. They took advantage of that.

Like every day, dusk descended on the village at a particular time. A rural darkness enveloped the whole place. A hazy darkness in which one couldn't recognise anyone. Some trees and shrubs stood motionless on the field, as if in some unknown trepidation. The sky was absolutely clear, and there was no breeze either. There was a fine dust in the air, like a false mist, kicked up by the hooves of cattle, making it difficult for people to breathe. Bhuban Gayen's trusted cowherd, Paban Malek, who had been with them for a very long time, returned just then with the herd of cows that had been grazing all day. Hidden among the cows were some men, who were moving on their knees. Some of them had bags in their hands or on their shoulders, some had sacks and baskets on their heads. As the herd entered Bhuban Gayen's open doorway, after having walked about a mile, wonder of wonders, these people, who were on their haunches, rushed inside the house like the cows. And one of them then shut the door and stood there. There was a country pistol in his hand, which was known as a 'machine' in the village. The other men ran into the interior of the house, some to the first floor. All of them had some kind of weapon in their hands. One of them held a chopper at Bhuban Gayen's granddaughter's neck, while another man did the same with another grandson. Two men herded all the women into a room, and latched the door. Another man asked Bhuban Gayen, 'Where's the gun? Give it to me, or else I'll cut the two children up!'

The whole house resounded with the uproar of wailing and screaming. Not being able to figure out what was happening in the house, or why, some people walking on the road outside stopped and stood in front of the main door. Why was there such a fracas in the Gayen household at this hour, when it wasn't a fire or something like that?

The wife of Bhuban Gayen's son Sisir had not yet been locked up with the other womenfolk. She gazed in terror at the men holding weapons at the throats of her daughter Shipra and her elder brother-in-law's son Kishore. Crying, she implored, 'Don't kill them, take the gun!'

They were killers and armed robbers, they could do anything. Killing people was a routine matter for them. How could the children be saved unless the revolver was found! There were no men in the house other than Gadai and Paban. Bhuban Gayen was immobile with his arthritic knees. Paban and Gadai did not know how to use the firearm. Fearing for the children's lives, Sisir Gayen's wife blurted out, 'The gun is hanging from a nail on the wall behind the cupboard upstairs.'

'What about the cartridges? Where are they?'

'Inside the big brass pot in the cupboard.'

It was clear that the man who found the double-barrelled gun was adept at using it. He loaded two cartridges into it and then held it at Bhuban Gayen's chest, and said, 'Hurry up, and give us all the money and jewellery.'

Someone who rode a bicycle didn't know how to ride a motorcycle. Similarly, every job required a different knowledge and experience. Observing half the people in the gang of robbers, it appeared they were still novices. Not knowing exactly what they ought to do, they were running hither and thither, and shouting. And the other half were searching all over the house, looking for things to take. When they found something of value, they put it into a bag. One man was making the women remove the ornaments they were wearing.

It was just past dusk. The village was full of people. There was no more time. If a job like this wasn't completed in ten or twelve minutes, it could be dangerous. The one who was standing guard at the door shouted, 'Draw the net now, there are too many flies buzzing around.'

For people in the film world, the word 'pack-up' meant that all activity ceased as soon as the word was uttered, and everyone was restless to return home; 'draw the net' was the equivalent word for these robbers. It meant, 'stop now, no more, let us leave'. The meaning of 'flies buzzing around' was 'people have arrived to help the victims, be ready to fight'.

Although they had entered the Gayen house with thumping chests, carrying some rustic weapons, now that they had a double-barrelled gun, all their fear and apprehensions vanished. And they had as many as fifty Belgian cartridges. Those were enough to kill even a tiger, let alone humans. The one with the gun in his hands opened the front door, fired two rounds over the heads of the folk assembled outside, and roared out, 'Move aside! Get out of the way, or else you'll die! And your wives and children will weep!'

The top brass of an army could be vanquished if a crowd of people bravely stood firm, but when a crowd began fleeing, they never looked back, and if someone fell down, they were trampled. That's what the crowd did. They ran away. There's no point getting into danger on someone else's behalf! If I survive, so will the family name! Just run!

And these intruders, who were not part of the crowd, crossed the road diagonally, and stepped down into the adjoining paddy field, which lay in darkness that stretched to the horizon. It was like a sea of tar all around them. Who on earth would find them in that sea!

⚮

It was 8 p.m. now. It was the day of the Gazi Baba mela in Ghutiari Sharif. The fair was held every Thursday. A special feature of the fair was that it wasn't just Muslims who came there, many Hindu devotees came too. Rooms were available here for a night's stay at a cheap rent. But not everyone came to have fun in the rented room with a woman for hire. Some came here seeking relief from illness or grief, for peace of mind.

There was a large pond beside Gazi Baba's mazaar, where people set flowers afloat. They believed that if the flower floated around in the water and then returned to the person's hand, any wish of theirs would be fulfilled.

A qawwali group sat on a cemented dais in front of the mazaar. The members of the group of singers could be engaged in various professions for survival, whether as butcher, or cook, or a tailor, or pickpocket. But on this day, they came here to reveal their musical talent. And it wasn't as if all those songs were just a loud, hoarse, tuneless roar. One saw some people there who were really gifted artists, who could entrance the audience if they got the opportunity.

There were plenty of shops, restaurants and eateries here. Everything had come up essentially on account of Gazi Baba's mazaar.

A Down-train had stopped at Ghutiari Sharif. Lots of people got off the train, but there were a few special people too among them. They did not head towards the mazaar. They walked in pairs along the rail track, going eastwards. After walking for about a mile-and-a-half, they arrived at a level-crossing, where they hit a road that ran north-south. On the northern side, the road curved to the east after a distance, and then ran parallel to the railway line.

There was a gatekeeper's cabin at the level-crossing. There were a few people sitting and gambling there, one of whom raised his eyes and observed a group of men of dubious character who were walking along the rail track; they climbed up to the road on their left and headed eastwards. He hurled a query at the last two people, 'Who's that? Give your name and address!'

Without stopping, one of the men replied, 'I'm from Belgachhi. I had been to the mazaar to fulfil a vow.'

'Which house in Belgachhi do you live in?'

'The Laskar house. Abu Bakr Laskar is my uncle. Do you know him?'

No, he didn't know him. But the answer seemed all right. The man who was gambling had been suspicious seeing their gait. But it was okay now. They weren't outsiders. They were locals. If he stuttered while replying, or if he began running, one would know he was up to no good.

The road running parallel to the railway line was at quite an elevation. And beyond that was an open field. There were a few small villages far in the distance. As if they were in the middle of a sea. Like small islands.

The pair that were walking ahead of the others stopped and looked behind, to be sure that the pair walking behind them were their own men and no one else. They then got off the road, and descended to the field on the left. The pair of men who were at the rear too looked behind, and followed the others to the field. Their eyes were sharp, their ears alert, and they were prepared in mind and body. These people were no longer ordinary folk, they were warriors who had plunged into the sea of death. Whatever was in their fate would happen now.

As they walked through the field, they arrived at an acacia grove. The trees had been planted around a pool that had been dug to store water for cultivation. Each one took off his clothes and folded them neatly and packed them into a bag. They tied the bags to their waists. One of them had a larger bag. He took out some pieces of iron from that. They were joined to make a few pipe guns. One of the men had the barrel of the stolen gun strapped to his back. The butt of the gun was in another bag. The two were joined to make the double-barrelled gun usable. The eleven miscreants, armed with four pipe guns and a manufactured firearm, sat in silence in the shade of the acacia grove, counting the hours.

This was a vast field. But it would be gone after a few years. A human settlement would come up there. But that would happen in 1979, shortly after the genocide in Marichjhampi. Those who would be able to escape from that fatal island were the ones who would build a village here, and give it the name Pother Shesh, or journey's end.

The field seemed to be asleep now, covered with a sheet of light mist. There was a fine, moist coating on the seated men. A pleasant breeze blew from the southeast. It was a lot like the panting breath of a terrified creature. A dog moaned plaintively in some faraway village. It sounded very sad, as if it was lamenting the departure of a loved one. Shooting stars coursed through the sky like arrows from time to time. The stars spread across the sky shone like newly minted coins.

The moon would rise at 1.15 a.m. tonight. Which was why the darkness was not so intense at this time. After a while, a train was observed racing along the track. Shortly after that, a man was spotted advancing cautiously from that direction towards the acacia grove. The man with the double-barrelled gun pointed it in that direction and watched him closely. When the man was about a hundred yards away from the grove, he uttered some sounds. The man with the gun asked, 'Who's that?' He replied, 'It's me, bhai.'

Addressing him as 'bhai' meant he was one of their own. He walked ahead. He had a bundle in one hand, and a pitcher of water in the other. When the bundle was opened, there were *rutis* and some alu tarkari inside. He gave each person two rutis and then served the alu tarkari over that, and then said, 'I just averted what could have been a calamity! There's a fucker, he never visits me. For some reason, he arrived today just as I finished making the rutis. I ran with the bundle of rutis. Wouldn't he have suspected something if he saw me making so many rutis!'

The man with the gun enquired, 'Is everything all right?'

'Yes.'

'So there's no problem?'

'No.'

'I had asked you to get a ladder. Did you get that?'

'You don't need a ladder.'

'How will we climb over the wall?'

'Someone will lift me up on his shoulder. I'll get to the top of the wall and clamber down the tree on the other side, and open the front door. All of you can then rush in through the door.'

'But the door has to be broken. I asked you to bring an axe, where's that?'

'Oh, I've hidden it beside the railway line. I'll pick it up on the way.'

Like there were matchmakers for marriages, *khonjdars* or spotters, were required for robberies. The man with the *rutis* was such a spotter. He lived in the village here. So he knew everything about the household in question. He had worked in the house for a few months. As a result of which, he knew even more. A thumbnail account of which room the safe was in, and which one had the gun, how many people there were, how many knew how to use the gun, whether there were more weapons in the village, what the relations between the household and the village folk were like, how many people there were in the village, how brave they were, and so on. All this information was vital to completing a job successfully.

The ruti man was about forty years old. He was bald, very thin, and less than five feet in height. He had a runny nose. Such a man had set out to commit a robbery. Looking at him, one would think that if he was a thief, he would probably be stealing bananas, radishes and suchlike from farmers' fields. One of the men was observing him closely. He couldn't see him clearly earlier. Now he observed that his right arm was severed at the wrist. It was that arm that he had bent like a hook, slung the ruti bundle on, and brought with him. The man would climb over the wall before anyone else, clamber down a tree on the other side and open the door.

'Will you be able to do it?'

'I will,' he replied. 'I'm used to it. So what if I don't have a hand, I have an arm, don't I? Sure, I can do it. I have to.' And then he muttered, 'If the fuckers had swiped at my throat instead of my hand, I would have been saved, and they too would have been!'

After they had finished their meal, all of them lit beedis. One person sat with his face covered, while all the others sat closely around him, and that was how a matchstick was lit. Or else the light from the fire could be seen from afar. Why was there light in the middle of the field! If someone spotted that, they might get suspicious. The village folk would then arrive in silence and surround the band of robbers. That was why the flame was concealed, a beedi was lit, and then one beedi from another, until all the beedis were lit. And thus, did they exercise caution even as they smoked.

The man with the gun stood up after that. He said, 'Get ready, everyone. It's time to go.' They all stood in a row then. They invoked their personal deities inwardly. Needless to mention, almost everyone was a devotee of Ma Kali. One member of the group remembered Allah the Compassionate. And another one was himself unaware of whom he invoked.

One could say now, with no doubt whatsoever, that the intensity with which they thought of God at this moment was quite impossible on the part of ordinary devotees. In a little while they were going to jump into a game of life and death. And in that game, the slightest mistake, or lack of alertness, or bad luck, could lead to a disaster of such proportions that a man could become a corpse the very next moment. If he was shot in the chest, the death was an easy one. But if he somehow happened to get caught by a bloodthirsty mob, he would suffer a slow, painful death.

This was why they implored inwardly, 'O God, Ma Kali, protect me. I'm very needy, Ma. That's why I'm doing this job. Please see to it Ma that no one is killed by me, and no one kills me.'

After they finished praying, the gang walked ahead in silence. The leader walked in front, he was carrying the double-barrelled gun. Beside him was the spotter, who showed the way. This was a time in which even the most daring robber trembled in fear. The path from the hideout to the house in question seemed to be a most difficult and impassable one. Once they crossed this, and jumped into the targeted house, all their fears would vanish. Each man alone was equal to a hundred.

This house too was a two-storeyed one. There were nine-foot-high walls on all sides. One man sat down in front of the wall. The spotter climbed onto his shoulders. The seated man then rose up slowly. The spotter got to the top of the wall, and descended down the neem tree on the other side into the courtyard below. He then unlatched the front door silently. He laughed inwardly. He had vowed for years on end to enter this house in such a fashion, with a gang of associates. That had been fulfilled today. One by one, all the gang members entered the house.

It was 11 p.m. now. The moon was supposed to rise at 1.15 a.m. That meant they would have a couple of hours of relative darkness. The last train of the day had gone down the nearby railway line a little while ago, making the earth tremble and raising a virtual dust storm. The entire region was fast asleep after a hearty dinner. The dog that had been moaning in some faraway hamlet was also quiet now. The dogs of this neighbourhood were silent too. Dogs had a keen sense of smell. Perhaps they had sensed from their scent that the denizens of night who had walked a great distance in darkness, without any fear of snakes or scorpions, and arrived at this hamlet now, were not afraid even of a tiger, let alone a mere dog. In fact, the master of the household where they were guests now was a more terrifying creature than a tiger as far as the people of the locality was concerned. There wasn't the slightest bit of kindness, or compassion, or forgiveness in him. His will was the law and his word was the last word in the region.

An uncle of this man was a powerful political leader of south Bengal, who had close relations with the state president of the current ruling party. Thanks to the powerful uncle, his nephew too was a powerful leader in this region. A man had once stolen some spinach from the nephew's land. He had severed the man's hand for that trivial offence. No police complaint was filed in this matter. The police station refused to file a case the moment they heard the name of the man in question. They had advised that it wasn't wise to be in conflict with a crocodile when one lived in water.

Severing someone's hand for a bit of spinach! The leader of the gang had thought the tale to be an exaggerated one when he had heard it from the spotter. The man had then raised his right arm— on which he had slung and brought the bundle of rutis tonight— and shown it to him, 'See this! What do you say now?'

'But weren't you working in this house?'

'That's right. That's why I was angry, and left the job. What else could I do? Work like a donkey all day, and when it came to providing food, all one got was stale rice. And if there was the slightest laxity in work, one got a thrashing.'

The leader stood next to the door with the gun. The spotter was beside him, with a powerful flashlight. If any outsider heard the screams of the members of the household and rushed towards the house in order to help them, the spotter would shine his flashlight, and the man with the rifle would shoot at the person. Besides, the spotter was a local. If he went inside the house and someone recognised him, the poor man would be in trouble.

Nine men advanced towards the interior, leaving the two to keep watch. A man was lying on the open verandah of the ground floor, just at the foot of the stairs leading to the first floor. He was currently working in this house. Custom dictated that he be caught and tied up. But that meant waking him up. If the man woke up now, his screams would wake up everyone in the house. That would be the end of all their plans. One of the gang members, whose status in the gang was next to the leader, silently signalled to two others to stand next to the sleeping man, and to grab hold of him and tie him up once shouts and screams sounded from the first floor. But not before that.

Seven men climbed up to the first floor. They would suffice to overcome the woman and the solitary male there. There was a low wall in front, at the top of the stairs. They could see the courtyard below from there. A door led to a room on the left side. It was a strong door, and had been latched firmly from inside. But one could break down the door with an axe. They had that too. But it was a bit difficult to do that right now. There was a gun in this room, as well as a man who was deft in using it. He would wake up as soon as the axe hit the door.

Two or three gang members discussed the matter. After that, two of them, one of whom was slightly inexperienced but very brave, and the other not so brave but highly experienced, crossed over the low wall on the first floor and dropped down to a parapet over the verandah. They walked along the parapet to the open window on the southern side of the house. There was a light burning in the room on the first floor. They could see a man lying on his back on the cot. Next to him was his five-year-old son, and beside his son was his wife, on the window side.

The brave man whispered to the experienced one, 'I'll shoot him. If I kill him, there won't be anyone left in the room to fire the gun. There won't be any problem in breaking the door down with the axe after that. Shall I shoot him?'

'You want to kill him!' The experienced man exclaimed.

'He won't die. Such people don't die easily. He'll be wounded. And if he dies, that's fine. There'll be one son-of-a-swine less in the country.'

'It's a 12 bore cartridge! What if some pellets hit the child?'

'Hmm. That's a problem.'

The brave man stood on the parapet, inserted the barrel of the pipe gun through the window, and waited with bated breath for either the father or the son to move away from one another, so that he could then shoot. The gun that was placed in a corner of the lighted room was visible. It was a really valuable asset. His eyes shone greedily as he wondered how soon he could lay his hands on it.

This was an unbearably suffocating situation. Eleven men were standing still in their respective positions and counting the time. It was like a battle that had begun and yet not begun. Their palms were sweaty in excitement, their hearts thumping loudly.

And then there was a sudden reversal. The boy sleeping between his parents suddenly began to cry. His mother woke up to the sound of his cries. She sat up, and asked, 'What happened?' 'I need to shit,' said the boy amidst sobs. The father scolded him, 'Be quiet! Why are you crying? Your Ma is taking you to the bathroom.'

Just another moment! The woman would surely open the door now. The gang members standing at the door would pounce on her at once, like hawks on the hunt, and tie her up. But all their calculations went awry. The two men who were standing at the foot of the stairs, beside the sleeping servant, were not aware of the drama taking place on the first floor. As soon as the random sounds of the child crying and the mother's query reached their ears, they assumed that the operation had commenced. They grabbed hold of the servant. And he screamed for his life, 'O God, they're killing me, help!' At once, the eyes of the alert master of this household moved to the window on the southern side. He could see the barrel of a gun pointing at him, and the heads of two men. He was a powerful leader of the region. He was always mentally prepared for an attack by his political opponents. Hearing the distressed cries coming from below, he figured out that the assailants had entered the house. In the flash of an eye, he rolled off the bed and lay on the floor. The one with the pipe gun fired, but that was of no avail.

The man wasn't so badly injured that he couldn't use his gun. He crawled to the gun and picked it up.

The man with the pipe gun needed at least thirty or forty seconds now to load another cartridge in his pipe gun. But it would take only a second or two for the bullet from inside to reach him. The battle could not be won. He would die. Retreat was the sensible option now. That was useful in every battle. Advancing one step, and then retreating two steps. Figuring that out, he jumped down at once from the parapet. The other man too did the same. It wasn't easy for someone to jump down from the first floor to the hard cemented courtyard below. But of course, these people were no ordinary folk, they were robbers, whose cries made people tilt over in fear. Seeing the two, the others too rushed down the stairs.

They now exited through the front door, and ran back the way they had come, towards the railway line in front of them. Once they crossed the rail track and descended into the field below, they would be free of danger.

The muddy path was no wider than ten feet. There were large ponds on both sides. The railway line was about eight hundred metres away. And then the vast, boundless field. But the villagers woke up to the loud shouts from the household and the gunshots. They picked up the spear, lathi, chopper, or *bonti* kept close at hand and rushed out like floodwaters. Their numbers could not be estimated owing to the darkness. It could be a hundred, or even a thousand. It was vital for the gang to descend into the field. But they could not advance towards the railway line now. There was a mob of about three hundred people gathered there. They were picking up stone chips from the track and hurling them at the robbers. It was impossible for the robbers to disregard the stones raining down on them and advance. And behind them, the master of the house was firing one shot after another. He had climbed up to the roof of the house with his gun. Although he missed his targets in the darkness and the bullets went this way and that, how could one be sure that would happen each time? The plight of the members of the gang, who had all arrived here from far away, was like mice caught in traps. People in front of them, people behind them, a pond on the left, a pond on the right. There was no way of escape.

The gang was armed, although not adequately. They could fire and clear the way in front of them. But there was the possibility of loss of life in that case. These people were terribly poor, like the robbers, and extremely simple, and foolish too. One of the gang members reflected on such matters. If they are intent on dying, there's nothing we can do. My life is precious to me. But before that, one ought to explain the matters to them.

He said to the man with the gun, 'Stay behind me, let me try to deal with them.' And then one of the eleven-member gang advanced with his pipe gun raised high, ahead of the others. He hurled a piercing missile of words at the men throwing stones. 'Fuckers, do you want to die? Move away! Clear the way for us! Or else I'll shoot!'

'Shoot!' one man in the samaritan mob shouted out. 'Fire! How many will you kill? But we won't spare you today!'

The pipe gun man said, 'Hey fucker, if the bullet hits your chest, you'll die, but have you thought about what will happen to your wife and children? Your children will starve to death. The babus won't give you any rice. Move away!'

The mob figured out the truth hearing the sound of gunfire, and seeing the resulting flash of fire. The men stopped throwing stones and moved away from their path. It's true, who will feed my children if I die.

But let us return to the servant in the babu household; he had consumed toddy in the evening, and then dinner at night. Who knows whether out of intoxication, or loyalty to the provider of the food that he had in his stomach, he came chasing after the robbers from behind with a lathi in his hand, leaving the other villagers behind.

The spotter, who had brought the rutis, was standing with a flashlight beside the man with the gun. He had nurtured a hope for five years. The hope had almost been fulfilled. Once the gang members had broken down the door and tied up the Sapui scion, he would enter the room, with his face covered with a gamchha. He would land a monstrous kick on the householder's face. That would have surely come true tonight, if it were not for the fucking servant!

The ruti man could never forget that frightful day. His severed arm would not let him forget. Nor could he forget the officer in the police station, who had forced the ruti man to state in his testimony, 'No one severed my arm. All such talk is false propaganda. I am a servant of Sapui Babu. I lost my hand in the hay-cutting machine, while chopping straw to feed the cows.'

Spotting that servant coming now, all the rage of the failed ruti man was directed towards him. He ran ahead and landed a powerful blow on the temple of the servant with his heavy flashlight. Losing his balance, the man fell into the pond.

22

Kumar Mondol

The district police headquarters had received a telephone call two days ago, 'We've caught him, sir. What should we do now?' An experienced, middle-aged police officer from there had arrived today at the police station in this remote region of south Bengal. The bald, fair-skinned officer, who had successfully cracked many cases, was sipping a cup of tea now, and trying to study the body language of the twenty-five-year old recently apprehended criminal clad in a lungi and vest, who was sitting in an ungainly fashion, with his knees bent, in a corner of the room. That was vital in the preliminary stage of an investigation. The interrogation would begin once he had studied him adequately, by *norom* and *gorom*, i.e., soft as well as hot methods. The mob had employed some of the hot methods, and some of that had been employed in the police station, too, over the last two days. The criminal's aching joints still bore testimony to that. There were black bruises on the palms of his hands from cane blows. There was a swelling below his left eye from a punch, and a cut with blood clotted on it.

The officer put down the cup after he finished the tea, and leisurely lit a cigarette. There was a large, thick register on the big table in front of him, a ruler, a paperweight, a glass of water, an ashtray, a small brass cannon, a Kali idol and other such sundry items. There were two large steel cupboards along the wall. On top of the cupboards were a coil of thick rope, a few lathis and some disused fans from olden times, which used to produce more sound than breeze.

The officer stubbed the butt of the cigarette in the ashtray, and drew the register towards him. He turned the pages, as if looking for something. And then he looked at the criminal sitting in a corner of the room, and ordered him in a calm voice, 'Stand up.'

The criminal whimpered, 'My legs are aching terribly, sir.'

The officer paid no attention to that, he picked up the lathi in front of him and struck him with that. 'Stand up!'

The criminal propped himself on his knees and rose up with great difficulty. At least two hundred lathi blows had landed on the soles of his feet during the last two nights. As a result, his feet were swollen and throbbing with pain. His legs were trembling.

'Stand up straight!' Another blow with the lathi. 'Absolutely straight!'

The officer had come from the district headquarters, where there were records detailing all the crimes and criminals in the district. And when those who had committed criminal acts under multiple police stations were caught, reports had to be sent to the headquarters from the local police station. The former's powers to investigate a case directly extended to the entire district, and if necessary, beyond that as well. From what the criminal who this officer had come to interrogate had confessed during the preliminary stage of third-degree methods, it was learnt that they had organised daring criminal acts in places that fell under eight police stations in south Bengal. All of these were crimes under Section 384 and 385 of the Indian Penal Code.

The criminal's inability to stand up straight made the officer furrow his brows in annoyance. Addressing a constable dressed in a white uniform who was standing nearby, he nodded his head, and said, 'Straighten him up.' The constable picked up the lathi from the table and tapped the criminal on his back and kneecaps, saying, 'Straighten up, straight, straight I said! Stretch yourself!' He made the half-mauled criminal stand up straight, exactly as the officer wanted.

'State your name, your real name.'

The criminal groaned, and said, 'My name is Kumar Mondol, sir. People call me Peto. I got the name at the time of the terrible famine, when I ate the flesh of a dead goat belonging to a babu.'

The officer rebuffed him. 'I'm not interested in how you got your name. State your address.'

'The village is Uchhepota, under Gosaipur post office, and Notunhaat police station, district—'

'That's enough.' The officer said, interrupting him. Now tell me since when you have been committing robberies. Which are the places where you have committed robberies so far? Who are the people in your gang, and where do they live? What's the name of your leader? What weapons do you people possess? There's no hurry, I have a lot of time. Tell me everything one by one. No one will hit you if you tell me the truth. Cooperate with us. Tell us where the weapons are. We will make you a state witness. You'll be released very soon. But if you don't cooperate with us, we'll thrash you and break your bones. We'll get the order for police custody, and beat you every night. Do you want that?'

'No, sir.'

'Then tell the truth.'

'I told you whatever I know.'

'You didn't say everything. You've concealed some things.'

'No, sir. I don't know anything else.'

Everyone in Kumar's village knew him to be a more or less decent person. He drove a rickshaw in Calcutta. He didn't have a mother, and his father was quite aged. He had a wife and two daughters. Kumar's father, Nabin Mondol, earlier possessed two bighas of paddy land. He had pledged that in the year of the famine, and had not yet been able to reclaim it.

That was the year Kumar's mother died. He was about eighteen then. Unless there was a woman in the household, who would gather twigs for the stove and cook on the occasions when some rice was obtained? Who would fetch a pitcher of drinking water from the tap that was a couple of miles away? Considering all this, Nabin got his son Kumar married to a poor and unfortunate girl from a nearby village. Kumar began driving a rickshaw in Jadavpur shortly after his marriage. Old Nabin too, let alone any others, didn't know that Kumar had covertly become like this. He only found out when people caught Kumar, tied him to a lamp post, and beat him till he was half-dead.

Notunhaat had a bus service. There were many large shops there. There was a rice mill, a warehouse, a fish wholesaler and a cinema hall. A major canal flowed by Notunhaat, and this eventually joined the Vidyadhari river. Boats plied along the canal, bringing various commodities to Notunhaat from Satirhaat. And some goods from Notunhaat too went to Gorerhaat.

There was a weekly market at Notunhaat. The marketplace was extremely crowded on that day. It was open for business only for a couple of hours in the morning on the remaining six days of the week. There was no electricity here yet. The cinema hall ran on a generator. The rice mill too was powered by a diesel generator. Petromax lamps lit up all the big shops in the evening. The other shops had kerosene lamps. There was a narrow wooden bridge opposite the marketplace to allow people to cross the canal. A gambling session with cards commenced late in the afternoon near this bridge, under a shishir tree on the canalside. The shopkeepers in the marketplace were the players, and their game went on until evening.

Such a gambling session was in full swing one day, and one of the players was Abani Purkayet, who was a member of the local panchayat, and the secretary of the market committee. All that

Abani and his partner needed to win this hand was an ace of hearts. That was the card he got too. Victory was certain. And just then, his eyes espied something in the distance, on the canal. It was about half-past-four in the afternoon now. The sun that had descended upon the western sky had a shiny appearance. The bright sunlight fell on a boat that was advancing along the canal. The mound-like load of roof-tiles from the Sonar Bangla Tile Factory which the boat was carrying assumed a golden hue. The price of each tile was a rupee and twenty paise. The tiles were strong too, they didn't break if they fell out of one's hand.

Whose tiles were these? Who was building a house with a tiled roof?

This was one of the poorest parts of south Bengal. Eighty per cent of the people here were unable to find two square meals a day. No clothes, or footwear, or oil to apply on one's hair. It was doubtful whether any village here had even five houses with tiled roofs. All the houses had earthen walls, with roofs of thatch. A tiled roof was a symbol of affluence. Which meant paddy in the granary, cattle in the cowshed, and fish in the pond. Someone who owned ten or twenty bighas of paddy land. But such a person was also the cause of jealousy, anguish and rage for many people. It was not wrong for a man to possess wealth in this country. However, the means of accumulating wealth in all countries and at all times was both wrong and criminal. When people toiled all day digging earth, slogging like a donkey, and yet could not afford two square meals a day, everyone ought to know that the mutual conflict, hatred and suspicion that existed between the rich and the poor would continue to flow in people's minds like the mythical subterranean river Phalgu.

Abani Purkayet was not really rich, but he could be called a medium farmer. He had inherited about ten bighas of land from his father, and obtained about five bighas following Operation Barga, on account of being associated with the party. There was a saying that when a man sold oil, there was always some oil on his body and head even if he didn't want it. Besides, on account of being a member of the local panchayat, he was able to earn a little bit from here and there. He also owned the rice mill in the marketplace.

Some of the rooms in Abani's house still had roofs of thatch. He wanted to do up all the rooms with brick walls and tiled roofs. It didn't behove the dignity of a leader to have a thatch roof now. The thatch had to be re-laid before every rainy season, and that was a bother too.

He couldn't take his eyes off the boat with the tiles going down the canal. While the cards remained in his hand, his eyes were captive to the flash of sunlight as it rebounded off the tiles.

The name of the card game they were playing was 'Twenty-nine'. This involved bidding, like in an auction. One of the players reminded him, 'Where are you, Mr Member! Make your call! I said eighteen. What about you?'

'I'll stick to eighteen,' Abani said absent-mindedly.

'Nineteen.'

'Okay, nineteen.'

'Twenty?'

'I'll pass. You choose the trump. And I say double.'

'Double's fine!'

The boat had now arrived near the wooden bridge. Two dark-skinned, bare-bodied men were punting the boat using poles. The canal's depth was limited. Oars were not required here. Abani called out, 'Whose tiles? Which village are you going to?'

One of the boatmen replied, 'Tiles for Uchhepota.'

Uchhepota was a small village. Thirty or thirty-two landless farm labourers lived there. Who had the means to build a tiled roof in such a village? Abani Purkayet found it strange. He couldn't think of a single person in that village whose kitchen stove was lit twice a day.

He asked again, 'Which house in Uchhepota.'

'Nabin Mondol's.'

It wasn't just Abani now, but each one sitting at the card-playing session who was startled. They knew Kumar Mondol's aged, decrepit father, Nabin Mondol, to a greater or lesser degree. It was just recently that Kumar got married to Kyalaram's daughter, Aduri, who used to forage for vegetables in the marketplace. After that, Kumar began going to Calcutta. But a lot of other people too went to Calcutta and rode rickshaws there. None of them could feed or clothe themselves properly. And here he was, making a tiled roof! No! The whole thing seemed suspicious.

Abani Purkayet's card-partner Koilash voiced the same thoughts. 'What's this we're hearing, Mr Member! So many people have spent their lives riding rickshaws. Not a single one of them could buy a rickshaw for himself after providing for his family, everyone rides rented rickshaws. And here's this chit of a boy, Kumar! He started riding a rickshaw just the other day, and he's building a tiled roof now!'

Ani Naskar joined the fray now. 'The job will set him back by at least two-and-a-half-thousand rupees. You can't get a bamboo pole these days for anything less than ten or twelve rupees. He'll definitely need about fifty of them. And then there's the mason, nails, ropes, and so on, and that's not cheap either. I don't know about you people, but I think Kumar is doing something fishy.'

Banamali Mridha, another shopkeeper from Notunhaat, joined in too. 'That's what I think too. I saw him buying a whole sack of rice the other day. And lots of other things too. How can he afford all that?'

Another man from the group added, 'A few days ago, I saw Kumar walking towards the station with a huge bag. I could make out that it was very heavy. No one who carries such a bag drives a rickshaw. I think Kumar has joined a gang of thieves or smugglers.'

It emerged in the course of the discussion that it was not he alone, quite a few people had seen Kumar heading towards Calcutta carrying a large bag on different days. Some suspected that it might have contained ganja, or opium, or suchlike, which had arrived in this country from Bangladesh via river. Some were of the opinion that he might be trafficking tiger or deer skin too.

The Bangladesh border was not very far from here. It was only twenty or twenty-two kilometres away. It was true that some stuff from that country was being smuggled into this country via the rivers here. Which then reached Calcutta by train. That included the skin of deer and tigers from the Sundarbans too.

Abani said, 'Keep your eyes and ears open. Whenever anyone spots him carrying a bag like that, just let me know. '

Kumar was unaware that all around him a lot of people were keeping a close watch over his movements. Reports of what he ate, where he went, when he left, when he returned, and for that matter, news of his wife's gold earrings and four saris too reached Abani Purkayet.

One morning, Kumar left his house carrying the conspicuous bag, walked past Notunhaat, crossed the wooden bridge, and got into a van-rickshaw to go to the nearest railway station. Abani Purkayet and some others accosted him, and said, 'Open the bag, let's see what you carry everyday.'

Kumar had no way of fleeing then. It was morning time. There was a crowd there. Someone unzipped the bag. And at once they were wide-eyed in astonishment. The bag contained two pipe guns, two large flashlights, a chopper and some cartridges. After a public thrashing, he admitted that the weapons were not used for any great objective, but to commit robberies. Kumar was not a rickshaw-driver now, he was an armed robber, but he had not yet become a seasoned criminal. Kumar was yet to acquire the skill of cooking up credible tales. And so, after a bit of thrashing, he blurted everything out. The people then took him to the police station.

The officer who had come from the headquarters heard the whole story in detail once again. The fat register on the table now had Kumar's name and address recorded in it, together with a photograph. The officer opened the register, showed Kumar the photographs of all the notorious criminals of the district, and said to him, 'Tell me which of these people are in your gang.'

There were a few hundred photographs in the register. Kumar could recognise only one person from among them. That was Badal. The officer figured out the gang was a recently formed one. Badal was the driving force. Novices were not so alert, so it wouldn't be difficult to apprehend the entire gang. It was only Badal who was swift.

'Where can I find all the members of your gang? Where do they live? Where does Badal live?'

Kumar replied, 'I don't know where Badal lives. No one knows that. But the others come to the top of the overbridge in the Baruipur station around dusk. They chat for a while and leave. They are all from various places. They used to drive rickshaws in Jadavpur, that's how I became acquainted with them. But I don't know where they live. Nor do any of them know where I live.'

The preliminary interrogation was over. The officer called the officer in charge of the police station, and said, 'Let him be here for a few days. I hope we'll be able to recover all the stolen goods he has hidden. And keep a watch on the railway station from tomorrow. Alert the informers.'

23

The Hut by the Canal

Badal's father, Haldhar, was an armed robber. But that was almost like being a day labourer in those days. It wasn't like it is nowadays, with country bombs, revolvers and pipe guns in virtually every house. Such weapons were not plentiful. The tools of trade of robbers were lathis, spears, choppers and a flaming torch. When the moon was waning, Haldhar would apply some soot on his face, carry such weapons, and set out with his group in some direction. After leaving their respective homes at dusk, they walked two or five kosh across fields, so that they could finish the job and return before sunrise. That was their limit. So there were also instances when they robbed a house twice the same year. If they were lucky, they got a gold ornament or two. But it didn't matter if they didn't. Paddy, rice, ducks, chickens, bellmetal and brass utensils, clothes—in short, they took whatever they could, and thus managed to eke out a living. Once the moon began to wax, they concealed the spears and choppers in the haystack, and acted like decent folk, and sat at home, pretending to be dim-witted good-for-nothings.

No one in Haldhar's village knew that he was a robber. His wife prepared muri, and he went from village to village selling that. That was apparently what he did. Haldhar's identity came to light the day his wife went to the Gajon Mela in the Kachari Maidan wearing the sari that belonged to the wife of Bibhuti babu, of Suryapur, her favourite one, which she had received from her parents. Observing the marks and symbols on the sari, Bibhuti babu's wife realised that it was the one that belonged to her, which was stolen by robbers the previous month. She voiced her suspicions to Bibhuti babu. And after that, Bibhuti babu secretly enquired about whose wife the sari-clad woman was.

After that he, together with a couple of people from his own village, searched Haldhar's house. They discovered that it wasn't only the sari that had been stolen, but also a bell-metal plate and two glasses belonging to Bibhuti babu. There were also a few more sundry items of his in the sack in which all these items had been stuffed and brought. The sack contained lots of things stolen from all the other houses. After a thrashing, Haldhar confessed to what all he had stolen, and from where. The more Haldhar confessed, the more the crowd of people there became excited. He was beaten to death that day. Badal was sixteen years old when his father died. He too became a robber after a few years. But not one like his father. Instead of carrying choppers and flaming torches, he equipped the gang with country bombs, pipe guns and flashlights. And in a very short time, he became a famous man in the region. He attacked the houses of all those people who were involved in the killing of his father. He couldn't find Bibhuti babu, but he was able to shoot his son and injure him.

Badal was caught by the police. But he was fortunate to have been apprehended. If he had fallen into the hands of the public, his plight too would have been like his father's. He was in prison for four years, without any trial. Although he was notorious, he didn't really have much money; after all, one couldn't do anything major when all one was carrying were country bombs and pipe guns. So he couldn't employ a good lawyer, and he didn't obtain bail. Charge sheets were prepared for some of the cases. Witnesses failed to turn up for many of the cases for which charge sheets had been prepared. And in the cases where witnesses turned up, their testimony was not adequate to sentence the accused for the crime in question. So Badal was finally acquitted and released.

But rural Bengal had undergone a change by then. All those who were Badal's enemies were the local leaders or workers of some political party or the other. After being released from prison, Badal got word that he would not survive if he returned to his village. Bubhuti babu's son Anup would hack him to pieces. So he went to Jadavpur instead, and began driving a rickshaw there. He got married too.

Just like it was impossible for a tiger that had tasted blood to be a herbivore, it was difficult for a person who had fallen into the temptation of immense amounts of money to be satisfied with meagre earnings. Badal had made the acquaintance of some robbers while in prison. He joined up with some of them after his release and did a couple of jobs too. But he was keen to form a gang of his own again. No more pipe guns this time, he would equip the gang with expensive guns. His gang was formed, and they managed to obtain two rifles too, one of them double-barrelled. Once they had five or seven 'original' guns, they would take up a major job. So that after a couple of such jobs, he could sit idle for the next few years. That was why he attacked the houses where wealthy folk lived. Where there would be money, as well as a firearm. It didn't matter if there wasn't much of the former, but getting the latter was very important.

Badal was advancing slowly, and according to plan, towards his desired goal. But calamity suddenly descended upon him because of the thick-headed Kumar. Fuck, everyone got thrashed, but how many could digest it! After all, it was the one who could digest it who was the smart one. What kind of man are you if you get thrashed and vomit everything!

Kumar had got caught, but that wasn't really an issue; if the gang survived, it wouldn't take long for all the members to contribute and get him released. But the gang couldn't survive. After just a bit of thrashing, Kumar spilt the beans, and then the police carried out their raid and hauled up everyone.

Badal no longer lived in a rented house in Jadavpur. He lived in his father-in-law's house in Jhinkipol. But he didn't tell anyone that, or show them the place—except for 'Jibon'. The two of them had lunched together today in that house, and then gone to see about a job in Haroa. That took them quite a while. By the time they completed the work and returned, the police raid at the Baruipur overbridge had commenced. They caught all eight of them. But Badal's eyesight was very sharp. He saw the scene on top of the bridge from far away. So he did not advance any further. He grabbed the stranger's arm, that is to say, Jibon's, and they slipped into a narrow lane.

They ran down the lane, and after reaching a safe distance, Badal stopped to get his breath back. He said, 'Thank God I hid the two rifles. Or else we would have lost everything. They won't be able to bear the torture they will be subjected to in the lockup. They will confess.'

There were drops of perspiration on the stranger's brow. Wiping that on the sleeve of his shirt, he said in a despairing tone, 'Fuck! Just my luck! From the frying pan into the fire! There was already a case in my name, and when I did a job so that I could get the money to deal with that, I was named in another case. And I did this job for you in order to get out of that one—now your boys will tell the police my name, won't they?'

Badal put his arm around the stranger's shoulders. There was compassion in his touch. 'Don't look back. Just keep looking ahead. If you come down with cancer, why would you be afraid of a common cold or fever? If you're caught, they'll reopen the first case, which they overlooked so far. You'll be sentenced to death, or to life imprisonment. So if you go to prison for that case, the sentence for all the other cases, whether there are ten or twenty of them, will be served in a single instance. You can't be hung twice, or be sentenced to life imprisonment twice. You should think now about how you can leave behind a lot of money with Kali, so that she can get you a lawyer when you are caught, and bring you beedis, chire, a gamchha and lungi, and so on.'

'Who's Kali?'

'I mean the one you live with. What's the name of your wife? Isn't it Kali? All the rickshaw-drivers in Jadavpur who know her call her that.'

'Her name is Surabala.'

'Whatever happens, she's the one who will help you. Who else can you trust besides her?'

After a pause, Badal continued. 'Have you managed to save anything? Or did you blow up everything? Listen, what we do is terribly wrong. But blowing up that money on booze, women and gambling is even worse. You mustn't do that. Save money.'

Badal walked in silence for a long time. There was no one around. He wanted to get as far as possible from the site of danger. They were heading towards the next railway station. They would take trains to their respective destinations from there.

Badal said, 'I had almost sorted everything out. After completing a couple of big jobs, I planned to move to some other district, change my name and so on, start a small business, and leave this line. But all the plans were thwarted. However, I'm not one to give up. I'll organise another gang. Since you're with me, it won't be a problem.'

❧

Surabala was all alone at home one morning, and feeling terribly restless. She had no idea where her husband had gone off to yesterday without telling her anything, and why he hadn't returned yet. Surabala was very scared and worried. What if he didn't return?

Golok Sardar had left the same way one day. Surabala was very young then. She did not know how to bind him to her. She didn't know how much a man was needed in a girl's life. Sukumari, the unfortunate wretch who was a member of a jatra troupe had said—a man is like a massive tree whose roots are deep in the earth and whose head is in the infinite sky, while a woman is like a weak creeper that can fulfil its desire to reach the sky only by relying on the tree. Surabala understood the meaning of these words now. There was nothing lacking in her efforts to tie the stranger down. Yet for some reason, she felt that she could not tie this man down, who was always restless and difficult to understand, with bonds of love.

Surabala no longer went to Jadavpur. She hardly kept herself informed about happenings in the faraway city. If at all she passed the station while on a train, she merely raised her eyes and cast a glance outside. But she never got down there. After all, who did she have there?

Her husband did not return that day, nor on the following day. Surabala was convinced that he wouldn't return. He was lost to her. And then he suddenly arrived after a long time, and left again too. His coming and going was like the proverbial storm.

When it seemed that Surabala had reached the limit of her endurance, and the restlessness was driving her insane, she observed a black dot far away in the harvested paddy field. That was a head. Of a man who was walking in her direction. But he wasn't coming by the route people normally took. This was the path her Ma took when she returned after collecting cow dung from the fields. The path cowherds took when they returned with the cows after they had grazed, or womenfolk took when they returned with the chuno fish and snails foraged from ponds and canals. As he neared, she observed that it was none other than the man she loved. But why was he coming by this way? Where had he been? His eyes were bloodshot, his hair was dishevelled, and he looked exhausted. He looked as if he had suffered some cyclone, flood, or war.

Her husband had arrived from across the canal. He stopped and stood at the canalside for a while. He was gazing at the other side, as if he was looking for something. What was that?

Surabala's hut was across the canal from him. A twin-roof of thatch over five bamboo posts. Surabala loved this place. The air within the wattle-and-daub walls of the shanty had the smell of the body of a strong and hardworking man. He was the man who had built the hut. Narad Sardar, the flautist in the jatra troupe, who was her intimate friend Sundari's husband, had named the place 'Taj Mahal'. 'Surabala's lover built this for her!' But she hadn't realised that it was a joke.

This was the only dwelling on this side of the canal. There were paddy fields on three sides. The hamlet of the Kaora folk was about two or three hundred yards away on the right. Pagla Sardar's house was in the middle of the hamlet. Surabala could not stay all by herself in her canalside hut when her husband was away. She felt scared. So although she was there all day, once it began to get dark in the evening, she returned to her Ma. Her Ma's house had a room and a verandah. The thatch on the roof was rotting. They were done for if it wasn't re-laid before the rainy season. At least one kahon of thatch was required for the twin-roofed structure, which would cost seventy or eighty rupees. Where would they get so much money? Surabala's father wasn't able to go out for any work now. He had been suffering for long after a thorn from a date palm had pierced his foot, and it had become infected and turned septic.

It hadn't become very dark yet. Surabala was gazing into the distance as she sat dejectedly at the door of her shanty. That was when she spotted her husband. She had risen in surprise and exclaimed, 'What happened? Why did you come this way? Come in!'

For some reason, the man stupidly asked, 'May I come in?'

'It's your house! Why do you have to ask? '

'No, I meant, is everything all right? Was there any trouble?'

'What trouble?' Surabala asked in astonishment.

"Did someone come looking for me?'

'No! Who was supposed to come?'

Feeling reassured, he now took off his clothes, wrapped a gamchha around himself, crossed the canal, and came over to this side. Surabala studied him closely. He had a long and deep scar on his back, with a blackish bruise mark all around it.

'How did you get this cut?

'Oh, this? I grazed it against a tin sheet. Couldn't see it in the darkness.'

'Where did you go to in the darkness?'

'I had work.'

'Work indeed! What work ?'

'Cutting tree branches, plucking fruits.'

'At night?'

'That tree can only be cut at night.'

'I can't make head or tail of what you're saying!'

'You don't need to! The less you know, the better off you are.'

Surabala paused for a while, and then she asked, 'Do you steal? Swear on me! Tell me honestly, are you a thief ?'

'Chhee! Do I look like a thief! I swear on Ma Kali, I don't steal. Stealing from sleeping folk is a sin. If I have to take something from someone, I'll call him, wake him up, and then take it. Can you get me a glass of water?'

For ordinary folk, stealing and robbing were synonyms. Because the words were similar in meaning. But for those who traversed the criminal world, they were not. They viewed robbery as a heroic act. While stealing was a most shameful misdeed. This was why thieves lived with their heads lowered while in prison, while the robbers roamed around twirling their moustaches. But even more honourable than robbery was murder. And the most honourable of all were the Naxalites, who were political prisoners.

With her limited intelligence, Surabala figured out that even if the man didn't steal, he definitely did something which wasn't easy, or simple, or everyday.

The man spent that night with Surabala in their hut, and left the next morning for Madarhaat, which was a market for babu folk.

He bought twenty kilos of rice, five kilos of potatoes and a chicken. He bought Surabala two saris. Spent almost a hundred rupees in a day. It was probably the first time in Surabala's life that so much money had been spent in one go, so she was both alarmed as well as incredulous. She asked in trepidation, 'Where did you get so much money?'

The man replied, 'I have more.'

'Where did you get it?'

'I earned it, I work hard.'

The man forbade Surabala from going out to sell toddy after that. He said, 'I'm working, am I not? There's no need for you to continue that business. Stay at home.'

Surabala couldn't believe her good fortune. The kitchen fire was lit twice a day now. Rice was cooked for lunch and dinner. There was also some vegetable curry to accompany the rice. Which was why Surabala was worried about when her happiness would slip away.

Sometimes the stranger left home after lunch. He never said where he was going. Sometimes he returned late at night, and sometimes he didn't return until a day or two later, and he was in great spirits then. He bought things lavishly. One day he spent a lot of money and bought four giant prawns from Madarhaat. Surabala was stunned to see that and complained, 'You wasted such a lot of money!'

'Why wasted! We'll eat it, won't we?'

'That money would have seen us through four days.'

'Yes, I know that. But when I saw the prawns, I wasn't able to control my greed. I've heard people say that a malai curry made with such prawns is apparently delicious! I've never eaten that in my life. Who knows when I might die, I might as well have it now.'

The stranger knew that in the line that he had chosen, a ruthless and cruel closure was always stalking you.

A whole gang got caught a few days ago. They were turned into lumps of flesh by a mob. One of the robbers had asked for water before dying. Apparently, the irate public then pissed on their faces.

A few days later, returning home in the morning, the stranger put a pair of earrings on Surabala's ears. She was stupefied. Such earrings were the stuff of dreams of any girl in the Kaora hamlet. The mistresses of the households where they went to work wore such earrings. Where did the man get something so expensive! It wasn't just the earrings, he had brought two saris as well. The kind babus' wives wore. Surabala seemed to feel an inward twinge in alarm. A dark shadow fell over her face.

The same day, he gave a substantial sum of money to Surabala, to buy thatch for re-laying her father's roof, and to take him to a good doctor. Observing all this, Surabala realised, whatever the man might be doing, she wasn't capable of stopping him. She was a helpless, powerless woman with a scorched fate. She remained silent, resigning herself to fate.

A salt-water canal skirted Surabala's village. It was about knee-deep. The canal was full of small fish. Girls and womenfolk from the Kaora and Bagdi communities would be there the whole day, catching fish using scoop-nets. That's where the stranger had built Surabala her hut.

Surabala's father's hut was a very small one. It consisted only of a room and a verandah. Because they were squeezed in together with her parents and siblings, despite lying next to a virile man, Surabala had not been able to appropriate from the night the pleasure for which every nook and cranny of her mind and body hungered all night long. This hunger lashed her. She would get into a blind rage at the most trivial thing and start quarrelling with her parents, siblings, neighbours and even her man. So the stranger had no option but to build a separate shelter for themselves as soon as he got the opportunity.

He had thought that if he managed to get hold of a big sum of money, he would set aside half of it so that it could be used to fight the legal battle in case he got caught, and start some business with the other half. He would quit this profession. But the situation in rural Bengal nowadays was not good. Because of inter-party conflicts, everyone had weapons, and there were robbers all around. All those who were party workers during the day turned into robbers at night. Someone could enter your house with a gun at any moment. Fearing that, people did not keep too much cash at home. And so, even though Badal's gang had risked their lives and carried out some daring acts, they had not been able to obtain very much.

The stranger had no idea when Badal would take up some big job. But he didn't like this daily labour kind of existence. A question arose in his mind from time to time—how long can you go on like this? The tiger that hunted everyday could be caught in a snare laid by a hunter. What would happen then? And what would happen to the woman whose life had become part of his life of uncertainty?

The stranger had been away for two days and then returned today. Surabala observed that he looked as if he had both run a marathon race and lost, as well as escaped from a tiger's claws. She did not say anything. Neither did the man. He took off his shirt and went and sat on the grassy bank of the canal. He plucked the grass absent-mindedly.

Surabala went and sat beside him. The stranger now asked her, 'How is Radhanath related to you?'

'Which Radhanath?'

'The one who returned after serving time in prison.'

'He's like an elder brother since we're from the same village.'

'Do you people have any conflict with him ?'

'No! Why do you ask?'

'If you ever ask him to accompany you to the court, or to prison, will he agree?'

'He might go. But why would he have to go there with me?'

'Since you don't know anything about that.'

'Why do I need to know ?'

The man paused, thought about something, and then said, 'The times are very bad nowadays. There's fighting, murder and injury all around. The police pick up whoever they like and frame them for someone else's crime. I'm not saying it will definitely happen, but if the police catch me someday and lock me up in jail, how will you find me? But if Radhanath accompanies you, he'll show you where the jail is. You can get me out.'

Why was he saying such ominous things! Surabala's throat turned dry in fear.

After a while, the man continued. 'Be very careful with the pillow I brought the other day. There's some money inside it. It'll come in handy when we are in difficulty.'

Neither of them spoke after that. They sat gazing at the salt-water canal like statues. Dark clouds had gathered in a corner of the sky. They floated along and obscured the moon.

24

The Vengeful Village

Badal had assembled a gang again. He was a man of action. A seasoned criminal. He had been in prison for a long time, so he was acquainted with many jailbirds. One such man was another former gang leader by the name of Aahbali. He had just recently been released from prison. All the tools of his trade had been seized. He was empty-handed now. That's why he had joined Badal. The man was extremely devout. He prayed five times a day, and observed the Ramzan fast.

It was time to operate outside the district now, things were getting too hot here. That's why the gang was going to Bardhaman. All the planning for this outing had been done by Aahbali. The stranger was like a neo-literate before them. He didn't really know or understand anything as yet, whereas they were experienced. They knew how to conduct themselves in different situations.

The experienced Aahbali disassembled the two rifles with amazing dexterity. He would reassemble them again at a specific place. He put the butts of the rifles in a large bag, and the two barrels were inside his rolled-up prayer mat. There was a bag with a few flashlights, another bag with four or five pipe guns, bullets and a few knives and choppers. There were seven gang members. Seeing them, and the clothes they were wearing, anyone would think that they were a group of ordinary men from the village who had come to the city to work and were returning to the village now after a few months in the city.

A man from the village in Bardhaman district that they were heading to had come to show them the way. He was responsible for ensuring that they journeyed safely. The same man would accompany them till Bardhaman station once the job was over, where they would board the train on their return journey.

The train journey from Howrah to Bardhaman took about two hours. It took them another hour on a bus headed westwards. After that they had to take a south-bound van-rickshaw for about five miles. Finally, they had to walk for about two miles on a muddy path on which van-rickshaws were unable to ply. It took them about eight hours in all to reach their destination. They had boarded the train at nine in the morning, and it was evening now.

Bardhaman district was famous for paddy production. There was only green and more green as far as one's eyes could see. That was something delightfully pleasing. The gang members walked for an hour along the boundary ridge between paddy fields. And then they reached the village.

Forty or fifty households belonging to the Bagdi community lived in this village. None of them possessed any agricultural land, they were all landless. They worked as daily labourers, and fished, and thus somehow eked out a living. If they got the chance, they went to a nearby village and pilfered bananas, taro, radish, papaya, and suchlike. They also bent the half-ripe paddy stalks, and cut and stuffed them into sacks. The name of someone or the other from almost every household graced the red register in the police station in that connection. That was why the police as well as the brahmin and kayastha folk of the area viewed this Bagdi hamlet with venomous eyes.

The small village was surrounded by paddy fields that lay in knee-deep water. Tender shoots of paddy peeped out a few inches above the water. If one bit into this paddy, a milky liquid emerged, which was delicious. Forgetting the pain as the sheaves scraped their tongues, cowherd boys who were dying of hunger gobbled a lot of this.

It was the Bagdi householders who were once the owners of all the land here. Their ancestors had driven away tigers and bears, cleared the forest, and taken possession of the land. But the land was grabbed from them through cunning and devious litigation. The land was now owned by Roys, Sens and Bhattacharyas, who lived in the rising villages a couple of miles away. The people of the Bagdi hamlet now worked as daily labourers on the land they had once owned. They were perpetually hungry. Poverty never left them. That was why they stole whenever they got the chance. Boys, girls and womenfolk cut and tore away ripe and half-ripe paddy in darkness and slipped away. But they inevitably got caught one day or the other. And when that happened, if it was a male, he was thrashed badly and locked up in jail, and if it was a girl or a woman, she lost her honour.

The people of the area were seething with anger now after suffering all the beating and humiliation. Enough, no more! They were ready for a final do-or-die battle now. They wanted revenge. Who knows how, but they had got in touch with Aahbali, who belonged to another district. And Aahbali had got in touch with Badal. The screenplay for a nocturnal drama was scripted through their joint efforts.

The name of the man who had come to show them the way was Bhuto. He was in his thirties. His body was stunted from malnutrition. He was short, his head seemed oversized, and his belly was swollen. He had a muddy complexion, the hair on his head was reddish for lack of care, and his teeth were yellow. He had a sister. She had turned fifteen last Boishakh. But no match had been found for her as yet. It was very difficult for girls from this Bagdi hamlet to find grooms. When the boy's party arrived to view a girl, they hemmed and hawed and sought to find out whether the girl had ever got caught while cutting the babus' paddy in the darkness of night or the desolation of noon.

Bhuto had a brother who suffered from night blindness. They had lost their mother, but their father was alive. Although no one knew where he was. A few years back, they had heard that he was roaming the streets of Bardhaman town like a lunatic. Bhuto had gone there looking for him, but despite a lot of effort, he couldn't find him. Bhuto was married. His wife was going to deliver a child in a few days. It was their first child.

The seven-member gang from the city of Calcutta arrived in the evening and went to Bhuto's house. It was an earthen house, but a two-storey one. Bhuto said that several years ago he had managed to pull off a gold necklace weighing twenty-five grams from the neck of a brahmin lady while returning from some mela, and run away; the house was built with the money from that. Or else they only had a small hut earlier. And no one else in this village had a two-storey house.

The gang members spent the night on the upper floor of Bhuto's house. Their operation would commence after eleven at night the next day. Aahbali opened the large bag he was carrying, took out two heavy bundles and gave them to Bhuto. 'Put these away somewhere safe for now. Grind them well in the mortar-and-pestle tomorrow. But not the two together. In two separate mortars. Or else it's dangerous.'

The stranger realised that the two bundles contained the raw materials for preparing country bombs. Carrying bombs for such a distance by train or bus was extremely risky. They could explode in the jostling crowd. That's why the raw materials had been brought instead. They would sit here and make the bombs that made a loud sound. These bombs were unequalled when it came to frightening people and making them scatter. The stranger knew that such country bombs were used whenever there was the possibility of too many people being present. He had seen bombs being prepared a few times earlier, and made some himself on a couple of occasions.

Excluding Bhuto, there were six outsiders. But actually, they were really associates. The main job would be undertaken by people of the village. Their numbers were large, and their body language said out loud that if they could only enter the oppressive landlord's house, they wouldn't even leave behind the plates from which he would eat the next day. They would take away even the clothes the people were wearing. And they would tear, break and destroy anything that they could not carry away.

Once the darkness turned dense, the village folk came in a group to meet the squad from Calcutta. This was an entirely new experience for the stranger. So far, if they happened to stay in a house and made it their den for the operation, they had to be covert, so that no one found out. But here, everyone was being informed, 'They are here!' People were coming to see them after having got the news. And they were delighted to see them.

The stranger had heard from someone the story of some daring and restless youths who had astonished the whole country just a few years ago. He had thought then that if at all he was compelled to walk this fiery path, he should do that, or be able to do that, by loving people like they did. But fate seemed to be mocking him now. He had used guns, bombs and knives lots of times, but he had never savoured the satisfaction of inflicting even a single body blow on a genuine enemy of the people. Now he felt he had reached the right place. The blow that he would land today would weaken the landlord's economic foundation to some extent at least.

When an entire village, regardless of age and sex, was prepared to risk everything in order to bring destruction upon this household, however powerful they might be economically, or socially, or politically, they were definitely not friends of the people. There was no moral hindrance in being cruel to such people. The stranger felt overwhelmed with joy that he was getting a chance to participate in such a worthy job.

A villager said, 'We planned for years to finish off the fucker, but we couldn't, dada. We don't have any arms. Just some lathis, spears and choppers. Can we confront guns with that? We need guns to confront guns with. But now that we have guns on our side, we'll teach all the fuckers a fitting lesson. We'll catch the old bastard first and tie him to the coconut tree. And then all of us will hit him to our hearts' satisfaction, until we are out of breath. And then we'll attend to other things.'

They had to eat at night. There wasn't enough rice to feed six people in Bhuto's kitchen. And even if there was, why should he alone spend so much! The whole village helped out with alms. A fistful of rice from someone, two potatoes from someone, a slice of pumpkin from someone. It was like a village festival. A hunting episode. Rice and pumpkin curry were cooked. That was served on banana leaves, and everyone ate together.

One man said, 'None of us sleeps at home at night. We are at the bamboo grove, or the banana grove. But you people should stay at Bhuto's place. You have nothing to fear, we are keeping watch, and besides we have trained dogs. If anyone unknown approaches, they'll bite their faces off. They can't come anywhere near the village so easily. Just stay a bit alert.'

The village lay amidst the vastness of paddy fields in water, surrounded by mango, blackberry, palmyra, coconut and various other kinds of trees and plants, and was as secure as a small island in the Sundarbans. One could spot anyone coming or going from two miles away. There was only a single muddy path leading to and from the village. No vehicles plied on the path. If one walked on that path full of muddy slime, there was every possibility of falling down. Almost every male in the village had a police case in his name—of theft, snatching, armed robbery. But it wasn't easy to catch them. The difficult terrain was most irksome to the government servants with their secure salaries. Some powerful people of rural Bengal were thus somewhat helpless before this Bagdi hamlet. As a result, the hearts of the poor, weak folk of the Bagdi hamlet thumped with courage and the desire for vengeance. We shall definitely avenge the dishonour of our mothers, sisters, wives and daughters, and the oppression heaped upon us for long years!

The next morning, after chewing on a bit of muri, with onion and green chillies, Aahbali said to the stranger, 'I'm relying on you. The raw materials are ready. Sit down and get some bombs ready.'

The stranger was stunned. How did Aahbali know that he had learnt how to make bombs? Had Badal told him that?

He said, 'With the amount of raw material we have, you can make at least twenty. How can I do that all by myself?'

'Just take the trouble and make them. After all, no one else here but you knows how to do it, all of them are almost novices. We can't do without bombs for the job today. Two- or three-thousand people may attack us. The man is a political leader here.'

'You had told us that the landlord was a usurer. That all the people of the area were against him, and no one would stand up for him. But now you're saying he's a leader!'

'*Arrey*, it's landlords and usurers who are the leaders today! People fold their hands respectfully when they are around such folk. But they don't stand by their side when they are in danger. Who will come to die when bullets and bombs are raining? But it won't do to be complacent because of that and sit idle. We have to be prepared. I've made a calculation of how many people there are in the village. Even if everyone comes, the fifty cartridges and these fifteen or twenty bombs will lay them low.'

After a pause, Aahbali said, 'I surveyed the place in advance a few times. If we can remove the ornaments and jewellery that the womenfolk of the household have on them, it'll be a kilo. People say that the old master of the house has six or seven pots of silver rupee coins hidden away somewhere. Let's see what fate brings us. Start making the bombs now.'

Bhuto's fifteen-year-old sister Sudha never smiled, her eyes brimmed with tears. That girl, who was an image of melancholy, had ground the raw materials for the country bombs using the hands she ground turmeric and red chillies with. The kind and benevolent girl who had been born to serve and honour her loved ones had turned into a mini version of the avenging Phoolan Devi now.

Bhuto had strained the ground chemicals finely using a mosquito net, and his pregnant wife had swept the floor in a corner of the cowshed, and spread out a mat and prepared a working place. Bhuto's whole family, no, an entire hamlet was mobilised now towards a specific goal. They possessed nothing, but they were united, they had fierce courage, and fired by that, they wanted to pounce upon an extremely powerful enemy today. None of them were the kind who read books and pamphlets, were steadfast in dedicating their lives to an ideology, or were workers of a particular political party. They knew nothing about the revolutionary theory of annihilation of class enemies, and about surrounding the city with the villages. But they knew—may the person, or the people, who used cunning and guile to strip our wives, sisters and daughters naked, and molest them; those who took away our fields that brought golden harvests, the means for our survival—may the fucking bastards perish! For that reason alone, there seemed to be a kind of uncanny resemblance with the Naxalite movement.

The stranger was now free of any fear or doubt. They would succeed, they would definitely be victorious. The fervent desire of so many people had to be realised. He sat down to make the bombs.

A group of villagers were sitting on a pile of hay in the cattle-shed and observing the bomb preparation. Through the admixture of two apparently harmless looking substances, one whitish, and the other rust-coloured, something terrifying was created. It looked like an ordinary ball of string, which, when thrown, had the power to defeat and shatter formidable opponents.

All the chemical raw materials were poured into a large enamelled plate with raised edges, wetted with petrol and then kneaded like sattu. The bomb was made by taking a lump of this dough and filling it with hooks, ball-bearings, pieces of glass, nails and suchlike. Seeing these, a battle frenzy rose in the hearts and minds of the Dalit folk of the Bagdi hamlet. 'We'll teach a lesson to the bastards today! The dues built up through long years of untold humiliation and oppression had to be settled. They would recover that together with interest tonight. Yes, dues. Fuck, I had cut a bunch of bananas, and he beat me all through the night. And then registered a police case too. I rotted in jail for four years as an undertrial on fabricated charges of armed robbery. My daughter starved to death. My wife went away to a brothel in the city. My household and family were all destroyed because of them. I will avenge everything today. In full measure!'

As the man spoke in rage and agitation, he suddenly lit a matchstick. He wanted to light a beedi. But he couldn't do that. A spark somehow flew and landed on the heap of kneaded bomb-making chemicals on the enamelled plate. There was a terrific explosion at once. A huge ball of fire rose upwards, emitting a cloud of white smoke. The thatch roof of the cowshed was a blazing inferno. Its red flames reached the sky.

There was a half-made bomb in the stranger's hands then. It fell off his hand and landed on the floor. It exploded. Its shrapnel flew in all directions. Those who were sitting and watching the bomb-making were all injured to a greater or lesser degree. The injuries were minor, but they were terrified. Nine bombs which were ready had been placed in the feeding trough lying on the floor of the cowshed. If those exploded now, everyone would die. They ran for their lives in whichever direction they could. A great, tumultuous commotion had erupted in just a moment.

The stranger too ran for his life. He managed to exit the cowshed with much difficulty and threw himself on the courtyard outside. The entire right side of his body, which had been turned towards the plate of bomb chemicals, was burnt. A layer of skin hung down from his face, arms and legs. The scorched skin had the acrid smell of gunpowder. White flesh peeped out from the gaps between the scorched skin.

Hearing the sound of the explosion in the cowshed, and the shouts and screams of the terrified people there, everyone came running out of the main room of the house. Where did they have the time to look towards the injured stranger then! He lay in the courtyard. People skirted him, they picked up any pot or bucket they could find, and ran to the pond to fetch water. The pond was nearby. So the fire in the cowshed was controlled quite soon. Meanwhile, the stranger rolled on the courtyard floor in the agony of his burn injuries, like a burning snake writhing. 'Ah! I'm dying! Ooh! I'm dying!' After the fire in the cattle shed was put out, he was carried to the main room. The burnt man was laid down on the mat on which they had rested earlier.

'Alcohol! Bring alcohol!' A man ran and brought a pot of cholai liquor from somewhere. 'Drink it. It'll ease the pain.' The stranger drank the whole pot of liquor quickly, as if he was drinking water. All the burns really seemed to turn cool then. He lost consciousness within ten minutes. His moans of agony stopped.

The bomb-making chemicals had got burnt. The bombs had exploded. Who knows how far the sound carried. Who could say whether it hadn't gone past the brahmin and kayastha hamlets and reached the police station? A good endeavour had been interrupted. They had to lie low for quite a few days now. They would not be able to realise the plan. They had to start afresh all over again. There was no point remaining here now. All the gang members wanted to leave the place as quickly as possible. None of them were the stranger's friends or kin. Nor were they political comrades who considered a friend's danger their own and sat holding him to their bosom. They were all criminals. Nothing was supposed to be dear to them other than their own lives and their own interests.

Observing their restlessness, one could guess that once they were able to flee this danger, they would never return here.

Aahbali said to Bhuto, 'There's nothing for us to do here now. We should leave, what do you say? Keep him here for a few days. We'll go to Calcutta, arrange a vehicle, and come to get him. We can't take him on a bus or train in his present condition. What do you say?'

Some people, maybe Bhuto too, had a doubt—these people were lying. They won't come back. But what could he say!

The gang members left in the evening. But they gave some money to Bhuto, 'Use this money for the medicines and so on. We are there if more is required.'

Meanwhile, the burnt man gradually regained consciousness. He understood everything, but was unable to do anything. He had fallen into danger many times in the life that he had chosen to lead. Like during the incident in Loharpara. But he had been fit and active in mind and body then, while he felt terribly useless and helpless now. And this place was like a foreign land to him. All the people around were strangers.

But what was the scorched man to do now? He realised that grave danger was encircling him. Here were strangers who were in anguish about their next meal, whom the police were constantly looking for, and who couldn't sleep at night out of fear. A half-burnt man like this was a burden on them.

The stranger had drifted out of consciousness again. When he returned to his senses, it was late at night. He saw that Bhuto's wife, his sister and his almost blind brother were fanning him continuously from three sides with palmyra-leaf fans. It was true that the breeze brought a bit of relief to the pain from the burns. But how much? Would mere breeze suffice for someone who had suffered burns on an entire side, with a layer of skin peeling off like a banana-peel?

Of course, someone arrived in a little while with a tube of Burnol. The medicine shop was far away. It had taken him all morning and evening to get there and come back. But the burns the stranger had suffered could not be healed with merely a tube of Burnol. The tube was empty by the time a little bit of the ointment was applied everywhere.

When the burnt man was unconscious, he did not feel anything. But once he returned to consciousness, he felt as if an ocean of pain had taken over his whole body. As if he was being cremated on a funeral pyre. But there was nothing he could do. He was terribly helpless today.

'Water! Please give me some water!'

Bhuto's sister Sudha, who was an image of melancholy, and the one who was most saddened by the failure of the mission, brought water and held it to the scorched man's mouth. 'Drink, dada, here's water.'

The stranger drank.

'How do you feel now, dada? Is the pain any less?'

'Nothing's less. I'm burning away.'

'Be strong. It'll come down in a little while.' There was empathy in Sudha's voice.

The frightened and worried people of the hamlet had all gathered in the courtyard. They conversed softly and in muffled voices. The stranger realised they were having a secret discussion. As he lapsed from consciousness to semi-consciousness, his sense of hearing could not discern all the sounds. But it wasn't difficult for him to gather that they were all trying very hard to reach a consensus, to find a way to be free of the danger that had befallen them.

A person's soft voice wafted to the stranger's ears. 'Look, Bhuto, we have no other option before us re. Fuck, our fate is scorched. Can one do anything! If the sound of the bombs exploding reached the babus' hamlet, do you think they will still be sitting quietly? No re. They must have informed the police station all right. They must be on their way here. They will surround the hamlet before it's dawn. Tell me, where can we hide him in such a situation? Can you do that? We are bound to be caught. Don't we know the kind of thrashing the police dish out? This man will spill out everything about us. Another case will be registered in our names. That's why I say, if you want to survive ...'

Another man said, 'It's the rainy season now. The river is full to the brim, with a powerful current. If we simply throw him into the river, the current will take him somewhere or the other. No one will come to know anything. Who will know which village the dead body is from? The man is not from this area either, so no one can identify him.'

After a spell of silence, Bhuto's voice could be heard again. 'Bhai, whatever you're saying is correct. But I don't know why, I'm unable to agree to your proposal. Here's a man who's still alive. He'll probably survive if he receives treatment. Will you just throw him into the river? No, bhai, I can't do that.'

Bhuto was a soft-hearted man. '*Arrey*, this isn't the time to be kind and compassionate. Danger is at our heels. It's the time to think of survival. Someone get some liquor! Bhuto will return to his senses after a couple of glasses. Hey, someone go and get some liquor!'

After a while, someone spoke again. 'What's the point of feeling bad? Do you think we like doing this? But there's no option besides this now. It's all the fault of our fucking fate. Every time we make a plan, some hindrance or the other comes up. Who knows how much longer that fucking Bhattacharya will torment us. So many people die, but those bastards don't. It's as if God has forgotten about justice.'

The liquor arrived. Pure cholai. When you swallowed it, it burned and pricked your throat as it went down. A drinking session commenced, aimed at boosting Bhuto's courage. The people were not ruthless or cruel, but their circumstances had made them like that. Bhuto went into the room to take a look at the burnt man. The poor creature. After all, he too had parents. They would all weep.

The stranger gnashed his teeth and lay as if he was dead. He did not moan or groan. If everyone realised he was awake, their voices would become even softer. He would not have any way of knowing how things were going. If he heard and understood everything, he could at least be a bit prepared at the final moment. Maybe he could try to survive.

Bhuto was not getting high on the liquor. Everyone was waiting for his response. Whatever he said now would decide things. A man's life was hanging in the balance. Anything he said now was like a bullet fired from a gun, which could not be turned back once it had been fired. Bhuto would have to carry the responsibility for what he said now all his life. He was the one who had brought the man from Calcutta to Bardhaman. It was his responsibility to take everyone back safely at the end of the job. How could someone who was supposed to protect a friend be the reason for his death?

The scorched man was silent. Given the agony he was going through, he only wanted to moan 'Oh Ma! Oh Baba!' But he did not stand to gain anything if he did that. He was as good as dead now. His opinion was like that of a dead man. It was of no consequence to the living.

Bhuto's voice was quite agitated now. The liquor had indeed boosted his courage. 'Look, bhai, what you people are proposing is not right at all. They said they'll be back with a vehicle in a couple of days. We need to wait until then. If they do come, and ask where their man is, what will we tell them?'

'I understand that. But what if the police arrive before that?'

'How can we be sure that they are coming? What if they don't come?'

'If they don't come, that's good for everyone. But what if they do come?'

No one else said a word. It was as if the contrarian question had choked their voices. What if they did come?

The nocturnal breeze whooshed over the marsh now. It seemed it wasn't a breeze but a deep sigh that emitted the undead man's chest. The tips of the long stalks of paddy emerging from the water, together with their tender ears of grain swayed in the breeze like the bared hood of a snake. As if the entire universe was rocking from its very foundations out of an eerie fear. A dense tar-like darkness hung over everything. No infant was crying now, no old man coughing, or any dog barking. There was no sign of life anywhere. It was as if everyone in the poor village surrounded by trees and greenery had died before the descent of dusk. And those who were sitting in Bhuto's courtyard and whispering, and those moving about, were only the ghosts of the dead folk.

After a long time, Bhuto's recalcitrant voice could be heard again. 'Why are you all so unreasonable? You tell me, when they return and ask where their man is, what will we say?'

One man then said, 'We'll say he died. What more can they say after that? We'll say that since we couldn't keep a dead body, we threw it into the river. So tell us what you want to do now, Bhuto.'

'What can I say then? Do whatever you think is best.' Bhuto had finally surrendered in the face of everyone's combined onslaught. 'All right, let's go and throw him into the river.'

A little while later, a man arrived carrying a bier made of bamboo laths. Sudha and her sister-in-law stopped fanning the stranger, they rose and stood on one side with distraught faces. They did not know what to do. It was only Bhuto's blind brother, Budho, who, perhaps because he was blind, and thus seemed to see things much more clearly than those who possessed sight, realised what was about to happen, and thought about whether that was appropriate. He began to lament loudly. 'Where are you taking him?' It was only a meaningless wail now in the context of the present situation.

It seemed like the man who had brought the bamboo bier would have been happier if he didn't have to do the task. He asked in a voice full of diffidence and worry, 'O dada, can you hear me? Wake up. Wake up and lie down on this bier. We will take you to another place. It's a nice place. Wake up.'

The stranger knew what the better place was. He also knew that all his entreaties and humble pleas and appeals for his life were futile. The whole situation was unfavourable to him now. A unanimous decision had been taken regarding him. If he failed to cooperate with them now, the liquor in their bellies would make them turn violent. People often did things out of fear, which they were unable to do with courage. They felt extremely vulnerable now, under siege, terrified. The man realised that it was best for him not to be hopeful of survival. He ought to wish for an easy death. So he rolled onto the bier. 'Let's go, bhai.'

Four men lifted the four corners of the bier onto their shoulders. This was a strange funerary journey. The community had declared a man—who still breathed, and who could survive if he received some treatment and care—to be dead. And those who were carrying him on their shoulders were also dead. Dead out of fear.

There were no chants or cries of *'Hori bol'* on anyone's lips. No one was customarily scattering khoi, or popped-rice, on the road. No grieving lamentation. Who knew that death was so destitute and miserly! A life was coming to a close accompanied only by the splashing sound of four pairs of feet ploughing through water.

The stranger lay on his back and gazed at the sky. It looked like a huge outspread black umbrella with thousands of perforations made by moths, through which one glimpsed light. Was that Orion? And was it the Ursa Major there? Were those stars Ashwini, Bharani, Krittika, Magha and Pushya? The stranger had heard that there was a morning star in the sky, which guided sailors who had lost their way. Which one was that? No, he would never learn about that now.

Gazing at the sky aboard a palanquin of death carried on four shoulders was an incomparable experience in a human life. Who else had experienced this! Life—the meaning of the name Jibon—was indeed the name of a journey. As well as that of an experience. Ought he to be grateful to God for granting him a taste of such an experience? O life, you fulfilled me, with every iota of all the beautiful elements on earth, with everything firm and liquid, ambrosia and poison, truly fortunate am I!

The left side of the stranger's chest still thumped loudly, and announced, 'I am alive!' But those were mere words. The present situation denied his claim. Now he was an absent man. The sky full of stars, the green paddy fields and the fluttering breeze were all lies for him now, devoid of meaning. He had only a few more breaths left. And then it would all be over.

His body would sink in the unfathomable waters. The river surely had a strong current during the rainy season. The stranger could swim well once. That skill which he had acquired was of no use now. He was immobilised now after the burns.

The stranger felt a bit drowsy now. It was because of the rhythm of the moving bier perhaps. Naughty boys fell asleep in their mothers' laps to such a rocking. He missed his Ma terribly now. As if she was calling out to the small, naughty, uncontrollable boy, 'Come back, don't leave me and go, my precious. Come back!'

Come back! Could one really return merely by someone saying so? All the paths to return had been closed one by one. He would never be able to return. The immortal phrase sung by the valiant freedom fighter, Khudiram Bose, *Ebaar bidaay de Ma*, Bid me farewell now, Ma. The logs on a funeral pyre call out to the one, 'Hurry, hasten!' The impetuous flow of the crazy river calls out to me, 'Come!'

The roar of the furious river that was in spate following the rains reached the stranger's ears now. The crazy waves sped over the bank. He could hear their murmur, as they lapped the shore. The left side of the stranger's chest thumped loudly. Only a few steps more, and then, *splash!* He began counting. One, two, three, four.

25

The Aborted Rebirth

Like the monstrous roar of a thunderclap, a scream suddenly shot through the darkness, enough to make the very earth quake and eject all the fears of the century—'Bhutoooooow *re*, stop! Don't go any further! Stop!'

'Who is that?'

'It's me, Budho.'

'What happened?'

'Wait, I'm coming.'

Why had the night-blind Budho come running like a madman through the woods and waters in the darkness of night? Why? There were two more figures behind him. One was Bhuto's five-month pregnant wife, and the other, the underage 'woman', Sudha.

Bhuto was on the side of the scorched man's feet. He sat down on his haunches now, like a firm post. The pulls and tugs of the three men were unable to uproot the post. He wanted, he really wanted in his heart of hearts for something incredible and miraculous to happen, so that this sordid journey was halted. It was as if that miracle was advancing, holding his blind brother's hand.

Budho came and stood before them. And then he cast his blind eyes towards the darkness of the sky, the earth, the water and the air, and the four men, and screamed out in rage, 'You bastards, are you even human? Does human blood flow in your veins? You couldn't pluck even a hair off the man from the babus' hamlet who forcibly lay with your Ma and sister, and this boy, who's come from far away for our sake, you're taking him away to kill him because a danger has come up? Aren't you ashamed? *Chhee! Chhee!*'

It wasn't only Budho, Bhuto's wife, as well as the baby in her womb, seemed to echo him in unison, '*Chhee! Chhee!*'

Someone mumbled, 'But ... he won't survive. Maybe a day or two, and then ...'

'Will you live forever? Maybe another year or two. So why are you alive? Tell me, don't you hope for something?'

Another man said, 'We can keep him, but what if the police catch him?'

'That would be the best thing. If he goes to jail, he'll receive treatment.'

'What if he tells them our names?'

'How the fuck does that matter? The police are looking for you for five or seven cases, so that goes up by one now. How does that matter?'

All these were Bhuto's own thoughts. So he didn't say anything. He turned around, and turned the bier around. He pushed hard and moved it forward. Seven pairs of able legs returned the same way they had come, splashing through water. While going, their hearts had thumped with fear. Now courage raced through their veins. Let's see what happens. Snakes, leeches and insects were squashed under their resolute steps. They cut their feet on snail shells. Yet they moved ahead. A faint stream of light was visible in the eastern sky. The sun would rise in a little while.

The night was over, but the day had not yet begun. This time was known as *'brahmamuhurta'*, or the moment of creation. According to Hindu scriptures, this was a most auspicious moment. There was no better time than this to begin a good endeavour.

Was that really true?

After all, prisoners sentenced to death were made to bathe, wear new clothes, and then hung on the gallows at this time. So how was this an auspicious moment for them? However, it was true that the day was indeed an auspicious one for the hangman. He received a large sum of money as his wages for just half-an-hour's work. It provided him the means to enjoy himself with alcohol and meat for a few months. Perhaps that was why it was said that one person's destruction was another one's salvation.

At this time—just before the pregnant night delivered a new day, at the junction of the immemorial past and the eternal future—nature was draped in a thin black veil of mystery. This was a time when everything in the world was opaque, it lay on the border between seeing and not seeing.

The entire solar system stood still and waited now. The birds in their nests had not begun their chirping. Before being extinguished, the faint stars in the sky gazed pensively for the last time at the earth's fields, mountains, marshlands and people.

People! Seven people on earth were walking at this time. They were walking as if they wanted to reach another world. Visible in the distance was a small village in the middle of the field, sleeping under the canopy of tall palmyra, coconut, mango and blackberry trees. Asleep, but definitely not in deep sleep. Years of history bore witness to the fact that the people of the village slept like horses, standing, with their ears alert, like that of dogs. And when they sensed danger, they fled like swift-footed foxes.

One of the seven people was afflicted with night blindness. As soon as the darkness of night descended, his eyes shut. But now, as the darkness moved away, slowly, little by little, light returned to his eyes. After long hours of blindness, he was once again able to see the faces of beloved people in the beloved world.

They were walking. None of them said a word. Their heads were downcast. Was that out of a sense of guilt? Or because of the inability to fulfil a promise made to the girl by the name of Sudha?

They were walking, but one man had ventured on the longest journey on earth without walking a single step. He had seen the two poles of life. The man reflected, he had been on the verge of non-existence. But the world would have continued just as it was. Summer, rains, winter and spring would continue to arrive. Flowers would blossom on trees and fruits would appear. Birds would sing. Everything would remain, only I wouldn't be there.

He felt depressed after thinking along these lines. I'm not there, but everything else is like before. Not even a single leaf fell off a tree in grief. The earth did not stop rotating even for a second. Not a single drop of salty water rose up in any ocean. My coming and going could not make a scratch on the flow of time.

The stranger reflected, he reflected deeply. It seemed something had gone wrong somewhere. Someone seems to have been pushing me along. I was constantly moving ahead at his will. I could not bury his imposed will beneath my own. That was the mistake.

The man reflected, since I was able to return from certain death, I will begin everything afresh. Not with the identity of others, nor upon the foundation established by others; I will walk on the path made by me till my end. My first task now is to return to the spot under the overbridge in that railway station. To be born again in that dark womb, like a snake shedding its skin, like a worn-out garment, discarding all my inheritance, boarding the train that has halted there, and moving ahead ...

When the train stops one day at some unknown station, I'll get down there and lay the foundations of a new life.

As the blind Budho, who had regained his sight, walked on, he suddenly raised his eyes and saw that their village was not so far away. Two hundred yards at most. The surroundings were clear now, but the mango, blackberry and kadamba trees that surrounded the village, and the banana grove and bamboo clump, were still shrouded by darkness.

As they advanced further, they spotted some men in khaki uniforms, with lathis and rifles in their hands, waiting in the darkness. They had conducted a routine search operation in the village, and not finding any males there, they were about to go back to the police station when they sighted the returning party and stopped. Who were these people? Where were they going with the dead body?

The man lying on the bier sensed that it had stopped swaying. The sound of seven pairs of feet moving suddenly came to a stop. Someone whispered to someone, 'Cops!' And at once, like a meteorite falling from the sky, his burnt body dropped to the ground, full of muddy slime. 'Flee!' A tiny word, but as a result, the sound of feet trampling tender green paddy stalks and running wafted in the early morning air.

There was silence for a while after that. And then the sound of feet and people's voices again. The scorched man saw quite a lot of people standing around him as he lay in the muddy slime. They had khaki uniforms on, and lathis and rifles in their hands. They swore at the fleeing people, threatening them. 'Stop, or else we'll shoot!' But they did not stop. No one fired a shot either.

And the man lying on the ground could not return to the place he wanted to return to.

The Runaway Boy

From the winner of the Hindu prize 2018 and the Shakti Bhatt Prize 2022 This powerful trilogy of semi-autobiographical novels begins in East Pakistan. It tells the story of little Jibon, who arrives at a refugee camp in West Bengal in the arms of his Dalit parents escaping from the Muslim-majority nation. He grows up perpetually hungry for hot rice in the camp where the treatment meted out to dispossessed families like his is deplorable. When he is barely thirteen, Jibon runs away to Calcutta because he has heard that money flies in the air in the big city. His wildly innocent imagination leads him to believe that he can go out into the world, find work and bring back food for his starving siblings and clothes for his mother whose only sari is in tatters. And once he leaves home, through the travels of this starving, bewildered but gritty boy, we witness a newly independent India as it grapples with communalism and grave disparities of all kinds.

'In evocative and imagery-rich writing, Manoranjan Byapari introduces us to the devastating realities of mid-twentieth-century India: hunger, caste violence, and communal hatred. Jibon's experiences in his tortured world remind us of the distance we have come, and how far we have yet to go.'

—Dr Shashi Tharoor

'Manoranjan Byapari is an outspoken, fearless and unapologetic writer. His writings seethe with anger and indignation, and The Runaway Boy is no different. It is a gut-wrenching account of caste atrocities, dirty politics and crippling poverty that no discerning reader should miss.'

—Hansda Sowvendra Shekhar

'The Runaway Boy is a piercing tale of human determination, shorn of hackneyed sentimentalism, and set in an unforgiving territory of death and desperation. Cuttingly frank, deeply political, and singular in feeling, this is an incandescent universe of long sufferings and small, fleeting joys. Manoranjan Byapari does not confirm abstract theories the better-fed cultivate about the poor; he holds up a mirror that reveals, instead, through the pangs of a boy seeking hot rice, a world that feasts on the soul, and where hell is not a faraway place as much as everyday reality.'

—Manu S. Pillai

The Nemesis

The second part of this extraordinary trilogy takes us into the late '60s and early '70s when the rumblings of liberation grew louder in East Pakistan and refugees came pouring into India, seeking asylum in the camps of West Bengal. The Naxalite movement too was gathering momentum; the CPI(M), which had broken away from the Communist Party, itself split with the formation of the CPI(ML), and a bitter power tussle ensued between its factions and the ruling party led by Indira Gandhi. Amidst this bloody battle, we find a twenty-something Jibon in Calcutta, driven to rage by hunger, inequity and a naïve, contagious nationalistic fervour.

This burning torch of a novel is a compelling portrait of a youth negotiating the streets of Calcutta, looking to seize a life that is constantly denied to him.

'Manoranjan Byapari's epic narratives tell you more about our society than any number of studies by social theorists or political psychologists. Immersed in a world of caste violence and congenital poverty, here is fiction with the unmistakable ring of contemporary Indian history.'

—Jeet Thayil

'A remorseless account of Jibon's saga of survival. Haunted by hunger and disease in the deep forests of Dandakaranya. Caught between deadly party wars and police atrocities in a city torn apart by the Naxalite movement. But even in this harsh world, Jibon will experience the first tender stirrings of love and desire. A book that will shake you to the core.'

—Poonam Saxena

'In the shape of a novel, Manoranjan Byapari serves us a great outpouring of pain and a hundred fierce cries for justice. This book ought to be on syllabi across the country so we may better understand how structural violence works at the intersection of caste, class and law enforcement.'

—Annie Zaidi